A Secret in the Ashes

Thea Atkinson

First edition 2025

Print ISBN: 978-1-0689100-9-8

Get updates and sneak peeks and more when you join my readers' group

Dedications

There's nothing more unnerving than a shy girl sitting in a corner
with a book.
This is for you, babe. I see you.

i

"SOME MEN ARE COMING. You need to get out of town."

The voice coming from the cell phone wasn't just familiar. Kit knew exactly who it was.

But it had an edge she didn't expect, an urgency that did its best to crawl down into the safe spaces she'd carved in her heart, a place where she tossed all those things she didn't want to think about.

She stood beside her kitchen counter, staring at the cell phone in her hand, and for just a single moment, she squeezed her eyes closed.

A reel of memories washed over her, bringing in flotsam of every kind. Heart-wrenching moments of childhood joy, when she and her younger sister played head to head over tiny dolls or stared at picture books and tried to discern the stories they were telling. Ava had been like a doll back then, with porcelain skin and pigtails of curling black hair that Kit loved to comb and curl around her finger. Her chest ached thinking of those memories as the overlay of later clips blotted out all those images and replaced them with the gray, grimy ones of addiction and death.

All she could think then was that she shouldn't have answered the notification. She knew better. And yet, she'd given in to the urge to answer. Like every other time Ava called.

She inhaled slowly, letting the steam rising from the dishwater in her kitchen sink mist her face. As the tap ran over the glasses and the smell of lemon and mint drifted up to fill her senses, she imagined the froth of bubbles growing into a cascade of soft pillows. The sizzle of a lamb chop on the stove suggested oil was peppering itself over the wall.

All very normal things for a normal day. Things she desperately wanted to cling to, because those words—that voice—had stripped the day of pleasure.

"Kit?" came the voice again, this time more urgent. Demanding.

She opened her eyes to peer down to read the identity of the caller from the silver letters on the screen.

Private number. A different one from the last time, different even still from the time before that. She hadn't had one of these calls for months. And now, just out of the blue, this. Most times, her sister didn't speak at all, just breathed into the phone for a few moments or Kit hung up. This time, the edge in her in her younger sister's voice was unusual. Granted, it had been a few months since Ava had called, and maybe that sense of dread Kit felt at hearing her voice was normal now.

As she looked down at the screen, the words blurred. Her palm felt sweaty. The backs of her eyelids stung as if someone had tossed a handful of sand into them.

"Kit?" Ava said, her voice bloated with emotions that were hard to ignore, bringing up all those memories. All those times Ava needed her. All those times Kit was there for her. All those times it had been foolish to be so. "Kit, are you there?"

Oh, she was there all right, just like she'd been when their parents died, when Kit had petitioned for guardianship even though she was just a couple of years older, when Kit had scoured the streets for Ava in her pajamas because the girl had taken off again. Just like when she'd done unspeakable things to save her younger sister from herself and from men who would use a teenager for all the wrong reasons. Yes, she was there, but Kit's throat was so tight she wasn't sure she could even speak. She had to drag words to the tip of her tongue by sheer will.

"Are you high?" Kit asked into the phone, and even as the sentence came out, her knees sagged.

Of course Ava was high. God only knew what sort of drug she was on this time, but her sister had to be under the influence of something. After months of silence, when Kit could pretend she had a normal life, a lonely one, maybe, but at least one that wasn't painful, this call shattered it all.

There was another long silence before Ava spoke again.

"I know you can hear me, Kit, so just get out of town." Her voice was pained and sad and urgent all at the same time. "Go anywhere. Take a vacation."

A vacation. As if there was no rent to pay, no groceries to buy. No Internet, phone, or light bill. Ava's world had none of those things. Just days without consequence, nights without concern. What must it be like to live a life where all you had to worry about was how to achieve your next self-medicated escape?

She stared at the phone for a long moment, trying to see the screen through the wash of water filming them. In a flash of time, she relived every other call she'd received from Ava since she'd left. The gutting moments of fear in the months after she'd accepted her younger sister's guardianship. Images replayed of her parents lying on stretchers, emergency lights cutting through the dark city streets, their urns sitting on the desk of a brusque funeral director. Ava nowhere in sight to help carry them home on the bus.

In that same instant, she was alone again, watching a seventeen-year-old Ava slam the door as she left the house for the last time.

All that whirled through her mind, tearing through like a hurricane and leaving rags of ruin in its place. She'd thought all that agony was over. That she was finally free of it.

Now here Ava was again, calling because she needed something she could only get from her older sister. Because like every other time, that sister came to her rescue no matter what it was. Surely, Ava expected that.

But whatever she'd gotten herself into, this latest tactic to get attention was a bridge too far.

Kit cleared her throat. Swallowed the hard lump back down her throat. Gathered the tatters of her courage.

And then she hung up.

For three days, Kit clung to the brittle hope that Ava's call was just another manipulation. She buried herself in routines, pruning her garden and tending her apartment, all while expecting a knock on her door that would herald the sudden appearance of a sister who would look beaten and ragged, hollowed out from hard living and needing that hand Kit had pulled back so many times already that it was difficult to count.

Granted, it had been almost seven years since she'd caught sight of Ava, and she couldn't be sure how Ava would look. Was her hair, so opposite to Kit's own, still black and tangled like the wild thing she was? The last time she'd seen Ava, her body had been lean but not gaunt. Had addiction and stress hollowed her out, stealing the curves from her body? Kit couldn't know, and she hated imagining the once-clear skin turning a sickly gray, the bright, inquisitive eyes transforming to something rheumy and lifeless.

Her only contact had been those calls. One every few months. Calls when the silence became unbearable, enough to remind her that Ava hadn't grown up or grown out of her addictions.

She wished it could be different, but the one thing she had learned the hard way was that Ava could not change. For her sanity, she'd had to give up.

So now, as tough as it was to hear Ava's voice, as much as she wanted to see her, the longer she clung to the hope and the longer no knock came, the more the hope soared. No men came. No Ava showed up at her door.

Cutting Ava off had been the right thing to do. It was liberating.

Once her body started to unwind from the tension, it felt as if she were floating.

She woke rested on the fourth morning, and it took several moments before she realized she'd not woken once in the night with a feeling of dread clenched around her insides.

A glance into the mirror after her shower showed a woman whose circles didn't ring her entire eye socket. Her hair looked more lustrous. Heck, she even looked thinner.

Maybe that call had been the last straw, the one that finally freed her from the guilt she'd carried for years because she'd thrown Ava out with the hope that some tough love would force adulthood and responsibility on her.

She stepped back away from the mirror, inspecting her naked body. A bit of chub here and there, mostly in the hips and bust, but not bad. If she pulled her ginger hair back, her cheekbones looked higher.

For the first time in years, she felt pretty again. When she leaned forward, inspecting closer, she noticed her tear troughs still showed a bruise of semi-circle. Nothing a bit of makeup couldn't fix. And today, she felt like fixing it. She felt like doing all the things. Maybe she'd even wear the short, flirty skirt she'd bought last year that she'd never found the courage to wear.

A quick dig through the bottom of the vanity tossed out an entire bag filled with old makeup. She blew off the dust and tugged at the zipper where it was stuck with a tuft of cotton ball fluff.

She pulled her hair back as she stared at her reflection. She could pull this off. It had been a while, but it couldn't be that difficult to mask a bit of redness and discoloration.

Once she was finished, she tilted her head to catch the bit of natural light coming in over her shoulder. The mirror showed she'd selected the perfect shade of blush. The smoky purple shadow she'd selected showed off the deep greens in her eyes. Lush eyebrows got brushed and gelled to a perfect sweeping arch the way the social media gurus suggested. Her lips even looked fuller, traced with a pencil a shade darker than the lipstick.

She stood back and nodded at herself. She'd been complacent too long. She'd taken her life back from Ava years ago but had never really lived it.

That was going to change. Today.

No men were coming. No one was going to sneak into her house late at night and abduct her for God knew what reason all because Ava had been a bad girl and they needed to punish someone to make her pay.

She laughed. Oh God, the thought that men would come at all. If they knew Ava's backstory the way she did, they'd know just how useless Kit was as leverage.

And if they did come? Well, then they'd confront a real woman. Not a shadow. Not anymore.

When she strolled from her apartment, she felt reborn. The day was as crisp and bright as only an autumn day could be. She stopped to pull a few errant weeds so they wouldn't drop seeds into her garden and come to life again in spring. The last of her late-blooming black-eyed Susans trembled beneath her palm as she drew her hand over the tops, feeling the velvet of their petals, testing to see how much longer they might last if no frost came to claim them.

Life could be good without Ava. She had this ground, these plants, something to nurture that wouldn't kick and claw at every bit of love she tried to give. Life didn't have to mean an aching hollow deep in her throat, the feeling of dread knotted at the base of her spine.

Three lazy Susans even had the flush of bloom still. Several stems clung to buds that would open within days. She hated to leave them to the ravages of a possible cold snap. She cupped the buds thoughtfully.

Her apartment was already filled with the last of her cuttings, brightening her space and making her lonely home a bit more cheerful. Usually, she would cut these and add them to the table in the kitchen, a bit of yellow sunshine as the days grew shorter.

But she didn't need them there. Not now. But her work area could use some cheering. The readers who came into the shop to settle with laptops and tablets or to buy a new release might enjoy a bit of summer on a brisk autumn day.

Reaching into the depths of her slouch bag, she dug through for the small penknife she kept there on a chain in case some weirdo tried to accost her. Keys just didn't seem like enough of a weapon in a pinch, so she'd long ago slipped the blade into her purse.

With a flick of her wrist, it clicked open. The blade caught the early morning sunshine and grinned back at her.

No men were coming. The threat had never been real. It was an imagined danger, made to manipulate her.

Her gaze narrowed sharply, her fingers bleaching out around the handle as Ava's voice tried to cut through her hard-won sense of peace.

"No more," she said.

A quick swipe, short and concentrated so the cut would be clean, and three stems came free in her hand.

She closed the knife, dropped it back into her purse, and examined the blooms with a critical eye. It was a good cut. Low enough down on the stem that she could prune as needed to fit them into a lovely vase and arrange them how she wanted.

She knew just the perfect place for them. Right beside the cash register.

She wasn't paying attention when she stepped onto the sidewalk to head to the bus stop and slammed into a large, hard wall of muscle. The flowers crumpled between them, broken stems barely held on to the blooms with the same tenacity that had them budding this time of year. She blushed, feeling foolish.

"I'm sorry," she said automatically and backed up.

Fingers dug into her elbows. A masculine voice said, "No problem, sweetheart," in a way that made her stomach curdle.

Yanking her arm back, she peered up at him. He wasn't much taller than her, but the beefiness of his shoulders spoke of more fat than muscle, the kind that might have been testosterone fueled once but had gone to jelly. His leer was so obvious she wondered if he understood the finer points of conversation at all.

And to think she'd apologized to him for crushing her flowers.

"I have to get to work," she said as she tried to brush past him.

He stepped in her way, and she froze. Panic razored through her. Ava's voice ran through her mind in combat boots, kicking at the safe corners. She peered up at the man, careful to inch away as casually as she could. She knew all of her neighbors, and this man did not belong.

The smile she tried to offer, a nonchalant, polite one, was as tough to paste onto her face as a full mask of geisha makeup.

"Excuse me," she said, trying not to show her panic. "I'm in a bit of a hurry."

Once more, she dodged sideways, dropping the flowers to the asphalt. A glance toward the bus stop that was still two blocks away. No one was there. No one was behind her. Most of her normal commute buddies had probably grabbed the earlier bus.

Should she run? Make a break for the house? Dammit, what did a woman do in this situation? It wasn't like he'd done anything yet. He could be a perfectly normal bloke on the street, just a bit of a bully or a crass misogynist, and there wasn't a law against either of those things.

And yet, her heart pounded hard enough to make it difficult to breathe. Surely those things were the same sorts of rationalizations other women had made and ended up dead in a ditch or culvert somewhere. The same sorts of things they thought as they waited until the last moment to save themselves. If she'd learned anything from all those crime documentaries she loved to watch in the evening, it was that most women were too trusting. They didn't want to hurt someone's feelings and waited till the last second to run...and then it was always too late.

"You know," he said, as though he hadn't heard the dismissal in her words, "I hate to see a woman walking alone in a neighborhood like this." He easily caught up to her. "We probably have the same commute." A glance toward her apartment made her throat go tight.

Sidestepping him, she pushed on, not glancing back. "I doubt it."

This time, he kept pace with her, brushing against her a little too intimately. "A pretty thing like you shouldn't walk alone this time of day."

It was almost on the tip of her tongue to snap back that she walked alone every day, but she clamped down on the words. The last thing she needed was to give him any information about where she might live or that she might live there alone. And then a thought struck her. What if he'd seen her leave her apartment? What if he already knew?

She pulled her purse close to her chest and broke away once more, stepping up her pace enough that her heels clacked noisily against the sidewalk.

"What's the hurry, sweetheart?" He caught up and kept pace with her, no matter how fast she walked. "You scared of me?"

She picked up her pace. The bus stop didn't seem to get any closer no matter how fast she walked. Her hand slipped into her purse, feeling for the knife. Dear God, what if she had to use it?

"Hey," he said, grabbing for her elbow and yanking her to a stand-still. "What the fuck, lady? You can't be nice to someone trying to make conversation?"

She swung on him, the knife in her hand, mouth screwed into a snarl. Surprise of surprises, the knife just seemed to leap into her grip. Like a pro.

"Let go of me," she said in as calm a voice as she could manage. "Right the fuck now." Oh, she sounded badass. Ava would be proud. "Let go or I'm going to use this on your voice box."

She expected him to back up, hands raised in an act of sudden contrition as he realized he was indeed scaring her. At the least, he'd back away out of fear. Because she sounded tough. She felt tough. Oh, the adrenaline. The feeling of power. There was no way he'd mess with her, and if he did, he'd get a hellcat to wrestle if he wanted to drag her into some van somewhere.

He laughed. Loud, braying barks of laughter. Enough that he bent over and slapped his thighs as he tried to catch his breath. She stood there like a dolt as he shook his head at her.

"Girlie, you gotta open the blade if you plan to slice a guy's voice box."

She swallowed hard, humiliation burning her cheeks like a brand as she glanced at her hand. She'd brought the knife out, all right, but it was still sheathed.

He straightened up, heaving the kind of sigh a person let go after enjoying a good laugh. Squared his meaty shoulders. Leveled her with a pitying look. The shaking of his head suggested exactly what he thought of her.

"I just thought I'd walk you to the bus stop, sweetheart. You looked like you could use a bit of flattery." He skimmed her body with an assessing gaze that did nothing to make him seem like the gentleman he professed to be. "Woman like you, dressed up in clothes that might have fit a year ago. Thought you might need a good lay. Help you get your groove back." He snorted and swiped his thumb over his nose as he raked her with another assessing look that made her feel decidedly naked.

She wanted to make some snide remark about her doubts that he'd be a good lay at all, but those weren't the words that came out.

"I want you to leave me alone," she said in a small voice. Gone was the momentary bravado. She wasn't tough. If this was the real deal, she'd have been scooped up and dragged into the back of some Bundy-esque vehicle. Maybe even murdered. Her shoulders drew inward. "Please."

His expression hardened, making his features look ugly. His tone was even uglier. "It's not always good to be alone in a busy city," he said, all trace of congeniality gone. "Never know what sort of man you'll meet when you're alone, walking the streets." He jerked his chin toward the bus stop. "Sitting in a shelter all by yourself, vulnerable. Alone." He pulled air quotes and tagged them around that last word. "Might be nice to have company at a time like that."

He turned around and strode off without looking back, but Kit had the horrible sense that he was laughing at her. She swayed on her feet, slowly breathing out of her nose as she tried to reclaim her sense of calm. Some sense of normalcy.

But all that pounded through her thoughts like a mantra was Ava's warning, and she knew she might not feel safe again.

ii

FLINT HATED JOURNEYING TO the mortal realm. It was a land where the very air smothered the most natural of magics, where cold steel and metal sliced and diced the energy of the land, where everything was covered in plastic film and a simple thing like bending light took a surplus of energy. And it stank there.

The last time he visited the mortal realm, he'd been commissioned to collect a stash of cursed objects from a fae sorceress who did dealings with the Shadow Court. He hadn't expected trouble but had brought a cadre of his father's best along with him. Just in case. His instincts had proven correct. When he arrived, a monster hunter had already been there, succeeding in taking down the sorceress and grabbing the stash from the witch's hand.

By the time the mortal ran off with the bag of relics, he'd already used up a week's store of magic trying to blast the human out of existence. The stash remained out of reach. A failure that did nothing to help his case as he stood in front of the fae who'd ordered it done.

So the thought of going there twice in as many weeks didn't just piss him off, it made him murderous. Didn't matter that it was his father who asked this of him. Didn't matter that it was a simple assignment. Better for him to be bound in Erachne's gossamer threads and let her feast on him for weeks than go back there again.

But there was no turning down the master of the Shadow Court.

Which was why he stood in front of Terran in the library his father used as an office and did his best to cloak the simmering rage from his gaze. It was a pretty enough space, if you liked that sort of thing. A fireplace crackled and died with the wave of a finger. Books lined two walls and stretched up beyond the boundaries of the physical space, aided by the magic inherent in the property Terran had built the manse on.

But his father used the large chamber because he wanted the energies all those books created. "Power in knowledge," he always said. And he used the inherent magic in that power to add to what he gained from the land, as well as his own natal magics. The master of the dark fae world already possessed enough power to rival the king's, but somehow seeing him reclining casually in a large leather chair in front of that fireplace, he seemed even more dangerous.

And as he aimed his steely gaze at Flint, it was with a considerable amount of disapproval. "You haven't said anything."

Flint resisted the urge to glower at the news that he was expected to go back to the cursed place. "Why not send Blade?"

His father's jaw ticked to the side. "Because the mortal female is crucial to our success."

That wasn't an answer. Not really. But Flint pulled out the word *crucial* from the reply, added it to the fact that they were in the library, and gathered his father needed someone he could trust. Someone predictable who took orders well.

Which left Blade out. The Dark Enforcer, as unpredictable as he was violent, did what he wanted.

"And Stone?"

His father raked him with a glare that would shrivel a lesser fae. "Your brother is occupied already."

Flint was sure his lips all but disappeared as he pressed them together to keep from snapping back. Dropped his gaze to his boots to remain silent. Father, Terran might be, but he was just as likely to punish his sons as any other soldier. No fae got to the pinnacle of power in an organization like the Shadow Court by showing mercy. The only time Terran showed any emotion at all was for Mica, but then...Mica was a different story altogether. They all coddled the youngest. The youth was even given a tutor of knowledge instead of a warrior's training like the rest of them had.

The creak of leather as his father shifted in his chair was the only thing that could drag his gaze back up, and even then, it took a massive effort to hide the simmering resentment that tried to plaster itself over his face.

"And what exactly am I to do in the mortal's anemic realm?" Flint asked and refused to flinch at the sound of bitterness that came out in his voice. Let his father know the extent of his request, asking him to go twice when he knew what it would cost him. All while his brothers remained in the Iron Realm.

Terran held his gaze, not a single emotion on his face to reveal whether he was angry or disappointed, but Flint suspected both. His father was at his most dangerous when he was calm. He was just as terrifying in his quiet movements as he was when he tore the throat out of someone who displeased him.

"I told you," his father said. "Watch her."

Watch her. Not watch over her or watch for her. *Watch* her. Surveillance. That meant lengthy hours in the mortal realm. Keeping out of sight. Hiding in the shadows. Something Flint was good at. Better than any of his brothers. But it was also one of the most difficult and energy-consuming magics.

Flint squeezed his eyes shut as a sigh built in his chest. The choice was obvious. He didn't have one. He would go. Because his father asked it of him. Because he was a good soldier. And because his blood oath to the Shadow Court meant something to him.

Another creak of the chair leather, indicating Terran had leaned back, relaxing into his knowledge that Flint had surrendered. "I need you to stay in the shadows," he said as though Flint needed the reminder. "And keep her in your sights."

Terran tossed one knee over the other, his hands and fingers still as death on the arms of the chair.

Flint's gaze flicked to those hands. Powerful. As quick to violence or magic as he'd ever seen. Maybe the quickest. Those hands had done violence to many fae and many mortals over the centuries. His father preferred to commit the acts with his own hands, not his magics. Vengeance was a personal thing, he always said. Magic was for cunning and manipulation.

It was a credo Flint understood. That had been instilled in him since he'd been a young male in the earlier part of his first half-century. That year had been his testing. Even then, his father hadn't balked at the orders he gave Flint to execute a favored mistress. Terran's brutality was a truth that had kept the entire organization in line for centuries, longer even. He wasn't sure there even was a time when the Shadow Court didn't echo the darkest parts of the Iron Realm.

"I can manage to remain hidden," he told Terran. "Gathering shadows and bending light doesn't take the sort of power that wielding magic does."

He thought of the blasts of power he'd shot at the human in Lilah's lair as he tried to wrangle the artifacts back into his control. It had taken him days to recover his magics enough to ride the portal to the Velvet Boar and back into Fae. Now, his father was asking him to leave. Again.

His father nodded without comment, but his eyes flashed with a silver gleam that suggested he was satisfied. They all had their own natal magics. No one was sure what the master of the Shadow Court had at his disposal for his unique powers. They only knew he wielded a lot of power, and he wielded it ruthlessly. Almost as much as the king they were trying to overthrow.

"This female you want me to watch," Flint said. "You don't want her for the pleasure taverns?"

A lantern flickered beside the bookcase behind Terran. If it was a show of power, Flint didn't balk. He wasn't about to show any sign of weakness in front of his father.

"She's insurance," his father said.

"Meaning you are leveraging her."

A shrewd narrowing of those heavy-lidded eyes. "Your brother has found someone who meets our requirements. She's in the cells below right now. Ava Ashe, her name is, not that it matters in the end. The woman you are to surveil is her sister."

They'd talked about this, so it was no surprise. In the quiet of this very room months earlier, when the seat of Terran's power, the hub of it, was secured against any unfavorable ears. Flint and two of his brothers had begged their father not to involve a mortal in fae business. It was too messy. Too many things could go wrong, the least of which was the frailty of a mortal in a land of magic. Anything could happen before the assassin even met the king.

In the end, Terran wouldn't be moved. Stone was to leverage a skilled monster hunter from the mortal realm who had no connections to anyone. When the assassin died—or was removed, as was most likely—there would be no messy ties to clean up. A nice easy hit. No ties to the Shadow Court. Just a quiet coup.

But a she? That was new.

It was difficult to hide the surprise in his voice. "Stone acquired a female to do this deed? And you approved it?"

This time, the narrowing of Terran's gaze suggested he'd tired of Flint's questions. "Stone thinks Ava is a better choice. A female of some skill, he said. Someone who isn't on the radar and won't be missed. He brought her to Fae through Blade's portal. But she was somehow taken from the Velvet Boar before he could escort her here."

"And Blade?" he dared to ask. "If he let Stone use his portal, then what does he think of the switch from male assassin to female?" He couldn't imagine the Dark Enforcer would think they'd have any chance of success using a mortal woman. They didn't have the fortitude, the strength, to stand against the king, let alone take him out. While Stone might believe differently, the Dark Enforcer's brutality could add weight to the decision.

Terran's foot bobbed as it hung over his knee. "Your brother approves."

Of course he would. Any other time, Blade would disagree, but now, because Flint would have to leave Fae, Blade would smile at his father and nod his agreement. It was maddening the way his older brother manipulated them all.

He resisted the urge to pinch the bridge of his nose. He'd brought two females from there just two nights earlier. It had been a happy happenstance, he'd thought at the time. Something to soften the edge of his failure in retrieving the relics. But this was too much of a coincidence. Those women he'd dragged all but kicking and screaming from the tavern. But one of them...one had been far harder to manage.

"From the Velvet Boar, you say?" he asked, suspicion rising to his throat like a knife's point.

"I'm beginning to think you aren't listening."

Oh, he was listening. He just couldn't believe the impossible coincidence that he'd somehow abducted the same assassin that Stone had acquired. That he'd delivered her to his father as a prize without realizing who she was. The same woman sitting in his father's cells as they spoke. Really. What were the odds?

But apparently, despite Blade's interference, fortune had been on Flint's side when he'd taken those women from the tavern, because one of them had tried to alert the captain of the King's Guard—a fae Flint paid well for information—that the king was in danger. She needed to warn the king of a betrayal, so the captain had told him, a bit of information he'd relayed to Flint the moment he stepped into the tavern.

The chance encounter was the impetus for him trussing up both her and her barmaid friend and delivering them to the cells in his father's manse. And that meant he had information that just might change the outcome of this loathsome request.

No female hunter, no surveillance of her sister. Flint could stay in Fae.

"This hunter," he said carefully so as not to incriminate his brothers. Blade, he didn't care about, but Stone was a good soldier, and involving him in any negative way might call unwanted attention to him. "She tried to betray you. Whatever vow she made with Stone, she tried to break it."

The way his father's fingers dug into the arms of the chair suggested he'd not known that bit of information, and how could he? Stone couldn't have known it. Blade wouldn't have said so unless it benefited him somehow. And Flint hadn't had a chance to tell him, just to bring the women to the dungeons in anticipation of this meeting.

Encouraged by his father's silence, Flint continued to build his case. "We should just kill her," he said, pressing on. "Send Stone back for the original hunter. I would be happy to execute the woman for you right now." His teeth caught in his lips as he smiled and thought of the delicious punishments he'd mete out before he ended the hunter. "She can't be trusted. She deserves to die."

A moment of tense silence pulled the energy in the room taut before Terran leveled his gaze directly at Flint, holding him fast with a baleful stare. "It is up to me to decide the moment of the assassin's death, and for now, she is more useful alive. For good or ill, she is the one we are going with. She bested her mentor, according to Stone. A man named Gideon who is heavily involved in the Network." He rubbed his chin thoughtfully. "He's actually the one who suggested her sister as leverage."

Flint pulled to mind the female he'd trussed up along with her barmaid friend. She'd been attractive for a human, well-shaped. She and her friend might have been good sport if he'd had a mind to enjoy them, but he'd wanted to get them to the cells, a gift to soften the blow of losing the artifacts. And since his tastes ran to entertainment that tended to break mortals, he counted his blessings for that decision.

He was so lost in thoughts of things that might have been that he almost missed his father's next words. It was only because his father let loose a long-suffering sigh that he was able to wrangle his focus back to the moment.

"The woman I want you to watch is Kit Ashe," his father said. "When I face her sister in the cells, I want you in place in the mortal realm, a clear threat that the huntress can't ignore. You will be the wedge into her submission, and your brother, the Dark Enforcer, will be the hammer."

Flint forced his voice to stay even. If he had to leave Fae, he wanted to be sure it was worth the risk. "And you're sure you can trust Blade?"

Terran stood, and it was so sudden that, despite himself, Flint took a step backward.

"Your brother swore the same blood oath you did. If he thinks this Ava Ashe female is the better, more useful assassin, then I trust his judgment."

Meaning if the brutal and unpredictable Dark Enforcer saw her as lethal, that was all that mattered.

While Flint fumed, Terran gestured to the bookshelves as though they had ears and eyes, and it took a moment to realize his father was drawing his attention to the books that sat there. Histories and diaries and catalogs of objects so old the gilt edging and runes on the spines were worn. Most of them had slid onto the bookshelves over the years by an ancient creature who tutored the royal family, a male his father employed to tutor Mica because his youngest brother could not control his magic.

Others had been stolen from the Iron Court's library and placed on these shelves long before Flint was born. The very sight of them bored him. Bored Blade. Some said there were important bits of history there, things that his father could use against his enemies. Flint knew it was the inherent power of knowledge that bid Terran to store them.

It was only Mica, the book dragon, who seemed enamored of them, but that wasn't why Terran was drawing Flint's gaze to the shelf. Rather, it was to remind him of the blood oath he'd taken, recorded there on Terran's flesh and bound in magic within a leather-bound volume, a signature of sorts and a listing of the atrocities he would endure if he broke the vow.

It wasn't necessary. Flint didn't need reminding. He took his oath as seriously as true death. But he trained his gaze on the shelves anyway, a reminder to his father that he would always do as he was bid.

And as he skimmed the shelves for that thick leather volume, he was sure one of them rocked itself loose to hang on the edge of the shelf. He eyeballed it, waiting for it to fall, but it clung to the shelves as if it had claws. Flint blinked, testing his vision, and when he focused again, the spine had dissolved out of view. A gap remained where it had been, the books on either side collapsing toward each other.

Exhaustion, Flint thought. He'd spent too long in the mortal's plastic-filled and iron-clad world.

"Besides," Terran was saying, and his voice caught Flint's attention, drew it back to his father. "Mica's tutor agrees with the choice as well. He says the Ashe woman will be the perfect assassin."

So, his fate was sealed. Blade. Stone. His father. Mica's tutor. What argument was even left?

"So everyone thinks a mortal woman with emotional ties is preferable to a male who has a decade more experience in killing?"

Neither would be his choice, but he was just a soldier. Soldiers followed orders made by those who had more information.

Still, it was clear by the way Terran's jaw seesawed back and forth that, while he'd decided to employ Ava Ashe, he wasn't happy about the reminder that she had loved ones who would miss her. And that was why Flint was here, after all. To take care of those dangling threads.

"I use what I have available to me," Terran said. "If our traitorous hunter has a sister, then that sister makes her more controllable."

Flint nodded. There was a beauty in that. "And when it's over, you want me to erase that sister?"

Terran nodded and sat back down into the chair. "Whether we succeed or not, we can't have her looking for Ava Ashe once it's all over. We can't risk the consequences for the fae world should it come under mortal scrutiny."

It took everything Flint had not to sigh in resignation. Such a task might take weeks. He'd be outside Fae and out of touch with the magic of the realm for longer than he could stand.

Terran stretched one leg out, propping his heel against the wool carpet that cushioned the boards. "You will remain in the mortal realm until this is over or until I call you home." His hand roamed to the handle of a handheld mirror sitting on the table beside him. Its face was black. "I will be able to find you through the glass whenever I need to."

When he plucked the mirror from the table, he pointed it at Flint and the surface wavered into an image he recognized well. It was the scorched and razed property of the fae sorceress, and he suspected the looking glass had come from there, collected by the cadre as they scraped the property for relics.

"When you find Kit Ashe, do not let her out of your sight. If she runs, you chase. If she sleeps, you watch her. If she dies, it would be better for you to take your own life than return home to Fae."

It was a shock, that last comment. Flint did his best to hide his reaction behind guarded eyes, but it didn't matter. There was no more discussion, it seemed. His father waited for a nod or a bow of dismissal because that was what he expected.

Flint gave them both and gave them freely, because in that moment, he knew that human or not, Kit Ashe was important enough that his father was suggesting her mortal life was worth a fae's immortality.

And that meant Flint would do whatever he was asked.

Even if it meant he died in the process.

$$iii$$

FLINT ARRIVED NAKED AND sweating in a back alley of the city. The portal through to the earthen realm had been unexpectedly painful. No one had told Flint the gates in the Shadow Bazaar had gone rogue. The builder, Maddox the Warrior, had apparently died and left a realm that straddled a cluster of others in chaos.

The gates ate as much magic as they gave to throttle him through. The anemic wheeze of a tavern's neon sign reflected in the asphalt from the main street and fingered its way into the alley where he landed. Bruises swelled beneath his skin. His mouth tasted of copper.

Thankfully, the bartender of the tavern was an abstinent vampire and recognized a creature of magic when Flint staggered inside. He gave Flint some clothes and a leather jacket and let him rest in the back room until dawn, giving him time to regain enough strength to stagger out before the homeless vampires decided to test his mettle.

He was still weak by early afternoon, but he felt his magic like a budding bloom beneath his skin.

It took a full five hours after that to send his light out to find the pulse of energy that matched the one his brother emitted and from there to train it to find the hunter named Gideon.

The dwelling looked ordinary, with a small porch and a door with a welcome mat. But Flint knew a fortress when he sensed it. Energy spiked all over the place, and that energy, that mortal magic tinged with some white magic, came from the garage.

His decision to approach the garage was swift, a warrior's instinct made without conscious thought. Pulling shadows around him, he moved quickly to the door, knowing the male inside would be ready for him.

And he was. Gideon stood in the open door even as Flint pivoted toward it. A line of salt seamed the threshold. A hatchet in Gideon's hands put tension in his biceps.

Ludicrous. So ludicrous Flint couldn't help the laughter that coughed through his throat.

"Even if that legend was true," he said, "the salt line would just keep me from coming inside, not from hurting you. And trust me"—he lowered his head, bullish and threatening—"I would like to hurt you."

Not a single flinch. Foolish or foolishly brave, Flint couldn't decide.

"What do you want?" Gideon demanded. The man might have made a good assassin after all, but it was too late.

"Information."

"Do I look like a fucking Encyclopedia?"

Flint edged closer. A pulse of energy came from inside, a faint whiff of magic older than the mortal kind, not just white witch magic. Something more insidious. The hunter used wards, he was sure. But were they elven or goblin? Black magic?

"What you look like," he said, knowing exactly how terrifying he looked, "is a lamb before it falls to the butcher's hand."

"And you look like someone about to get a hatchet in the throat." Gideon raised the blade, mocking a heaving toss. His biceps flexed.

Flint smothered the snort of derision that wanted to climb his throat. There was a time for bravado and a time for truth, and the truth was that he could end this bug with a single squashing swat. "You think a little toy like that can threaten me?"

"Cold iron." Gideon said this like it was a victory. "You fae don't like cold iron."

Flint's shoulders moved in a casual shrug. While the male was versed in lore, it seemed he was sketchy on details. It didn't surprise him: the entire world of Fae had worked hard to keep an allure of fairy magic that the mortals might doubt as well as celebrate.

"A rare few of us have an affinity for cold iron," Flint said, divulging enough to enlist trust. Painting the possibility that he might be able to resist with the right fae but coloring the moment with the knowledge that he would not survive the resistance with him. "But I'm not here for discussion of natal magics. I want Kit Ashe's information. I want to know how to find her."

Nothing. Not even a blink in reaction.

Flint sighed. "Don't make this hard, mortal."

"There is no easy button you can press that will make me betray Kit," Gideon said.

Flint canted his head, studying the man. "But you betrayed her sister, did you not? You gave her up to the Shadow Court to save your own skin."

That got a reaction. Subtle, perhaps, but the way Gideon's shoulders sagged, the way the hatchet dipped just a bit, spoke of a man piecing himself back together after a hard fall. He felt guilty about that betrayal, that was for certain. That was how Flint knew he wasn't going to just surrender more information than he already had.

At least not under threat of violence. This man was a hunter. Hunters lived with the threat of violence. But they also lived with something else, a quality Flint could use to his advantage.

"That's not entirely how it went down," Gideon said, his voice so low only fae ears could hear it. A test, perhaps. To see what sort of magic Flint was capable of, maybe to ascertain he was fae.

"I'm not interested in easy," Flint said, picking up a thread that would be easier to follow, sensing the man might reconsider if he thought he was helping Kit instead of betraying her. Didn't matter which he believed. He just cared about expediting the task.

Gideon planted his feet wider.

Frustrating. At this rate, he was going to be all night, and he was already tired. "Listen, hunter. While hard might be enjoyable for me, I don't have the luxury of drawing this out. She's in danger. I've been tasked with watching her."

Every word of that was true.

Gideon's eyes narrowed. "Fae don't lie."

It wasn't shaped as a question, but Flint heard the query in it just the same. He didn't respond. Diplomacy wasn't his strong suit, but he knew when to shut his mouth and lead with violence and when to shut his mouth and look as though violence was imminent.

When the man lowered the hatchet, he knew he had him. Whatever Stone had done, however he'd threatened the man, it had made a lasting impression. It was clear Gideon wanted to believe he was doing the right thing.

The best part was that Flint didn't have to waste a single bit of magic on the hunter.

But the weapon didn't get dropped. Instead, it rested beside the man's thigh. His throat bobbed. "Promise you're there to keep her safe."

If she runs, you chase. If she dies, you take your life.

Flint crossed his arms over his chest. "Fae don't give vows easily and rarely to mortals."

"I know."

The sigh of frustration was real, but it couldn't hurt to offer the truth as it already was. "I promise if Kit Ashe dies at my hand before her sister completes her task, I will take my own life."

"That's not enough."

Flint couldn't hold back the roar of rage that rumbled free. It came with a flare of energy that burst the lights in the man's bunker. "I can't promise more than that, hunter. Humans are frail. She could fall down a flight of steps through no fault of my own."

Gideon's answer was a lifted brow. Flint should kill the man where he stood, not pander to his whims. And yet...this was what his father wanted.

It was difficult to marshal that rage back inside, but he managed to soften his voice. "I can't tell you I'll guard her forever. My words as I said them are to ensure you I mean her no harm for a given period of time that protects us all from a hastily made vow that might extend far past a mortal's given time."

Gideon's mouth twitched, and Flint wasn't sure if he found humor in the explanation or if he was mulling over the sincerity.

"She is running out of time, hunter," he growled, wondering if he should just tear the man's spleen out and extract the information from his blood, except he doubted Gideon would surrender the information even under painful force.

Flint's huff of exasperation made his throat hurt. Gentle prodding was getting him nowhere. "Take the vow or leave it. I'm sure I can find another way to locate Kit Ashe. She might have a friend. Perhaps a customer where she works..."

Gideon's face paled. It was clear he fully expected Flint to commit whatever violence necessary to get his way. And he wouldn't be wrong.

The man grunted out a street name and number. Somewhere in the city center. Lots of public transport, including buses. Gideon grinned wickedly at that. Flint could get to Kit, but it wouldn't be easy or comfortable, that was what that smile suggested.

Flint knew what buses were. He knew what cars were. Contraptions surrounded by steel and diesel fumes weren't the most inviting mode of locomotion, but it had to be done. Walking to his destination would use up reserves he'd need to keep himself cloaked. Using magic to get there would do the same.

"I'll take a cab," he said.

"Good luck paying the driver." Gideon turned on his heel and closed the door. Locks of every sort sounded on the evening air. A drifting waft of ozone crackled, a sharp punctuation on a final thought.

Flint stared at the barricade and groaned silently to himself. He wanted dearly to teach this Gideon a lesson in power, but the damned Blood Gate had taken more out of him than he'd realized. Merely keeping his temper in check was enough to deplete his magic.

Using any more precious energy on this hunter would be satisfying, but it would also be a waste. The hunter must have realized that. In light of Gideon's stubbornness, he wondered if his brother Stone had been right to swap out the assassin for a female one, even if she was the woman's sister. A mortal woman just couldn't have that sort of fortitude to stand against such a threat of violence. Human females just weren't made for it.

If he needed any more proof of that, he only had to remember how Ava Ashe had run when he'd confronted her at Lilah's. Faced with an ambush of high fae, the woman had fought back very little before escaping with the cursed objects.

So Flint left Gideon's house behind and took one of the hateful contraptions because hailing a cab proved more difficult than it seemed. He sat as close to the front as he could, so the occasional waft of evening air could relieve the horrible pinching feeling of his skin. And he held himself stiffly, bracing against the waves of energy coming at him from the gears and pistons and flimsy iron coating of the vehicle, because it was necessary to expedite his surveillance. It made him hurt all over.

In the end, it was well past nightfall by the time he stood on the sidewalk in front of Kit's house. At first, he was worried Gideon had duped him and given him the wrong address. Everything was quiet. Even the trees remained unmoving in the light breeze. A tidy garden lined the sidewalk up to her front door, and the dying flowers nodded beneath the moon's light. Quaint. Not the sort of place a hunter would live.

But it was the Ashe house. The mailbox said so. He scraped his hair away from his face, combing it back with his fingers as he regarded the abode and the surroundings. A spindly, city-bred poplar tree reached for the sky from the small bit of grass between her house and another. From there, he watched every flicker of movement from the silhouette inside.

She had a pleasing shape, the woman he surveilled. If the shadows on the curtains were any indication, she'd make a good sale to the pleasure taverns in the Iron Kingdom, fodder for those perverse fae who enjoyed the frailty of humanity.

Perhaps when this was over, that would be the way he erased her from existence. A disappearance like so many other women of this world.

He could make a good bit of coin for her sale, judging by the size of her breasts. Blade was the one who did most of the scouring for indentured mortals since he loved the earthen realm, but Flint was sure there would be room for one more mortal at the Velvet Boar.

Or perhaps he could put her on auction in the Catacombs of Dread, where the purchase of human flesh was about more than the deviance of fae/human coupling. The value of properties there went beyond mere coin, and the things they subjected the items to once won were commensurate with the bids.

With a renewed sense of interest, an almost calculating sense of possibility and potential for what this trip might mean after all, he leaned against the poplar tree and gave her more thorough study. No haste. Just careful, deliberate watchfulness as the thin branches cast fleeting shadows over the yard and facade of the building.

She moved with a quiet energy that surprised him. Her ribbon-like aura trailed through the chimney and out the cracks in the windows and door. If he looked hard enough, he could see the color of it, a pale yellow like creamed butter.

He canted his head, curious. A shift of her hip as she reached for something, the gentle sway of her hair when she turned. Those things electrified the pulse of that energy, calling out to him in ways that made him lean forward, eyes trained more intensely on the window.

She paused at the glass behind the veil of curtain. A faint glow of light from within outlined her curves, delicate yet firm, a sculpture caught between fragility and strength.

Fuck. This was going to be more difficult than he thought. She wasn't just some vulnerable female with yielding, full curves. He recognized exactly what she was.

Dangerous things came in many forms, but mortals were never one of them. Soft. Breakable. Entirely beneath his notice. But this one, this one was a threat. That was the only explanation for the way her presence coiled around his senses, demanding attention he could ill afford.

He straightened, tension bristling under his skin. Hesitation could kill faster than any blade. He exhaled sharply. Threat or not, vulnerable or not, it was time to make the first move.

With a twitch of his fingers, he summoned a sliver of magic—just enough to stretch the edges of his power. The faint ribbon of energy coiled through the air, weaving toward the door.

He pushed a whisper of force into it, and it flared briefly as it struck the wood, the knock muffled but sharp enough to beckon her.

He waited silently, leaning against a spindly-trunked poplar tree until she came to the door. Alert. Ready. Eyes narrowed to see better through the darkness.

When she pulled open the door, she stood framed by the soft light spilling from inside, her gaze combing the darkness like a blade skimming over a strop. He remained still, daring her to find him, to see him as clearly as he saw her.

For a fleeting moment, her eyes seemed to lock on his, her posture straightening as though she'd caught the breath of his presence in the night air. His jaw clenched in reflex. That focus—it was too intense for the powerless human he expected to find. It pierced deeper than it should have, unsettling the foundation he'd built with centuries of violence.

A low grumble moved up his throat, straining toward that inquisitive gaze. She didn't react to his unbidden groan. He knew then that she hadn't heard him, hadn't seen him, and yet...she held herself stiffly, angling the way a warrior would as she looked out into the night, making herself as small a target as she could. Ready for whatever lethal energy she sensed in the night.

She'd seen violence before, and she hadn't pulled away from it. Perhaps violence was a thing she knew and expected.

A smile tugged his lips, but he couldn't say if it was from relief, pleasure, or something else. He just knew he was compelled forward, advancing on her as he walked with the shadows, pulling them around himself with each step until he stood right on her stoop.

Silent, careful treads up the stairs. He angled himself off to the side, hiding out of range of the play of the light coming from inside that cut a neat triangle on the painted wood but left hard edges of shadows spilling over the porch. He stood there in that darkness, and he looked at her.

Lush auburn hair spilled free in places from a messy bun tied at the top of her scalp. The stray hairs framed her face, reaching for and kissing a few freckles that dotted her cheeks. Each strand caught the golden light from behind her. It was magic, the way they seemed to breathe in the air currents, moving like weeds below the surface of a lazy river.

Her green eyes narrowed as she swiveled her head left and right, searching the night. Stopped right on him.

There was an electric, tension-filled moment when he thought she'd seen through his magic and found his face. He fought the urge to suck in a harsh breath.

The way the porch light caught her eyes was like a burst of magic. With the halo of light rimming her hair, she could have been from the fae lands. The small tilt to her nose gave her an almost elven appearance.

His hands itched to travel her features as he studied her. The thought of sending her to the pleasure taverns or the catacombs suddenly tasted like bitter ogre's ale in his mouth.

"Who's there?" she whispered.

His stomach clenched at the sound of her voice. It was the stroke of soft fingers against his cheeks, of frenzied fingers tangling in his hair, of a hand on his chest that stilled his heartbeat and kept it from pounding through his ribs.

A knot tied deep into the pit of his stomach. This was not going to be easy. It might even destroy him.

Because he wanted her.

Not for his father. Not as leverage for the Shadow Court against her sister. Not for any duty that had been hammered into him over centuries.

For himself. His to devour. His to break and reshape the pieces into something only he could claim.

The moment sharpened into perfect clarity as she stared right into his eyes without seeing him. In that electric silence, he knew he wouldn't let anyone else touch the edges of her fear, taste the power laced within her pulse, or break her spirit into shards.

No matter the cost. Even if it meant forfeiting his soul for a single breath of her despair.

Watch her when she sleeps. Follow her if she runs. Die if she does.

Those words rang through his mind like a death knell. His oath. His vow. In perfect harmony with his desires. So perfect that he knew with a quiet certainty that no path he took would leave him unscathed.

Whether he honored his blood vow or shattered it into pieces, the cost would be the same—torture, death, ruin.

And he knew exactly what it was going to cost him as she stepped back into her foyer. He understood the breadth of the test of this task as he brushed past her, a quiet shadow she couldn't shake, to steal his way into her haven.

And he was ready for whatever would come as the door clicked shut, sealing her fate.

iv

IT WASN'T MUCH. NOT at first. The faintest tingle on the back of her neck, lifting the downy hairs on her nape. Something Kit could easily dismiss as a stray current of air fingering its way in from the bedroom window she always left slightly open. The sort of movement so subtle, only the finest of hairs could feel it.

But the sensation lingered throughout the night. And it grew more persistent. There was an urgency in the energy of it, a feeling like she was missing something, that she'd forgotten to turn off a burner on the stove or left her curling iron plugged in. It was the slightly off-kilter vertigo of an ounce of wine too much before crawling between mossy-hued flannel sheets.

She'd jerk awake just as she drifted off, sensing something, some energy standing over her as if an intruder had broken in and was lying in the bed next to her, felt but unseen.

At those times, her eyes would fly open. Drunk on a dream she couldn't remember, she flailed about on a surge of instinct that wailed at her from her very marrow that she was in danger.

Nothing. No one. Not a single anomaly in a room she knew so well she could trace the shadows in her sleep.

All the dizzying shift in mental states made the night pull out like warm taffy in sticky strings of disorientation and exhaustion until inevitably, oblivion called out to her again. That siren's call from the shadowed rocks of the Stygian Sea gave her grateful, but fearful, surrender.

In that hazy state between wake and sleep, when her body refused to obey the sluggish murmurs of her mind, her skin felt swollen and feverish.

And in those moments, just before she'd slip beneath the waves of consciousness, a sensation like a feather brushing her skin lingered over her face and throat, static electricity drawing goose flesh to the surface of her skin.

The featherlight touch drifted to her wrist as it lay atop the blankets, and for a terrifying moment, she swore she saw the faintest outline of fingers brushing her skin, feeling for her pulse.

She smelled ozone, sharp and pungent. The scent of it prickled her nostrils. On its tails came the fragrant aromas of cloves and woods and earth.

Struggling her way to the murkiness of consciousness, she struck out, flailing like an exhausted swimmer until she broke the surface. Yanking her arm back as if burned. A bolting movement for the lamp. Jack-knifing herself upright. A boxer lunging from the mattress before the count, ready with a snapping right hook.

Light swam over the room as the light clicked on. She swept her gaze across the bedroom, her eyes so wide and overwhelmed by the sudden brightness that she pressed her fingers to her eyelids, forcing them to stay open.

Sure enough, she was alone. Like always. But if her heart rate was any indication, the shadows held threats her eyes could not see.

At least she didn't have to try to convince herself it was just her imagination. The empty room proved it for certain. A sigh scraped free of her throat. It wasn't that she wanted something or someone to be there, but it was disappointing to realize that the adrenaline soak of dread and fear could take her right back to the days when she'd lived so close to the razor's edge that she felt bloody all the time. And all from one damn phone call.

Some men are coming. You need to get out of town.

Who these men were or what they wanted went unforgotten at the time and in the face of her own anger. Now, she wondered what her sister thought these men wanted from her. Was it money for drugs she'd stolen? Revenge for Ava being a dick?

In either case, bothering Kit would get them nowhere. She was a bookshop clerk, not a high-priced lawyer, and it would be hard to get any sense of vengeful satisfaction from an estranged sister.

The truth was probably the simplest explanation. Occam's razor and all.

Sagging against her headboard, with her nerves still frayed like old wire, she tried once more to remind herself that it was highly unlikely there were any men at all, let alone planning to break into an apartment in the dead of night to demand cash from a woman wearing cheap, wine-stained pajamas.

She flipped the sheets off her legs, considering padding across the room to where she kept her purse on the bureau. She had a knife in there, the medium-sized penknife that she'd used to threaten that bully outside her house.

A flush crept over her skin as she recalled that incident. It hadn't gone well. She was too unpracticed at violence to make a knife work. She pulled her feet back into the sheets again. She was being ridiculous. The fragrance of cloves and pine was just residual aromas from the spices she'd used at dinner.

She fell asleep again, finally, to conflicting thoughts about purchasing a weapon. Just in case. And her dreams were filled with shadows and figures looming over her, examining a pistol the size of her mattress.

By the time dawn invaded her room, slipping around the edges of the curtain and stealing across the old wooden floorboards, she felt like a ragged strip of dirty linen.

She made her coffee like an automaton. Poured it in a mug and spilled more of it into the sink than into her cup. Eyelids barely holding their own against the sandy grains of gravity, she swayed on her feet for a moment before putting down the mug and stomping into the bathroom for a cold shower.

She peeled the pajamas away, dismissing the brush of air across her skin that felt so much like a gaze tracing the lines of her body. It was nothing. She swallowed down the unease that crept over her with each movement. Just the echo of a restless night and the unwanted heavy dread Ava had left behind.

Nothing a little ice-cold water and a hot towel couldn't fix. And it did make her feel a bit better. Maybe not rested the way a good night's sleep could, but at least she didn't feel like she'd fall asleep in her coffee.

Which, apparently, she did not have time to top up because a glance at her cell phone indicated she was late. Very late. Again.

She grabbed the closest skirt from the closet, panties, shirt, and ballet flats and squeezed into and shoved on everything as she ran through the apartment. Her purse and keys were stolen from the foyer table on a flyby to catch the bus, a warm sweater stuck in her elbow and trailing along behind her.

It wasn't until she was already at the bus stop that she realized she had forgotten her travel mug half-filled with coffee on the counter.

She dropped her head back, frustration prickling along her hair-line. The day was shaping up to be a doozy. "Great. Just great."

"What's that?" said a voice from beside her.

She hadn't heard a soul come up next to her and snapped her head to the sound of the voice. Rattled. She was so damn rattled, and he was just an old man with white hair and age spots on his face. There wasn't a single curve to his spine. He smelled of cloves and woods and might have been handsome in his prime. His eyes, bright with an amethyst glint of light, blinked at her. She tried to match the voice, a strong rumble of a sound that had no business coming from such wrinkled lips, but she couldn't.

She gestured to the space between them, waving away the comment. "Oh, nothing," she said to the man standing beside her. "Just forgot my coffee." A smile pulled at her mouth. No sense being rude just because she was having a bad day.

"One thing about coffee," he said in that disconcertingly powerful voice, "there's always a shop on the corner."

A chuckle moved through her chest. "That's true enough."

She found it hard to meet his gaze. The intensity of it was un-nerving. It begged a sudden exclamation that she knew him from somewhere and that he was waiting for that moment. The way an old schoolmate knew your name but you'd completely forgotten they existed.

He wasn't a customer, she didn't think. Nor was he a neighbor, and yet...

"Do I know you?"

A dip of his torso in a slight bow and she thought he might answer, but the bus heaved along the curve and shuddered its doors open.

She stepped aside, waving him in front of her. He shook his head and swept his arm toward the stairs. Even that gesture seemed too youthful.

"Females before males," he said, and a gleam lit his eyes.

She canted her head at him as she angled her feet toward the bus. What a strange thing to say. "Females?"

His head dipped, a subtle nod that would have seemed demure if not for the flare of his eyes, an almost smoldering glint that hinted at things done in the dark between two people. Things that he wanted to do to her. And it completely froze her.

"My apologies," he said in a husky voice that shouldn't be doing the things it was doing to her insides. "I sometimes can't find the right words for your world."

Without thinking and before she could stop herself, she was reaching out to touch his hand. An encouragement. A moment of understanding from a city native to someone unfamiliar with the cultures. But when she did, his hand shot out faster than it should, and he gripped her wrist. A hum of warmth streamed up her arm. Flustered, she yanked her hand back. Her eyes darted to his. They weren't downcast. They were aimed like flashlights right at her. Something in her chest squeezed tight.

Behind him, a streetlight flared and died with a loud sizzle. A flicker of light sparked at his side, faint at first but unmistakable, like the edge of a firefly's glow. She blinked, but it didn't vanish. It pulsed softly, matching the faint thrum of her quickening pulse.

"Ladies before gentlemen," he said, making her drag her gaze back to his.

She blinked, confused for a moment, then dipped her head demurely. Right. The bus. "That's so sweet of you. Thank you."

He leaned forward, not much, just enough to charge the air between them. A flutter tickled her stomach, as though the butterflies inside weren't sure they liked the way he was edging into her space. And when he spoke again, it was in a throaty, almost lustful tone that made heat swamp through her core.

"It's been many a decade since any woman has thought me sweet." A wicked grin then, showing white teeth, so white the little points in the canines looked vaguely threatening.

She wasn't sure what to say to that. Thankfully, she was saved from replying by a growl of impatience from the driver.

"Lady," the driver called out from inside the bus, "I should have pulled out by now. Are you getting on?"

"Yes," she said, hastily spinning around and nodding. "Yes, of course. I'm sorry to make you wait."

With a quick step, she boarded and slipped a handful of coins into the fare box before hurrying to find an available seat. This time of the morning, most were already taken, and she was mindful to look for a spot only if it wasn't the last one available. She wanted to be sure he had a place to sit when he boarded.

As luck would have it, she found a fully empty bench at the back. Turning to wave the old man down, she stumbled slightly as the bus jostled into motion and caught herself on the seat's edge. She might be worried about the man's welfare, but apparently, the driver wasn't. It took a moment to regain her footing and scan the aisle, and in that time, the poor gent might have already lost his balance. She tossed a glance over her shoulder, checking to see if he'd found a seat, to wave him toward her.

But he wasn't there.

A sliver of unease worked its way under her skin. Maybe he just hadn't had time to get on. She slid closer to the window, checking for the old gent on the sidewalk. The bus rumbled beneath her, its vibrations rattling the bench and sending fumes spiraling in through the cracked seals.

As the transit lumbered into traffic, her gaze darted to the sidewalk and then back to the aisle when she heard a commotion at the front. Maybe he'd just been stuck down below on the boarding area and was just now making his way into the aisle. She certainly caught his scent moving through the cabin, that strong aroma of forested glens and holiday baking.

She was prepared to wave him over, but it was someone else who had boarded in his place—broad of shoulder and towering to a height that nearly brushed the roof of the vehicle.

He wasn't just handsome. He was perfection. A beautiful predator in a man's skin. Brushed-back black hair curled around his ears. His unbuttoned leather duster flared open as he prowled down the aisle, revealing dark clothing that clung to a frame built of sharp, unforgiving angles.

She could barely tear her eyes away.

And then, as if he sensed her eyes on him, his gaze locked onto hers. His gaze shuttered, focusing on her with riveting intensity. Something primitive and instinctual came to life in her. Heat surged from her chest, rising up her neck in a molten wave. He was looking at her—not past her, not through her, but *at* her. She felt the way a mouse might as a cat's gaze found it in the grass.

Even as the bus jerked out into traffic, a smile spread across his face, and for the briefest moment, his eyes gleamed with unnatural light—too bright, too sharp, like the violet underbelly of firelight caught in a blade. He halted beside the seat in front of her, and strangely, the man sitting there, a large man himself, vacated the spot and shuffled all the way to the back of the bus.

With a long look that was as impossible to meet as the old man's had been, the stranger slid onto the vacated seat. Safe behind his back, she lifted her gaze to his shoulders, trailing over the lines, marking the thick, corded power in his throat. A bodybuilder, maybe. The black ink peeking up from his collar suggested a larger tattoo below his shirt. An incredible urge to peel it away, to trace the lines below, made her fingers itch. She clenched them tight over her purse.

Heat wavered off him like eddies of water on the shore. She pulled her eyes back to his nape, watching the place just behind his ears, where his pulse thrummed at a rate that made her own start to race.

God, he was gorgeous. Even from behind. But where had the other man gone? Not that she was complaining at the view, but the old guy had been standing right behind her, smiling with those sharp, white teeth. He should be somewhere on the bus or on the street. She leaned sideways, her gaze sweeping the seats again, but all she saw were tired commuters and empty expressions. The vehicle jolted over a massive pothole, and a harsh grind of gears rattled the floor. Her heart stuttered, a breath catching sharp in her throat.

Her phone buzzed from inside her purse. She fished it out, and as she did, something caught her eye from beneath her sleeve. Pulling the material back, she peered down at the inside of her wrist.

There. Right there in a small cluster, like a constellation, were five dots joined together with thin lines that glowed with an almost bioluminescent purple shimmer. She blinked as she tried to work out where she might have come into contact with glow stick paint and came up empty.

She rubbed it, expecting it to smear or come off onto her fingers. Instead, it heated up, warming her skin as though a curling iron had touched down on it. Unnerved, she rubbed harder, shook out her hand as if that could cool it off.

The dots got brighter. The links joining them smudged, creating inky black lines along the edges with subtle depth and thickness, like echoes in the shadows of her skin.

She stared down at the mark, scrambling to make sense of it, and caught a good look at the screen of her phone.

That was when her heart rate really ratcheted up. She thought she was going to puke.

The message said, *Be careful. He's watching you.*

Another private number. Different than the one from earlier. Ava couldn't have ditched her burner already and got another. Plus, her sister never texted. She barely even spoke when she called.

This wasn't television or the movies. She wasn't Adriana le Cerva, for heaven's sake. But those words...they stared up at her, goading her. Her hands trembled. Her throat hurt in ways that made it tough to swallow. Determined to remain calm, she blew out a long breath. Pressed the OFF button.

With her heart hammering in her throat, she scanned the faces around her, searching for threats, for evidence that someone was indeed watching her. She forced herself to draw in her breath slowly, purposefully. Whoever had called knew her number. Burner phones could be purchased anywhere.

She pulled the cord, anxious to get off, to get moving, to get to the safety of her little bookshop as soon as she could. A place where she could think things through and find some calm to work out exactly what might be going on, whether it was a manipulation by Ava or something else.

In her haste to exit, she was already standing before the bus groaned to a stop. She brushed past the stranger in front of her. As if drawn by some compulsion outside her own interests, her gaze darted sideways to him. His head tilted as though he were listening to something only he could hear. And then, impossibly, his lips curled into a smile that whispered one thing.

He knew.

-The End-

Kit out There in the Darkness

KIT

THE NAILS DIGGING INTO her throat needed to be clipped. That was all Kit could think the moment she swam to consciousness. It was a stupid, absurd thought to bob to the surface, because the fact that there was a hand around her throat at all should have had her in a full-blown, adrenaline-soaked panic.

But it didn't. The too-sharp nails and what sort of grime might be embedded in them, that thought took all her mental space. Her brain might as well have been suspended in some green gelatin dessert for all the good it was doing for her. There was just nothing to fire the muscles into resistance against the very real danger that she might choke to death.

It took far too long to get past the thought of those pointed things embedding into her skin. Battling the surface tension of consciousness was just about all she could do. She tried to shove through the slick of it, her limbs shrieking at her mind to do something.

Eventually, the demand for air fired her lungs enough for them to act on their own, and she gasped around nothing, wheezed in a small funnel of air. Instinct dumped itself into gear then, accelerating the panic that had been sitting on the sidelines waiting to see who would lead the troops out of Armageddon.

She flailed and pinwheeled with her arms, twisting with her entire torso, and yet...nothing. All her brain could shoot off for signals were blanks. Nothing responded. She couldn't move. She couldn't catch a good breath. A landed herring would have had a better chance of batting away that hand from her throat.

That was when the second thing slid in from the sidelines past her wheezing, coughing attempt to feed her lungs oxygen. The realization that she was lying down. She wasn't on a soft bed with a nest of blankets to bury into. The place she lay was hard and unforgiving. Something round and fist-sized jabbed into her back. Instead of warmth, a damp chill trampled up her spine in rubber galoshes.

And it was dark. No. That wasn't accurate. Pitch black described it better.

Her nostrils flared with the damp stink of earth and rot, the scent of ancient, forgotten things. This wasn't her comfortable bed, and it was not her house. She wasn't lying on the stoop, having passed out before she could jiggle the lock of her apartment door. Not the bookshop, either. She would know the aromas of those places. She would know the air, how it tasted, how it smelled. She'd know the feel of it brushing her skin.

Inside somewhere, though. Because there was no breeze. No birdsong. No traffic hum or exhaust fumes clinging to the back of her throat. Just an unending aroma of ozone like the stink of too much bleach. Of atop that, the smell of woods and damp stone.

Inside her chest, ants began to chew through her resolve. She was about to scream, but an unfamiliar voice cut through the miasma of confusion and shock.

"Hurry," he said.

Oh sweet Jesus, not just in the dark, but not alone either. She tried to twist her head to see the source of the voice, and only realized it was coming from somewhere below her chest when he spoke again.

"The magic is wearing off," came the complaint. "Be careful. You know what he'll do if we damage her beyond repair."

"What's a corpse going to do?" drawled another voice, eliciting laughter from several more, and this time her entire body convulsed with the realization that there wasn't just one but several sets of hands now roaming her body in the darkness. "What's he going to do now except feed the Darkness with whatever magic he has left."

"I wasn't talking about him," came the voice, but all she could think of was the one word that snagged her mind.

Magic? Was that what they called roofies now? Because she was most definitely drugged. And while she might not be able to see where she was or how many revolting pricks had decided to take advantage of her paralysis, her brain had at least sorted that fact out. And that was something to hold onto in the chaos of confusion.

Was she supposed to be screaming inside now? Screaming out loud? Should she be able to struggle?

Because she couldn't seem to do any of those, and that was worrying her more than the unknown amount of men she could feel like spectral energies all around her.

Her mind tried to raise a flag to her limbs. It fluttered off in the distance, trying to catch her attention, barely able to break through the clouds, but it was there. She could almost make it out. If she focused. If she ignored the cold on her back, the brush of stinking breath above her. And one thought came back to her out of the darkness.

Someone had been watching her. A stalker of some sort. Maybe several of them. And now they'd taken her and drugged her.

Sweet Jesus. Would she feel everything they did to her?

She supposed she might be grateful later that she wouldn't remember any of this, but that didn't help her right now. Whatever they planned to do to her, would she feel pain, pressure, terror? Because God knew she was pretty terrified right then and it didn't seem to evaporate in the least. It was her first time being roofied. Would her body store the trauma and feed it back to her later in bouts of panic she couldn't explain?

And then why the hell wasn't she already forgetting things? Why could she even remember that she was being held here by...oh God, was it six men?

She thought she was going to puke.

"It's not a corpse I'm afraid of," the owner of the hand drawled, slicing through her frantic thoughts. "Don Sidhe will have our balls if we deliver her dead."

Don Sidhe? The term had a ring to it, like mafia, but it also didn't sound like it had any roots in any language she knew. It almost seemed as though she'd merely heard it in English, but had been spoken in some other language, something ancient and forgotten. Like Aramaic or Latin. And what was this worry that they would deliver her dead? Was that a hope she could hang onto? That they needed her alive, or was it more frightening because it meant that whatever they did to her, there would be no hope of a peaceful end?

This wasn't just a gang of thugs looking for a quick good time. Fears of trafficking bobbed up to the surface as a stubborn bit of flotsam. She swatted at it, trying to shove it back down beneath the waters. Because she needed to hang onto this peculiar calm until it allowed logic and reason to leak through. And then she could work out a way to escape.

The hand around her throat let go, finally, and those fingers, calloused and rough, skittered over her belly, poking into her belly button, exploring her. As if they had all the time in the world to do so. No worries about anyone watching, obviously. So where was she? In a mausoleum in the graveyard in the middle of the city center or a damp cellar somewhere in an abandoned crack house? Dragged there after they'd dropped the roofie into her drink at the bar.

Except she hadn't been at a bar. She'd been at work. Hadn't she? And who carried roofies into a bookstore to drug a simple clerk?

Some men are coming.

Her mind bucked up at the thought. Ava's warning, stomping through her mind on rubber-soled combat boots. Ava had tried to warn her. She'd called after months of silence to drop that one cryptic message, and Kit had ignored it.

And now she was paying for that. Or was about to pay for it. She didn't think they'd done anything to her yet. She would know, wouldn't she? She would feel different. Ugly. Hurt. Ashamed. Rage?

Something. Not just this deafening numbness.

"We have to be quick." A guttural voice. The first one, she thought. She could feel him leaning over her.

"You be quick if you want," said another. "I plan to savor it."

Hands. Not just one. Not just on her throat, but moving over her body now. Two sets of palms, twenty fingers, if she counted right. She couldn't see them, just feel the clammy, creeping progress down her torso.

But this time, her ribs flinched at the touch. Hope sent up a red flare through the darkness. She tried to move and managed to twist her torso ever so slight to the side. Victory, however small, pulled at her lips. Then something tore—fabric ripping, and the sudden jerk of her torso under the effort sent a spike of terrifying clarity through her.

Sweet heaven. They were undressing her, taking her clothes. Her sweater. Her pretty bird-shell blue sweater.

Oh God. The terror came in full force, then. She was wrong. So wrong. It was much better to feel that numbness. She couldn't breathe for the panic, the dump of adrenaline that had her shivering harder than the chill in the air demanded as it brushed against bare skin. Rough fingers pushed beneath soft cashmere—that sweater, the one she'd pulled over her head that morning... or yesterday?

Kit's stomach turned. *When* had she put it on? She couldn't remember, and that bothered her as much as the cold that tightened over her ribs.

That they dared touch her body as though they owned it.

She *saw* herself then—straining against the hands, the flimsy bra that was useless against their pull. Lace snapped through her mind: pretty, delicate, the exact shade of blue as the cashmere. She'd chosen it on purpose, hadn't she? A gift from Chester over a year ago. When life was normal and her sister was content to call and breathe into the phone.

Her vision swam, slowly sharpening the shadows, creating grey ash of the dark coal. The musty stink of dirt and mold clung to the back of her throat, thick and sour, and a faintly metallic tang whispered cement basement.

Sweet Jesus. If she could smell, if she could move, then maybe the drugs were wearing off. And if the drugs were wearing off, then she could fight back.

She just had to distract them. Delay it all. Find a way to appeal to their humanity.

"Please," she said, daring to try out her voice. "Don't hurt me."

A long, drawn out silence. The hands skimming her skin halted.

"Fuck," said the voice, a gritty thing, like nails on stone. "Now she's awake. You want a broken body on your hands? You know how fragile they are when they fight back."

Fingers probed her belly button again, poking in so deep she winced. "So give her more magic," came the answer. "She won't fight then."

More drugs. They wanted to keep her helpless. She couldn't let that happen.

"I won't fight," she said, pleading. "Please. Just let me go. I promise I'll be good. I won't tell anyone."

A long-suffering sigh and then a response, but not to her words. She might have said nothing.

"I've already used up too much magic. You do it." Something like a flicker of a tongue over her belly. Rasping like a cat's. Wet. "Unless, of course, you want me to have the first turn."

"Who said you would get a turn at all?" A waspish reply that had her trying to roll over, out of reach of those greedy fingers now pinching her belly fat.

"You can't just use her up and force me to watch without a taste. That's not fair."

"If I let you go after me, there won't be anything left to bring to him. I know you. You're a greedy sonofabitch."

The pinching of her belly chub turned rough. "I'll be careful." The voice was pleading even as the touch got more painful. She winced as he begged. "Please. She has such lovely skin."

That was all she heard, all she needed to hear, before her body erupted, every limb jerking at once, and thank God for it. Kicking. Flailing. Pinwheeling. She didn't hold back. Just let go with a frantic, animal instinct.

There was no plan, no precision, no rhythm, like in the fights she'd seen on TV. Kit wasn't a fighter. She was a quiet bookworm who liked wine and reading into the small hours of the night. And yet here she was—thrashing, clawing, struggling like a cat in a cage to wrest herself from the grip of hands that shouldn't be mauling her skin.

The men fought back. Grabbing her arms, grappling for her legs. She managed a scream that tore through her chest, burned up her throat. She felt ragged after it erupted, but she let it fly with all the energy of a hurricane shredding a windsock.

The hand with the nails clamped down over her mouth again. She tasted earth and something funkier, as though he'd been eating pungent cheese with his fingers. The back of her throat closed down in a suction as it fought the bile that started to rise. She groaned deep in her chest, a sound that rumbled through the air. She needed to reclaim her wits. She needed to calm the fuck down or she wasn't going to live through this no matter how badly they needed her alive.

Her core trembled at the force it took to remain still. She had to convince them she was submissive. It took almost more than she could bear to stem the tsunami of panic.

A moment of silence, then. Shivering, her teeth rattling around her tongue, she finally found the courage to do nothing.

Tentatively, the hand moved away from her mouth, but she felt the imprint of those nails in her cheeks. Could still taste the funk on her tongue. Her breath was the only noise she heard, and it was moving in nasal wheezes and coughs. She didn't dare hope they were thinking of letting her go. Every inch of her body hummed with electric fear and hope that her compliance might help change their minds.

She prayed for it like she'd never prayed before. Willed it. Sent out a thousand manifestations into the universe.

Then one of them sighed theatrically into the belly of the darkness. She felt his exhale on the small hairs of her body.

"We could both go at the same time," he said.

This time, when she screamed, it hurt her ears. She barely felt the rocks on her back, the cold dampness of the floor on her bare legs, the grooves that caught her hair as she writhed and flailed about.

The backhand came swiftly across her cheek, striking with enough force to bring fire to her face and clamp her teeth down over her tongue. She tasted blood. The urge to cup her cheek and rub away the pain made her hands itch, but she couldn't move her arms. Someone was holding them down now.

The drugs were completely gone. She felt it all. Right down to the razor sharp terror of all the things they would be doing to her and a body that was now fully aware of the atrocities committed upon it. And with no hope of memory loss to disguise the trauma from herself later. The urge to beg for more 'magic' was so strong she parted her lips to plead for it, but another blow came, knocking her jaw to the side.

A popping sound ricocheted in her eardrum. Whoever he was, he didn't care what he struck out at, so long as what he hit was her. Blow after blow rained upon her until she was doing everything she could to curl into a ball.

Everything went darker after that. A blissful, swallowing well of shadow came up to claim her for a long, peaceful moment before she was vaguely aware of climbing that ladder again. Rung by aching rung, she ascended to a consciousness that seemed oh so far out of reach. Her chest heaved and yet it didn't move a single inch up or down. The darkness remained, but she knew it was one of reality and not of consciousness. She could make out a scuffling noise, coming from beside her, somewhere in the pit of shadow.

Barely suppressed roars of rage and grunts of pain drifted over her too, rousing her to full consciousness. Blinking even though she couldn't see a damn thing, she strained her vision into the shadows.

Wet noises, as though someone was striking something soft, filtered through, followed by groans. The sound of bone on bone, of large objects colliding with another. Multiple footfalls, too many to account for one or two men, too many voices cursing and growling.

They were fighting, it seemed. Fighting over her.

Which meant she was alone. She felt it in the way her limbs felt free, the way her breath pulled in nothing but stagnant air.

No one had her pinned.

She rolled to the side, bruising her shoulder against the crush of what she knew now was stone. Scrambling as best she could to her feet, she bit down on the pain. Stuffed it in. Told her mind to shut down anything but the thought of survival because she knew that was what was at stake. Life. Breath. Blood.

But it was dark, so dark, and her legs were a newborn deer's. She wobbled. Fell against something hard and pointed. The edge of a desk, maybe? The corner of a bit of twisted metal? Whatever it had been, it had been large enough to put an ache in her leg that still hurt. A slow, wet trickle cut a path down her shin. Blood. She sucked in a hiss of pain as the razor-like pain ate away at her resolve. The sound of that alone was as loud as a bullhorn in the darkness because it was different than the other noises of battle.

All scuffling stopped. The tense silence pulled every hair on her body to a quivering stand.

"She's up."

The words struck terror into her chest. She had to move. Now. If she didn't find a place to hide in, to run to, she might never get another chance. And she needed this chance. Of that, she was certain.

Gathering her courage, she felt for the shape of the thing through the shadows and decided it was a bit of metal. Hard and cold, but not sharp. Just clunky and edged enough to catch her leg as she tried to edge by. Hopefully it was a furnace of some sort and would provide adequate defense.

She inched forward, in the opposite direction of the voices. As quietly as she could, so she wouldn't draw attention to her position, she drew circles in the air, rippling outward, aiming for the side of the thing she'd bumped into. If she could find a way around it, she might be able to orient herself. She could use it as a defensive block at her back, leaving them to navigate around it themselves, maybe inflict more damage as they rushed to catch her. Because they were coming. She could hear them even now, realizing she wasn't where they'd left her, the curses ripe and ready on their tongues, blaming each other.

She had to keep going. Get around the furnace. She'd run, then, if she could. Duck and hide if she couldn't. Darkness could be her friend if she didn't freak out. If she was in a basement, there would be a door. She just had to find it.

With each, faltering step, adrenaline swamped in deeper. She felt it as a flush of her skin, a prickling of her nostrils. Instinct coming alive and firing her senses.

Silent, now. She had to be a ghost in the dark. She struck out with hands waving gently in front of her chest, below her hips, above her head. Water pooled beneath her tongue, demanding to be swallowed down, but she resisted because she was scared they'd hear and that would pinpoint her position. Holding back made her throat ache.

But she kept on. She felt with her feet, gaining an inch at a time, sweeping her hand out in front of her, advancing painstakingly into the darkness.

She was sure she could make out a bit of cotton white somewhere at the end of the dark tunnel. A flare of cautious excitement sparked in her chest.

But then, calloused fingers closed down around her wrist and that hope became a tamped down wick on a candle. Gone without an ember's glow in the shadows. Just smoke and the stink of petroleum.

A yank and she staggered sideways, lost in the darkness, no orientation in the shadows. Just that hand on her wrist, the breath on her face.

"Oh, no, pretty thing." A guttural, almost animalistic throatiness to the voice. It was the same voice from earlier...but different. "You aren't going anywhere until we've had a taste."

That was the moment she felt those pinprick teeth sink themselves into her chest.

She cried out, but not enough to drown out the words hissed into her ear by another person.

"And where you're going after, you'll be crying for the gentleness of our company."

Before the Darkness Descends

Kit

SOME MEN WERE COMING.

They were coming and Kit needed to get out of town. That's what Ava had said on the phone...what? Last night? The night before? It was impossible to remember anymore, since Kit wasn't even certain she'd had a full night's sleep since. One thing she was certain of was that her sister's voice had a sterling sharp edge to it. A hook that sank into the monkey part of her psyche, where her brain caught hold with the tenacity of a marlin.

It made standing alone at the bus stop on her way home from work, long after the sun had dropped behind the curtain of buildings, a bit too unnerving.

And just why Ava would deign to speak to her after all these months, weeks, years, of doing nothing but breathing into the line or leaving dead air was a mystery. Her sister was no stranger to trouble.

She courted it the way a dog sniffed at another's backside. But this time, whatever trouble she'd got herself into had urged her to speak, and those few words were like a punch to the gut. A rope tightening around Kit's throat and cutting off her air.

And it was enough that Kit hung up before she could even think it through. A reaction, she was now regretting, because another text popped up on her phone this morning. From another private number. Telling her she wasn't safe. For a manipulative tactic, it was a pretty awful trick. Even for Ava.

It had been years since her younger sister had left, or had Kit tossed her out? She wasn't sure of that anymore either because that moment was chaos of emotion where both of them were yelling but not hearing a thing. Some words were said. Someone tossed out the pedo term. Someone got angry. Someone—likely Ava—had yanked neatly stacked books down from the shelves and stomped on them. Yes, Kit thought. That was definitely Ava.

Seven long years ago, and Kit was older now. She wasn't the same young adult in charge of a rebellious teen, both of them grieving the loss of their parents. And she hoped with every tension-filled, silent phone call, that Ava had matured too. But this last call proved otherwise. Just what Ava thought she could gain from a vague threat like that, Kit couldn't understand, and didn't want to. It was too painful to consider the things Ava might have got herself into.

And though it felt good at the time, hanging up did nothing to assuage the feeling of dread that followed, the sleeplessness, the sudden rapid firing of her heart for no reason. A fluttering, hammering sensation that amped up far too much as she stood beside the bus shelter, too scared of being trapped inside to step out of the cool air.

Even the little retail therapy she'd indulged in after work—a shopping stint she could ill afford—had done nothing to smooth down the hackles of her nerves. It might have actually made things worse. Because now instead of taking the bus the same time as the rest of the nine to five working world, she was waiting for transit long after eight with a purse loaded with things she didn't need.

And no one was waiting with her.

Night had already crept over the buildings and begun to leak onto the asphalt. Every shadow felt sentient, and it wasn't just the chill in the autumn air that had her shivering. Hugging herself for warmth did nothing to ease it. She wasn't sure anything could at this point, except maybe a nice hot shower and a tall glass of wine. Something she planned to do as soon as she got home. If she was lucky, she'd be sleeping by ten.

But for now, the best she could do was edge closer to the wall of the shelter, letting it buffer the breeze that tugged strands of her hair across her mouth and slid cool fingers down her neck. It didn't help that the bus was late. Didn't matter how many times she told herself she was just tired and overreactive. She'd taken this transit for years and knew the way the fog lingered over the sidewalks as it rose from the manhole covers. Just because it looked like a shroud clinging to the air tonight didn't necessarily mean a horror show was going to come to life in front of her. If the street lamps barely cut through the mist, it wasn't because the weather was conspiring to turn her into a victim of some psychotic slasher.

But tell that to her nerves as a dog somewhere barked in a high-pitched note of urgency or the cat that yowled on the heels of that frenetic barking.

Dammit. Even witching hour couldn't be more nerve-wracking than this dead time after rush hour and before night shift workers headed out. She shifted her weight, the toes of her sensible shoes catching and rolling over a small pebble. Huffing impatiently, she glanced down the street one more time, groaned nearly out loud when nothing met her gaze except the same parked cars and the same streetlights flickering against the foggy air. The same boutique shop doors caged off from theft.

With that same prickling along her neckline. It was enough to make her huff in frustration as she dragged her eyes over the street again before checking her watch for the time.

That was when she caught sight of a tall figure leaning against the lamppost just across the street. She was sure he hadn't been there earlier, but now, he acted as though he was part of the scenery and had all the time in the world to study her. Her gut knotted at sight of him.

His broad shoulders and hard lines spoke of power. Almost like a bull mastiff. Even from this distance, she caught a gleam in his eyes, a flicker of color—purple, maybe—in their depths.

She shouldn't be able to see all that from across the street. There was just something altogether wrong about the way he held her gaze with the sort of boldness that came from believing you couldn't be seen.

Fighting back the clump that lodged in her throat, she tried to break the lock he had on her gaze. Tried to pull attention away, to look at anything but the way he straightened up when she caught his eye. But she found her attention snagged the way a cobra handler had control of a snake. Rising from the basket, weaving back and forth, she felt the same sort of mesmerizing trance for all of three seconds before a long, slow grin broke out over his face.

The audacity of it broke the hold, finally, and she cut her eyes to the street again, tugging her coat closer. A habit more than anything, even though her therapist said she did it to gather a sense of safety and comfort around her because she lost it all during her formative years.

The relief she felt when she saw those much anticipated headlights piercing the gloom of the night's street, pulled a moan from her. The exhaust was a welcome thing as it drifted over the air, mingling with the stink of brake fluid as gears shifted. She shuffled impatiently, anxiety climbing her spine, urgency chasing it.

She edged toward the curb prematurely, and for a second, she thought the crunch of boots on pavement was her own feet moving across the pebble-strewn asphalt. But the weight of it was all wrong. The pace was off, the noise too distant.

Her fingers caught on her purse strap at the sound, ready to dig inside for the tiny blade she had stowed inside. She wouldn't make the same mistake she'd made with the bully from earlier. This time, her knife would be snapped open. Let someone try to attack her then.

Except she couldn't find her knife in her bag. And there he was on her side of the street already, stepping out of the shadows as if he was made of them, striding straight toward her with calm, unhurried confidence. His leather jacket flared out as he stalked toward her, grasping for the air like wings. The sound of his footfalls didn't quite match the way his boots struck the pavement. The effect was eerie, as though she was watching a movie where the sound wasn't synced.

And that stare. God. It held hers with a ruthless intensity. Unrelenting. Just as bold as it had been from across the street. If she'd even managed to burrow into her bag long enough to put her hand on the elusive pen-knife, it had fallen back into the depths the moment he tilted his head at her. An invitation of some sort, a greeting of one acquaintance to another.

Her stomach dropped. Her pulse hammered. She thought she smelled a faint waft of chlorine, an ozone-like smell that prickled her nostrils.

There was something about him that looked vaguely familiar, but she knew she would have remembered him if she'd seen him before. She'd have picked out every minute detail of that magnificent body, that prowling stride. She'd have marked it the way an antelope took note of a tiger's movements.

All she needed was the same opportunity for escape that an antelope might have at the last moment. She just needed the few more moments that it would take for the bus to pull up to the curb. The few seconds it would take for her to flee up the steps.

He was still a few yards away when the transit screeched to a stop a few feet from the bus stop exhaust fumes, sharp and persistent prickling her nostrils. The doors hissed open on their pistons. Metal glinted at her, dirty and black from constant exhaust and street grime of a thousand thousand boots scuffing the filth form the city onto its treads.

She all but ran for the boarding platform, clutching her purse, trying not to look like she was running from the devil because that sort of behavior only made her look more like a damsel. She'd seen the movies. Read the books.

He was beside her long before she had a chance to lift one foot onto the boarding platform. How he managed it, she had no idea, but she felt him there like an undercurrent of electricity, the way the air feels before a lightening snap.

As if drawn by some magnetic pull, her gaze flickered to his. A flash of purple moved through his irises, strangely visible in the dim light, as though sparking from within by a magical energy. A memory lit up somewhere in the depths of her mind. She'd seen that sort of eye color before, hadn't she? Those eyes would be hard to forget.

He was so close she could catch the faint scent of cloves and something sharper, like scorched wood, coming off his skin.

"Did I scare you?" he said in a low, throaty voice.

His gaze was as intense as a touch, lingering a bit too long on places it shouldn't. Some dark place inside her blinked its eyes open like a leviathan in the depths of the Mariana Trench. A reaction she'd thought comatose beneath the weight of the ocean.

Up close, he was absolutely and damnably gorgeous. She floundered over a reply, and ended up saying all the words all at once. A ramble. Nothing intelligible. She would roll her eyes at her own awkwardness if she could tear them from that handsome face.

Impossibly, mercifully, the corner of his mouth hitched up in amusement, not mockery. A gift for the rousing beast she'd thought slain for years.

"Are you going to climb aboard?" he asked around the heartbreaking, achingly wicked grin. And oh Gods, the way her heart hammered then.

She almost forgot to grab for the railing in the fluster of the moment, and when she did, she missed it entirely. Too much of her own weight propelled her forward with nothing to catch herself on.

When her foot missed the first step, it came down on the asphalt of the street too hard. The metal stair cracked into her shin. She winced from the pain, buckling over automatically. Bright stars winked at her from behind her eyelids.

For a second...just one...a memory far more sharp overrode the pain.

Like lightning flashes, shuttering images of a young woman hanging from the rafters of an old gym came at her. Sneakered feet kicked out in the memory, their owner strangling beneath the coils of rope around her neck.

Kit gasped despite herself. Impossibly, the remembered salty taste of semen threatened to make her gag. She wavered on her feet, reaching out for something to hold onto. What she found was a hand, firm, large. Callouses rubbed against the softness of her own palm as another arm went around her waist. The way it slid over beneath her jacket to lay atop her sweater too intimately for a stranger was lost in the face of how amazing it felt. The ground settled beneath her feet. Everything stopped spinning.

Warmth, delicious warmth, spread through her spine and ignited a line of fire that climbed all the way to her neck. And yet she shivered. Some part of her feeling as though a creature of prey had claimed its supper, that sense of ownership coming and going in milliseconds, yet time felt like warm taffy being pulled out into a gooey string.

Compelled to look up, she sunk herself into his gaze and locked onto those eyes as though they were an anchor she could toss into a raging sea. And then...as if by magic, those images roiling through her mind's eye just stopped. A tap shut off with a dying squeak as if he'd somehow quieted the storm in her mind.

No killer here, surely. No stranger looking to do her harm. Just another weary human looking for a ride home.

She tried to smile back at him, but it was as natural as a puppeteer pulling on a string. Instead, she just stood there, one foot on one step and one lower. He smiled, his canine teeth just a little pointed, denting into his lip and making the fullness of them seem even more lush. She wanted to run her thumb over that bottom lip.

Awkward, so damn awkward. It took a beat before she remembered herself and was able to jerk herself back into the present.

The bus driver groaned behind the wheel. "Lady," he barked. "Are you trying to get on or get laid?"

"I'm sorry," she gushed out, gathering her purse against her chest. "I didn't mean to hold you up."

She rushed up the steps, then. Favoring the leg that she was now sure was bleeding beneath her slacks, and hurried to the nearest seat. Everything in her wanted to sag and let go, and she couldn't find a seat fast enough.

She'd had herself so worked up, the adrenaline washing in and washing out all her energy, leaving her to scan the bus aisles with a weary eye.

There. Two unoccupied benches in the middle of the bus. Bright blue seats with cracks in the benches, but side by side and away from a cluster of giggling teenagers hanging onto the rail.

Heat moved up her throat. They'd seen her reaction, she was sure, and were mocking her behind their hands. It made her chest ache. Eyes down, she hurried to the one farthest away from the girls and shoved into the seat closest to the window, silently, maybe foolishly, inviting him to push in beside her.

He didn't. He stopped a row ahead of the one she selected and on the other side of the aisle. Her heart dropped. Of course, he would slide onto a seat of his own. Of course, he would stay as far away as he could. He didn't know her. He probably had a lover waiting impatiently for him at home. He'd have to, a man who looked like that.

And because he looked just exactly like that, she found herself watching him slide onto the bench and settle with his arms crossed over his chest into the one closest to the aisle. Barring anyone from sitting with him at all. He kept his gaze fixed straight ahead. Not one glance back to where she sat fiddling with the purse strap.

Warm air from the heater brushed against her cheeks, and when the air felt cool against her skin, she realized she was blushing furiously. He'd probably seen it. No wonder the driver had made that comment. She probably looked like one of those teenagers.

But it was a relief, really, to have him sit somewhere else. She sighed quietly, relaxing into the bench. With him facing the front, she could draw her gaze from that one knee that angled out into the aisle, leveraging him against the seat as though he wanted to bolt back out of it. It was strange, the way he sat there, so stiff, as though the very seat he perched on was painful. When she traced that line up to his shoulders, she noticed they were one solid block of hard muscle.

His back was deliciously broad, the muscles in his neck thick and corded even though his frame was wiry. The leather duster he wore seemed from another century, faded and cracked in places but supple looking enough that she wished she had touched it when she had the chance. It gave off a strong scent that mingled with what had to be his own, one that reminded her of hot spices.

He wore the collar turned neatly down, and from her angle, she could make out a slight point to his ear beneath the lush mass of black hair. Pushed straight back in one sweeping cascade, his hair curled in places that begged for a finger to tangle into it.

She found her fingers running through her own locks, smoothing the dry ends, feeling for the softness closer to her scalp, making of her own ginger-colored hair a surrogate for that black mass that she wanted so desperately to knot in her grip. It had been so long since she'd been with a man. She'd even forgotten what it was like to hold a body close to her own.

Surely she could be forgiven for spinning fantasies about him during the ride home. To make the ride go faster, to calm her over-heated nerves. Imagine him as dark and brooding man in the racy romantasy book she had stashed in her purse.

The fantasies might have played behind her eyelids the entire way home, but the bus stopped again and the teenagers exited the middle door as a bunch of rowdy drunks pushed their way down the aisle from the front.

Laughing. Slapping each other on the back. Good old guys having a good old time mid-week. She watched them dispassionately, her gaze nothing more than the disinterested glance many transit riders gave newcomers, but one of them caught her eye. His head canted to the side as a slow smirk played over his features.

She caught sight of a tense shift in the stranger's body posture. He angled himself just slightly more toward her. His hand dropped to his thigh. Clenched once. Then splayed over his knee.

She should have taken the moment to push out into the seat next to the aisle, but because she was too preoccupied, it didn't occur to her till too late.

A Purse is not Enough

Kit

Some things can never be taken back, and Kit knew the second she met the drunk's eye, that she'd gone too far with a simple glance. His wicked smile pinned for a heart-stopping moment between his brash stare and the stranger's powerful energy coming off in waves. By the time she glanced away, dropping her gaze to her bag on her lap, the damage had already been done.

So she edged over on the bench, praying he'd just ignore her and grab onto the rail with his buddies, guffaw amongst themselves like most too-drunk rabble oblivious to anything but their own voices until they reached their destination and got off. But that wasn't going to happen and she knew it. She didn't have to look up to sense him bee-lining his way down the aisle right toward her.

Unnerved, she rooted hasty fingers inside her purse, digging through the interior. Wafts of spearmint gum and ink fled the inside like down feathers shedding a summer goose as she sorted through the tubes of makeup and plastic wrappings from her lunchtime sandwiches.

It wasn't like she was going to take anything out of her purse. She just wanted her hand on that pen knife. Maybe if she knew where it was she wouldn't feel so anxious. Maybe if she looked busy, they'd pass her by. Maybe if she didn't look up...

No such luck. A heavy weight shoved at her, forcing her to push over into the seat next to the window, trapping her there as he fell onto the aisle seat. The bench jostled beneath him, vibrating through her. His companions found spots right beside him, hanging onto the rails and laughing too loudly. Looking down at them. Leering.

She swallowed hard, pressed closer into the side of the bus. His shoulder pressed against hers too intimately. She did her best to lean away, out of touch, but he just leaned closer. She thought she heard a low growl coming from somewhere, but dismissed it quickly as the drunk placed his arm over the back of the bench, crowding her.

"Hey beautiful," he said, a wave of booze assaulting her nostrils. "You look lonely here all by yourself."

"I'm fine," she said in a clipped tone. Pushed closer to the window, only to end up tightening the man's hand on her shoulder cuff.

Up ahead of her, the stranger from the bus stop turned in his seat. She was pretty sure she heard that low growl again. Except she couldn't be hearing anything because neither the drunk nor his companions seemed to notice. If they did, they were oblivious to the tension that crackled through the air.

Her gaze darted to the driver, looking for some sort of help. She caught his eyes in the mirror before they went back to the road and her stomach dropped. Maybe he was forbidden by protocol from interfering. Maybe all he could do was pull over at the next stop and give her a chance to get off.

Which was exactly what he did, thank heaven. The bus began an obvious, careening swing toward the curb. The brakes squealed. A hiss of pistons cut through the air, wafting in the smell of diesel as the doors wheezed opened.

The driver flicked his gaze back to hers in the mirror. Get off, those eyes said.

Her eyes cut to the window to the darkness outside. There was no official stop, no shelter to wait in for another bus. Just a lot of sidewalk. The buildings looked dilapidated.

But this was it. The one chance she had to get off onto an unfamiliar street or stay on the bus with these strangers leering at her. She swallowed. Ava's words raced to mind.

She hauled her purse strap over her shoulder, deciding quickly. "This is my stop," she said, painfully aware that she'd have to climb over the drunk in order to get off the bus. He certainly wasn't making any move to let her out like most passengers would.

She started to get up, her stomach sick at the thought that the guy might grab her as she tried to get by. But she tossed the belly of the bag behind her so it would at least cover part of her back while she kept her arms over her belly. It wasn't much, but it would have to do.

Gathering what courage she could, she looked down at him. "I need to get off," she said, more insistent now, her voice a bit shrill for her tastes.

His blink was too slow. "Honey, just say the word and I'll happily oblige you," he said, slurring his words together.

His buddies snickered. One of them said something that sounded like get'er done, Buddy.

Those words, that insinuation. It all made her mouth taste like salt and musk. Memories of ropes and kicking feet tried to steal their way in again. Her chest felt entirely too tight.

Flustered, panic razoring through her like shards of glass, she started the distasteful climb around his knees. Pushing at his legs, squeezing between his shins as she gripped the back of the previous seat, she was acutely aware that her back was to him. But she didn't care if he groped her ass now. All she wanted was to get off the bus before she completely lost her shit.

Because she was going to lose her shit. Any second now, all those disgusting, shameful memories were going to wash her overboard, and she was going to end up curled up in a snotty, snarling mess of tears.

And sure enough, a hand slid between her thighs, so hot she could feel the sweat on the palms. For a gasping instant, she froze. Thought and reason fled her, leaving her mind a slate of black stone as civility and disgust warred to process the assault. She was just gathering her wits when a blur of movement invaded her peripheral vision. The heated fragrance of cloves and smoke and something else, something like ozone, washed over her.

The invading fingers jerked out from between her legs. Suddenly, there was plenty of space to swing around in. She was open, liberated somehow, and yet the first thought that came to mind was the worry that those fingers would end up somewhere else.

She panned the bench behind her, expecting to see the drunk tucked into his seat but still leering at her. All that met her gaze was a hard seat's hard edge and an abandoned wallet.

By the time she realized what the scuffling sound was in the aisle, the drunk was being hauled off his feet and hoisted into the air.

He hadn't said a word, the stranger. Whatever he'd done to the drunk's companions, they were fighting each other to get off at the stop. The drunk was hanging from massive hands by his throat. His legs kicked out like a marionette, and for a heartbeat, she saw Ava there, floundering, strangling, her eyes straining in their silent plea for mercy. Kit's hand went to her throat in reflex. She thought she couldn't breathe.

And then that image, too, was gone. She was left dragging in air through a wheeze in her throat, standing so erect her back ached. Her fingers fluttered to the base of her neck. Her pulse was a rapid fire in the hollow of tiny bones. The rumble of the bus beneath her feet seemed to match the vibration trembling in her core.

This...this was unexpected. Even as she darted a look at the driver, who was looking back in the mirror, she could hear the man strangling beneath the grip that held him. And where were the man's buddies? Fled to the streets, apparently. She could see them pointing at the bus window, yelling for help.

If she didn't do something, anything, right then, that man was going to die. No one was gong to help him. Jaded city gazes might be desensitized to violence, but this was ridiculous. The drunk might be a thoughtless prick, but that didn't mean he deserved to strangle to death. Whatever he'd done in his life—whatever he'd done to her in just the last few moments—didn't warrant the way he was kicking out, arms flailing as he struggled to suck in air.

And she couldn't just let him die. Not right in front of her. No matter what he'd done. But she was stuck between the seats, and the man's legs kept thrashing and catching her in the shin every time she tried to squeeze out into the aisle. No matter how much she waved her arms over her head, knowing...knowing the driver could damn well see her and what was going on, he was doing nothing.

The sound of the man fighting for air was sickening. It raised every hair on her body, set off an alarm so loud between her ears that everything came back muffled.

A gritty, stoic determination had painted itself onto the stranger's face. The cords in his thickly muscled throat strained with effort. There was no compassion in that expression. No hint that the grip would slacken at all.

Kit's purse fell with a thunk to the floor of the bus the moment a miraculous opening presented itself between a kick and a swing. She used it to wrestle out from behind the seat, pushing past the flailing legs into the aisle. The drunk landed another unintentional kick, this time to her thigh. The muscle spasmed in reflex, temporarily dead-legging her. She sucked in a hard breath. But the man's eyes were bulging and bowing out of the fight was not an option.

In a heartbeat, the world shrank down to that narrow place. It almost seemed like someone else's hands reached for the stranger's elbow. Someone else dropped all her dead weight into the pull as she let her feet fall out from beneath her. Dropping back, she did all she could to yank on an arm that seemed made of iron girders.

But even her weight couldn't dislodge his grip. Her voice when it erupted from her throat was a shrill whistle. Urgent. Commanding.

"Stop," she yelled. "Stop. You're killing him."

The stranger turned his head to her so in what seemed slow motion. His eyes narrowed as he skimmed her with a heavy glance, one that made her stagger back at the brutality she saw in those depths. She let go instinctively, a small bird finding itself pinned by a hawk's examination.

Predator was the word that came to mind. She'd been right the first time. He wasn't a gorgeous stranger seeking a ride home. He was a violent, ruthless creature.

She couldn't even see the driver anymore, just hear him talking in hushed, rushed sentences to someone.

The radio. He must have called his dispatch. But she couldn't wait for help that would come too late. She threw herself at the stranger again, clawed at his elbow, trying to dislodge his grip from the drunk's throat.

"Stop," she sobbed this time. "Please stop."

Wrenching hard, too hard and too ineffectively, her hands slipped from his elbow to the where bare wrist showed at the cuff of his leather jacket.

She felt a shudder go through him the moment she touched skin to skin. His hands fell away from the drunk's throat so suddenly that the poor bloke collapsed into the aisle in a puddle. Panic still held his features prisoner, and he lifted shaking hands to his throat as he gasped for air.

"What the hell, man?" he finally got out in a coughing fit of words, all the while finding the strength to crab walk backward, worming his way up the aisle toward the nearest exit. "Are you crazy? You almost fucken killed me."

It was clear he was suddenly, keenly sober. Fear was written in his gaze, and Kit was feeling for the seat behind her because she knew he was right to be afraid. The stranger had the look of murder in his eyes, a look that didn't lessen as he turned that piercing gaze on her.

She blinked. Was that something glinting in his fist? A knife maybe? Was he coming for her now? She staggered back, feeling for the backs of the bench seats as she inched away from the stranger, desperate for something to support her because her legs were failing in that regard. And she needed to get to the door. Like yesterday.

From the corner of her eye, she saw the drunk fall out of the bus, rearranging his shirt and tugging it down over his beer belly. The driver was rapid fire talking into the radio. Someone was going to be coming soon. Someone would sort this all out, but by then, it might be too late.

She might be dead.

What was a purse worth compared to that? She left it where it lay, as she back-stepped toward the exit, keeping her eye on the stranger who was canting his head at her as though he was trying to make a decision. Her mouth was too dry. She couldn't swallow. When she thought it was safe to turn her back to him, she spun around and raced for the exit.

She hated to just leave the driver to face all this, but he could hop off faster than she could. And if he knew what was good for him, he'd do just that.

She had made it within steps of the exit when something flickered in the side of her vision, some color. Or light. A presence, maybe. Some instinct buried deep in the monkey part of her brain pulled out an automatic shoulder check. The aisle was empty.

Blinking, confused, she turned back to the exit.

And her heart dropped. He towered over her, blocking the way out.

Her purse dangled from his hand. She had to drag her eyes up from that massive fist clutched over the handle to the eyes that had already locked on her face. Everything in her felt like it was bound to massive bars of lead.

"You are uninjured?" he asked.

She was painfully aware that the driver hadn't pulled back out yet, that the doors were still open. A breeze made its way down the bus, moved her hair. She smelled exhaust in it.

"I..." she breathed out very deliberately despite the trembling in her core. "I'm fine."

Her chin lifted on its own as she caught his gaze. The last moments replayed in full color behind her eyelids. She forced a calm into her voice that she didn't feel because she knew anything else would mark her as prey.

"I just need to get off."

She looked askance through the window, double-checking to make sure the gang of thugs was long gone. Then ahead to the driver. She caught his eye in the rear view, and he jerked his chin at the door.

"Yes," she said, nodding in shock. "I'm fine. It's just that...just that this is my stop."

She had to swallow down the unease as he aimed those violet eyes at hers. For a moment, she didn't think he was going to let her by. She angled her body sideways, trying to prod him into doing the same so she could pass. A subtle, but insistent hint to move the heck out of her way.

She tossed him a half-hearted smile, a careful encouragement to suggest nothing she'd seen was out of the ordinary. That she could keep a secret.

"He won't hold the doors for long," she said, pointing with her elbow at the driver, who she had a feeling planned to sit there until the grim reaper himself pushed her out of the exit.

"Lady," the driver urged, turning around in his seat. Both eyebrows were raised in an urgent suggestion. She had to get off. Now.

"Yes, thank you," she said, directing her comment to the front of the bus. "Just a moment." A nervous twitch of her mouth as she tried again to urge the stranger to move aside.

It took a long moment, but he finally dropped his gaze before stepping aside to let her to pass. She pulled in a bracing breath, slipped her fingers beneath the strap of her purse. He relinquished it without comment, just that same hard and unnerving stare. Her throat worked on a swallow before she gathered the courage to edge by him.

A flutter moved through her belly as she touched down on the last step. She was free. Things would be OK. And then, his voice stopped her, seizing her heart mid pump.

"I would have killed him," he said in a low voice, drawing her gaze to his face again. His eyelids were shuttered, but the gaze was direct. "If you wanted me to."

She didn't know what to say to that. All she could do was nod. He didn't need to confess it for her to know it was the truth. The ruthless energy was coming off him like heat from an open flame.

But he had let her go and she was on the last step, finally, just inches from freedom. She gripped the railing, faced the open doorway and the dark city streets beyond it.

And yet...yet something compelled her to look over her shoulder once more. He stood where she'd left him, his gaze pinned to her face as if he'd hadn't taken his eyes off her. His gaze dropped to her throat, and though it was a relief to be out from beneath that intense gaze, it was somehow more dangerous for him to be watching the way her pulse was hammering in her neck.

But she had confronted men like him before. One thing she'd learned was that no matter how terrified you were, you couldn't show that fear to a predator.

If she could do it for Ava, then she could do it for herself.

"Do you make a habit of killing men for women's pleasure?"

She expected him to be chagrined, to show a bit of embarrassment that he'd been called out, but his jaw clenched and he shoved his fists, still curled tightly, into the pockets beneath his long duster jacket. The gaps between the buttons strained open and she caught sight of the tight ridges of muscle between the fabric.

"I don't kill for anyone's pleasure but my own," he countered with such a lopsided, innocent-looking grin that it might have taken her breath away if the man smiling hadn't just tried to kill someone. "But I might be persuaded to rip out a throat or two...for the right female."

Something moved in his eyes, a glint of crystal kaleidoscope gems, she thought, the way a raven's wing caught the light and reflected an iridescent sheen.

She worried for the poor driver. He'd pull out into traffic and be left with this psychopath. But she nodded silently, swallowing down her unease. Then she turned and fled down the last step to the pavement.

Outside, her breath came much easier. Cigarette smoke drifted over the breeze to prickle the small hairs inside her nose. Traffic had begun to congest again. Late shift workers in their skirts and sneakers plowed over the sidewalks like dozers, not stopping, shouldering their way past each other. A woman walking a dog too big for the city was bent, scooping up its deposits from beneath an anemic poplar.

She thought she caught sight of a prostitute clinging to a dark corner.

Normal things. Things that might make her question everything she'd just seen. Except her eyes stung. Her breath had ice shards in every inhale.

But at least the drunks were gone, and that meant she could make her way to the next bus stop, hop on and ride the rest of the way home. She'd sit as close to the front as she could and cling to the last shred of sanity she had in her until she could scream the craziness into her pillow before she went to sleep. If she went to sleep.

Her shoulders still hadn't found a release of the tension when the bus gears engaged with a loud groan. As it pulled away from the curb it drew eyes like a magnet. She wanted to be sure it was gone because the electricity of the night was still there, clinging to the air like ripe fruit.

From inside, the windows were lit with a bright white light that cast a hazy glow, a palm of illumination that swept aside the darkness and reached for her as she stood on the sidewalk. And there he stood, facing out, watching her.

His features were set in such a possessive, fierce expression that she shuddered.

Late Blooming Mums

Kit

She didn't sleep all night. Her skin felt too tight and too sensitive after the events of the ride home. Every brush of the flannel against her legs was too much sensation and not enough.

And the worst of it wasn't because she was afraid. It was because she couldn't stop thinking about the stranger's piercing gaze, the sound of his voice. The way...oh God, the way he looked at her like he would devour her.

Pent up fear and energy, the dump and release of adrenaline married to the sizzle of that man's voice was enough to delight her in the safety of her own bed. No judgment there, alone in the dark. No threat. Just her and the sweating heat of too many blankets and the smothering press of need.

By the time two A.M. came around, she'd realized the only way she would catch a few hours' rest was if she gave in to the shamefully guilty pleasure of touching herself.

And it was the stranger from the bus whose image came to life beneath her eyelids when she clamped them closed, her fingers roaming her breasts and stomach before finally, achingly, bringing herself to climax.

Even then, her finish was unfulfilling. Hollow. Like being starved for a decadent dulce lece cheesecake and finding only graham crackers in the cupboard. The rest of the night was no better. The restless thoughts that kept her awake mated with the shame and guilt so nicely that she spent most of the night wondering what sort of woman would lust after a violent man like that.

She'd had one partner in her lifetime, and that felt like a century away. He'd been soft in the middle too. The soft round belly beneath her navel felt comforting each time it brushed against the fullness of his.

Chester was soft everywhere, if she was truthful with herself. An office guy who sat behind a desk inputting numbers into accounting systems, filing papers away in metal drawers. His tongue tasted of paper.

But he'd been kind. Cooked delicious, decadent meals for her. Bought her flowers.

He was nothing like the teenaged boy from her senior year who raced his car in vacant parking lots every weekend, a boy she ached to kiss every time she caught sight of him in the hallway. The first boy to sink a finger inside her after one date with a desperate urgency that made her breathless.

She'd been racier herself then. His forceful, experienced touch excited her. But her inexperience turned him off. She caught him kissing a popular girl the next day in the hallway and that was that.

He got the girl pregnant before prom. If they stayed together or kept the baby, she had no idea. All she knew was that the years after graduation, when she became guardian for her wayward sister, she might have had other dates, other opportunities to find happiness. But Ava...Ava had struggled more than Kit with their parents' death, and any hope of finding a partner dissipated like a heroin high cut with baking soda.

She tried so many ways to make a safe home, one that her sister could pull about her and thrive in, but that wasn't in Ava's nature. The more Kit tried, the worse Ava got.

Her own grief got scheduled for a time when Ava didn't need her so much. She dropped any pretense of believing she could find a man who would survive the whirlwind that was her sister's daily life and battleground of home.

So when Chester asked her out two years after Ava had left for good, with his full lips and broad, almost feminine hips, she'd accepted. And his gentleness made her first time easy. Foreplay was lengthy. His thoughtfulness showed in the way he plastered them both with lubrication, slicking it over them both in a languid way that made her want more, beg for more.

He pressed in slowly, giving her time to relax and adjust.

His lovemaking was a turkey and stuffing feast for a conscience that desperately needed self-medication. They rolled around beneath sheets in the dark as though both of them had glutted themselves on carbs and sugar. Tryptophan leaked into his seed.

Despite his tender ministrations, his patient and plodding work, she could never finish like he did. In the end, she began to pretend enjoyment just so she wouldn't hurt his feelings.

By the time he left her, declaring himself conflicted by his own gender identity, she was ready to accept that she could never find love, anyway. She wished him well, hoped he'd found happiness. He deserved every bit of love and affection that a partner could shower on him. She didn't ache with resentment. She wanted him to find love in any way he could claim it.

But Chester was long gone and Kit had been on her own, growing plumper but more experienced with self-pleasure. Self care, she thought they called it now. Such a nice, clean and supportive term. By the time she'd realized she would be on her own, she started to lose weight for herself and not some man. She claimed her health and wellness like a warrior.

And yet, there were nights when her pillow claimed a dampness that had nothing to do with the weather. Mornings when her eyes took a bit longer to compress with a cold cloth.

The stranger from the night before reminded her of the young Kit, the one in the back seat of that Mustang with her jeans splayed open and a young man's fingers buried in her sex. A thrill of possibility made the air electric, putting a tingle in the small of her back.

But while the thought of him brought back memories of the way she'd been, the things she could have become, she also knew the stranger from the bus was far more dangerous than the boy in the Mustang. And that was what she was aching for: something forbidden and untouchable, as salacious and unrepentant as Ava had been, a way to reclaim what had been taken from her.

She wasn't drawn to *him* exactly, she didn't think. She was drawn to the kind of passion that could make another person commit whatever acts were necessary to keep a loved one safe.

At least, that's what she told herself, even though the mere thought of the things she'd fantasized about over the night would alarm the daylight Kit.

So she dressed in the morning with more flair than usual. She took her time applying the makeup she'd purchased with the last of her money, carefully masking the dark circles in her tear troughs that had etched themselves in nice and deep over the long, restless night.

The mirror showed she'd selected the perfect shade of the blush. The smoky purple shadow she'd selected—a coincidence?—showed off the deep greens in her eyes. Lush eyebrows got brushed and gelled to a perfect, sweeping arch the way the social media gurus suggested.

Her lips even looked fuller, traced with a pencil a shade darker than the lipstick.

She stood back and studied herself. It had taken months of work to lose fifteen pounds. Months of suffering and determined work that a few insensitive words from a stranger could tear down like a tissue in the wind, because no matter how much weight she lost; she'd still see a chubby girl in the mirror.

But she looked good. She knew she did. She looked healthy and that was what mattered. Not a number on a scale and not a few extra pounds. And it didn't matter if she never found a partner. She could be enough. She didn't need a man to complete her.

Her shoulders sagged as she let go the tension that had built throughout the night and since Ava's call. Things would be ok. She'd taken her life back from Ava all those years ago, but never really lived it.

That was going to change. Today.

There were no men coming. She laughed to herself at the thought of it as she pulled on the same pretty sweater as the day before because it was soft and comforting. Oh God, the very idea that men would come at all. If they knew Ava's back story the way she did, they'd know just how useless Kit was as leverage.

And if they did come, then they'd confront a real woman. Not a shadow. Not anymore.

When she strolled out from her apartment, she felt reborn. The day, crisp and bright as only an autumn day can be. Traffic hummed by. Her neighbors slammed out of their front doors and called to their kids. Revved their car engines into life.

She stopped to pull a few errant weeds so they wouldn't drop seeds into her garden and come to life again in spring. The last of her late blooming Chrysanthemums trembled beneath her palm as she drew her hand over the tops, feeling the velvet of their petals, testing to see how much longer they might last if no frost came to claim them.

Life could be good without Ava, she thought as she examined her garden. And life was good just the way it was. She had this ground, these plants, something to nurture that wouldn't kick and claw at every embrace she tried to give. Life didn't have to mean an aching hollow deep in her throat. The feeling of dread knotted at the base of her spine.

She was about to straighten up and head for the bus stop when the crackling of fallen leaves suggested a booted foot had crushed them. Her nape prickled. All determination to put the past behind her abandoned her as the trauma of the night before pounded back into the space between her temples.

It felt like it had rocketed into damn space as Ava's voice slammed into her skull.

Some men are coming.

She came up swinging. Her movements, unnatural and unfamiliar, were impossible to control. She nearly twisted her ankle because she whirled around too fast. Her slouch bag fell from her shoulder so smoothly it might have been practiced, except she knew it was blind luck.

Thank God for blind luck. She used it, went with it, swinging out in a forceful, sweeping arc. Stretched to the limit of its strap, the purse claimed all the air she could give it, and she leaned out, automatically, the way a batter gave thrust to a strike.

A blur of movement, too swift to coalesce into anything solid, met her gaze. She adjusted quickly, thoughtlessly, twisting the other way as she hauled the bag to the reverse, giving the blow all her weight as she spun in place. And then...then the bag fetched up into something solid and immovable. A small exhale of air was her only reward. A sound she might have made herself from the exertion.

Too late, she realized her own balance shifted too fast. Inertia an inevitable thing. She twisted painfully, her back twinging. A muscle spasming as she kept going even as the bag stopped short.

Some men...

She ignored the pain. Brought out her elbow. This time she swung with her arms, flinging them out to her sides. Straight as they were, her purse strap slid down and fetched up on her wrist. It was weightless. Nothing in there anyway except a few almonds. Her new lipstick. But holding onto it would hinder her if she had to get away.

She'd just leave it. Let it drop. It was nothing to her own safety and something inside her told her very clearly...

She had to run.

But then firm hands dropped down onto her shoulders, and full-blown panic took her. Someone was shrieking in her ear and it took a brush of fingers across her cheeks to realize it was her.

"Some men," she shouted, the only words that would come to her aid, the only syllables clanging around a mind emptied by panic.

"Not men," a male voice said. Soothing. Calming. "Just one."

A shudder ran through her and stilled. Like magic. One more trembling shake and she could see again. The horrible tunnel of pinprick light opened up and daylight leaked in at the corners of her vision.

She blinked. Stared up into the face she'd fantasized about the night before. Here. Standing right here in broad daylight. The morning sun slanting over the chiseled angles of his jaw, turning his face into hard edges.

Her nerves were a frayed mass of wire, hackles on a cat being rubbed the wrong way. And yet...

And yet his voice, his eyes. They were enough to draw her breath out in tiny, puffing inhales. A bloom of exhaust mushroomed out around her face. She exhaled the nerves into the miasma of it.

"You," she said. She wasn't sure if she should be relieved or just as terrified, but she scanned the street, looking for signs of other neighbors, just in case. Witnesses in case she needed them. She might have even taken a step or two backward. "What are you doing here?"

Some Kind of Masochist

KIT

THE MAN IN FRONT of her had tried to kill someone the night before. And while he'd done it to help her, there had been a ruthlessness in it that bordered on terrifying. The thought that he was standing right outside her house was nerve-wracking.

"Well?" she asked, pressing on even though her windpipe felt like it was closing. "What are you doing here?"

"I'm charged with watching something precious," he said.

An incline of his head and nothing more, but it was enough to put all those wiry nerve endings, each hackle on the back of her neck, into a frenzy of activity. It didn't matter how exciting it had been to think of him during the underbelly of a long sleepless night, the real shape and size of him standing in the light of day was completely different.

He was a beast. A magnificent beast, but a beast.

She stepped back too fast, and she knew he took note of it by the way his jaw ticked to the side. Something primitive and possessive passed over his face. His piercing gaze swept over her head to heel before locking itself down over her pulse. She was certain it had started thrumming in time with the one she saw beating in his throat.

"I didn't mean to scare you," he said, edging closer.

She swallowed. "I'm not scared."

She tried to aim for a strong tone to carry the weight of the words and disguise the quake in her knees, but the breathless catch in the statement gave her away.

His eyes shuttered. "You're lying," His voice was warm molasses, as though he was pleased to know she was afraid.

Her chin lifted, sudden defiance at being caught in the lie making her braver than she might have been. "Do you get off on scaring people?"

His throaty chuckle surprised her. "I get off lots of ways," he said in a husky tone. "But I think that's a bit too intimate a question for strangers, don't you? Especially after last night."

There it was, that mention of threat and danger, reminding her of how she'd felt at the drunk's innuendo, and she knew he was enjoying this. He did get off on intimidating people and he was laughing at her behind that stoic expression, damn him. She stalked closer, a sparrow flapping in the face of an eagle.

"You bullies are all alike." She sucked the back of her teeth to show him what she thought of that, then she gathered her courage again and spun around, putting her back to him. It was risky, a move she might not have made if they were anywhere but a dawn-lit street with cars whizzing past.

She would walk away. Right then. She wouldn't engage with him a moment longer. Just head to the bus stop and go to work the way she did every weekday. And then she'd refuse to bring him to mind ever again, not even in the darkest, most lonely part of the night.

He snagged her elbow before she even got a chance to turn all the way around. Even through the sweater she wore, she could feel the heat of his palm creeping in to invade her skin. The way her knees bagged was a pretty good sign that her body remembered exactly how she'd thought about him in the quiet of her bedroom, the weight of her blankets pinning her to the mattress.

"Maybe I am a bully," he said. "But mark me, I'm not like anyone else." His eyes glinted like the centers of amethysts.

With a glance over her shoulder at him, she steeled her spine, dropping her gaze to the place where his hand lay on her arm. His hand was bigger than she remembered, or maybe it just looked large against the delicate curve of her elbow. His knuckles were calloused and the skin thick. Not just a predator, but a fighter.

And he held her like he thought she belonged to him, as though he planned to pull her close, sealing the gap between their bodies.

God. She wasn't sure what she would do if that happened. Her wires were all mixed up and crossed over each other. Both fear and residual excitement from the night before mingled in a dangerous cocktail. She had to replay the image of those same hands squeezing the life out of a man's body so she wouldn't feel the zing of pleasure that zippered up her spine.

Instead of taking the hint, he advanced a step, claiming the small space between them with a fluid, graceful motion that had her taking in a sharp breath.

Her gaze panned up to that face, to hold his stare with the best unaffected expression she could manage. As her eyes met his, he cocked his head to the side in quiet challenge, and damn if he didn't look even more gut-wrenchingly gorgeous when he did that. Damn her stupid, deprived body.

"You should let me go," she said, trying to keep her voice even despite the way her heart was hammering, the way her core had begun to tremble.

Something crossed his expression, a waver of resistance, perhaps. But at least he did uncurl his fingers from around her elbow, only to cross his arms over his broad chest. Then, surprisingly, he propped one elbow on his forearm so he could run the knuckle back and forth beneath his nose. Drawing in a long breath as though he was inhaling her scent from his fingers, he watched her with hooded eyes.

Astounded, she stood there, blinking, not sure what to say when his nostrils flared, only that confusion entered the battleground of already complex emotions roiling in her chest.

And that little bank of heat that fired up into the lowest parts of her belly, just made things worse, because feeling anything other than disdain or fear for him was just ridiculous. This was not a gentle man, and she knew it. He was no Chester.

She shrugged herself out of range, angling away from him, intent on heading on to the bus stop. Even then, she didn't hear him make a single move. She felt his eyes burning into her back, raising prickles of static on her nape.

She halted. Breathed through her nose. And then, because she was obviously some sort of masochist, she pivoted on her heel to confront him.

"What are you doing here, anyway?" she demanded, crossing her arms too.

"I already told you."

"Yes," she said, hugging herself tighter. "A guard of some sort. Like security?" She swept a glance around the very rural area, nodding her head in the direction of a cat cleaning itself half a block away under a poplar tree. "I hope the kitty over there appreciates the safe space you made for him to wash his balls."

He didn't take the bait, nor did he bother to follow the direction of her gaze, just remained as stoic as before. The only shift in his features was a slight play of movement at the corner of his mouth.

"I didn't say I was guarding anything. I said I was watching."

A cold chill swam over the back of her neck. Her tone grew sharper. "Well if you're going to lurk about in a residential neighborhood, you better let people know you're here. Otherwise, they're like to call the police."

It was as clear a warning as she could give without accusing him of something nefarious.

His response was to advance on her, his lean frame closing the short distance she'd put between them. It was all she could do not to step back again, showing her fear even though her entire body felt tense and tight, coiled to run.

"You know I'm here," he said softly. "Isn't that enough to keep the hounds at bay?"

"You're hard to miss this early in the morning. But I'm not the one you need to worry about."

Bold, he skimmed the back of his fingers up the sleeve of her sweater. And even though she couldn't feel his fingers on her skin through the fabric, she felt as if she was raising up on her toes, being drawn upward by a marionette's string. If she went any higher, she was going to float away.

He leaned in, filling the space between them with the scent of cloves, radiating heat that spread over her cheeks. He was close enough now that she really could see the violet flare in his eyes. The hue was unnatural, she realized. There shouldn't be light glowing around the pupils. No human being she'd ever met had such other-worldly striations in their irises.

"Are you saying you don't mind me...lurking is it?" His fingers reached her collar, and he pinched the soft fluff of material between his fingers.

For some ridiculous reason, her head angled sideways, inviting his touch, goosebumps straining for his fingers. His breath mingled with hers. Joining together as if in a fist too tight to undo, a mating of sorts. The pleasure a tension begging for release.

She smelled ozone. The dying light in the street lamps blurred, and she was sure for a second that she saw lush foliage in their place. Castles rose up in the background, their stony facades holding court with the moss and vines gathering like mist around them. It was enough to make her head swim. She felt like she'd bolted back an ounce of strong tequila.

He inhaled sharply, his nostrils flaring before he smoothed the collar down over her shoulders. The gesture felt like a reprieve of some sort.

The tightness in her throat was difficult to swallow around. "What I meant is that I see you," she rasped out. "I've warned you. Others may not be so nice."

This time when she stepped away, she put her purse against her chest, a barricade that didn't make her feel any safer but that she hoped was a signal that she was done. That she wanted—needed—to keep him at a distance.

She was beginning to think he would advance on her again; he had a sort of possessive look on his face, but the then, surprisingly, he darted a look over his shoulder. Whatever he saw there made his body go rigid.

"Be careful today," he said as he stepped back. "Your city is filled with danger."

Your city. Not *the* city.

Some men...

His hands dropped to his sides, but she noticed they were clenched into fists. When he followed the direction of her gaze, he shoved them into his pockets. Out of sight. But they bulged there, showing the shape of his knuckles against the fabric, pulling the front panel of his trousers taut.

It took a moment for her to realize he had an erection. Right there, out in the open, with the sun leaking down over the rooftops to find his mass of black hair and rigid shoulders. He was hard for her. Her. A chubby, ginger-haired bookworm who fantasized about bad boys in the gloom of her apartment.

A moist heat coiled down low in her belly. She parted her lips, deciding she would tell him exactly how she felt about the way he drew such an unwelcome fit of yearning from the pit of her belly. But then he offered a slight nod, a half-smile that suggested he knew some shameful secret about her.

And then he pivoted and walked away. She was left to stand there, watching him, thinking back to the night before, knowing...God, knowing... that his was a violence that ran like a seam of gold beneath the surface, glinting at the faintest bit of excavation.

And while she knew some things were best left buried, the thought of excavating that gold shivered a line of delight up her spine.

Survival of the Fittest

FLINT

FLINT WAS NOT GOING to survive this assignment.

The first night, when he'd slipped into her apartment and watched her every movement had been a trauma of sleeplessness and confusion. He'd had to settle into a chair in the corner of her bedchamber just to keep from pacing. His own mixture of hatred for the mortal realm blended with that odd attraction he felt for her, cast a weary pallor over every moment that ticked by as he pulled from the life force of the plants to fuel the magic he need to pull shadows and bent light over himself, to hide in plain sight.

He'd been exhausted as he followed her to work the next day. Dropping the magic that kept him cloaked was a relief from the constant vigilance of maintaining the illusion of invisibility that was necessary inside her apartment.

It all made him acutely aware of how fortunate a thing it was that his father had sent him for this task and not another lesser fae. A weaker warrior wouldn't have been able to remain undetected. Because she was already cocking her head at the shadows and narrowing her gaze at light that bent just the right way to hide a full-grown fae within its prismic embrace.

But the second night. That was the real trial. By the second night, he was exhausted and on edge. Following her home at a good distance to drop his magic without detection was like a hot bath after a long, filthy, bloody battle. He was hungry and thirsty and far less willing to hold his temper when another of her kind decided to assault her. Under *his* watch. Under *his* guard. They stank of arousal and cheap mortal ale and the thought one of them touched *his* charge near sent him mad with rage.

Unfortunate, that, because it made her see the monster in the mortal form he tried to hide within. As anxious as he'd been when she'd confronted him, giving him a chance to measure her reaction to him, he wished suddenly that he'd not spoken to her at all.

Because it hadn't gone well. While so many fae females would have courted the violence in him, she shrank from it. She hated him, he could see it in her eyes. But she'd stood up to him anyway, and it was so unexpectedly exciting that he'd forgotten to get off the damned iron horse until it stopped at the next shelter. He'd had to use too much magic then, to run back and catch her before she boarded another one of the nasty mechanical beasts.

He could have happily settled quietly into the same chair that night too, mulling over the conflicting emotions that made his skin feel too tight, his hair stand on end, his chest ache in ways that put his temper in a foul mood. But the damn female put out the lights and tossed and turned until he realized with shock and excitement exactly what she was doing beneath those sheets. By the time he recognized the scent of arousal, it had coiled around him like a kundalini serpent.

And oh gods, the torment he suffered then. He would have mauled himself into a state of ruthless lust if he'd thought he could do so without attacking her. By the time she moaned out loud, he was a sweating, clammy mess with an erection that would have impressed the most jaded of youthful fae.

As it was, it terrified him. Mostly because he knew right then that he wasn't going to get out of this commission without breaking several life-threatening vows.

The thought of her lying there, touching herself while he sat powerless was enough to compel him to drop his cloak again the next morning, when all he'd meant to do was simply follow her to work and hide in the shadows. Seeing her pause and fondle the flowers. God, the thought of those fingers on his own flesh disintegrated any resolve he had to remain hidden. He'd let go the facade and approached her. And in the end, all he did was manage to scare her more.

Turning away from her, pretending he was just happening by as she left for work...that was tough. Every instinct in him told him he needed to stay with her, keep her in sight each moment.

No. He was not going to survive this commission. She was a test of his magic and a trial for his soul.

To make matters worse, he was still starving. Time and circumstance had not given him opportunity to grab the smallest tidbit of food, and he was never at his best when he was hungry. He was short-tempered and careless.

By now, his hunger was a need amplified by the scent of savory lamb and rosemary now sizzling on the stove, sending out plumes of fragrantly oiled mist as she de-glazed the pan with a pour of bold red wine. The potatoes, roasted in thin layers and melted together with some shamefully decadent herbed cream, were impossible to resist. The moment she turned to stir the gravy, he snatched a hot stack of potato and cream and stuffed it into his mouth.

Despite the searing pain on his palate, he closed his eyes against the sin of the taste. He chewed it slowly, savoring the nuances of flavor, knowing it might be the last thing he ate for hours. It took every ounce of willpower not to steal another. And he told his stomach to accept that a single potato was enough to fill the aching hole within.

It took some doing, but at last his belly agreed and hushed itself to a whisper. But it didn't go quietly. At one point, his stomach growled its resistance so loudly that if she hadn't been humming to music, she'd have heard it. By the time she'd given up peering into the shadows and given herself over to the cooking and the music, she was singing along to the words, some sensual, rhythmic tune where the male vocalist's voice reminded him of melted butter.

Now, all he had to do was resist the nearly irrepressible want for drink. It had been too long since he'd enjoyed a dram. He watched those long fingers leverage the cork back and forth on a bottle of something called Bordeaux until it sighed itself from the bottle. The scent, the sound of that release and the way it poured like molasses into the glass had him longing for a blast of strong fae ale.

Wine was something for the weakest of fae, a drink they gave children or the aged, but he'd gladly have sold his boots for a drink right then. Hard as all that was, he ached as he watched her with something more acute than mere hunger and thirst.

Like some randy untried and celibate recruit stationed in a whorehouse, his cock stiffened each time she wrapped her lips around a piece of dripping meat. It twitched when she made the softest of moans as she took it in her mouth and found savor in the taste.

All of it was enough to buckle his knees. The urge to yank her out from behind that primly laced table and throw her onto the bare boards of it was almost more than he could manage. Fantasies of feeding her his cock like those mouthfuls of lamb came at him in unrelenting waves until he swayed in his boots.

Oh, how he wanted to spread her legs. The thought of filling her, of tasting her fear with each brutal thrust made his ears ring. She'd cry, he knew. Beg him for mercy. He fantasized about his father giving him permission to break her when this was all over, and how he wanted that.

And he hated himself for it.

Because with each comfortable, familiar fantasy, one more persistent came to torment him. Each harder and harder to bear.

It was in the way she ran her fingers over every spine of book in a bank of shelves, as though she knew each one by touch, finally pulling free a hefty paperback with silver foiled lettering.

It had everything to do with the way she dropped down into a large chair in front of a fireplace that gave no heat, and slung her leg over the cushioned arm. A glass of wine in one hand and her book in the other.

The glass of wine fit snugly in the curve of her fingers. The cherry-tart bite of scent that drifted to him from the glass each time she swirled the liquid to find its legs made his mouth water. On her lap, she balanced a small dish of chocolates that she'd set out before she'd begun cooking her meal.

She dipped into the stash time and again as the pages moved, the only sound in the room, an achingly lonely noise that made him want more than anything to fill with cries of her pain and pleasure.

Each plunge of her fingers into the bowl as she plucked out a cream-filled decadence was an agony for him. He could almost taste it through her, feel the same ache of delayed gratification during that brief moment of introspection as she took a moment to examine it before popping it into her mouth.

Each time with a small murmur of delight that made something deep inside him draw tight, a pucker of raw skin around a salted wound.

The way her mouth pulled on the flavors nearly undid him. He'd had to close his eyes against the sight of it, and so he didn't groan out loud, he concentrated on the other things in the room. The way her apartment was filled with books. In piles on the floor. On shelves where they companioned small statues and candles that all looked vaguely magical.

Like the way her entire home smelled of dusty pages and vanilla. The candle from the table emitted a fragrance very much like the smells that came from the kitchens in his father's manse. The fragrance clung to her and wrapped its smell around his throat like cloying fingers and squeezed just a bit too hard.

He rather liked that sensation of losing his breath, of catching it as though he were on the cusp of orgasm. It made him think of the pleasure taverns and the few human women he'd taken to bed with a violence that left him reminding himself why he loathed the frailty of human flesh. They were not made for the likes of him. Mortals like this were more suited to lovers in the spring or summer courts, where the delicacy of magic was a gentle thing.

Not for the brutality of the Shadow Court or the Iron Kingdom.

And though fae of all creeds patronized their pleasure taverns explicitly to taste of the perverse pleasures of human fae coupling, his disappointment rose every time he indulged and left them broken in ways that would shame even the most hardened and brutal soldiers in his father's organization.

Those disappointing, unfulfilling escapades were the reason he'd long ago given up mortal women and decided to stick to merely taking them from their realm and supplying them to the Shadow Court. A good bit of coin could be earned for the right female. A good deal more for the right kind of man. And the master of the Shadow Court sold them at an even higher price, not caring where they went so long as they benefited him.

Humans and mortals were products that enabled Terran to acquire wealth and power, a means to make his father happy as he grew more powerful.

That was what this woman should be to him.

If Ava Ashe refused his father's demands, he couldn't imagine the things the master of the Shadow Court would ask of him, then. There were no empty threats when it came to Terran. Either Ashe did as she was bid or this woman would die.

At least that's the story they told the female monster hunter. The real, unglossed truth was they were both loose ends his father would need to tie off. Ava Ashe, her sister and the mentor named Gideon, who had betrayed Kit to Stone and set this whole situation in motion, was why Flint was here.

This woman wasn't just leverage. She was a promise fulfilled should Ava go back on her word. His dispatch here was the blood that sealed the magic of the vow.

Watching her savor the chocolates, the way her lips pulled together, the little moans of pleasure she made when it melted inside...all that made him want to do right by her. When it came to it—when his vow demanded her death—he would make it quick, he decided.

He could do that much for her. That was the lie he told himself. But another part of him, darker and desperate, wanted her to go out gasping, her lips shaped around his name. She'd find pleasure in her death, he'd make sure of that, so much pleasure that her heart would simply give out from the joy of it.

There would be no pain, as much as he'd enjoy that. Not for this one.

His throat bobbed beneath a hard swallow as he considered all the ways he could bring her that pleasure, and yet even that thought made his heart clench. It felt wrong thinking about her death. Fury gripped him by the throat at the thought of anyone doing her violence.

The thought must have pulled a sound from him because she froze mid-turn of a page. Looked up. Looked over at him.

He stilled, every muscle locking. What had given him away? A creak of leather beneath his weight? Was his breath too loud?

The dish of candy tumbled from her lap, and one rogue chocolate rolled across the floor, stopping just shy of his boot. It took every bit of willpower he could muster not to nudge it back toward her.

She looked right at him. Gold flecked her eyes. The soft hollow of her throat moved more rapidly, its pulse hammering beneath her skin. He felt his cock twitch.

"Hello?" she asked.

Oh gods. The fear in her voice made him hard. He prayed for the strength not to drop the pretense of invisibility. Not to pin her, terrified beneath his gaze as he prowled toward her. His intent to claim her right there on her chair as evident in his stride as in his eyes.

And damn if his breath didn't catch as she rose slowly from the comfort of that plush seat. Her eyes on the space where he stood, held all the fear he wanted to see, that would drive him to climax if he was inside her.

His fists clenched in effort as she inched toward him, eyes narrowed. His magic was slipping. His heart rate quickened.

She was coming for him. Coming at him, and he wasn't sure he could resist taking her.

The Terror of a Decision

FLINT

If FLINT DIDN'T DO something soon, she would walk right up to him. Bending light and shadow might have been part of his magic, but he could do nothing about his physical presence. He was a solid thing, just like she was, and solid things took up space.

She kept coming. His heart kept pounding and his fists kept clenching and unclenching. He had to do something to distract her. And he had to do it before she reached him.

So although it took a surplus of energy that he would have to rest to reclaim, he flicked a bit of magic toward the window. The resounding slap of magic on the glass was enough to produce a ticking sound. She jumped. Startled.

And thank the gods, it stopped her dead in her tracks. She swung her gaze toward the broad expanse of glass covered in velvet curtains.

For a moment, he thought she wouldn't take the bait, that she'd turn right back his way. But then, as if in answer to his prayers, another sound echoed through the room. A thwack on the glass from the outside.

Her head dropped back as though she couldn't believe how foolish she'd been to be nervous. She groaned in annoyance at herself and the noise at the window.

"Damn pigeons," she said out loud. "It's just birds you dumb-ass. Gawd."

She chuckled, a forced sound that carried her over to the window to peer out the curtains. Watching her go, training his gaze on her spine and the relaxed bow to them, he almost sagged against the bookcase. He didn't move again for another hour, and each joint felt like it would seize up entirely while she sat reading and sipping wine.

By the time she finished and headed into the water closet, he could barely feel his legs. Movement never felt so delicious as it did the moment she disappeared into the bathroom and he could pull his shoulders back, arching just enough to feel the kink in his spine crack free.

This was not going to be as easy a commission as he thought.

Water ran loudly in the other room. He knew he should just take the breather to move more freely, stealthy as a vampire to exercise his legs and get his blood moving, but he found he was drawn to the doorway that separated them.

She'd left it open, satisfied that she was alone in the apartment. A good sign, he thought, especially after the botched meeting during the morning. She hummed the tune from earlier, uncaring of the few off-key notes or the way it strayed off the main tune as she ran the water and tested its temperature with her fingers. Though it was a simple thing, it entranced him.

He found himself filling the opening of the door, his throat tight and aching as he indulged in the compulsion to watch her. He'd never found excitement in voyeurism, but in the short few hours, he'd found the smallest things a curiosity in ways that made his chest hurt.

Now, for example. The simple act of brushing her teeth, with white foam dribbling down her chin, the way she spit into the sink, sent a shiver of delight up his spine. The way she pulled her lips back and smiled into the mirror with a froth of that paste still clinging to her mouth. Oh Gods, the delirium of that.

He shivered as he watched and fought the urge to stuff his hands down his trousers so he could end the agony before it went too far and he couldn't control himself at all. Because it was ridiculously sensual. The desire to run his tongue over the foam and taste how it felt on her lips was almost as powerful as any drug he'd indulged in within the walls of the Shadow Court.

He was rapt long before she peeled her slacks and panties away and stepped free of them. By then, his cock was already a throbbing pain, and by the time she leaned into the shower, her ass curved to perfection over a rounded thigh, thrusting in his direction, he knew he wouldn't be able to resist taking her for himself when this was over.

With every moment that he stood by silent in the mist that rose in the bathing chamber, as she dropped her head back and gave herself to the warmth of the water, he knew this with more certainty.

His throat tightened at the thought of that neck arching toward him, surrendering to his mouth, his teeth. He wanted to press his fingers against that delicate, throbbing jugular, feel it beat beneath the calloused pad of skin, straining for the relief of pressure. Wanted to bring her to the brink of death with his passion, sink his teeth and his cock so deeply into her that she could break in half if she didn't surrender.

There was violence in his need, a brutal, primitive thing that pushed out every other thought. No vow existed. No worry for the generations to come or the consequences they would face should he break the oath that had held him bound to the Shadow Court for most of his life.

And at the same time, he wanted to fold her into his arms and cradle her against his heart so she could match her rhythm to his. A gentle touch, a rose petal against the damp stone of his heart.

Both unequivocally and opposite desires. One large pillar of salt that he couldn't deny begged to seep into wounds both old and new. What kind of monster wanted both of those things in equal measure? What sort of beast living in the shadow wanted to drag the light into the darkness?

All he knew was the more he saw, the more he wanted.

And then she went to bed. And watching her sleep became its own kind of torment.

He clung to the shadows in her bedroom. The urge to inch out of the darkness and stand over her, daring her to wake and meet his gaze, gnawed at him.

Shadows hid him well, but it was his own lust that betrayed him in the end. The moonlight pooling across her skin was too much to resist.

One step. Another. A hair's breadth away from her bed, and the sound of her breathing caught in his ears—soft, vulnerable. She shifted in her sleep, a hand curling against her chest, her pulse a visible flutter at her throat.

If she opened her eyes now, he would have to kill her.

Or fuck her.

In the torment of his thoughts, he imagined she would fight him either way. And he was tempted to wake her just so she would see him standing there, struggling not to brush the backs of his fingers over the light fuzz of hair on her arm. And then he could find out which of those things she would beg for.

Under the spell of that same deviant torment, he forced himself to watch her breathe. That rise and fall of her chest, her nostrils widening as she caught the scent of him in her sleep. She knew he was there. Somehow, in her unconsciousness, her body cried out to her to wake the hell up and face the threat that loomed over her.

A single thrust with his blade or slice across her neck and she'd be dead, he thought. One step. A slight movement of his hand. If he chose to do her harm, she'd be powerless against him. Dead in an instant.

Helpless. She was so damned vulnerable.

His fingers curled around the blade in his fist. And when had he pulled it out, he couldn't know. But it was there and it felt heavy and cold in his grip. It felt naked without a sheath of flesh.

His chest hollowed out at the thought of touching her with it, of drawing a thin line down her chest, of watching a bead of blood rise to the surface, begging for his tongue.

Something about that made him lean in closer, skimming her body beneath the sheets with a swift glance, taking in the softly open mouth.

And he discovered something in that movement. It was the hair, he decided, that drew his attention. Its fawn-red hue spread over the stark white cotton of her pillow in ways that made him think of the Shadow Trail at sunset. The violence of the color against all that white, blinking at him like the blood and starlight that was so much a part of that deliciously brutal place.

One leg stole its way outside the blankets as he watched, curling a delicate foot into the folds of the mossy eyelet comforter. He stiffened involuntarily, bracing himself for that moment of decision as she opened her eyes and saw him standing there, uncloaked.

But she didn't wake. The moon was a caress across her face, and since here in the city he felt so unconnected to nature, the pull of the light was too much to resist. His knuckles were drawing a line down her forearm before he realized what he was doing. Velvet, he thought, so achingly soft that he fought not to close his eyes against the luxury of sensation.

Breath caught in his throat, jaw impossibly tight, he waited to see which it would be. Tempting her to wake, wanting to be pressed into making that decision for her.

But there was only a soft sigh. A twist of her head so that her mouth parted as it faced him.

He skimmed her skin with a languid gaze, taking his time roaming the length of each limb that reminded him of the storm-stripped tree branches of the Shadow Trail. The calf atop the sheets possessed a delicate vein pulsing near her knee, one last bud doing its best to survive without the gentle rains that might sustain it... that was the sight that worked on his gaze, pulling him closer as the calf tensed and let go, suggesting that somewhere in the depths of her dream world she was running from something. From him, maybe. A monster surrendering to the glee of the chase.

He'd like to chase her, he realized. While his was not the sort of magic that allowed him complete and utter transformation the way his brother Blade had. The Dark Enforcer owned a magic few fae possessed due to his mother's hellhound bloodline. He was more brutal than any fae Flint knew. Shifting into an 'other' wasn't a glamor for him. It was part of his nature.

But there was something of the predator in Flint too, a feline creature that enjoyed a good hunt. Something that rose to his throat when he looked at this woman. This frail human woman.

Kit, his mind insisted. She is Kit.

"Kit," he whispered.

She stirred at the sound of his voice, and he froze. Terror for the first time in his many centuries, a claw raking over his heart. Please don't wake, he prayed. Please stay asleep. Don't force the decision on me.

Her eyes blinked open. The hand beneath the pillow pulled free and planted itself on the mattress.

"Who's there?" she asked, her voice sleep hoarse and afraid.

His cock twitched at that note of fear. He pulled the shadows and bent the light quicker than she could register, and yet a whisper of movement shivered through the room as she propped herself upright.

She strained to see through the darkness, her eyes owlish. He could see her clearly, that throat a rigid column that showed every swallow so acutely he had to fight the urge to run his finger along the muscles that pressed against her delicate skin.

"I have a gun," she said. This time, stronger. "I have a gun and I'm not afraid to use it."

She sat up straighter, her hands in position, as though they aimed a pistol into the darkness, as though she could see.

"If you're here to steal something, I beg you. Just leave. No one will get hurt."

Oh, so foolishly brave. There was no gun. There wasn't even a blade by her bedside. She was a trusting sort, believing herself safe in her home. She even left the window open the tiniest crack. The breeze moved her hair. His throat felt too thick to swallow.

"I'm begging you," she said. "Don't make me shoot."

Then she waited. He could see her counting in her head, the way her gaze scoured the darkness, as if it would simply peel back and reveal any threats lurking inside. Her throat bobbed, and he almost groaned at the terror she was holding back so bravely.

Smothered as his magic might be here in the earthen realm, those skills were as much a part of him as his breath. She'd not be able to cut his outline from the shadows he pulled around himself.

With a painstaking slowness, she slid her legs free of the bed and swung her feet to the floor. Her bare feet touched down silently, so silently he felt a surge of pride in her composure.

Just like she had just hours earlier when she'd unwittingly let him brush past her and took up his surveillance from within, she looked directly at him.

His fists clenched at his sides, the struggle to reach for her a real thing as difficult as a physical battle.

That alertness that he'd seen claim her body in that moment pulled itself back over her as she searched the room with unseeing eyes.

"I know you're there," she said in a hoarse voice. "I can see you."

A Bean for your Thoughts

Kit

THE ONLY THING WORSE than wearing a short skirt to work was wearing a short skirt to work and having to balance on the top rung of an ancient wooden stepladder after a night of near endless sleeplessness. Right then, Kit was doing all three. Fingers stretching for the elusive first edition just out of reach, she did her best to keep her knees together and thanked her lucky stars she'd decided to wear tights and flats to work that morning.

Knowing that the man below her was an older gentleman, she might not have given it a second thought. But she'd barely slept. She'd tossed and turned all night, dreaming of someone standing over her. At one point, she'd thought she saw someone standing over her bed.

And damn Ava for sending her those messages in the first place. Now, everything was a threat. A man walking by offering a lovely chat. An old man looking for a book. She felt like everyone was watching her.

Whatever she was being watched for, she had no idea. But at least today, she managed to get the key into the bookstore lock without dropping it from trembling fingers the moment she dug it out of her purse.

Yesterday, it was a struggle to take a breath. Yesterday, innocent strangers were rapists and murderers, the worst of the worst, with some hidden agenda to torture a woman for no reason except to get back at her younger sister. Yesterday, she'd almost seen a man kill another.

Today, she felt more confident. No men were coming. No one was watching her. The mere thought of such a thing happening to a quiet bookworm who worked in a bookshop and barely went out was as real as a sharp twist in a dark crime thriller, and Lord knew she'd read enough of them to know that if she was in danger, she'd have been in the back of someone's trunk by now.

Even so, the moment her keys found their way into her palm, she breathed a sigh of relief. She fitted the key into the lock and jiggled like she did every day, working the mechanism just right to get it to click over into just the right place to release the door to her pressure. It came away with a rattle. When it swung open, the scent of old paper and wood polish drifted out at her.

Calm came with it. That was the thing about books. They had a way of making everything right again. One look inside the store, where paperbacks and hardcovers and even leather-bound tomes lined every wall, with display cases catching a fairy hint of light and the overstuffed chairs invited a weary body to rest, and her shoulders relaxed.

Stepping inside any bookstore was like walking into the inner sanctum of a cathedral, a safe space where sanctuary came in the form of a thousand fresh starts awaiting the worst of sinners. So, being inside the bookstore where she'd worked for the last five years had the same effect as a good dose of prayer and confession.

It was nothing short of miraculous, really, the way the library shut out all the noise of the last twenty-four hours. She'd seen threat in every exchange until she'd stepped inside the shop. Every corner held a shadow.

Now, she was standing at the top of the rickety ladder, trying to get at a book just out of reach for an older gentleman who wore the most toothful, benevolent smile she'd ever seen, she thought the only threat from him might be an accidental peek up her skirt.

And just as she glanced down, those bright blue eyes flicked to the side so fast she knew he'd been staring at her crotch.

Great. There went her faith in mankind. She just hoped there weren't any holes in her tights. Not that his eyesight could be great at his age, but it was just...awkward thinking some old geezer might be imagining what you looked like without panties.

The ladder creaked as she made a hasty adjustment, closing her thighs together a bit too late to make a difference. Her stomach made that little flip-flop thing it did when she found herself a bit too high off the ground.

Whatever had possessed her to drag this old thing out was beyond her. She should have left it in the back room, told the old guy there was no way to get to the particular book he wanted.

But after the events of the last twenty-four hours, she found herself looking down at him, examining him with an almost clinically detached eye.

"I can almost reach it," she said, and a wicked thought overtook her. Maybe it was the result of all that impotent fury and fear at her sister for scaring her, but she let her thighs sag open. Just a little. A scrap of retribution for all she'd put up with.

Here, she wanted to say. *Take a good look, you old codger and know it's out of your reach.*

He was looking somewhere to the right, as though something had caught his eye that she couldn't see, and for a second she thought he might have been motioning to someone, but then his gaze flicked back to the ladder. He tilted his face upward, expectant, ready to respond to her comment.

She knew the moment he caught sight of the world beneath her skirt, because his cheeks bloomed into two red poppies.

"Do you want the gilded spine one?" she asked sweetly, feeling strangely victorious. "Because I'm not sure I can reach the leather bound one."

His gaze jerked away to pin itself to the paper laden counter where several old first editions already sat beside the register. He smoothed his silver hair back. He was very attractive for an old guy, to be honest.

Something electric in his posture made him think he had a spark that even younger women might enjoy. Charisma, she thought. He was probably some gold digging bitch's sugar daddy. Being used for his money, but very certain that he was using them instead.

"I'd like the vellum, please," he said with a grin that somehow, right then, seemed unabashed and dare she say...younger? His eyes glinted. "There's a lot of power in skin."

Was that a comment about her legs? Despite her stubborn attempt to seem bold, to make him pay for something a disgusting stranger had done to her, she felt warmth spread over her cheeks.

She started to correct him about the binding—there was a difference between leather and vellum—but unease shivered over the back of her neck. Something about the way he'd said skin didn't sound remotely sexual now that she thought about it. It sounded...unsavory.

"Mr. Castor—"

"Just Castor," he said, flashing that smile again. A bit of a point to those canines. She was put in mind of the old gent she'd met at the bus stop that morning. His looked very similar. "I don't confess my name to many," he said. "But for you my dear..." His gaze slid slyly toward her thighs and she clenched them tighter, with a jerk.

"Castor," she said. "That's a Greek god, isn't it?"

A low, dark chuckle, very uncharacteristic of the jovial-looking face. "Not quite a god, no. That was his twin. Castor was his mortal brother, but he does share Pollux's immortality."

She felt as though someone had just stroked her cheek. "Yes," she said, flustered. "I remember that. Brothers to Helen of Troy weren't they?"

His throat bobbed as he swallowed. "In the stories, yes. So many myths coincide and cross over one another that it's a tangle at best." He skimmed past her to where the book still rested on its shelf. "Do you think there's a set price tag on the vellum? Or will I be able to barter?"

It was an adept shift in conversation, diplomatic even. She took in the frayed edge of the spine, running her gaze over the length.

"I don't see a price, but none of the used books have any on them anyway."

If she could just gain one more inch. She stretched again, testing the distance. "Castor was one of the Argonauts, wasn't he?"

"You're asking me as if I know the story personally," he said, his tone dipping a bit, like he was offended. "Do I look that old?"

"Oh gosh," she said, peering down between her shoulders. "That wasn't what I meant. I just figured you must have read the poem since you knew the legend. Most don't."

His movement below her sent the dust motes swirling into the air. She held back a sneeze. The last thing she wanted was to upend herself on this ladder. Dizziness was already doing laps in the space between her ears.

"Indeed, I've read it. It's likely the reason he shows himself to warriors in danger." His eyebrows furrowed. "At least, so the legends go. The ancient Castor is also said to be a harbinger of important news."

Ever so carefully, she scuffed her feet a bit wider, a terrifying movement meant to strengthen her balance point, but that made her vision swim. God, she hated this rickety old thing.

She wobbled on the step, and the resulting creak from hinges she swore were rusted made her heart leap up into her throat. She yanked her hand back, resting her palm on the spines closest to her to steady herself. Waited till her heart rate normalized before she spoke again.

Defeated in this one small task. But at least that damnable creaking had stopped.

"I like that last one," she said, breathing to calm her nerves, deciding conversation was really helping. "You know. The thing about news."

She eyeballed how just out of reach that book was. Just like most things seemed to be in her life. "I could use a bit of good news."

His voice, husky now, not sexual but darkly foreboding. "I didn't say good news, my dear."

A flutter went through her chest at the low-throated way he said it. She swallowed. Maybe testing her limits on this old ladder right then wasn't a good idea after all. She tried on a smile to hide the anxiety welling up beneath her voice box.

"Well, Castor, I don't think I can reach that book for you. Not with this ladder. Not with..."

She was about to admit to the vertigo swimming over her vision, the bubbles in between her ears, but for some reason, she felt as though confessing that to him was dangerous. And that was ridiculous, wasn't it? He was old. And yet...there was definitely something off about him and after this morning...

She stepped down a rung. Breathing came just a little easier then.

Just how spooked had that bastard made her, if she was too nervous to even admit she was scared of heights to a kind old man who had to be at least in his seventies?

The prickling sensation of too much heat in her cheeks, of feeling as though she wanted to crawl into a dark space, settled over her. Pretty damn spooked, she thought, as she fought back the sensation.

Trying to keep her nervous sigh to herself, she peered down at him again.

When she'd arrived—an hour late because of that restless night — he was one of several customers clamoring to get in. As strange as it was for any customers to be waiting, let alone ticked off that she was late, it was odder still that he was the only one to actually enter. The others just filtered away, as though they were punishing her for not being there on time.

She'd smiled for him, grateful he hadn't commented on her tardiness. Offered to get him a cup of coffee.

"No thanks," he'd said. "It's not in my habit to accept food or drink from strangers no matter how pretty."

It was the compliment that sent her to the ladder. On a normal day, she'd have left the heavy old thing in the back, not positioning it as close as she could to the book he pointed at.

Climbing the rungs of such an ancient ladder to pluck some archaic first edition from the topmost shelf was not a favored task, and it didn't happen often. No one wanted anything from up there. It was dusty and smelled of old pages. They wanted new and fresh. They wanted trendy.

And she was ok with that.

"I'm afraid you might have to wait until my boss comes in," she told him now, this time with a huff of defeat. "Or someone with longer arms." She tried a light chuckle, but it did nothing to ease the sensation that he just wasn't right somehow.

"Are you sure you don't want me to try?" he asked. "My arms might just possess the requisite length." He stretched out his arm to give her a good look at his reach.

Clad in an expensive suit, his arm was longer than hers. He might just be able to grab the spine from the top of the ladder, but she couldn't say his legs were as sturdy as his arms seemed. He'd walked in steadily enough, but it had been a slow, determined stride, the kind seniors took when they were uncertain of their balance.

The last thing she needed today was for this old gent to fall and break something.

She offered him a conciliatory grin. "I'm sure," she said. "My boss would have my head for letting a customer climb this rickety old thing."

"Any boss who would decapitate such a pretty head over such a small thing should be in the bookie bushiness not the book business." He offered her a bright smile, but it made her clench her thighs tighter together.

So. Damn. Strange.

Giving him an anxious smile, she strained ever more slightly to the right.

Her fingers clawed their way over several dusty spines, aiming for that edition just out of reach. One more time.

"It's also a town, you know," he said amiably.

"What's that?" His voice startled her enough that she wobbled and had to bend back down to grab for the top of the ladder.

"Castor. It's a town. And a star."

She couldn't help a glance down. "A bean, too," she said with a grin. "You can't say I accused you of being a god, but at least I didn't say you look like a bean. Even if it's one that's both therapeutic and poisonous."

He waved the comment away good-naturedly. "I've never heard a summation of my character so aptly described."

She quirked her eyebrows at him and he reached out to hold the ladder, an offering of help that should have been welcome, but that made her flinch.

"I took no offense," he said hurriedly, his eyes trained on her face, obviously sensing her unease.

And yet he placed his hand on the middle rung of the ladder, anyway. Very near her foot.

"I was just ruminating on the many different ways that name has been used over the centuries," he said. "It's hardly unheard of."

"It is unique, though," she said, forcing her muscles to relax. It wasn't like he was going to push the ladder over and make her fall, but for some reason, she didn't feel quite so safe with his hand on the rung.

"You're my first Castor."

"Put a comma in the right place," he said in a husky voice, "and you'd have a sentence I haven't heard in a very long time."

A long moment drew itself out between them, and she swore she could see a thin membrane ticking down over his eyes. An involuntary shudder ran through her, even though the timber of his voice made it seem more like a shiver of delight than one of revulsion.

Then he stepped back, not so much shuffling over the wooden floorboards, but scuffing in a way that sounded like dancing.

"Maybe you should just come down," he said, dropping his hands to his sides, his head canted ever so slightly toward the corner, as though he was listening to something she couldn't hear.

And his posture changed, too. He stiffened up. She was sure she heard his heels click together.

"We can move the ladder," he said, all business again, the flirtation gone from his voice. "I'm sure we can wedge it into a closer spot without knocking over your display shelves." A gesture, half-heartedly toward the free-standing display of scented candles and bookmarks.

"I'm so close, though, and this ladder is so heavy."

Indeed, she just had to scrabble a micro inch more in order to get her nail embedded against the bottom of the spine. She was already up here. It had taken all her will power to climb the thing in the first place, fighting off waves of panic with each foot. There was no way she could do it again.

But if she could lean just enough to get hold of that lip in the spine. If she could do that, she'd be able to slide it out enough to get a good purchase on it. But what then? There was no way she was going to be able to get her fingers settled over both covers enough to pull it free.

She peered down, cursing her boss for not installing a slide ladder as things wavered below her. But then, no one ever asked for the books on the top shelf. She'd thought them tomes so old they were part of his own collection. The title wasn't even legible on the spine, but this old gent had seen it and wanted it.

"Can you move a bit to the right?" she asked.

A well-groomed eyebrow arched. She did appreciate a man who kept his eyebrows tidy. His even had the most graceful, lush shape.

"I'll pull it out," she said, explaining. "You catch it when it falls."

A slight bob of his head as he side-stepped neatly to the right in his spit-polished shoes. He was even thoughtful enough to check to his right before he moved, the sort of thing you do when you know someone is near and you want to make sure you don't step on their toes.

He nodded. Not to her, but the empty space at his side.

Strange. But it gave her time to measure the angle from where she leaned just enough to grab hold of a shelf for leverage.

The ladder teetered, rocking from the sudden movement. Her heart jumped to her throat. That familiar sensation of vertigo threatened to overtake her.

She braced herself. Not today. This was not going to happen today. It was just a ladder. She could do this.

She swallowed as a prickling sensation moved over her scalp, suggesting it wasn't just vertigo bothering her. Not even the height or the dust slanting in through the panels of windows in the front of the store, catching her gaze, and discombobulating her.

For a moment, she felt a dizzying, breathy sensation of falling...

But she was a hair's breadth from the book. And she hadn't come all the way up here to fail.

She reached out, straining every bit of fascia forward. She was almost there. And then...

That feeling. That feeling like a set of eyes was fixed on her every movement. Close enough that even at this height, she could feel the weight of study on her back.

But she just needed one more second. Her nail was already on the spine.

Distracted, she reached a little too far, her hand grazing the book's spine, and—her foot slipped.

The world tilted in a blur of bookshelves and beams of dusty sunlight. Her hand shot out instinctively. She grabbed for something--anything--solid. Something caught her hand.

Fingers. She got hold of fingers. She was sure of it. Instinctively, she held on tight, tangling into a knot of skin and bone. An arm went around her. The hard wooden floorboards loomed up. She braced herself for impact—

But that firm hold on her back warmed her. Steady. Invisible. She didn't topple over. She found her footing almost magically, and the ladder felt sturdy. Like someone was holding it.

She peered down, her breathing rapid.

Castor was cradling the book against his chest, and yet she couldn't remember yanking it free of the shelf. It looked...both wrong and completely at home in his embrace. Maybe it was the light and the way it was slanting in through the bank of windows at the front, but the book appeared brighter, limned in prismic color. It was mesmerizing.

"Ms. Ashe?" Concern in his voice.

"Yes?" she managed, trying to remember if she'd told him her name, trying not to feel panic over the fact that she'd felt so viscerally, the sensation of being caught.

"Are you alright?" He shuffled closer, peering up at her with those dazzling, almost unnatural looking eyes. "You look like you saw a ghost. I barely got underneath the book as it fell."

He hugged the book tighter. It looked much bigger in his arms than it had on the shelf. The edges looked frayed and ripply. Too thick for paper.

Vellum, her mind whispered. The pages were vellum. Unease tightened her throat. How had he known?

"I'm fine," she said, but the unease lingered, popping over her skin like soap bubbles.

"I'll just go put this on the counter," he said, hesitating, as though he thought she needed him.

"Don't you want to know how much it costs?"

He shook his head, his smile widening. "Cost doesn't matter when you find a prize this wonderful."

She gestured to the cash register. "Go ahead. I'll be right over." Adjusting her feet on the rung and grasping the edges of the bookshelf, she braced herself for the descent.

"Be careful," he said in a low voice. "You never know what sorts of dangers await in return for a simple, thoughtful act of kindness." His eyelids shuttered before he pivoted, a bit too sharply, a bit too adroitly for his age, and headed into the other room.

Such a curious version of the adage. No good deed, indeed, she thought and waited until he was out of range before she took the first step down the ladder. Not that she was frightened, but it didn't hurt to be cautious.

No sooner had she dropped her leg down than that prickling sensation came over her again. It was as palpable as a hand guiding her down, as warm as a hot water bottle pressed against tender muscles. The air suddenly smelled of ozone, like chlorine bleach.

But there was no one anywhere around except for the old gent at the counter. He stood in quiet contemplation, running his hand down the pages of the open book. A shadow in the corner wavered, but that could be any trick of light. A bureau or chair in the shape of a monster late at night. Nothing more.

She glanced at Castor again, watched as he flipped through the pages, his expression shifting thoughtfully with each turn.

"I'll check on the price for that," she said as she picked her way down the remaining rungs. With each step she felt better, less anxious. "It should be in the index."

A brush of her skirt, smoothing it down against her hips, making sure the flirty flare covered her bottom in the back. She'd put the ladder away later, after she dealt with Castor and the pile of books he'd stacked on the counter.

Except Castor wasn't there any more. The book wasn't on the counter. None of them were.

She swung around, scanning the bookstore in confusion, searching for him, thinking he might have stepped to the side or into the new books area. Nothing. She was alone in the shop.

She hadn't heard the bell ring to indicate the door had opened and that he'd left. Hadn't heard the scuffing of his shoes on the floor.

All that remained was a light smell of wood and cloves, and the very distinct impression that someone was watching her.

Bully for You

Kit

She had a hard time shaking the feeling that someone was lurking in the shadows, watching her for the rest of the morning.

She kept telling herself there was nothing to worry about from an old man with sticky fingers. Maybe a bit of anxiety as she notified her boss, and a bit of worry about how she was going to find the money to repay the loss if he demanded it of her. But not much more threat than that.

No doubt they'd had thefts before, but this was excessive. And strange. Unless those old books had been more valuable than she'd thought, she couldn't imagine anyone wanting them that badly.

Tapping her finger on the counter, she tried to remember the volumes and place them in her memory. Were they rare books, first editions, or possessing signatures from long-dead authors? Probably not. She'd have to consult the index she'd made all those years ago when she'd first been hired. She'd added to it often over the years and while she didn't have much occasion to pull it out, she kept below the counter, just in case.

In truth, that top shelf, with its tight grid of spines, could have been arranged there for any reason based on the eccentricities of her boss's whims. He was a bit peculiar when it came to his library. And though he had a soft spot for books of any kind, that trait didn't extend to preservation.

They could be invaluable first editions out of temptation's reach or battered old volumes he just didn't want to throw out.

Smoothing her hand over the counter, she tried to pull the memory back in case she was asked to describe Castor. But when she tried to imagine what he looked like, the only thing she could recall clearly were his eyes. Fierce. That's what they were. Like little laser beams.

Other than that, the rest just came as an avatar of every old man she had seen in movies and television specials. As though someone had painted him out of some notion of what an old world gentleman should look like. Maybe it was time for a cup of coffee. Something to cup in her hands as she gave it more thought.

The burbling drip filled the silence as Kit leaned her hip against the bar counter, staring at the steady stream of liquid, unable to shake the feeling that someone was behind her. And maybe because she was so lost in her thoughts, so well-shrouded in that coffee and clove aroma, the prickling sensation of someone watching her, she didn't notice the door to the shop open. Didn't sense any real movement behind her until a smirk-filled voice broke the spell and made her jump.

"You going to pour that or just stare at it?"

A mug came up in her hand without her thinking about it. Whirling around fast, priming the pottery for a hefty hurl, gathering thrust behind her head, she aimed for the door.

Her arm froze mid-air as she caught sight of the man standing just inside the shop, his hands in the air, palms out. That playboy smirk firmly fixed on his face, despite the way his eyes bulged from surprise.

Gideon. Of all people to come into the shop today, it had to be the bastard Ava had run to when things got too tough-love at home. She didn't exactly lower the mug.

He lowered his hands to his chest. "Whoa, Kit."

The posture might seem like he was surrendering, but she wasn't fooled. His chestnut eyebrows arched over blood-shot eyes. The ever-present grey slouch hat sat so far back on his head, it looked like it was falling off. High? Drunk? She could never tell when it came to him.

She swallowed the lump of adrenaline clogging her throat. Maybe it wasn't too late to let the pottery fly.

"What do you want, Gideon?" She dropped the mug to the counter beside her.

His eyes trailed to the percolator. "Coffee would be a good start."

She didn't bother checking the coffee counter. Her jaw clenched. "There aren't any clean mugs."

His gaze flitted to the stack of pottery, in warped and dented wabi sabi styles that coffee addicts paid big bucks for. Lips pressed together as he eye-balled the mugs her boss thought were kitchy, along with the four plump chairs and electric fireplace he thought customers loved.

Gideon was no customer, but he took to wandering the shop as though he was itching to find a good read and settle into one of those plush armchairs. Fingers trailing over a few of the fantasy stacks, he paused, pulled one out, and shoved it back in place. Continued his infuriatingly casual stroll.

He ended his jaunt beside her, his gaze pinned to hers as he reached behind her to pluck a mug from the stack. He held it up, titling the insides toward her to show her the inside. Mocking her with the perfectly clean interior.

She kept her expression carefully bland. What did she care if he knew she'd lied? Maybe he'd take the hint and leave.

With a casual flip of the mug, he upended it so it sat on its base on the counter. "Heard from Ava?"

So. Not leaving. Kit stiffened at the affected casual way he dropped her sister's name.

"That's none of your business," she snipped.

"Ah," he said. "Sounds like you have."

Was that relief in his voice or anxiety?

He wrapped his entire palm around the carafe instead of the handle like a normal person would and poured himself a full mug. Great. He was planning to stay longer than five minutes. She didn't think she had this in her today.

"And based on your tone," he said as he set the carafe down and aimed his red-rimmed eyes at her. "I gather she told you we broke up."

Kit crossed her arms over her chest. She knew him exactly well enough to know she didn't like him. She didn't like the way he was older than her, let alone her younger sister. She didn't like that he drank too much, and she didn't like that he smelled like he hadn't washed in days.

Even so, there was something pinching his expression. Like he wanted to say something, but wasn't sure how to broach the topic.

She moved the carafe back onto the heating element. "Your relationship with Ava is not my business," she said. "And what happens or doesn't happen between my sister and me is not your concern either." She paused a moment. "It never was."

He leaned against the counter, dropping one ankle over the other. He wore socks with cartoon frog characters on them. So juvenile. And a man his age. He had to be what? Somewhere in his mid-forties?

"Spoken like a woman who never threatened to interfere in our relationship," he said.

Fair enough. But she tried not to rise to his bait as his biceps flexed and bulged quietly beneath the charcoal t-shirt, a very Gideon thing to do. His gaze was always assessing, and even when he was relaxed, he looked like he was posing.

Dipping his mouth to the edge of the mug, he watched her over the rim in an analytic manner, keeping his cool as though she'd not just told him to go pound sand. Just like Ava would do. And blast if she wasn't pissed off all over again. But she'd learned a thing or two dealing with her renegade, rebellious sister, and she wasn't about to give him what he wanted so easily.

She poured herself a mug of coffee as well, taking the respite in the act to gather her thoughts and composure, because just seeing him on the heels of Ava's phone call and the strangeness with the books was enough to fray her nerves to a bit of raw wire.

And damn him if he didn't scrutinize her every movement as though she were guilty of something. As though she was the one who was making desperate, manipulative calls in the middle of the night. As though he was squeaky clean from blame. Him with that slouch hat. Those socks. That judgmental gaze.

"You're a bastard, you know that?" she said.

His gaze lingered on her, a certain knowing sadness in his eyes that would have melted her had it been anyone else. "I thought I was a pedophile."

She had to hide the smile that tried to tug her mouth upwards. So he'd heard that old accusation. Good. "I never said you couldn't be both."

He swirled the coffee in the mug, staring down into its depths. "You know it's not true, Kit," he said softly before he gave her a straight, bold look. "And just because I'm not easily bullied doesn't make me a bastard."

"So, I'm the bully?"

He shrugged. The t-shirt moved too taut over his chest, showing off the lean fitness of his body, just the way he no doubt intended. "You told Ava you'd never speak to her again if she 'carried on' with me. Isn't that what you called it? 'Carried on'? I'd call a threat like that bullying."

"Because you're too old for her."

"I'm not even forty."

She snorted at the comment. "And she's twenty-four. She was seventeen when she met you."

"It's not like I wooed and wed a child bride, Kit." The knuckles clenched around his mug bleached out. "Christ, she was a kid. Even I knew that. I just kept her safe so she could actually grow the fuck up."

He didn't say it, but she heard the accusation in his voice. That if not for him, Ava wouldn't have lived past seventeen. That she couldn't keep her sister safe. Not from dealers. Not from street gangs. Not from Ava's own damn vicious death-wish streak.

But that didn't mean he was any more qualified for the task. It had been a long time coming, and today...well, today was the day she told him what she really thought. He wanted to know about Ava? Then let him hear everything.

"You call encouraging her to troll the streets at night, keeping her safe?" She slammed her mug down on the counter. "She was no safer with you than with me. You couldn't keep her out of drugs and fighting either."

"I channeled her rage, at least. Used it for something."

"You call turning her into a street fighter, channeling her rage?"

She turned her back on him and took several deliberate steps away from the counter, because she didn't like the way her tone had gone shrill. And she didn't want to see the pain in his gaze, an echo of her own, she was sure. Loving Ava was like loving a feral cat. She had the scars to prove just how well her affections were received. She didn't doubt he felt the same, but he was obviously not in a position yet to give the beast free rein.

But she was. Dammit. She was.

The way he lingered beside the coffee counter, watching her, unnerved her. She didn't want to feel all this. It was bad enough she felt so damn guilty over hanging up on her sister, scared almost shitless, and most definitely sleepless over the cryptic phone call.

Now this. He had no right coming here and bringing all this up again. And to top it all off, his expression was so filled with pity that her knees were bagging.

"I didn't turn her into a street fighter," he said in a soft voice. "I just trained her to look after herself. She needed at least that chance." He hesitated, looking down into his mug before setting it on the counter. When he looked up again, his gaze was shuttered. "Do you have anyone to look after you?"

It was such a strange question, coming on the heels of the last twenty-four hours, that she almost gasped. Almost. She caught it between her teeth and held it there until she thought she could keep it from leaking free. He would not see her break down. She wouldn't let it happen.

When he pushed off the counter, his hands turned out as though he planned to comfort her, she took a step back, instinct a sharp and overwhelming urge.

"Kit," he said. Softness in his tone. A terrible, pitiful sound that broke her finally. But not the way he probably expected. Hell, not the way she expected.

She snapped one word at him like the popping of a stiff wad of gum. "What?"

He reacted like she'd fired a shot, his hands going to the back of his pants as if he had a weapon there. She knew better. He was a coward. Someone who couldn't even come to the apartment and tell her Ava was doing alright in all the time they were together.

As the silence drew out between them, he turned conciliatory. He sighed, his hands falling to his sides. "I know you hate me, but even knowing that, I still came. Because I'm worried. About Ava. About you."

His steps toward her were mincing, a man approaching a woman on a ledge. "I don't want to argue. I just want to know you've heard from her. I want to know what she told you. That's it. That's all I want and I'll be out of your hair."

Worried. As though he had a right to claim the same raw, wounding tears she had in her own soul, the result of years of loving Ava. As though he was in the same league.

She knew she should be compassionate. She knew she should admit to her own fears, bond with him over it. Find a way to figure out how to help her wayward sister. But what came out was a snide remark that soothed her aches for about the three seconds it took to spit free.

"I heard you dumped Ava for a younger woman. Is that what you call worrying?"

He pinched the bridge of his nose. "You know I'm not like that, Kit. I didn't dump Ava." His jaw was white at the edges. "And Shea is not my lover."

She sucked the back of her teeth, refusing to touch that one, and he raked a hand over the top of his hat, pulling it forward. She had the feeling he was about to wring it out in his hands.

"If Ava told you about Shea," he said in a tight voice. "Then when was that, exactly? Yesterday? Last week? Yesterday?"

"I don't have to talk to Ava to know what's going on," she said. "She calls me."

He perked up at the comment and she realized her mistake. Lifted her chin before he could accuse her of withholding information. "It's mostly just breathing. She rarely says anything, but I know it's her. She hangs up."

"If you don't first, I suppose," he drawled. "What did she say to you? Exactly?"

That some men were coming. That she had to get out of town.

But that's not what she told him, because this was Gideon, and he had taken her sister from her.

"You've been watching me," is what she said instead, her eyes narrowing as her brain picked up the comment and filled in all sorts of blanks. "How long?"

He toed the floor with his combat boot and she knew she was right long before he admitted it.

"Not long," he said, skimming her with a guilty glance. "A little while this morning. Getting the courage to come in."

She snorted at that. Gideon had more balls than a Chuck E Cheese franchise, and inferring that he was scared of her was the richest of ironies.

But at least she knew now why she felt eyes on her back, and that went a long way toward making her feel a bit more conciliatory. Relief like that had a way of making a gal feel generous.

"Ava is high most of the time," she said in a tight voice as she remembered the last call. It was hard to hang up on her sister, but it had to be done. But that didn't mean she didn't worry too.

His nod suggested he understood and she softened. Not much. Just a little more. Misery and company or something like that.

"It's too painful, you know?" she said. "I feel like I want to rush to her aid and have the doctors put her into a coma. Help her get clean. But that wouldn't fix a damn thing." Her eyes burned. She swiped away the sting. Lifted her chin. "There is no 'easy' button. There isn't anything that would fix a damn thing."

"I know Ava," he said. "I get it. Getting emotion out of her is like pulling cotton wadding through a needle. But it's in there. Trust me."

This said as though Kit didn't know her own sister. As though he knew her better, when he hadn't even been around the night their parents died. The night Ava slipped sedatives into their tea so she could run off to meet some jock.

She stared at Gideon's face, the earnest expression as if he could comfort her with some intimate knowledge about Ava that Kit didn't know existed. And somehow, his pity made it all worse.

She found herself in a direct line to the counter, lodged behind it because she needed something between them or she was going to scratch his eyes out. All softness left her. What remained was a hateful scrape exposing raw meat and she struck out because that was the only thing that made it hurt less.

"Oh, you know her so well," she said. What exactly did the two of you do out there in the dark streets," she demanded. "What were you two up to encouraging her to sneak out so she could meet you if you weren't grooming her?"

A cackle of laughter escaped his throat that sounded raw and hurt. "Christ, you're something. You've never given me an inch of quarter, have you? I've seen rabid beasts grant me more ground than you."

Beasts. As though he was some sort of lion tamer braving claws and teeth on a regular basis.

Her hand slammed down onto the counter. "I don't give you an inch because you don't deserve it. An adult man does not encourage a teenager--"

"She was pretty much of age when I met her," he cut in, his voice rising. "And when she came to my bed later, what happened between those sheets was between two consenting adults." He stressed the word adults like it was a weapon.

Her head lowered, bull-like. "You haven't answered my question."

He leaned his elbow on the counter, idly using his finger to push his mug closer to the carafe.

If this was a tactic designed to put her off kilter, make her break the unnerving tension by filling the silence with words he could use against her, he was going to be disappointed. Ava did the same thing. It had taken Kit years to realize just how well her sister used silence as a weapon.

But Kit wasn't giving in this time. She gave him as long a stare as he gave her. Finally, he straightened up and arched his back, cracking oil into his joints and scraped the hat over his head and back again.

She could see why Ava had found him dashing. He was handsome. She had to give him that. The hard-edged jawline covered in days' old growth. The beginnings of salt in the pepper of his hair. Another time, she might have filled the silence just like he expected of her, feeling too uneasy with her own sense of awkwardness to let quiet just sit there.

But just when she thought the stand-off would net her nothing, he broke. His sigh was a frustrated, weary one.

"You know, I kept Ava alive," he said. "Despite herself. That's all I did. And I loved her. I still do. But that's not going to be enough. It was never enough."

She said nothing, just watched the way his jawline went white as he wrestled with whatever it was that had brought him into the shop when he knew she hated him.

A sigh moved his shoulders. "I didn't just come here for Ava. I came here to make sure you were OK. And I can see that things are just fine for you, so I'll tell you what I know. I saw Ava about a few days ago."

He waited for her response, and the look on his face was enough to tighten her chest. Because it wasn't a question, not really, and yet it was clear his offer of information was because he hoped she'd return in kind. There was something he wanted, something he was holding back.

She looked at his face, studying every flicker of his gaze, every tic in his mouth. Her chest did a funny little thing where it squeezed and jumped at the same time, like a stress ball oozing over the top of a fist.

She swallowed, very slowly, ignoring the nagging feeling prickling the back of her nape.

There had always been something odd about the two of them, and it wasn't just the age gap. It was in the secrecy, the bruises Ava wore on her skin in places she couldn't hide. The cuts and abrasions that she'd explained away by insinuating they came from activities Kit didn't want to hear about.

There were times she'd accused Ava of covering for Gideon, and her sister had always laughed it off. Gideon didn't have the balls to abuse her, she'd say. Then that patronizing laughter as though Kit was being ridiculous.

But that didn't mean he wasn't violent. She sensed it in him like a bottle cap not screwed on quite right. She squared her shoulders now, sensing the way she always had, that Ava was keeping secrets and that Gideon was just one of them. That for whatever reason he was here, this was just another moving part to her machinations. And she was tired of it. Angry, even, that they would play on her fears so.

"Are you the reason she's gone?" she asked too sweetly, even as an eerie déjà vu swept over her. "Did you do something to scare her? Is she hiding from you?"

"Good God, Kit." He shook his head.

That was no answer. Her eyebrows gathering together, she said in a cold voice, "If you're not going to come clean, Gideon, then I can't help you."

Hard as it was, as painful as this entire ordeal, she had finally hit her own bottom. Let him worry about all the bruises her sister wore without comment, no matter how often she was asked. Let him feel the disgust at opening a box with the expectation of finding a few buds of marijuana and discovering a trove of strange looking teeth. Whatever Ava was into, whatever trouble she'd brought down on herself, Kit was done.

"If you have nothing to do with it, then she's yours to deal with. You asked for her. You lured her away from a safe home. You told her she was pretty, that she was special—"

"She's all those things," he cut in. "And she's so much more, Kit."

"Of course she is," Kit responded, heat in her voice. "But a teenager needs to hear those things from boys her own age not an adult man."

"This again," he said. "You talk about her as if she's still seventeen. You think I groomed her? We're talking about the same innocent kid I found higher than a weather balloon at a drug party, just about to fall prey to some monster? The Ava who might have ended up dead if I hadn't dragged her the fuck out of there and brought her to my apartment until she sobered up? An act, I might add, was pretty damn ballsy for an adult man."

His palm ran over the counter sideways, cutting through a thin layer of dust she didn't realize was there. "Oh, yes," he said. "That Ava. I didn't realize we were talking about the same girl who refused to tell me that night where she lived because she said, and I quote: "My sister thinks I killed my parents."

The gall of it. That he would bring up that horrible, intimate pain. She had to choke out the next words just to get them off her tongue.

"Get out of my shop," she said, picking up her mug. "Get out right the fuck now or I swear I will find a way to shove this up your ass sideways."

"You're making a mistake."

She shook her head. "I'm finally doing something right. I can't keep living my life terrified she's going to end hers."

Her voice broke on the last, but she held his gaze so fiercely it was he who cut away first.

His gaze dropped to the handle of her mug, where she was clenching so hard her knuckles were bleaching to a frightening shade of white.

"I guess that's the difference between us, Kit," he said. "I won't give up on her."

The scream that erupted from her tore her throat. Her arm came up, clenched around the heavy pottery mug, and she let go with everything she had.

But he'd already spun on his heel and was halfway across the floor. The mug crashed to the floor, spilling black coffee everywhere. It splashed up onto a shelf of second-hand books as the door chimed closed.

She stood there, chest heaving, tears stinging her eyes.

Because if Gideon had braved the store and her hatred of him, then the truth was too bald to ignore.

Ava really was in trouble. And that meant that the call she'd been trying to ignore had been real.

Slaking a Fierce Hunger

FLINT

GIDEON. THE HUNTER WHO should have been. The human male he had threatened on his first night here in order to get Kit Ashe's address. The bastard he should have ended because now he was sniffing around, suggesting things that were better left unsaid. That Kit might be in danger.

As if Flint might be that threat.

It took everything he had in him to remain concealed through the conversation as the hunter tried to wrangle information out of her. He burned to drop the camouflage as Gideon alternately baited and tugged on the leash of her control.

The way they talked, the way Gideon prowled toward her, insinuating the worst of things. The way he'd made her scream at the end, choking on her own tears as she hurled her mug at his back.

That was the worst. That moment, Flint almost choked the life from him right there in the shop. But he waited. Like a patient warrior did, like a good killer.

Flint held his temper on a tight leash as the coward fled out of range of the mug of hot coffee. Then he slipped outside, leaving Kit alone in the shop to gather herself while he hunted down the prick who made her cry.

He abandoned the pretense of being invisible once he was outside and out of Kit's eyesight. It wasn't needed as he struck the pavement, letting the light and play of shadow leak away from him.

Careful to stick close to the building, to ensure someone was in front of him as he removed the glamor, he let the cloak drop. Blending back into reality was swift, and to the mortal eye, seamless, a blur of motion from the corner of their eyes.

But his magic signature was something he couldn't disguise as easily as his appearance, and because the hunter was used to the smell and sensation of magic, he fully expected Gideon to sense a predator trailing his every step. The truth was, he wanted Gideon to sense him. He wanted the man scared. He was on edge from lack of sufficient sleep and he *needed* the man terrified.

But Gideon merely strolled around the corner as if he was completely alone in a city filled with humans. Leaving his back open, his hands stuffed into his pockets completely out of commission should Flint attack from behind. Ridiculous. Some hunter, this. As much as he hated to admit it, maybe Stone had been right to change assassins and swap out Gideon for Ava Ashe.

The traffic smelled of oil and tobacco, the sparse sidewalk like trash and rotten apples. But nothing else, no hint at all to indicate Gideon was anxious or spiked with adrenaline. It was possible the hunter was oblivious, or maybe Gideon was just good at cloaking his emotions. That sort of skill would be useful when hunting predators.

But Flint hadn't lived all these centuries just to trust a mortal's focus. He prowled around the corner, fully expecting Gideon to be plastered against the wall, the first move in a sneak attack.

What he got was a full out ambush.

Gideon leaped at him, a blade slashing sideways at the level that might have been his throat if Flint wasn't an inch taller. It was a good strike. A solid investment of training, but fast as Gideon was, Flint was faster.

He leaned back out of range almost leisurely. A smile played with his mouth as he eyeballed the hunter and the breath already coming in short bursts because the man was obviously under the tight fist of adrenaline.

This would be a joy.

"You're too slow, hunter," he said, lowering his head, a bull about to charge. "I told you when I first met you: I will enjoy hurting you."

No word in response. No word-play to tease out or taunt Flint. Just laser focus. Deadly intent maintaining his schooled movements, keeping every jab and parry tight and intentional.

He feinted right when Gideon came at him again, this time with the fist around the knife handle plowing the air. No doubt he thought he'd punch in and slash away, but Flint knew the tactic. He avoided it easily, a silent, grim line to his mouth.

When he came up again, he reached with a deadpan, languid grasp, locking around Gideon's throat as though the man was standing still. The human's eyes went wide, panic flaring as his hands clawed uselessly at Flint's fingers.

"For a hunter, you're woefully inept," he said.

Gideon's eyes bugged out as his breath cut off. It was clear he was trying to talk now, but that he was nowhere near done fighting. He kicked out when Flint lifted him off the ground, holding him above his head like a doll.

"Those pitiful monster hunting moves aren't fast enough for our kind, you know," Flint drawled. "Maybe for a lesser fae they'd work. I'm surprised you don't know that. Your protegee, Ava, was smarter. She ran from me."

In a sweeping, fluid arc, he slammed Gideon against the brick wall of the building. The sound of teeth clacking together almost pulled a grin from him. It was satisfying to smell the blood in the air as the man bit his tongue.

The knife Gideon clutched with such tenacity clattered along the sidewalk until it came to rest against a discarded apple core. Flint didn't bother trailing its path, but he noted where it landed. The glint of it catching the sunlight winked its presence from the asphalt.

The man in his grip still clawed at his arms, even though he was pinned to the building. Persistent little bugger. Refusing to just surrender. He had to know he couldn't win.

With a dispassionate eye, Flint watched him fight for breath, let him dig into his skin as his fingers crabbed their way up his shoulder to his throat. There wasn't enough energy in his hands to make it all the way, and he ended up flapping at Flint's collar instead. The beat of a gnat's wing against leather, the man himself no more than a beetle trying to flip over off its back.

How long might it take for the man to die? he wondered. By now, most other mortals would have expired. They'd have pissed himself by now.

Flint was impressed.

But he leaned in, all the better to take in every muscle flutter in Gideon's face, every second of dying light in his eyes.

"You don't have long, hunter," he said. "Your face is red. Your lips are a beautiful shade of indigo."

Gideon's fingers crawled back onto his collar and Flint looked askance at them as they found purchase on the fabric of his coat. They were long fingers, thick and calloused. The man spent long hours at labor. He might have been inclined to let a fellow warrior go, but the image of Kit's tear-flushed face came to him again, and he couldn't find the mercy in his heart.

"You hurt her," he said, drawing his eyes back to Gideon's face. "Maybe you shouldn't die so easily."

A hint of release. Enough for the man to drag in a breath. Victory flashed over Gideon's face.

"You're attracting attention," he rasped out, his voice already scraped raw. It would be more raw soon. "If you're going to kill me, I'd suggest taking the fight elsewhere."

Flint didn't bother looking over his shoulder. He could sense the two humans pausing in their stroll a few yards away. He noted the way Gideon's eyes flicked in their direction.

"They won't help you," Flint said. "And by the time someone else comes to do what they don't dare, you'll be dead and I'll be shadow again. Although what mortals think, I don't care. Fae lives are not bound by your laws."

He didn't grin. Didn't scowl. He refused to let a single instant of emotion inch over his features because he wanted every bit of energy he had within to come to bear when he punished this man.

"You once told me there was nothing that could get you to betray the woman inside." He canted his head at him. "And yet you betrayed her to me. That makes you a traitor in my world. Do you know what we do to traitors?"

Laying his forehead against Gideons, a lover's touch, intimate, he lowered his voice. "Your kind used many items perfected in Fae to inflict pain. The rat. The Iron Bull. The Judas Chair. None of them were created to cause death. At least, not right away. Torture is an easy route to confession. Death, an after thought. After all, what sort of inquisitor wants to kill their victims before they get what they need?"

He leaned in with his whole body, molding himself to Gideon, the anger so visceral it needed to be shared or it would set him on fire. "But in my world, death for treachery is a delicate, fanciful balance of the union between agonizing pain and the fleeting heartbeat of life."

He exerted more pressure, enjoying the way Gideon's eyes bulged. "I'm not looking for information from you, hunter. So guess which side of the balance will tip first?"

In answer, Gideon brought his knee up, but without oxygen in his lungs to fuel his muscles, given the awkward positioning against the wall and beneath Flint's body, the blow was weak.

Flint pursed his lips, thoughtful. A cold, icy draft moved through his veins.

"I tell you what I'll do," he said and moved his hands to the man's T-shirt. "I'll give you a chance to answer before I kill you."

Flint's fingers loosened, his palm slackened its hold. Just enough for the hunter to pull in a draft of air. No more.

Gideon sucked in a lungful. "Fuck," he said and used that bit of air he'd dragged in to slam his forehead into Flint's chin.

It had to hurt. It was a good solid hit and might have cracked Flint's bone, but he barely felt it. He barely felt anything except the all suffusing anger at this man for bullying the woman inside. His woman, he thought.

But the hunter felt the pain of the blow, that much he knew. Gideon drew back, a glazed look in his eye. That shot had cost him. The booze on his breath smelled stale, suggesting he'd had a drink perhaps an hour earlier.

Flint swiped his arm over his mouth, feeling the warmth of blood on his lip.

"Fuck," he said thoughtfully. "Is that what you wanted from her? Did you want to fuck her, Gideon?"

The man had the power to snort in derision. When he wheezed out the next words, it was to clarify his earlier response. "Fuck *you*."

Flint blinked. His jaw ticked to the side, the only movements he let his face show. "Are you offering?" he asked in a drawling voice. "Because while I prefer the female sex, I am not averse to tearing you a hole big enough to shit your heart through."

From the side of his eye, he noted more people had begun to gather. Soon, she might come outside to investigate. He didn't want that. He didn't want her to see the violence in him unless she was enjoying it with him.

So he let the man go, but he held him against the wall with his arm, pinning him against the wall as he pulled the light and bent the shadows. He couldn't cloak Gideon, but he didn't need to for what he planned.

"If you know what's good for the humans gathering, you'll remain still," he said in a cold voice.

The man's face bleached out. Flint had struck a cord. The creed of the hunter, he supposed. To protect the innocent. A weakness as far as he was concerned.

"Shall I clear the street?" he asked conversationally. "I haven't tasted human flesh for a long time. I might be hungry for it." He paused a moment. "Actually, I am very hungry."

"I surrender," Gideon said, letting his shoulders sag to prove his submission.

Flint stepped back, noting that while the man's posture was certainly complacent, his face was anything but. Even so, he'd take what he could. "The first smart thing you've done since we've met."

Gideon narrowed his eyes as he peered up into Flint's.

"You want to fuck her," he said, disbelief in each syllable. "My God. You want to fuck Kit."

Flint swallowed. What he wanted from her was something else, something he didn't quite understand. Yes, he wanted to fuck her, but it was so much more. He wanted to devour her. He wanted to break the seal of air between them like the cork on aged fairy wine. To savor the taking in long drafts that slaked a thirst so potent, he could barely swallow against it.

He skimmed the man's face with a raking study and he formed the answer as best he could.

"What I want from her is not your concern."

The hunter snorted. "Good luck with that. She has a thing about older men and younger women."

"Careful, human."

"You think you scare me? I know what you are. And I'm guessing if it was something powerful in your world, it wouldn't have been your brother who came to collect me to do your father's bidding."

Flint's grip tightened, his fingers itching to snap the fragile column of Gideon's throat. It would be easy. Too easy. She wouldn't mind, he didn't think. She'd likely be glad he was gone.

And yet, there were other ways. Crueler ways to see this man punished for hurting her.

"You flatter yourself," Flint said, threat rumbling through his voice. "My brother, Stone, is an administrator. What your kind would call a desk jockey." He leaned in, smelling the booze on the hunter's breath. "What I am is very different. I'm the muscle. I love being the muscle. And I hate this earthen realm. I hate everything in it. When I say I would enjoy killing you, I'm not being diplomatic the way Stone would be. I could have ended you at your bunker. I can end you now."

He took a long, purposeful breath, inhaling the man's scent and tasting a tinge of anxiety, finally. Not fear, though, that would come later.

"I have what I need from you," he said. "And if you aren't afraid of me then you are stupid."

"I stand by my original assertion," Gideon said with a cocky smile. "Except let me make it more clear. Go. Fuck. Yourself."

Flint's eyebrow arched at the foolish bravery. He had guts, at least.

"Again with that suggestion," he said. "I'm beginning to think you really do want me to give you a good reaming." He sighed theatrically. "It's just not my flavor, the male on male, though some do indulge in it." He leaned in. "But I'll tell you what I do like. Human skin. Human blood. It's been many many generations since I've tasted your kind." He snapped his teeth for emphasis. "For you, I might be persuaded to change my dietary habits."

"And Kit?" Gideon asked. "What will she think when she discovers you have a taste for human flesh. What will she say when you wheedle your way into her bed and decide to take a nibble on her neck."

It shouldn't have bothered him, but the thought of it, the mention of his teeth on her neck, the savor of her blood in his mouth as he took her. It was too close to the yearning in his veins. And that was too intimate for discussion with this bastard.

"Let's make sure my hunger is slaked before that happens," he said and gripped the man by his shirt, the wicked grin stealing mouth too insistent for him to resist.

Before Gideon could protest, he bent the man's neck sharply, bit down on his throat and buried his teeth in.

Of Frogs and Grimoires

KIT

THE FIRST TIME KIT realized just how much trouble Ava was going to be as a ward was two weeks after their parents died. She had already disappeared on multiple nights and come back slurring her words and looking glass-eyed. But two weeks in, when Kit had met with the school and social workers three times in as many days and been informed that if she couldn't handle the teenager, something more drastic would have to be done...Kit was at her wit's end.

Her younger sister was the wild child poster kid, and had been long before their parents slid into the car that fateful night, groggy from pills they had no idea they'd ingested.

Fighting, partying. Kit had known it would be hard—heck, even her parents only knew half of the things Ava did. She'd always believed her sister would even out with maturity, but she had no idea just how difficult it would be to hold a tornado by the tail as it blew itself out.

The fight they'd had that night had been a physical one. And Ava had been the undeniable victor. All those back of the school fistfights the girl had engaged in gave her the edge, even though Kit was larger, taller, and had a bit more heft to sling about.

Kit had slunk to her room, nursing a bruised cheek, salt from her tears making it ache all the more. Her ego bruised and battered much worse than her jaw. What business did she have trying to raise a teenager when she was still officially one herself? How could she mother a youth who was terrified of feeling love for a mother ever again?

That was the moment she realized she might not be able to hold on to her sister at all, no matter how hard she tried. Love wasn't enough for a girl like Ava. She fought it tooth and nail, as though somehow it made her weak. Ava fought in advance of pain. She struck out preemptively. And because Kit knew Ava was terrified of feeling emotional pain, Kit decided she would battle the devil until hellfire came to claim her. Anything to prove to her sister that no matter what she did, she was loved. She was family. All the family they had, and they needed each other.

The memory of it all washed over her now as she stood in the middle of the book shop staring at the spatters of black coffee on the floor. The fragrance of the java permeated the air, and might coat the air currents for hours. Comforting as it might be, all she could see was how much like a crack pipe and toot the cocoa-colored puddle looked. And just how she knew what they looked like was all thanks to her sister.

A groan escaped her, and she pivoted sharply to distract herself from thoughts of Ava inhaling smoke from a wrinkled cradle of foil. At least cleaning this sort of mess was something she could manage without having her heart cracked open. The bucket and mop in the back room asked for nothing in return. Soap and water as good a metaphor for scrubbing her sister's drama out of her life as any.

Steam rose hot and misting from the bucket in the back room as she ran the tap as hot as she could stand. Bubbles rose with the level of water till she feared she'd not be able to lift and carry it, so she shut it off long before it was full and dumped the old-fashioned string mop into the suds, lost in her thoughts. She swished it several times, watching the water turn brackish before dumping the water and starting again. As if Gideon coming in and putting her on tenterhooks wasn't bad enough, digging up conflicting emotions from the neat little grave she'd buried them in, now she had the unenviable task of washing out a mop that should have been clean before it was stored away.

She bit back a groan of impatience at the task and silently cursed Gideon for coming in. And when she dragged the bucket and mop out of the back room, sloshing water out of the sides and onto the floor, she had to choke back the tears trying their damndest to do the exact same thing. The ache in her chest made her ribcage feel so inflexible that she had a hard time bending over to squeeze out the mop. All this thought of Ava and her parents. Gideon reminding her of the trials of the early years. And now it seemed Ava really was in trouble and she was left as powerless as ever.

She blew out a long breath as she watched the tangled strings move over the floor. There were worse things, she thought. Her life wasn't that bad. She had a garden she loved to tend. Friends she got to see every so often for a theatre and dinner night. Enough money to buy herself a nice bottle of wine and a single lamb chop for dinner.

Life was good and maybe that was because Ava wasn't in it anymore. It wasn't like she had to squirrel her way through derelicts and drug addicts in a desperate midnight search and rescue mission anymore. Those days, thankfully, were gone.

She just had to change her perspective, was all. The coffee on the floor, for instance. It wasn't just a mess she had to clean because Gideon had goaded her into losing her temper. It was more evidence that she'd had a chance to tear into him in the first place. Words she'd not been able to say to him since she'd asked Ava to leave all those years ago.

Bonus point? She'd even got some on that pristine t-shirt of his. The thought of him strolling down the street with coffee stains all over his back put a smile on her face that she found difficult to let go.

She was still smiling when the door chimed again. "Careful," she said, only barely looking up from the mop. "We got a little coffee on the floor here, and I don't want you to slip."

The man standing before her was strikingly handsome, enough to pull her full gaze upward and let the mop sag in her grip. Auburn-haired and muscled like a pit bull. A predatory stance leaked into his posture. There was a lethal sense of power in the set of his shoulders.

Yet he flashed a playful grin at her, shifting the energy in the air to something that felt like a comfortable housecoat had been pulled over her shoulders. Dangerous, but only in the right circumstance. She decided right away that she liked him.

"Must have been quite a cliffhanger to make you toss a perfectly good cup of coffee at the door," he said.

A chuckle moved up her throat. "Let's just say the story was getting old."

His turn to chuckle, and it was both throaty and pleasant. It made her shoulders sink down to a normal place instead of hitching up to her ears the way they'd been with Gideon.

"What can I help you find?" She swept the room with a gesture. "I'm guessing you're not into cliffhanger endings, but if you're looking for something new, we have a BookTok section. Lots of trending reads there."

He skirted the wet spots and toed the bucket into a more discreet spot behind one of the large reading chairs. "Nah," he said. "Too many men with bat wings and feral claws there for me."

"Ah." she dipped the mop into the bucket and leaned it against the wall behind the chair, brushed her palms over her skirt. "So I'm guessing you're not into magic and romance."

Something in his expression shifted subtly, but it was too fast for her to make out. Instead, he shoved his hands in his trouser pockets—God, she loved guys in suits—and panned the shelves in the library.

"I wouldn't say that, just that I prefer my romance with lots of steam and zero drama."

Spoken like a man, she thought, even as she blushed but couldn't say why. To hide the heat creeping up her neck, she spun on her heel, her soft ballet shoes whispering over the wood. "You're a classics guy, then, I bet."

From beside her, his throat cleared. "What gave me away?"

He'd not made a sound as he'd moved. Was just there beside her. It might have been eerie if she didn't enjoy the feel of his energy so much. A faint whiff of wood smoke rose around her and she had to fight back the urge to inhale, just to take more of it in. He smelled of home and hearth, of protection and safety. Something in her stomach uncoiled.

"What gave you away as a literature fan?" she echoed. "I'm not sure."

"My age," he said with certainty.

He couldn't have been more than thirty. Just a few years older than her. "No," she said. "You don't look that old." A titter that made her want to roll her eyes at her own simpering girlishness.

"Oh," he said. "I'm old. Trust me." He stuck out his hand. "Maddox," he said.

Surprise and pleasure claimed her mouth, curving it up in a smile. Most customers didn't introduce themselves. Well. There was Castor, but that had been different. Hadn't it? Maybe she just looked especially cute today. Or maybe it was the short skirt.

Sticking out her hand, she said with a confidence she didn't feel, "Kit. I work here."

His auburn eyebrow quirked. "Do you really?" His eyes trained toward the bucket. "I thought you might be the maid."

She groaned out loud, a most unflattering sound. "That was a stupid answer, wasn't it? Of course I work here. "

Just a laugh, then. Not patronizing. A good, hearty chuckle that seemed just about perfect if she had to measure it.

"Oh, Kit. If I could tell you about the stupid things I've done in the last month...and I mean really stupid," he said. "The kind of things that would make you wonder how I'm even standing here breathing..."

A shiver moved up her arms and absently she rubbed at them. "Sounds dangerous."

He tilted his head slightly, as if to agree. "Oh it is. Very. Truth is, after all this time, I should have known better." There was an ache in his gaze as he canted his head toward the bookshelves. The theatric sigh that escaped him seemed painful for him.

"But I'm here now, in spirit if not body, and I need a book. Not fiction. Something with a bit of history to it. Something—I don't know—magical."

At that, he stalked toward the shelves, moving like a russet colored mountain lion, with steps that were as silent as if he was wearing soft-soled moccasins. Watching him was a joy. The rippling of muscles through the back of his jacket. A warrior in a business suit, she thought. It was almost so enjoyable she forgot he could turn around at any second and catch her watching him... until he did just that.

"You have a lot of old vellum," he said casually, as though he hadn't just caught her standing there with her mouth hanging open.

"Vellum?" She couldn't have heard him right. The coincidence was just too coincidently. "We do have some. But we have leather too. First editions. Some so old, I have no idea when they were bound because they were hand scribed." She pointed to the top shelf over to the right, where a row of spines peered out like eavesdroppers. And there, right there, in the same old phalanx of spines was the book Castor had been looking through.

She started. That couldn't be right. She glanced back at the checkout counter, back again to the bookshelf. A chill raced up her backbone. There was no way he'd climbed the ladder to put it back. And he sure as heck hadn't come back in to return it. Her jaw ticked to the side, thoughts racing.

Of course, the old gent had put the books back. Because of course there was no other explanation. And with Maddox standing there, watching her she brushed the event aside. "I doubt even my boss knows how old they are," she said, running a hand over her throat. "He bought a bunch of books a couple of years back from a collector's auction. No one wanted them."

"Too musty," he said, with a crinkled nose, and gosh did he look amazing when he did that. Just gorgeous enough to be a wonderful distraction.

"I like that smell," she said. "But you're right. Collectors now are looking for pretty edges. And vellum is difficult to store. It's why we have them over there out of the light."

She couldn't stop herself from going on about how to best archive them, the need of a rolling ladder, her desire to see them in the hands of readers who could appreciate them.

And through it all, Maddox smiled and nodded. At one point, he shuddered as though a cold wind had swept through him, but all she felt was the heat that came off him in waves. He angled himself toward a corner, his brow furrowed as though he was trying to stare through the wall. She was probably boring him to tears.

"Do any of those sound good to you?" she asked, realizing she'd been rambling, but as soon as she did, she realized she'd have to climb that damned ladder again. And her wearing such a short skirt.

Of course...maybe she wouldn't mind if he took a peek. Maybe he'd like what he saw. They could have dinner. Talk books.

The fantasy engrossed her so completely, she was grateful he'd already turned his back to her and strolled to the shelves. She fanned her cheeks as she watched him run his finger over a row of spines. He was taller than he seemed, she realized. Had to be at least six-three or four. She was willing to bet he'd only have to climb a couple of steps up that ladder.

"Your shop came highly recommended," he mused aloud, as though the words weren't really for her.

She remained silent, although she was dying to know who would recommend a small little out of the way second-hand bookstore like the one she worked in. His gaze started to roam along behind his fingers, darting faster as he moved along the shelf, those shoes whispering like velvet on velvet across the floorboards.

He stopped suddenly beneath the spot where Castor's sat. "Do I spot an old grimoire?"

Her brow furrowed, and tugged by that comment and the curiosity of it, her feet carried her the few feet that separated them. "A what?"

He pointed. "There. That's a witch's spell book, is it not?"

She blinked, aghast that such a thing existed at all let alone sat right there in the shop she worked in day in and day out. But she was intrigued, too. What exactly did a witch's spell book contain?

"You don't think that's what it is, really?"

His gaze shuttered. "You'd be surprised the sorts of things you find tossed away like garbage by folks who have no idea what they have in their hands."

There was no way that comment could have any relation to the things she'd been thinking about Ava, but a long swallow pulled at her throat just the same. An image flashed through her mind of Castor standing at the counter, running his hands over the pages.

She peered up at the shelf. "And you think that's what it is? That old book that's sat there for months without the teensiest show of magic. Without anyone suspecting a thing?"

Not completely true. Castor had asked to see it. He'd run his hands over it. Maybe he'd known exactly what it was.

She shuddered. "I can't believe we have a witch's book in the shop."

Maddox dropped his head back, gazing up into the topmost shelves, his gaze skimming the assortment of old books. "More than one, I think," he said in a husky voice.

Was he excited about that? She couldn't help stealing a look at him from beneath her lashes. And even as she did so, the answer came. He was the kind who just might pay good money for an old book.

And if any of them were, in fact, grimoires, then she'd be happy to get them out of the shop she spent over thirty hours in each week. All that bad juju. She didn't need more of it.

Better in his hands than hers. "Would you like me to get one down for you?"

He skimmed her with a quick glance, and she knew he was measuring her in some way. When his gaze moved over her shoulder, toward the ladder, she knew whatever he was mulling over, he'd made his decision.

"It might best if you don't lay your hands on it. Some witches protect their books with pretty devastating spells."

Sudden dread worked its way up her backbone as he strode past her. As he wrangled the ladder into place, she scrambled to relive her moments with Castor. Had she actually put her hands on it?

"So, by touch," she ventured, watching him set the feet into place, propping open the ladder as wide as it would go. "Do you mean hands on, full palm, or an accidental brush? Like...What exactly do you mean?"

His laugh came sudden and unexpected as he began his climb. "I mean I might not want to put a single finger on one unless I was wearing neoprene gloves and even then..." He let the words trail off as he inspected the spines visually, and while she felt her entire stomach roll over.

Her mind played out the exchange with Castor again, moment by moment, in an agonizing replay. Doing her best to remain calm, to breathe through it, she walked herself minute by minute slowly. Intentionally.

A nail. That's all. One single fingernail. She was pretty sure she hadn't done more than yank on it that way. It was ridiculous to even be nerved up about such a thing, but even so, her mouth felt very dry.

She was about to ask if that counted, when from above her, a grunt sounded. Hands twisting together in front of her hips, she dropped her head back to see him better.

He was looking down at her. "You look like you've been chatting with a ghost."

"Well, this is a bookshop, and I do touch a lot of books."

It took a moment before realization played over his features.

"I've scared you." His hand went to his heart. "Don't worry," he said and almost absently trailed that same hand over the spines, hovering an inch away from the leather. "You would know if you touched one. If you'd have put a single fingernail down on a book like that, you'd likely already be a frog." His half-hearted grin was not comforting.

She had a hard time swallowing. "And if I did and I'm not a frog yet?"

He peered down at her through his arms. Eyebrow raised, mouth set in a grim line, he said, "Then the spell would most likely be a delayed execution. And likely deadly."

Among the Missing

Kit

EVERY BIT OF ENERGY in her legs went to bags of water at Maddox's comment. Flippant, joking. He obviously had no idea what effect they had on her, since he turned his attention again to the books. She stood there, paralyzed, as a dozen scenarios moved through her mind at the speed of light.

She moved closer to the ladder. She found her fingers wrapping around the rung at chest level. Probably to steady herself. Her knees really did feel weak.

She was just about to ask for more when she heard the unmistakable sound of a book sliding across worn oak. It drew her attention upward, where through the gaps in the slats, she could see him pulling free the book Castor had been interested in.

With his bare hands.

Her breath came out in a flood. "I'm guessing that's not a grimoire?"

"Nah," he said absently as he flipped through the pages. "Something else. Something...interesting." He slammed the cover closed the way a teenager might slap down the cover of a nudie magazine. If they still even looked at nudies anymore.

"Not what I'm looking for," Maddox said, disappointment in his voice. "But very interesting."

Her fingers left the ladder and her head dropped back in relief. "Too bad," she said. "You're the second person this week who wanted to see it. I thought I might have made a sale." She tried to chuckle lightly, but even with the relief, her voice box felt tight.

"Second person?" he asked, and his gaze began a lazy journey throughout the room, as though searching for another customer. "Someone else came in looking for this?"

She wasn't sure why he was pressing the point. It wasn't a question, but she heard the note of urging in his voice just the same.

"Just someone who did the same thing you did. Looked inside and closed it again. The difference is..." Just what had the difference been? Castor hadn't put it back, nor had he told her he didn't want it. She just noticed it back in its place.

"The difference is that he didn't think it was a grimoire and you did."

"He didn't say it was a grimoire or didn't think it was?" His smile was odd, and his attention kept shifting to slightly over her shoulder.

"He didn't say it was a grimoire."

"Because it isn't," he said.

She shrugged, thinking perhaps that was the reason Castor hadn't actually taken it. "Apparently not, thank God."

With a shuttered expression, he held her gaze for a long while before he looked at the book again. A huff of thought before he climbed down the ladder, the book in his grip.

"I thought you didn't want it," she said.

"I didn't say I didn't want it," he said, tucking the book under his arm. "I said it wasn't a grimoire and it wasn't what I came in looking for."

Her jaw hitched to the side as she regarded him. "You're buying that?"

His grin came easily. "Unless you're going to give it to me."

There was no price tag on the book. She'd been adamant with her boss that they not put stickers on covers that couldn't be peeled off without ruining the material. Bar codes worked just fine for most newer books. But one that old? She'd have to look it up in the index.

She struck out her hand. "Here," she said. "I'll take that and ring it in for you. Would you like it wrapped?"

He hesitated long enough that she had to waggle her fingers. Eventually, after a long and pointed look at her palm, he handed the book over.

Spinning on her heel, she headed to the counter, tossing a question over her shoulder at him. "Maybe if you tell me what you're looking for I can help."

When he didn't reply, she assumed he'd gone back into the library to look over the shelves for whatever he'd come in for. No matter. She'd drop the book on the counter and look up the price while he dug about the shelves.

Her indexing system was the reason she won the job and she could make easy sense of the numbers penciled very lightly on the inside cover page. She'd enlisted her boss's help in the first few weeks, giving him a list with the code that he could put on the books he preferred she not touch.

For archival reasons, she'd always believed. But what if some of those books were dangerous? Like the witch's spell books Maddox had mentioned. It certainly gave her a new perspective on the grumbling old coot. She'd have to ask him when he came in next.

Not that it was likely to be anytime soon. He rarely came into the shop unless he had a new cache of books to add to the inventory. He was a collector for sure, but he was also a bit of a slacker. He appreciated the age of old volumes, but he wasn't great at storing them.

And that had been a problem a good number of times. Kit's type A personality required that she provide proper care for the books that were old and valuable. His absent-minded professor attitude had probably lost him a good deal of money over the years, because while he had an impeccable eye and a knack for finding valuable editions, his skills didn't extend to conservation.

He preferred to sell quickly those books that could keep the shop flush. His passion was in the acquisition, she always thought, and not in the maintenance. So it was a good thing the shop sold mostly newer books, the ones that kept the shop running, and a new influx of customers.

But the older ones, the first editions and special collections, were where the money was. Selling one of those could net enough to pay a multitude of bills.

She remembered the day he'd brought in a first edition of Jack London's *Call of the Wild* with a small handwritten note inside that he immediately slipped into an acid-free sleeve and taken to Sothebys. He'd bought her lunch that day and put a beautiful set of gold earrings into her purse.

But he came in for other reasons, too. She just never knew what he did when he barricaded himself in the back room or why he came so late at night.

Her hand stilled on the cover of the book as she laid it on the counter. The shop did OK for business, but on a regular day, she might have gone till noon before a single customer came in.

Now, today, two customers long before noon and both noticing the same book. Strange. Lifting one finger off the cover, she peered at the leather.

Definitely nothing out of the ordinary on the cover. A bit of worn gilt lettering that might have been language at some point, but now just looked like indecipherable shapes. The leather was worn and the gilt edging on the spine was a bit faded in places. In most ways, very much how an old book should look. But with the title an inscrutable mash of shapes on the front, she found herself squinting at the spine for the title. They refused to come into focus.

They didn't look like letters, to be honest. No matter what angle she peered at them, no recognizable word formed.

She'd have to resort to looking up the number in the codex.

"I'll just be a second," she called out to Maddox. "You keep looking. I'll have the price in a jiffy."

Bobbing down behind the counter, she ran her hand along the cupboard until a flexible journal with elastic around it met her fingers. She pulled it out and unwrapped the wide band that held it shut.

She had dozens of tabs in the journal, all designed to help order the old inventory. New books were in the computer and could be scanned. These old volumes needed special care, and she gave it. All she had to do was match the number penciled into the pages, identifying its provenance here in the shop so it could be traced back if need be.

With a plop and a flap, the journal landed beside the old book. Easier for comparison if they were side by side. Turning the cover over, she looked for the penciled in code, presuming it would be in an acid-free piece of paper just on the inside.

But there was none. No doubt it had fallen out when she'd dropped the book down for Castor to catch. She'd have to look for it later. Maybe close the shop after Maddox left so she could look without fear that an errant breeze from the door would float the paper somewhere she'd never find it.

Thinking of Maddox, she looked up, searching for him in the library.

"Have you had any luck?" she asked, raising her voice enough that he should be able to hear it even if he was over in the corner.

"Maddox?" she asked again when he didn't respond.

She waited a moment, not quite concerned, but curious. "Do you see a piece of paper on the floor in there?" she asked. "About the size of a sticky note."

Nothing. With a sigh, she flipped the pages. Maybe it was just inserted somewhere deeper into the book. Perhaps Castor had seen it and held it as he browsed the pages and put it back where it didn't belong.

Her fingers froze on the cool vellum within moments. Nothing. No note. No page numbers. No words. Nothing.

Not a single page had any writing on it. From start to finish, every recto and verso was empty.

A murmur of wonder moved through her throat. No wonder Castor didn't want it. The book was just an old empty journal that no one had written in. She snuffed out a bit of a laugh, all that buildup about the old tome's background to end up in such an unsatisfactory ending.

But at least she knew one thing. Old as it might be, the book wasn't terribly valuable.

"You know you can get a more modern journal that's easier to write in," she said, moving out from behind the counter and aiming for the library where she could catch Maddox's attention. "But if you're hellbent on buying this one, you'll need a special pen. Something archival quality."

She rounded the corner, her breath hitching as she expected to find him, head bent, fingers combing through the shelves.

But the room was empty. No Maddox. Not a shuffle of movement, not a creak of the floorboards. Her chest tightened, and she swallowed hard, straining to hear any sign that he was still here. Nothing. He hadn't even made enough noise to leave. She stood frozen, foot tapping against the wood, her brow pulling tighter with every beat of silence.

Gone. Just like Castor. What was with customers today? With a huff, she turned to head back to the register, thinking she'd have to climb the ladder again and shove the book back in place.

But the only book that met her gaze on the counter was the index. Her mouth twitched. She ran her hand over her hair, scraping aside the locks that swept over her eyes. Gone. That made no sense. She knew she wasn't imagining things. Tucking her hair behind her ear, she pivoted to face the bookshelves, scoured the top shelves, checking for the telltale gap in the phalanx of spines that would suggest maybe Maddox had taken the book without her noticing.

A cold shiver skated up her spine. The book—*that* book—was back in its place as if it had never been pulled free.

She wrapped her arms around her midriff, feeling far too cold all of a sudden. And there was the faint whiff of ozone again. As sure a sign as any that something weird was going on.

The shiver that ran up her arms was testament to it.

She wasn't sure she believed in things like magic, but magic wasn't the only kind of power in the world that could explain strange occurrences, was it? If Maddox and Castor both wanted to look at that book, and it wasn't a grimoire, then what the heck was it?

Something, she thought. Something powerful enough to interest two men. Mouth set in a grim line, she marched into the library and dragged the ladder back into place beneath the leather volume.

Bracing herself with a long breath, she climbed each rung, resolving not to look down. Instead, she forced herself ever upwards, and when the ladder tottered a bit with each heaving step upward, she pushed her fear to the back of her mind.

Because she was going to take another look at that book.

Balanced on the top step, she reached up and gripped it by the spine.

It refused to budge, the damn thing. She leaned just a bit more, hooking her toe into the ladder's slats for good measure, planting her palm against the shelves beside her. Getting herself good and leveraged.

The ladder swayed. Her breath hitched.

But dammit, she was going to do this. Bracing herself, she pinched her fingers around the spine.

Yanked as hard as she dared.

She thought she heard the soft whisper of the leather against the wood. Progress. Slight, but better than nothing.

Sucking in one more breath, she decided to stretch just a little more. She almost had a good enough space to slide her fingers in between the spines, right to the knuckle. Almost. What she lacked was the arm's reach to do so. Swallowing down her nerves, she gathered another millimeter from the fascia in her shoulder, rotating the cuff to free up any constriction.

Because she was going to look at that book if it killed her.

That was when she heard it. A thunk on the window. Hard enough to be intentional. Like someone rapping to get her attention. Probably Gideon again.

She recoiled back to a straight up position and dared a look over her shoulder.

The first thought that went through her mind was that she was probably mooning someone outside with her short skirt and that whoever it was, had decided to let her know.

Her second thought was more primal. Fear. It clawed its way up her throat with acidic fingers.

Because standing there between two parked cars, too far away to have rapped on the pane, stood that dark stranger who'd rescued her from the brute at the bus stop, who'd suddenly shown up outside her apartment. The one who fueled her fantasies in a dark, shameful way.

And he was staring right at her through the window.

The Flight of a Dove

KIT

HER HEART LURCHED AT the way that gaze held hers even from this distance. She told herself he could not see inside. The lights, the way the sun was slanting over the buildings...all of that would make it impossible for him to see her.

And yet, she felt as if he was drilling right down to her soul with that gaze. She clutched at the shelves beside the ladder, feeling dizzy. She might have hung there for hours, staring at his face, but that noise came again. A whack. A thud. Hollow and sharp at the same time.

She dragged her eyes from his to the window. A mourning dove, a pretty brown and pink thing with purple eyes, was flapping against the glass. As she watched, it pulled away, flying drunkenly over the roofs of cars parked along the street before coming straight for the plate glass again.

Right to a spot already covered in bloodied feathers. The poor thing was going to kill itself if it kept that up. No doubt it kept seeing itself in the reflection and felt the need to defend its territory. She knew it wouldn't stop unless she intervened somehow.

She glanced back at the man across the street. He stood placidly, hands in his pockets, his gaze shuttered as though nothing was going on. He was just going to let that poor bird ram itself over and over again into the glass.

"Bastard," she muttered, and scrambled down the rungs to the floor.

She was across the shop in moments. From somewhere down the street, the faint sound of a busker's guitar drifted over the sound of cars wheezing by. Laughter leaked out of the coffee shop next door and found its way beneath the cracks of the shop's threshold. And that awful thumping sound as the dove slammed into the glass again cut through all those noises like a gunshot.

She raced toward the window, waving, trying to scare the thing away from the inside. It dove straight for the window, right where she stood.

She flinched. Foolishly. Automatically. Even knowing she was protected by the glass, it was difficult not to duck instinctively. When it struck the glass, its breast flattened, spreading the plumage apart enough that she could see the greyish tinge to its skin.

"Stop," she said, spreading her palm over the window, hoping it would see her fingers through the glass and fly away. "It's not another bird, you fool. It's you. You're hurting yourself."

Wings spread over the breadth of her hand as it lay against the cool surface. The bird flapped so hard against the glass, its feet scratching the pane, bleaching out the red of its feet as it fought its reflection. She rapped the pane with her other hand. There were gaps in the poor thing's feathers now, and those plumes lost were sticking to the glass, caught and held by its own fluids.

Without stopping to grab her jacket, she raced outside to the sidewalk, and she slipped in something wet before she managed to get to the window. She scrambled to keep her balance and by the time she did, the dove had flown off. She watched it whistling with that peculiarly haunting noise its hollow bones made as they bore the bird through the air to a perch on a lamppost across the street. Right beside the stranger.

For just one second, his eyes grappled onto hers, then they shifted to the bird as though drawn by a tether to where it sat on the lamp post. Hands in his pockets, he eyeballed the poor thing as it tucked and plucked at its plumage. A soft pink hue coated the front of its chest.

Bleeding, she realized.

Unsure what to do, she turned to the window, trying to see if there was any way she could make the window less reflective.

Her own face wavered in the glass, caught by light and sent back to her along with all the other buildings, the cars, the people milling by. But that smear of feathers and blood and white excrement created a hole in the image, one that was disconcerting and sad as the mournful song of the bird who lost to it.

"Best wash that right away," said a man as he passed by.

He paused to examine the stain with her. She could see him in the window without turning around. "Nothing harder to get off than bird shit."

"Maybe tomorrow," she said. "Once I'm sure it won't be back."

"Do yourself a favor," he said. "Just kill the damn thing."

The cruelty of the comment left her staring as he shrugged and walked away, continuing on. She watched him go through the reflection in the glass, wondering how anyone could be so heartless. The poor thing obviously didn't realize what was happening.

She was so distracted that she didn't notice the bird again until it flapped past her face, so close, so fast, that she stepped back too fast and fell against the window. When the bird changed trajectory and came for her, she couldn't get her hands up in time.

It went for her throat. Or her chest. She wasn't sure. It just felt so damn frightening that she let loose a shriek and flailed about in a panic, arms, hands, and feet all going at the same time.

Tiny, scratching feet clawed at her arm and all she could think of was that beak aiming for her eyes. Rational or irrational, she squeezed her fist around whatever touched her palm and she flung it hard as she could.

The bird slammed into the glass with more force than it should have. Her hand went along with it, slamming the dove into the pane so hard she felt its breast break beneath her palm.

When it fell to the sidewalk, she was already on her knees. Chest scouring for air, bellowing in and out so fast she could hardly catch her breath, she kneeled on the sidewalk just inches away from the fallen bird. The poor thing lay crookedly on the pavement, its wings splayed wide, its neck clearly broken.

"Oh sweet Jesus," she said.

Tears stung the backs of her eyelids. She couldn't blink them away to save her soul. All she could do was let them stream down her cheeks as she lifted the dove into her hands, cupping it in her palms. "Oh sweet baby Jesus."

She felt a shadow move over her and looked up.

"Is everything alright, Dove?"

She blinked up at the owner of the voice. Broad of shoulder and towering above her. She tried to make out his face in the shadow, but it was impossible, backlit as it was, and with her eyes all filmed with water. And yet, she knew who it was even though she couldn't see that intense gaze. His voice sounded like warm chocolate and hot spices.. He even smelled like a hot cup of cocoa with a bit of clove and cinnamon sprinkled over the top.

Knowing who it was did nothing to calm her nerves. It made it worse.

"Poor thing broke its neck," she said, except that wasn't it, or not all of it, exactly. But she didn't want him to know how off she felt with him standing over her. How vulnerable she felt.

She scraped at the water pooling beneath her chin with the back of her hand. "Well. I broke it."

She sniffed, the tears threatening to break apart the rickety scaffolding she was trying desperately to put into place. She felt him crouch beside her, but didn't want him to see the ugly cry already working its way over her face. She didn't want anyone to see that, let alone this man.

"It would have killed itself anyway," he said, his voice low and throaty.

She shook her head, feeling combative. "You don't know that."

"I do."

He took the bird from her hands and laid it on the sidewalk at her feet. "I know something of death. This creature would have beat itself into that glass until it broke itself trying to get through the window."

She refused to look up. The way her face felt, she was sure it was twisted into something unrecognizable as human. But she couldn't let it go. He didn't understand. She could have avoided this.

"I should have put some sort of sticker on the pane," she said. "Let it know it wasn't safe. That the world it saw looking back at it was not real."

His quiet chuckle drifted over the air, a dark thing that reminded her of mossy places and earth.

"You think that's what it was doing, little dove? Trying to escape to somewhere new?"

"The sun makes a perfect mirror this time of day." She sat back on her haunches, staring at the body. "So, yes. I think it imagined the world it saw was real. Either that or saw itself as a threat." She tugged at the hem of her skirt. "All I had to do was shoo it away. It would be gone, not dead."

"That little bird was blind to everything except its own primitive need. You wouldn't have made a difference."

She did look at him then, but only because she refused to believe that. While everything about him was cast from shadow, the light scraping over him from behind, limning him in something that could be called a halo if she believed in such things, his eyes stood out like gems catching the light.

She swiped the tears from her face, met that gaze with a boldness she didn't expect she could manage. "Sometimes the only thing standing between life and death is another person's single act of kindness."

Even as she said it, she knew what had upset her. It wasn't the bird or the fact that she'd accidentally killed it. Not at all. But that wasn't a conversation for a stranger.

As if he understood her reluctance to say more, he drew back, pushing himself to his feet effortlessly and towering over her. He raked his hair back and followed it up with a swipe at the back of his neck. Bewildered, perhaps, or frustrated. Unsure of what to say to her.

Except there wasn't an ounce of insecurity in his demeanor. He didn't seem the sort who would be at a loss for words.

His was more of an energy that possessed the same kind of stoic presence as she'd expect from a Spartan warrior. His leather duster was spread wide as his hands stuffed themselves into pockets stretched over narrow hips and muscled thighs.

But when he angled himself just a bit to the side, and the sunlight moved over his features, playing across his skin like a painter's brush, she had to suck in a breath. He really was beautiful.

Not the sort of model material beautiful, either. His jaw was cut from Michaelangelo's marble, sure enough, with a lustrous sheen that would have been too perfect if not for the stubble clinging to his jawline in patches. Thick, lustrous black hair brushed back over his head, curled at his earlobes and framed the most intense and fierce looking eyes she'd ever seen. They'd looked violet before. Now they seemed made of amethysts themselves, with an icy glint that softened as he took her in.

No man on earth had any business being that gorgeous. And she was kneeling in dove shit and feathers, her short little skirt probably riding up in the back. Cheeks no doubt swollen from emotion.

"Thank you," she said, dusting herself off and leaning sideways so she could get her legs under her without committing some obscene act of exhibitionism. "I feel better now."

Expecting him to move on, she reached for the bird, intending to carry it into the shop to look for a paper bag or something. But as her fingers scooped beneath, his were there again.

She hadn't heard him bend down, no rustle of clothing or popping of knees. He was just there, and his hands were beneath the bird's frail, broken body, touching hers. A hum went through her. Singing behind her teeth. Ringing in her ears.

Flustered, she swept him with a glance. He was smiling at her. Tiny points in his teeth flashed. A whiff of danger tainted the air.

Like Castor's, she thought. Except this was no old man. No matter how mature that gaze was, it was nowhere near the ancient appearance of Castor's. Dangerous. Lethal. She sensed it in the way he held his shoulders.

"You were outside my apartment," she said, hesitating before she continued. "And on the bus." Determined not to be afraid, she opted to stick out her hand. "I'm Kit," she said.

He looked at her fingers waggling in the space between them, and for a second, she thought he would ignore her invitation. She was about to pull back, when his fingers curled around hers, an old world gesture, light and formal. A whisper of sudden longing crept up her skin.

"Kit," he said and her name on his tongue, coming from those lips, with that rasp of breath, her knees went to water. Her name seemed like a taster on his tongue. A flight of good ale or a sip of wine from an unfamiliar bottle.

Good thing she wasn't standing up.

"And you are?" She shouldn't encourage him, but all she could think was if she had to give a name to the police, she should make sure found out what it was.

"Flint," he said in a tight voice.

His jaw was clenched, as though he was struggling with the thought of giving his name, but it was perfect for him. That sharp jawline, the cut of his brow. But more than that, the sound of his voice.

"Flint," she repeated. "I never got a chance to thank you for what you did for me on the bus." Letting him know she recognized him. That she might have spoken of it to someone else. Because if she went missing...

He cut off her thoughts when his hands moved toward her. Too fast, she thought. She must have flinched because he drew back again, inclined his head toward the dove as it rested in her lap. "Let me," he said. "Kit."

There was no reason she shouldn't, was there? Would he get violent again if she refused him? Warily, she lifted the dove up into the space between him and he took it carefully.

The bird looked so small in his hands. Or maybe it just looked wrong, the way a giant might look holding a premature infant. She stood up when he did, feeling as though she didn't want to be kneeling in front of him. She just couldn't figure out if it was because she should run or...

She got up quickly. The dove didn't look right in his hands. He wasn't cradling it like he should. It seemed to her that vulnerable, delicate things should never be held by those brutal hands.

"You can't hurt it," she said, maybe trying to convince herself of the fact. "Not now anyway."

A glance up at him, and something froze inside her. In the seconds it had taken for her to stand, he'd closed the distance between them so tightly she felt like a cornered mouse...except no mouse ever felt like the cat was going to ...what? Kiss her?

Something was off about him, she realized. A thousand horror movies flashed through her mind. Documentaries of stalkers and murders, and she knew...just knew this man wasn't as beautiful on the inside as he was on the outside.

And yet, her cheeks flushed so hot she couldn't hold his gaze. Instead, she gestured to the door of the shop.

"In there," she said, trying to force her heart to stop that infernal racing. "I'll put it into a nice gift box. Bury it in my garden when I get home."

"Among the black-eyed daisies," he murmured, and her head snapped up to look at him. The way he looked down at her, like he would eat her...her knees sagged.

Some men were coming.

The words drifted into her mind like jagged bits of debris and she had to swallow down the unease that spidered its way up her spine.

"Maybe just give it to me," she said, shaking loose the cobwebs sticking to the images of all those horror shows. "I've already taken up too much of your morning."

But he wouldn't relinquish the dove. Instead, he strode toward the door of the shop, his long legs turning the yards of sidewalk into a few steps. Shouldering his way into the door, he held it open, inviting her to go ahead of him.

She hesitated. Her gaze flickered to the window. In its reflection, she saw herself with mascara streaked cheeks. Her eyes were owlish. The short skirt had turned almost half way around on her waist. She tugged it back into place. Blinked at herself. The pane showed nothing from inside. Just her face, her body, the street behind her, and cars whizzing past.

What bothered her the most, what made her hesitate, was that she couldn't see inside her shop. And that raised alarm bells. On a given day, she was in that shop unseen by the outside at various times of the day for the last four years. But now?

There was no way she was going to go inside that shop alone with him. The prickling along her neckline was too insistent. The brutal set of his shoulders, just a bit too unnerving.

She smiled, an affected thing that she had practiced for years as a shop clerk. "You go on," she said, smiling again. "Just lay it on the counter. I'll be in to look after it once I clean the window."

His throat bobbed on a long swallow and for a second, she thought he would decline, but then he swept inside the store and the door closed with a huff behind him.

She let go a long exhale, mindful that he could see her from inside and that she didn't want to look too relieved.

But she did feel as though she'd dodged a bullet of some kind. Swinging around to survey the streets, make sure she wasn't alone, she put her back to the window. It felt like every hair on her body rose then, and it was a struggle not to turn around. She wouldn't see anything anyway, but she had a feeling he was watching her. Her heart hammered loudly in her ears.

She had to breathe. Inhale normally. Exhale slowly. Get a grip. Wait for him to come out and then casually, but quickly go back inside.

But for now, because he was watching, she made a show of inspecting the sidewalk and even dared pivot to examine the window. That was the hardest thing. That moment when she felt as if she was laid bare to the eyes inside the shop.

Her reflection looked calm, at least. So she'd managed to gather some composure. When she noticed a woman walking toward her, she stepped out to make conversation, biding herself time, asking for the time of day, trying a soft sell of a new book, anything to delay going back into the store while he was there.

She all but heaved a sigh of relief when he came back to the door. The woman she'd cornered, a pretty brunette wearing yoga pants and a bulky sweater, gawked openly at him.

"I put it behind the counter," he said, his voice gruff. He'd known what she was doing, that was clear, and he was offended.

Well, too bad. A girl couldn't be too careful these days.

The pretty brunette ran her hand over her hair. "What are you storing in there, sugar?" she asked with a cock of her curvy hips.

He didn't answer. The way he grazed the woman with a dismissive glance was like a scalding spray of water. The woman cringed and shot Kit a look of pity. Instead of walking on, she lingered, her gaze stealing a path to the gorgeous man, who stood stiffly, as though he was irritated and was waiting for her to leave.

But she didn't. As though the woman sensed her unease, she lurked by the window, asking questions about the bird, suggesting ways to clean the glass. It went on so long, Kit was worried the stranger wouldn't take the hint, but he finally did. With a huff of barely concealed impatience, he pulled his duster closed and headed across the street. By the time he disappeared between two parked cars, Kit was ready to collapse.

"Thanks," she said.

The woman waved away the sentiment with a hand covered in rings. "Listen, I get it. I had a stalker once. Hot as Satan's unshaved balls in the middle of a Tuscan summer. But it don't matter how gorgeous they are if they're violent, honey. Keep that in mind."

Something squeezed in Kit's chest. It was difficult to smooth down the backward stroke those words put on her hackles enough to ask how the woman knew.

But the woman was already making her way down the street. Kit watched her quick stride, the way men coming toward her tried to catch her eye. With a sigh, she turned on her heel and fled to the inside of the shop.

She'd have to gather some cleaning supplies. Get the window nice and tidy. Then she'd put the bird in a pretty gift box they had stashed in the back room. On her way to the back room, she noticed the ladder still resting beside the bookshelf.

In the hubbub, she'd forgotten the book she wanted to take down. She glanced up, either habit or curiosity, but when she did, her feet halted in their tracks. Her head canted to the side as she grazed the shelf, training her eyes on the spot where the book was.

Where the book *should* be.

Because it wasn't there anymore. All that existed in its place was a two-inch gap in the Roman line of leather spines.

The Frailty of Humans

FLINT

KIT ASHE WAS AFRAID of him. That was clear right away. And it didn't detract from her allure one bit. It was smart of her to be afraid. He was a thing of violence and brutality. A soldier in his father's shadow army since long before her kind abandoned the caves and mud huts and moved into buildings made of stone and brick. He'd broken hundreds of mortal women like her a hundred years or more before he'd given up trying to enjoy them.

If she was afraid, then she just might survive him. And he wanted her to survive, he realized.

He watched her from inside her shop, the bird all but forgotten in his hands, and he knew the savor of her fear through all the layers of man-made materials that separated them.

The energy of it was a palpable thing that tasted of sour cherries and port wine. It possessed effervescence, and he could imagine it on his tongue, dancing with abandon as he took his time savoring the fullness of it. Not just this teasing sample gained from a current of air that wafted in from the open doorway. He wanted it in all its headiness, from the sweat on her skin, to the tangy pheromones in her ragged breath.

But as he cradled the dove in his hands and looked out the window where she stood, nervously chatting some slattern of a woman, he wondered what it would be like to break her, to hold her in his hands and feel her heart thrumming against his palms.

Normally, he would revel in that sensation, knowing that the release of it, the final breath of surrender, would be a wash of relief over his own skin. A gust of life's energy needling into his pores. His entire body quaked with the need to have her beneath him, on a precipice, taking the exquisite need for release and violence to the brink where he could hang on, when her terror would be at its height.

And then he would wash it away with one brutal thrust.

Strange, so strange, this need. He didn't understand it. Only that he felt it so acutely he could barely swallow down his need. He knew the sensation of fear. In all his generations of instilling terror, of using it for his father and his shadow court, living for it, he'd never found a flavor more enticing than fear. It made his throat tight and his heart beat faster.

But this one, this was different. It tightened his balls until they hurt, and it seeded an ache in him that went root deep.

Even the dove cradled in his cupped hands sensed his unrest and stirred ever so slightly. Its heart found a stuttering rhythm that pulsed against his thumbs. He wasn't a healer like his brother, Blade, or even a magical savant like his brother, Mica, but the creature's body felt the stirrings of his magic as he watched Kit through the glass. As he watched her and breathed too deeply. As he thought of her and what it might be like to crush her against him and test that fear.

And whatever last residual bit of energy that remained within the dove's cells responded.

It wanted to live.

He glanced down at it, frowning. The softness of the plumage, sticky in parts from its injury, was velvet against his palms. Fluffs of pin feathers had drifted through the air and landed in that small hollow beneath his nose as he'd stalked through the street and into the shop. They embraced the curves of his nostrils, tickled his skin. His nose twitched as he tried to relieve the itch.

The creature couldn't possibly survive the way it was. But Kit was stricken that she'd hurt it. The sight of her tears was a knife in his liver.

He'd been watching her for a full night and a day now, and he was so sure she could see him that he'd dared to assume a nonthreatening glamor at the bus stop just hours earlier. It wasn't much, a brief use of his magic that could be replenished if he was careful. But he needed to know if it was his own desire to be seen or if she could she recognize his energy. Would she respond to the old man with familiarity, as if she knew him? His heart had been hammering in his ears as he watched for the faintest light of interest in her eyes for the fae hiding beneath the glamor.

For a moment, he thought he'd noticed a brief flare of recognition, but then she'd given over to her very mortal belief in her own senses and treated him as the old man he presented. It was both a disappointment and a relief.

Clinging to the glamor had been like trying to hold onto a wisp of fog. Glamor magic was not his specialty, especially not when his natural self wanted to present as something far more vicious than an elderly human. But he held the glamor as long as he could until she boarded the bus. Watching her climb up the steps created a burn in his belly, a telltale sign that he was lying to himself. That this one meeting had fueled his desire, not dampened it.

Boarding the bus didn't seem too onerous, knowing she was sitting inside. When he sat in front of her, he felt her eyes on his back and smiled. She found him pleasing to look at. For the first time in generations, he let himself take pleasure in that, letting it shield the unwanted, prickling energies of the interior of the metal skin that surrounded him. He breathed in her scent of vanilla and sweet things. Lost himself in fantasies of things that should be devoured and licked clean. And by the time she pulled the cord, as he'd seen others do, he felt a little less unnatural.

She brushed past him before he rose to his feet, and there was a moment when she paused, confused, as if she noticed him. The rapid fire of his already hammering heart ratcheted up even more at the way she skimmed over him with her gaze. In the evening light she had been beautiful. In the day, she made his heart clench.

He followed her stealthily, not bothering to hide. If she would have turned around, she'd have seen him. But she was too intent on getting to her shop. He watched as she struggled with the door, completely oblivious to the man standing at the side of the building leering at her. Gideon. She had been so preoccupied, she'd not seen him. But Flint had. His reaction at seeing the hunter lurking outside, waiting for the moment he could pounce on Kit, was one of pure fury. And an almost irrational jealousy.

A smile curved his lips as he thought about Gideon now. Where he was. What he would do to him when this was over. The earthen realm would have to live with one less hunter to protect it. And the fae realm would gain another indenture.

One life decided, then, and another loitering out there on the sidewalk, pretending to examine the cracks as she waited for Flint to leave. She wouldn't come back inside the building till he was gone, he knew. It pained him to know she was so scared of him. He wished she still saw him as compelling. It would make things so much easier. But a hand dealt was a game begun, and he had to work with what he was given.

He watched mesmerized as the breeze caught a strand of her hair and blew it out straight. She must have caught a scent of something on the breeze because she lifted her chin, inhaling deeply. The way her throat moved as she swallowed down the fragrance of the air made him want to curl his fingers around the curve of her skin and muscle as he sealed his mouth over hers. He wanted to steal her breath. Take it inside him and roll it around on his tongue.

He dropped his gaze to the dove in his hands. She'd raced to its rescue and instead broke its neck. Something in him cracked when she did. He saw something more in her. A proclivity for violence, a drive that came out when she was threatened. And something inside his chest burned like a banked fire coming to life.

He'd known it was at death's door before he even picked it up. While he didn't mind letting it suffer until it found its death the way most things did, he knew she would mind the creature's suffering very much.

And that was the thing that bothered him. The thought of her agonizing one more moment over this wretched, already dead crea-ture, bore a hole in his soul.

So when the bird lifted its head ever so slightly, seeking a life it had no right to anymore, he clenched his fist over its body. The neck broke completely with barely any force. Gone. Just like that, a life force snuffed out and gone to black with barely a bit of effort.

So frail. Just like these humans. Just like her, he thought. He stared at it for a long while until a shudder moved through him.

She would need to come in soon. She'd need to finish her work. Ride home on the bus. And he'd need to be with her and watch her and make sure this sort of thing didn't happen to her. An errant swipe of some god's hand slamming her against her destiny. Breaking her neck.

He stashed the bird behind her counter the way she'd asked, and then he drew a long breath. She'd need to see him leave the shop in order to feel comfortable again. So he made sure she saw him as he struck again for the door and paused long enough for her to catch sight of him before he made a show of walking away.

But when she turned to the door with a relieved sigh, he slipped back in behind her, much the same as he'd done that first night, and he hid himself in shadow while she went about her day. She read, she chatted with people, she drank five cups of coffee with lots of cream and cinnamon. The pleasure he took in watching the simplest of her actions astounded him, and twice he had to fight back the urge to brush the soft fluff of the bird shell blue sweater she wore just so he could imagine taking it off her.

He followed her when she locked up and headed to the bus stop, a time when night was encroaching and he didn't need to hide in the shapes of darkness. He walked behind her softly, keeping his eyes on her as she took brisk steps. The way her hips swayed, the scent that trailed along behind her to wrap around his throat, was delicious agony. He boarded the bus with her, suffering the prickling energy of the cold steel as he focused hard on holding the invisibility so he wouldn't spook her yet again.

Disembarking at the stop nearest her house sent a shiver of relief over his entire body, as he shed the steel confines. He all but shook himself like a dog wringing water from its fur, and he inhaled the city night smells as though they were a balm.

It was all going so smoothly.

That was when she paused at the shelter instead of walking on. He halted with her, just to the side of her shoulder, almost touching. Following the direction of her gaze to the Plexi-glass shelter, he saw the same woman she did. Within its confines, the woman sat slumped, staring off into space. No jacket. Torn pants that clung to the bones in her hips in ways that made Flint's lip curl back. Oh, yes. He knew what this woman was.

But not Kit. She halted with her purse over her shoulder and she fidgeted her feet back and forth, angling her body slightly away so it wouldn't look like she was staring. So polite, his dove. So considerate. He was sure she noticed the track marks that climbed the woman's thin arms like a Jacob's ladder of puckered, red sores. He was sure Kit would stop to help this hapless creature.

And that was when he knew he would have to kill again.

What She Is

KIT

THERE WAS SOMETHING OFF about the woman waiting in the bus shelter, Kit thought. The woman sagged into the Plexi-glass walls, barely lifting her gaze to Kit as she stepped off the bus. It wasn't unusual for someone to avoid eye contact, especially this late in the evening when folks were long past rush hour and the darker things of the world came out of hiding. But it was the way she avoided eye contact, not actively as most people did, averting their gaze quickly and to some spot out of focus.

No. This woman stared ahead, right at her and right through her at the same time. Dead eyes, she thought. Dead eyes just like an addict might have after a hefty hit of something strong.

Or dead.

That thought ran shivers up Kit's spine. Surely, if she was dead, someone would have called the police. The driver would notice.

From the last step on the boarding platform, she glanced back at him. He already had his hand on the door pull.

"She needs help," she said, pointing at the shelter where the woman leaned a little too crookedly. A young woman, she realized, now that she felt safe to look more openly.

Barely more than twenty. Just a few years younger than herself. Ava, too. Her heart clenched around that thought. This girl didn't look anything like Ava. Her hair was the color of ash, not pitch. And Ava was curvy, with taut bits of muscle despite the drugs. This girl was scrawny enough that the t-shirt she wore, a filthy rag of a thing, looked like it belonged to a giant.

And why she was wearing short sleeves this time of year, yet refrained from hugging herself for warmth? Kit wore a sweater and still felt the chill.

She refused to step down onto the sidewalk. "We have to do something."

The driver heaved a sigh and looked back over the transit interior. He wasn't the same driver as the nights before and she wondered if they had to take some sort of training in detachment. There was no one else on the bus. It was a dead hour when most commuters were already home for the night. Almost absently, nervously, she dug into her purse, feeling for her phone. Her phone. If the driver wouldn't do anything, then she'd call the police.

"Lady," he prodded. "I have a schedule."

She whirled on him, then. "A woman might be dying out there and you're worried about your schedule?"

"I didn't say I wouldn't help," he snapped. "I said I have a sched-ule." He grabbed for his radio transmitter and held it up and stabbed the air between them with it.

"So you'll call it in?"

His sigh could have peeled paint. "You need to hear me do it? Get the fuck off already."

His bark drove her out the door, finally, and onto the sidewalk, but she was sure he hadn't been content with just snapping at her. The growl that tore the air between them was so fierce it made her pivot sharply on the asphalt before the doors closed, angry that he would be so unfeeling.

She was about to snap back, something about treating people with dignity and not growling at them like some beast, but he spoke first.

"You might want to get that throat checked," he said with his brows arched. "That's a nasty sound for a young woman."

Then the door heaved closed with a spurt of hydraulics, leaving her to stand on the sidewalk blinking in confusion. She watched the bus move into the traffic with barely three seconds of signal blinking into the growing dark.

A shuddering sigh moved through her. That prickling sensation of someone standing nearby moved over her skin. If this was what it felt like to see a dead person, then she believed right then that ghosts were real. The air was sharper than it should be. The smell of cloves and pine a bit too overwhelming.

But except for the woman slumped inside the shelter, she was alone. No pedestrians walked along the streets. The area was a bit too rural for a mass of people at this time of the day.

She should have been home an hour earlier, too, not carrying a weighted down purse filled with makeup she didn't need because she'd gone on a shopping spree. The dove. The stranger AKA stalker. Gideon.

She squeezed her eyes closed. Let loose a long breath through her nose. The shopping made her forget all that for a while. But now, rubbing her arms, she had to brave yet one more horrible thing today. Then make a decision about it.

Or did she? Maybe this wasn't all what it seemed.

She turned to face the poor wretch in the shelter. Just to make sure. Telling herself once she acknowledge her, the woman would speak.

The girl hadn't moved.

Oh God, she really was dead. Kit's belly turned over on itself as though a stone had dropped down into a deep well inside her. This couldn't be happening. She had to do something. Call someone. She couldn't just trust the driver to make that call. She was so close to home, too. She'd feel safer making it herself from the safety of her apartment. Things didn't...they didn't seem right. Night was prowling over the city and the dead hour would end. And she felt that damned sensation of being watched again. Again. Still.

Kit shrugged herself deeper into her coat as she eyeballed the woman, doing her best not to lose her shit. The woman might not need her speedy aid anymore, but she shouldn't be left to sit there for all the world to see, a loss of dignity she would never get back.

Exhaust fumes roiled about her feet and lifted to her nostrils. Some car down the block coughed into life, drawing her attention for an instant toward a dilapidated bungalow built on what was once the outskirts of the city.

That house leaned into the past, it seemed, the sills a wicked grin beneath the windows. Even in its run-down state, the rent was probably astronomical. She watched the owner, a narrow man with a bent back, toss a cigarette out the window before pulling out into the harried traffic.

Just like all the other cars passing by, and not a single one stopping to investigate.

Maybe she should move on too. Something wasn't right here. And it was more than just the tingle of unease prickling over her nape. More than just the way the world around her had started to seem 'off'. The smell of ozone kicked up like dust. But what if she was just being too cautious?

She found herself inching forward, clenching her phone in case she had to hit something with it or voice an alarmed 911 call. The young woman was definitely an addict of some sort. Track marks peppered her arms, raw and puckered. She couldn't just wait to see if someone showed up. She had to do something. With a flick of her thumb, she unlocked the screen. Light played up at her, making her blink.

"Probably not a great idea," said a male voice from behind her.

She whipped around, a cold chill instantly shooting up her spine.

Phone up over her head. Ready to come down on any part of anatomy that came too close. Up until a second earlier, she'd been alone with this girl. No one could have just walked up without her noticing. Not unless he had been stalking her.

All sorts of thoughts ran through her mind at once: was he the person responsible for this girl? Someone who might attack her? Why didn't she take the knife out of her purse instead of the phone when she got off the bus?

Flashes of the bully from the day before swam before her eyes. His mocking laughter. Her shame at forgetting to open the pen knife when she tried to defend herself. But she knew it wasn't him. And she was even more terrified because she knew before she even trained her eyes on the man's face that she recognized the voice. She could bring his face to mind even without looking at him.

She stepped backward, toward the shelter. A dead girl was far safer than a living stranger. Especially this one. He prowled toward her, those violet eyes taking her in with a single look.

She didn't have to be a mouse beneath a cat's eye to know he was a predator. It was there in his every move, every flutter of muscle in his stubbled cheek. That black hair raked back was lit from behind by the streetlights like he was edged in the brightest parts of a fire.

She'd not seen it in the first moments outside her shop because she'd been so worried about the dove. But now, in the growing dark, just like she had when he'd spoken and taken the dove from her hands, she knew him for what he was: a threat.

And her here with no one in sight but a dead woman. Had he killed her? Was this a trap of some sort?

She backed up again, felt the corner of the shelter dig into her back. Flint, his name was. And she'd told him her name. Fool, she thought. Too damned trusting.

"What are you doing here?" she asked, and curses formed on her lips at her stupidity. Don't encourage the bear, Kit. Don't poke it. But her nerves were ringing. "Are you following me?"

He paused, his eyes narrowing. "I wouldn't call it following exactly."

The timber of his voice was almost unreal. There was a clarity to it, a music that was too pure even though the sound was far more primitive than any a man-made instrument could make. It was like the symphony of a fire crackling, of ash being dragged across stone into a grate.

It put her in mind of sitting around an ancient fire, wolves calling to each other in the distance, the carcass of a hare roasting over a spit. But all she could think was that she was the diner around the fire and he was the wolf in the distance, waiting for her to come out of the light.

She didn't dare move. Didn't want to alert the predator to her fear. Unconcerned, his glance flicked to the dead girl and horror clawed at her throat at the truth she saw in his face.

She had a hard time breathing. Though she could barely trust her voice, she had to speak.

"You know her."

His gaze did not leave the young woman. She was sure it was pinned to her face, and the expression on his was unreadable. No emotion, she thought. And that scared her.

He spoke, finally, dragging his gaze back to Kit's. "I don't know her. Just what she is."

Despite her fear, his brow furrowed in confusion. He stepped closer, just a foot, but it was enough to throw the confusion running headlong into panic.

Her hands came up, defensive. "Stop," she said. "Don't come any closer. If you do, I'll scream."

His mouth twitched. Even with the dying light, she could see he was amused. She swallowed down her unease, forced herself to be conversational, to delay until someone came or she could find an opportunity to run.

She waved behind her at the girl. "She's dead."

An accusation she couldn't help. She needed to know, the way she had to look at a needle before it plunged into her skin as it drew blood, how he would react.

He shrugged. "She appears dead."

Inspiration flared. She held up her phone, showing him the screen. "I'm going to call 911."

The way he shook his head put a knot in her stomach. "I told you it wasn't a good idea." He took a step closer. "Put the phone down, Dove."

Dove. Oh, the endearment was not helpful in the least. It just made things worse. She shook her head, backing up, feeling behind her with her one hand, aiming to get around the shelter, maybe run. She felt like running. Every inch of her skin was trying to flay itself from her bones in an effort to depart this moment.

"Come now," he said, his voice a low murmur, his gaze on the woman behind her in the shelter. "As much as I would love to taste your fear, I need you to stay calm."

The comment did exactly the opposite. Everything in her began to vibrate. She stepped back again. Her heel caught a crack seamed beneath the shelter, drawing a line to the middle of the sidewalk.

She was sure she heard a noise coming from inside, but that couldn't be right. Any noise should be coming from him. The sound of a sudden intake of breath, the shifting of movement. She wasn't sure which way to look.

The decision was taken from her. He leapt for her the moment she fetched up against the Plexi-glass wall. She was trapped there. Traffic on one side, solid cement buildings on the other. Her heart rammed up her throat like it was on a mission to stampede straight out her mouth.

She parted her lips to scream.

He flew by her so fast he was nothing but a blur. Stunned, she pivoted, compelled to satisfy the morbid curiosity of why he'd not grabbed her.

And there she saw it. The girl. Standing. Her head was cocked at an odd angle. Her smile was one of victory.

"I've been waiting," she rasped out, dust in her voice. A snake's rattle in the tone. "It's time, Flint. They're coming."

And that was the moment he sliced a glinting knife across the woman's throat.

And What She Isn't

KIT

THE YOUNG WOMAN CRUMPLED like a paper bag. There was no blood. No death rattle. She just fell.

There was a moment when Kit thought she should scream, but it was a wooden feeling, like she was viewing it all from a thousand feet up. Her hand went to her throat, feeling for evidence of a scream on her throat because her mouth was open and her throat was hurting like a cheese grater was rasping over the skin.

But there was no vibration. Just a tea bag feeling in her knees, the sensation that she was being held up by something other than her own power. Shock. That's what it was. She'd heard about this level of numbness, of the body shutting everything down because it couldn't bear the weight of so much adrenaline, but had never truly understood it until that moment.

Everything in her bowed inward, her body curling into itself as she swayed on her feet in the middle of the sidewalk, trying like hell to do exactly the opposite and run.

Flint was doing something to the woman's body. Slicing into her neck. Sawing away at it with a blade the size of Crocodile Dundee's. Big as it was, as powerfully as his muscles moved beneath his jacket, it was clear he was having a hard time. When he did make a solid cut, the skin clung to the vertebrae by threads that seemed as impossible to get through as a block of cement.

She thought she saw some sort of electric light play over the knife, making it glow with heat. But that couldn't be right, could it?

And the woman's head...it should have come away by now. In the movies, the tender flesh separated so easily. This woman's skin kept coming back together with a bloodless determination to knit itself back onto its body. Though a red seam appeared in her neck with each slice, it dissolved as if by magic a moment later.

The blood should be spraying everywhere. Kit should have been half a mile away by now. She knew why she wasn't even as her brain shouted at her to move, to run, to hide, to scream. She knew that the battle to win over the blackness creeping in from the sides of her vision was more important.

Her body's reaction to the violence of those thrusts he made, heaving everything he had into the cuts, gathered a tingling sensation behind her ears. It was threatening to purge her stomach in the most violent of ways.

She felt herself swaying sideways.

Her body had decided which battle it was going to lose. She was going to pass out.

She couldn't pass out. She needed to fight back against the shadows creeping in. She had to stand.

For a second, the dizziness retreated. A smile tried to claim her lips, victorious. Fleeting but critical. She swallowed down the nausea. She could do this.

Just when she thought she might have reclaimed control, the woman's head came free with a pop. The stink of ozone erupted into the air like arterial spray. The woman's eyes traced a line right to where Kit stood. Impossibly, one of them winked at her. Then they went dead.

That was when she lost her stomach. She sagged over her knees, letting it come. The steam of it hitting the asphalt, the spray of it over her shoes. The smell... It dropped her to her knees.

"They've found us," the man said from somewhere way off in the distance. She put her hand up, hoping to make contact with the shelter wall. Needing something solid to grab onto. She had to get up. Get away. Right the fuck now. Sweet Jesus, why couldn't she move?

Her grasp met another hand instead. Fingers wrapped around hers. Hot. Electric.

For an instant, she felt safe, protected. But then she remembered this man had just murdered someone.

He had been stalking her. And he'd found her. Alone. Why the hell was she alone out here? Where were the pedestrians? The cars? The buses, for pity's sake?

His voice drifted down to her, urgent. Commanding. "I need to get you out of here."

She dropped her head back. It felt too heavy, like it might tumble right over her back onto the sidewalk. He was looking down at her, his expression pinched.

"Kit," he said.

She swayed sideways, her eyes going to the way his hand wrapped around hers. What was it that woman had said. She knew about stalkers. Oh, sweet heaven. This was bad. This was very bad.

Little bubbles popped in her brain like champagne. She was just beginning to register the other words: they've found us. As if *found* was a terrible, terrible thing. As if *us* was something intimate, that she was already a part of when she didn't even know who the heck he was.

She tried, oh, she tried to yank her hand out of his grasp, but he was so strong. That was when her heart rate really ticked up. A thousand scenarios ran through her mind. None of them pleasant.

"Let go of me."

"I'm trying to be gentle, Kit," he said. "But time is running out."

"Fuck time," she said. "Fuck you." And surrendered herself to the panic. She flailed out everywhere, in every direction, all at once.

"Stop fighting me," he growled. "You're going to make me hurt you."

She barely registered anything after that. But whatever happened, whatever he said, he finally lost control and let go a rumbling growl. A snap of light from somewhere behind them caught her attention, and she stopped moving. He murmured something about her being a good girl and wrapped both arms around her, holding her pinned in his brutal embrace.

"Good girl," he said as he hefted her over his shoulder. "Smart girl. You'll be fine now. Just you see."

His shoulder bore into her hips, making it hard for her to do more than crane her head upward. Something had happened while he was grappling her into submission. Something that made her wordless, that compelled her attention the way a horrible traffic accident pulls a passerby's gaze.

"She's alive," she said, her words sounding wooden to her ears.

His hand ran over her backside, lighting a fire there in her skin, beneath her tights. She was vaguely aware that she should scream, but she felt... calm.

Calm even while the woman stood up beside the shelter, head cradled in her arms. Calm as the scrawny body split right down the middle and slid away like snake skin. Calm as a large, incredibly beautiful man crawled out of the darkness between the seams and shook her off as though she were dirty clothes.

She was even calm when he canted his head at her, a smile of recognition on his face before he stepped free of the flesh that lay puddled and quivering on the sidewalk.

He was haloed in light, limned in an aura of silver. His hair, long and white as bleached bone, caught an invisible, unfelt breeze and splayed it out against the backdrop of city buildings and streetlights. She noted that he was nude. His skin shone with the iridescence of an abalone shell. His member was large and hard and though he was an adult, there wasn't a hair on his body except for his scalp.

"I should have been more clear in my message, Ms. Ashe," he said in a thick, multi-faceted voice. His tone, the sonic equivalent of a prism's light. "I told you the news was not good."

"Castor," she murmured even though this man, this being, couldn't possibly be the old man from the store. And yet it felt right to call him that.

"I don't give my name to many," he said. "In all my centuries I can't remember ever doing it so frequently." He tittered. "And to think Homer was the one before that." He shook his head in disbelief. "You might be careful how you use it."

The man holding her paused in his progress as he heard the exchange from behind him. He went rigid beneath her. She felt the way his muscles went taut before he swung around and all she was left with was the view of the empty street and the glow of lamplights as they reflected off the pavement.

She struggled against his firm grip. She needed to get down. She couldn't see what was happening behind her and that was scaring her.

Her neck ached from trying to hold it up. Blood was rushing in between her ears.

She pounded against his back and legs. Rock hard muscle met her fists, but she struck him, anyway. Kicked out in the front. Arched and twisted until he finally set her down with a frustrated sigh.

When he set her down, he did so with care. And when she tried to run, one swift motion, and she was snagged and pulled close up against his side.

"Not yet, Dove," he said and gathered her in against the heat of his body. She was shaking, she realized. Despite her terror, her traitorous body craved the warmth and melted against him like ice against a hot stone.

She thought she heard him suck in a breath. And while she was trembling like a lamb to the slaughter. His arm tightened, a seam of warmth running down her body, and she silently cursed herself for burrowing in further. For wanting that heat.

Castor tipped a finger to his brow, sketching a slight bow. "Ms. Ashe," he said. "I enjoyed our discussion. I hope you'll forgive me for leaving without saying goodbye, but my young charge called me home."

She was about to respond with something equally polite, an automatic habit, when she noticed a ticking membrane slide down over his eyes. It was so unexpected that she drew back instinctively.

Flint must have felt it, because he side-stepped so that she was slightly behind him. She was pretty sure, looking at the smile tugging at Castor's lips, that he had seen her reaction too and was pleased. Or smug. She wasn't sure.

"Your portal," Flint interjected, drawing Castor's eye to him and away from Kit. "That's some pretty dark magic, using mortal flesh as a build foundation."

"I note you recognized what it was," Castor said.

"That sort of thing has certain tells. The question is why? I'm no friend to the humans but I always thought you were partial to them."

"Alas, not just a portal, I'm afraid. I wish I could tell you otherwise. In fact, it's why I'm here." Castor swept his arm toward the place where the young woman's skin lay in a puddle. "One does what one has to in circumstances like this."

"And what sort of circumstance is this?" Flint asked.

Castor's eyebrow arched up an inch. "I would rather you ask what other purpose I cast the magic, but if you must know the circumstances..."

Flint's core stiffened. "My death."

Castor's sigh was long and weary, an answer as good as an agreement. "I have served many powerful fae in my day, but not so many as ruthless as Terran of the Sentinels."

There was a long silence after that, as though both men were contemplating those ruthless masters and what it might mean. Flint came to a conclusion first, and it shocked Kit.

"Do I have time to save her?"

"You have time to fight," Castor told him. "From where I opened this portal others are gathering. Six fae. You know them. The best of the Shadow Court save you and your brothers."

"Six," Flint said. "Is that all?"

"Your father expects you to come peacefully or he would have sent more to force you. Of course, I knew differently. One look at you watching this little mortal in the shop and I knew she had already stolen more than your loyalty."

He advanced, one predator facing down another, and Kit had a terrible urge to slip behind Flint's back. She wasn't sure which was the more dangerous, but her marrow responded by presuming the safer bet was the man who stood beside her. Man? Hadn't both of them used the word fae?

"Those who are coming believe I cast the magic for them so they could come through," Castor said with another lingering glance at her. The membranes in his eyelids ticked down again. She resisted a shudder.

"They can't know any differently. You understand."

His gaze on her was so hard she thought he was talking to her, but Flint answered. "I understand."

"You know who is coming," Castor said and adjusted the cuffs of the suit he wore, and that was when she realized he was clean. Clothed. She was sure he'd stepped from the woman—the portal—naked and bloody.

"You know what they want." A long pause before he said, "I have used the mortal's blood to cloak the battleground from human eyes beyond a certain perimeter. All they will see is the scene they always see. But within the barrier, all will be visible, so make it swift."

His gaze skimmed to Kit's, and she fidgeted beneath that intense scrutiny. "If you want her to live, then make it the battle of your life."

A thoughtful sound moved through Flint's throat. From beside her, he looked down at her with a stoic expression, his lips in a grim line. A movement from Castor drew her attention to the shelter. He was gathering the woman from the sidewalk. Propping her back onto the shelter bench. A snap of energy, like a bolt of lightning, jolted through her and she lurched like a puppet before sagging sideways again.

He looked askance at Kit, excluding Flint from his comment. "She does need her dignity, does she not?"

She might have nodded, but a heavy weight warmed the top of her head. A palm. Flint's palm smoothing down to cup her face. Gentle but with a possessive pressure. With his body, he angled her toward him, forcing her to face him.

She knew the hum of an electric change in the air, the calm before a hurricane. The suck of air before a tsunami and her palms went to his chest as if drawn there by invisible cords.

His eyes flared as if they held light within. A sad smile played with one corner of his mouth. It was a pretty mouth, she thought.

"Run, little Dove," he said in a husky voice, his eyes pinned to hers. "Before it's too late. I can give you some magic to cloak you, but don't hesitate. Go as fast as you can. Don't stop. Don't look back. No matter what you hear, keep going."

His thumb whispered over her chin, a moth's kiss as he held her gaze, and something odd moved through her chest. Pity, perhaps. Sadness. She might not understand what was happening, but she knew danger and threat when she felt it. She knew a victim didn't fight to stay when her captor released her.

And yet she couldn't move.

His throat bobbed as he took a deep swallow. He was struggling with the thought of releasing her, she knew. Confusion held her rapt.

"You need to go."

His gaze roamed her face, as if memorizing every line, every feature. It halted at her mouth. He licked his lips, as though he could taste her breath and found it as sustaining as bread.

"If you hear me call to you," he murmured. "Don't look back. There is nothing for you here. The cries will just be because I wanted your name to be the last thing on my lips."

And then the most incredible thing happened, something she didn't expect and wasn't ready for at all.

His arm scooped her waist and pulled her close, forcing her to arch upward and present herself to him. She was so surprised at the action that she didn't fight back. Not even when she saw his head and those glorious eyes flutter closed and knew...knew what was about to happen.

She watched him through wide, shock-gawking eyes, as his lips touched down on hers, fitting perfectly to hers. His tongue flickered in and teased out a moan from her that made her cheeks burn. She tasted his breath as he exhaled, felt the way his heart pounded against her palms. There was spice on his tongue. And heat. A hint of smoke.

She thought he let go a sigh and realized she was kissing him back. That the hands she had pressed automatically to his chest to hold him back had snaked up and over his neck. She strained into him shamelessly, sensing an urgency that took control whether her mind agreed to it or not.

Time stretched like a gooey bit of warm toffee. Gone was the night air, the sounds of traffic. She could have been back in her own room again, imagining his hair in her hands, the press of his weight on her. All that existed in that instant was the warmth of his embrace, the feeling of his arms locking her against him.

And then...then he pulled away like a man who had taken a long, slaking swallow of water. He brushed over the corner of her mouth with his lips as he eased away, a sigh of relief and release on his breath.

She was left to gape openly at him, trying to process the odd sense of bittersweet ache that had begun to build in her throat. Tried to sort through the confusion of her own response.

He cupped her jaw, a tight expression on his face. His lips pressed together in a sort of mournful half-smile.

Then he blinked, and the flare in his eyes changed. His gaze caught and held the light coming from where Castor stood. She watched, dumb-founded as a violet fire circled his irises. The bob of his throat suggested he wanted to say something more, but a ruckus behind her drew his gaze.

He was already stepping away from her.

"Go," he said. "I have work to do."

Then with a rough shove, he pushed her behind his back, stepping around her neatly to block her view of Castor and the bus shelter. Or maybe he was blocking her from Castor's view. She wasn't sure. She just knew she wasn't ready to let go. She wasn't ready for what she sensed was going to be the last moment she saw him.

But he was firm and the shove was enough to propel her backwards. She might have stumbled except for some force holding her steady.

Magic, she thought. Just like the hold she'd felt when she'd toppled from the ladder.

He'd been there then, she realized with a start. Watching her. Catching her. Not just a stalker from afar, unseen in the shadows, but right there in the play of light, just out of her vision. How long, she wondered. What had he seen. Heard. Known about her?

With legs quaking, she backed away as he gave her one last, lingering look over his shoulder. And then he pivoted sharply to face the bus shelter. He shook his hands out at his sides. Cracked his neck back and forth.

Preparing for war, she realized.

On the Run

KIT

COMPREHENSION DREW HER GAZE to the spot just beyond, where the battleground lay in shadows and smudges of buildings framing a small area. She'd not noticed how barren the bus stop area was. A vacant lot behind it, abandoned and dilapidated buildings on either side.

Castor was gone. The woman was gone. For a heartbeat, there was just her and Flint. She stared at his back, watching the way his shoulders rolled as he curled and uncurled his fists at his sides. With feet planted wide apart, and light gathering around his fingertips, his leather duster jacket flaring out, he reminded her of a Marvel character.

This was her chance to run. The last moment she might be able to escape. She parted her lips, thinking she should say something, but she didn't know what would be appropriate. Not when she knew she should be running for her life. Except she couldn't run. She was rooted to the spot by the image of him stretching his arms out to the side, the light flaring now and spiraling like two sparklers being held at arms' length in the inky darkness.

A sound caught her attention, a growl, she thought, rolling through the dark like a tumbler of thunder being poured over the sky. It was such a fierce, furious sound that it made her heart choke on the pump of blood it had gathered to fuel her escape.

And in that moment, when her heart ejected a blast of oxygen-rich blood back into her veins, she saw six men step through the shadows and into the light of the street lamp over the shelter. A cool wind moved over her hair. Her vision went gray and murky, as though a veil had been pulled over her face. Ozone prickled her nostrils. The aroma of cloves and forested spaces wrapped itself around her.

Magic.

Impossible, Improbable, but she was as certain of it as she was of her own breath. Cloaked, he'd told her. He would cloak her with his magic and keep her safe. Sure enough, she felt it like a heavy weight, a blanket of wool dampening the chill. She could almost smell him in it.

But he'd also told her to run. Because what was coming was enough to scare him, and whatever could scare a man like Flint had to be horrible indeed.

So she peeled her feet out of the grounding compulsion that had her stuck to the asphalt, and she aimed herself for the cars parked along the street. She ran quickly, as silently as she could, ducking behind one and another as she was able, mimicking the movements she'd seen in movies of soldiers strategically moving at pace.

Castor had been clear in saying he'd cloaked the battleground, but how far was the perimeter exactly? How far would she get before she wouldn't be able to see Flint anymore, hear his voice? How would she know if he'd survived?

An icy chill ran through her veins as she realized the answer. He wouldn't survive. He didn't plan to. He was going to fight until there wasn't anything left in him so she could get away. To save her.

Dread clutched her heart with sharp talons. She might already be too far.

Plastering herself against the side of the nearest car, she went as still as she could. Her heart was a din of hammering in her ears. Her breathing was coming in tatters and wheezes. The fight or flight squeezing out anything but the most necessary of oxygen, trying to keep her body light. She had to pee. The sudden spasm of her bladder all but overwhelming her.

But she had to look. Had to see if he was still there, if she was out of range.

She stole a look backward, scanning the darkness and the smudges of even darker forms assembling themselves into something that looked very much like a gang fight.

Flint's voice cut through the darkness even as she scanned the area, which helped her to pick him out easily against the shadows. She was relieved to see him still standing. A rigid column in the middle of the small lot, but flanked by six other large forms that looked as imposing as he did.

"You're saying my father sent you to collect me?" Flint demanded. "Why?"

The timber of his voice reverberated through her chest. She felt that strange longing that comes with the passing of one familiar moment to the next, uncertain one. He was safe. He was still alive. And she wasn't out of range.

But hearing him, she made a quick decision to drop down right where she was. From one heartbeat to the next, she palmed her way around the vehicle, an SUV of some sort, large with big tires. The back end of it would hide her well enough if she didn't move too suddenly. The stink of oil and gasoline a pungent invasion to her nostrils.

From the back, she had good sight of Flint and the men he was squaring off against even then. His fists curling and uncurling at his sides. Even from here, she could sense the violence in him. The threat of danger in all of them.

But she was still too exposed for her tastes. She needed to get to the side of the car, out of sight entirely, and then if she needed to, she could keep low, duck walk to the car across the street, and then the alley way beyond. She just hoped the cloaking Castor had put on the area would keep her actions invisible, reasoning that as long as she could see them, they could see her.

Moving slowly, keeping low, she held her breath and scuffed as silently as she could to the back quarter panel and splayed her hands over its cool surface. The magic adjusted like it was part of her, re-shaping itself to accommodate the shift in posture. It tingled against her skin, moving with her but creating a cushion of air that made each movement feel like she was pressing against a barrier.

Everything looked grey and murky. The streetlights had a film that seemed more purple than white. The yowling of a cat some-where down the block got muffled and transformed into something less piercing.

Once she was safely on the far side of the SUV, she adjusted her stance, trying to ease the ache of crouching too long in one spot. As she did, her ballet flat nudged something heavy. It made a metallic clunking sound. Panicked that they'd hear her, she slammed her palm down over the object, deadening the noise, but terrified she'd done so too late.

It was a tool, she realized, as her fingers curled over it. Long and solid. Hard. Cold as iron. With enough heft to make it awkward to lift with one hand.

Peering down at her feet and the object beneath her hand, she realized someone had been trying to steal the tires and had gotten caught in the act. She noticed for the first time that the car was propped up on a block. The tire half off. The discarded tools left abandoned.

A tire iron, that's what it was. It was certainly heavy enough to be one.

Thanks to the gods or whatever righteous soul who had caught them and made them abandon their theft, leaving this perfect weapon right where she needed it.

Emboldened by the presence of protective magic, she leaned around the bumper so she could see the bus shelter and the sextet of men. All of them were haloed in a peculiar glow, as though they were backlit by some great light that she couldn't see coming from behind them. Even as she watched, the limning shut off, like a passage way had closed. She could swear she heard it vacuum seal.

They were nothing but shadows then, until one of them stepped into a pool of light cast by a street lamp.

He was just as gorgeous as Flint. She suspected they all were, and she suspected they were all dressed the same as this one. He wore what looked like more primitive clothing beneath what she imagined were battle leathers. A chest plate and forearm bracers of leather that seemed as fluid as skin caught the light and revealed intricate etchings of symbols and runes.

His hair was loose and flowing, catching a gust of air and billowing out behind him like a Victorian lady's skirts. She couldn't tell what color it was, but it gleamed like burnished gold as the street lights teased it.

"Ava Ashe has angered him," he said. "He wants retribution."

"Ava Ashe has angered more than her share of creatures," Flint said. "What does that have to do with my father bidding my return, Sigard?"

Kit's head snapped up at mention of her sister's name. This wasn't about her at all. It was about Ava.

And Flint knew this. Knew these men.

She bottomed out onto the pavement at the words. A sickening sense of betrayal clawed its way into her belly.

Her instincts had been right. Flint was involved and Ava must have known he was coming, was going to watch her, keep her in his sights until what, though? She still didn't know what was going on or why these people wanted Ava or her.

A snap of ozone moved through the air. It met her nostrils with stinging clarity, drawing her attention away from her own thoughts. The other man, this Sigard, had used magic, she guessed. He was holding a weapon of some that hadn't been there a moment earlier. At least, she thought it was a weapon by the way he brandished it.

Sigard jerked his chin at Flint. "He wants the Ashe woman." The baton in his hand grew two feet. Silver runes sparked up in silver tracings along the handle, but she was more rapt by his words than the sudden enhancing of a weapon.

The Ashe woman. Sigard was talking about her. This was what Castor and Flint were trying to prevent. Her abduction by strangers.

Well, if he or anyone else came for her, she would fight. She wasn't about to just walk off hand in hand to some unknown demise.

Shifting her position, she pulled the tire iron across her knees. It was heavy. It was solid. She'd use it.

Because she was not going to run. Not when Ava was in trouble. Not with Flint out there, taking whatever threat was meant for her.

Bracing her back against the bumper, she inhaled in and out slowly, measuring her breath, gathering her courage and her calm.

Knees up, balancing the tire iron in the curve between her thighs and hip, she dug for her phone.

She could call the police. She could call 911. Report a woman's body being found. Even if the police couldn't see the fight, it might still draw unwanted attention, and maybe it would gain Flint time.

But her phone wasn't in her pocket. Neither was it in her purse. No matter how much material her fingers roamed over, feeling for the telltale shape of her phone, all she came away with was the square edge of a book and a lipstick case.

And she knew without checking inside that the last time she'd seen it, the phone was in her hand. She'd been about to call for help for that woman Castor had murdered.

The woman. Her eyes squeezed closed at the the thought of her. If she had ever been a person at all, she was nothing but a mass of skin and bones now. And that phone of hers was likely sitting on the ground somewhere beside her unmoving body.

Her head dropped back against the vehicle's taillights, frustrated, as she imagined how close and how very far away it was right then. Her breath was pluming now, visible to her as the temperature dropped further. If she leaned out to check for her phone, would those plumes just look like exhaust?

But she wasn't sure, and she needed to know if her phone was anywhere nearby. Because if it was, it was evidence of her presence. And she had the feeling that might be all it took to light the fuse of the banked tension in the air.

Maybe she'd dropped it somewhere between the bus shelter and here. It might even be just around the taillight of the SUV.

She'd never know unless she looked. So, swallowing down her nerves, she turned over so her belly pressed against the cold car.

The chill of the metal bore into her stomach, making her shiver beneath her sweater. Her hands shook as she splayed them out over the rear quarter panels. Bracing herself against the car, she tried her best to peer around the tire without being seen.

There. Right there at Flint's feet. A small rectangular chunk of plastic. She didn't need to see it in the light to know the color was turquoise. That the little "I practice shelf care" sticker was coming unglued from the back

She was praying the thing wouldn't ring or beep with some stupid notification when Flint kicked it aside. It skittered unseen by the others into a pile of discarded newspaper littering the base of an rusted dumpster. She almost blew out a breath of relief but cut it off abruptly as a rat scurried out from beneath and tore off into the shadows.

No one noticed either of those things and so she eased the air out of her lungs as scanned the area for Flint. She caught sight of him still barring the way, blocking her from view. With both hands curled into fists at his sides, he looked to be holding his anger in check and struggling to do so, but at least the posture suggested the threat hadn't ramped up to violence.

Yet.

The light gathering around them had increased, all colors of it snapped and sparked, throwing off enough light that she could see he'd discarded his leather jacket. It lay in a puddle nearby.

He looked terrifying, even from behind, with no facial expression to signal his rage. His shoulders were square, the muscles in his neck strained in cords against his skin. His voice, when he spoke, was low and threatening, and yet it cut through the air as though it was amplified by electricity.

"Who are you to demand my obedience, Sigard?" he asked. "Last I checked, my father had you relegated to the Guild, tending to the training of the young ones." He snorted this last as though it was the worst of insults.

"I have no quarrel with you, Flint," Sigard said, his hands coming up, placating. "Your father tasked us with bringing you home. He was of the mind you'd be pleased to hear your commission has ended. And yet I find you reluctant." He tossed a glance at Flint's fists. "And armed."

"I'm always pleased to return home," Flint said, his voice thick with suspicion. "But I've never yet required an escort. What has changed?"

Sigard advanced and the others behind, immediately formed a sort of phalanx. Flint raised one fist, a tight ball of energy by now, glittering like molten silver on his hand.

"Careful, Sigard," he said. "A warrior might think he's being threatened."

Sigard halted, straightened his hand back behind him, signaling to the others to remain still. "We are not here to threaten you. Merely to fetch you."

"I haven't been fetched since my mother unbound me from her umbilical cord and plopped me in the cradle. And my commission was very specific. It had only one ending."

He lowered his head, and though Kit couldn't see his face, she knew exactly how terrifying it looked by the involuntary step back Sigard made as Flint spit out the next words.

"You will have to fight me, Sigard. There is no other way out for you or way home for me."

"You would go against your father's wishes?" Sigard said, disbelief edging his tone. "You? Your father's most staunchest warrior? What happened to you here?"

"My father wants the leverage dead," Flint said. "And I can't let that happen."

One of the men stepped forward. "You have it wrong, Flint." Sigard tilted his head, confused. "He wants the leverage brought to him."

A long pause. The energy curling around Flint's fists paled. He raked a hand over his hair and the locks glittered in places as though some light was running through him.

"I don't understand."

Sigard propped the butt end of his staff on the ground. "The woman he sent you to surveille," he said. "Your father wants her delivered to Fae. Her sister has been sentenced to watch her die."

The Ruse

KIT

THE SHARP HISS OF her own breath at hearing the words was enough to force Kit to stuff her fist into her mouth. Die. Sister. Good God, they were talking about Ava. Ava was alive. Ava was in trouble. And Kit was going to have to watch her sister be killed.

That was what Flint was doing here. He'd been watching her, waiting for the moment when he was ordered to collect her and bring her—

Where exactly? She supposed it didn't matter. The main thing was that Flint had been sent to betray her from the very first moment. She might have wondered if his 'protection' was all a ruse, except his reaction to the statement was cold and terrifying, even though he never made a single move. It was in his voice, a promise of violence so sharp it cut through the air.

"I'm not going to let that happen, Sigard." The light in his hands grew brighter then, renewed. It sizzled and snapped and sparks flew off from it like a holiday sparkler. Even the smell was the same.

The man named Sigard shuffled his feet, the only indication that he was just as affected by that ruthless tone as Kit was.

"You don't have a choice," he said as the other men clustered closer to him. "The same as we don't."

Flint's head cocked to the side. "You have a choice. The one I'm giving you now. Return to Fae. Or die here."

Sigard hefted the staff from the pavement and drew it across his chest. "You know we can't do that," he said. "You know the consequences of our betrayal of the Blood Vow. Your father won't just kill us. He'll torture our entire families. He'll string us up for generations and peel our skin from our bones. He'll come for you too. You know this."

Flint's shrug was cold. "I've made my choice," he said. "Must I make yours, too?"

"You would break your vow for a mortal woman?" he jerked his chin toward the parked car, and Kit's heart sank. They knew she was there. They'd probably known all along.

A soft, dark laugh rumbled free of Flint's throat. "You have no idea what I will do for this mortal woman." He advanced a step toward Sigard. "I would tear my heart from my chest and sear it over an open flame for her should she be hungry. I would sever a vein should she thirst. I would swallow my own soul, carry it to the Stygian Darkness and offer it to Aiofe herself if meant she did not have to see the other side."

His head lowered and Kit had the feeling that whatever the men saw in his face, it was terrible to behold. They retreated quickly, huddled closer together. But it didn't stop Flint's advance. He stalked toward them with a lithe but deadly grace. "And I would take your souls with me," he said. "Because I'd want you to watch my agony and know that you had this choice in this moment and chose to oppose me."

He halted. Lifted his hands in front of his chest, outstretched. "Compared to that moment," he went on, "a broken vow is nothing."

Kit wasn't expecting the sudden eruption of violence that came next, but it was made abundantly clear that she had been right to be terrified of Flint.

And it wasn't because he fought back so powerfully, the way she might have expected. No. It was in the way he faced off as each man came at him, a quiet, confident, lethal calm descending over his entire body.

They took him one at a time at first, testing him. Throwing punches. Bringing down and hacking sideways with weapons that looked ancient and lethal. Nothing landed, and it was clear, even to Kit, that the men did not want to hurt him. They wanted him to concede.

But conceding meant giving her up, and it was also painfully clear that he wasn't going to do that.

A choreograph of movement was Flint's response. That was all they got from him. Like he was an adult playing soldiers with children carrying rubber swords.

There was no rush, no sense that he felt harried or hurried. If a blow landed, he made no sound. Neither did he retaliate. He merely danced, ducking under the first's swing, twisting his body as smoothly as a bend in the river, coming up again to spin out of reach.

At first.

Then there came a moment when the testing was done. It was a shift in the energy, a change in the way the men looked at Flint, who was circling them now. She thought his gaze landed on her for a second and something in her heart cracked.

He was going to die. Right here. Right in front of her.

And he was going to do it for her.

She clenched the tire iron, knuckles hurting at the pressure with which she gripped it. She was safe. He'd given her a head start. He was taking all those blows so she could escape.

But before she realized what she was doing, she had risen to her feet. Her little ballet slippers creaked with the movement. Her short skirt clung to her backside. A breeze moved over her hair. For an instant, she felt as if she'd stepped inside the pages of a book.

Fae. Magic. Portals.

Impossible as it was, Castor had indeed pulled down a cloak over the area, sealing them off from human eyes. Flint's magic was the reason she felt as if she was cocooned inside a greyish film, why she smelled ozone and caught glints of lightning like bursts snapping free of Flint's fingers.

It even explained the way the men, including Flint, moved. They were warriors from some historical fantasy movie come to life and yet each thrust, parry, and duck, was done in deadly earnest.

Sigard fell back, sweeping his arms out to direct the others to do the same. The phalanx broke apart, each warrior taking a defensive stance as the battle broke, giving them each a moment's respite. Sigard was bloody, she thought. So were the others. She couldn't see if Flint was injured, but he seemed to be favoring his left arm. The shoulder on that side hung just a little lower than the right.

"Just come with us, Flint," Sigard urged. "You can have her as you like, more than us if you want, for all the time it takes to bring her back to the Shadow Court. We don't have to try to kill each other. The Stygian Darkness does not need another fae life."

Flint halted his predatory circle around the men. "I can do with her what I like?" he asked in a very low, very dark tone.

Sigard nodded, and even from where Kit was hidden, she could see the relief that bowed his shoulders. This was coming to an end, was the thought painted over his expression. He could stand down. And he needed to stand down. She could see how winded he was even though each movement had appeared so effortless.

"Your father just wants her alive," he said, holding the staff across his chest. She noted the end was broken, that it had split into a sharp and jagged point. The runes didn't light up quite so well anymore. "You know him, Flint. Probably better than anyone. He doesn't care what shape she's in so long as she's breathing."

Flint's hands dropped to his sides. The light faltered, and encouraged, Sigard went on.

"I know you enjoy their flesh. I'm a blood drainer, myself. My magics work on it. There's plenty to go around. We have a semi-healer with us. He can fix her as many times as is needed. There's no need to break your vow to have her."

"Your healer," Flint asked, his voice laced with curiosity and her heart squeezed. "How good is he?"

"Very good. It's why your father sent him with us."

"And he's not angry?"

"Your father wants you home as much as you want to go."

"Do not let her out of your sight," Flint said, raising his voice, an odd tenor to the lilt of it. "If she runs. Chase her. If she sleeps, Watch her. If she dies..."

He paused there, and Kit's breath caught. She held it, not daring to a single hiss free that might obliterate the sound of his words. If she dies...

What then?

But Flint never finished. He shook his head as he regarded the man facing him. The light in his hands flared again. "Those were my orders, Sigard. That is the vow my blood is obeying. If it wars with my Blood Vow, then so be it."

The men were gathering together, sensing the same shift Kit was.

"But you're free. The surveillance is over."

"It will not be over until she is dead," he said. "And even then I will set fire to the clay feet of any god who takes her from me. And I'll make of their hollow shells a pot to hold my piss until the Stygian Darkness claims me."

Flint dropped his head back momentarily. She saw his chest expand, his arms outstretch. Whatever he was gathering had the men scurrying to raise their weapons. But as fast as they were, Flint was faster.

He moved like a tornado. The others surged forward as one, their movements unnaturally fast, like flickering flames. A flurry of strikes followed, each one faster and deadlier than the last. Flint's body was a blur of precise, lethal motion. His fists connected with sharp snaps of bone, his blade cutting arcs of silver through the night. He seemed untouchable, unstoppable—a predator unleashed.

And Kit couldn't stay in the shadows anymore.

She stared, wide-eyed, as Flint sent a razor sharp line of light into the throat of the one he'd called Sigard. The man froze in his tracks, the staff dropping from his grip. When it fell to the pavement, star bursts of energy crackled upward into the air. A rumble like thunder stampeded over the floor of the heavens.

But before Sigard's head even fell from his body, landing on the pavement with an obscenely wet thunk, his body crumpling in a pile, Flint had aimed himself at another.

Sigard's death shot the rest of them into action. They charged enmasse at Flint, who, though outnumbered, held his own against their blows. He took several, most of them connecting with a snap of magic, some of them from a violent skin to skin contact.

But he stood and he prevailed and she was sure he would win. She even took a step forward, excited, drawn by the violence and the energy of victory.

But then one of them lunged, swinging a blade wreathed in a faint blue glow. Flint parried, his muscles straining as sparks flew from the clash of steel. He pivoted to disarm him, but another fist slammed into his ribs.

Flint grunted, staggering.

She must have cried out. Her lips were parted. Her chest hurt. Too late, she realized she must have cried out because one of them flicked his gaze to where she stood. She blinked. Everything was so clear. Too clear. It hurt to see the entire scene so perfectly, she was certain the cloaking had failed. Flint's magic was gone.

Flint followed the man's gaze, and she saw horror weave itself onto his expression.

That was the opening they needed, and they took it.

Even as one of them peeled himself away from the throng and ran fast, so fucking fast, toward her, she saw Flint lurch in her direction. His movement was jerky and awkward, so different than his usual lithe gracefulness that she doubted the evidence of her own eyes. She stood too long, unmoving, and that hesitation showed her a blow coming from behind. One of the unnamed men took him at the back of the knees.

Flint staggered, fought to remain upright, but another struck his back, driving him to the pavement.

He rolled. His belly exposed. His arms were in the air as though he was about to make a fancy flip back onto his feet.

But he was too late. Fast as he was, they were just as fast. And the next time a weapon came down, it was straight through his belly.

A scream tore through the magic in the air, piercing her ears in a note too shrill, too loud to be coming from anyone else's throat but hers.

The tire iron fell from her grip. It clattered to the sidewalk, whacking her on the foot as it landed. She would leave it there. She would run to him. There had to be something she could do. Maybe offer herself. Maybe beg for his life.

But someone stepped in front of her, and his form blocked the battleground from her view. She couldn't see Flint anymore. Just this magnificent but terrifying looking man who was cocking his head at her.

"You must be the leverage," he said.

And then everything went black as something heavy and fragrant pulled itself down over her head. She thought she smelled manganese and ozone.

And in the next second, all she smelled was fear and darkness.

Flint out there in the Darkness

FLINT

THE TASTE ON HIS tongue was blood. That was the first thing Flint thought when he came to life. But it wasn't her blood, at least. It was his own. He knew the taste of it well after all these centuries. The days of his trials when he'd had to consume his own flesh to stay alive, when his magics were too depleted to slip into the Earthen realm and steal a mortal child or two to slake his hunger and feed his magic.

But that he was lying face-down suggested he'd lost a battle of some sort. He just couldn't remember fighting or falling.

A groan built in the back of his throat as he tried to push himself upright. He bit down against it, deadening it before it could slide free. If he'd somehow managed to avoid revealing himself a fit of sleep-deprived, starving madness, then he didn't want to alert her to his presence.

He just hoped he was still cloaked.

Because he was in her chambers, that much he knew. He could smell her. Smell the bed she slept in. The light air of her natural perfume lingered in his nostrils. The ache in his belly that had taken residence there days earlier and not given him a moment's respite still swelled into a bloated, balloon sized need.

He managed to push himself up enough to put an arch in his back. A cobra pose, so the human yogis called it. The same name, strangely enough, that his tutor had taught him before sending him out into the forests of The Shadow Trail, forcing him to kill, feast, kill, to live for forty days and forty nights alone.

A swamp of images came at him, stealing the power in his biceps.

He fell again face first with a huff, silent, and choked it down so he wouldn't frighten her. It was bound to happen, this collapse. He'd been on his feet for days and nights already, watching her. It was damned lucky beyond a god's fortune that she hadn't stabbed his very visible back while he slept comatose on her floor for...how many hours; he wondered.

It certainly felt like a lot of hours. Days, even. This sort of clumsiness was for newborn colts testing their legs for the first time. Not for a centuries old high fae.

Rolling over took all his energy, and it was not graceful. Completed only by a bucket full of energy, heaving himself with his core, flinging his legs and arms over. Holding his breath against the effort. Grunting like a fat pig foraging through a trough of rotten vegetables.

Movement was agony, but he had to move. He had to get up. He had to make sure she was alright. Each muscle screamed in protest, his ribs grinding as he pushed upward, every inch forward a battle against his failing body.

His gaze raked the ceiling, searching for the light fixture that should have been there and finding a canopy of light bleeding into a starless sky. A breeze moved over him, taking the skyline with it and leaving behind a cavern ceiling filled with stalactites.

That was when a dirge of howling began. And that was when he realized he was not in her bedroom at all.

He was not in her world. He was not in his.

"Took you long enough," said a female's voice.

He dropped his head sideways and caught sight of a pair of black leather boots. His gaze trailed upward, tracing the leather, the laces to mid thigh of a gorgeous female. Fire red hair spilled around her shoulders, framing a face that was as chiseled as his own. Bright flame red eyes with snakes of silver coiling around her irises.

Not fae, his mind whispered. Not human, either.

"Where is she?" he croaked out, alarmed that his voice was not clear and full, but more alarmed at Kit's absence. *Die if she does. Chase her if she runs.*

He shook his head free of the hammering of those words on his mind. Those words would not help now.

The creature squatted beside him, her head canted sideways. Perplexed. "Wouldn't you rather know where you are?"

Swallowing was like trying to tame fire with a thimble of gasoline. "Kit," he said. "What have you done with her?"

He tried to get up, but she pressed him down with a single palm. Strong. She was incredibly strong. No fae could do that to him.

"Don't you recognize me, Flint?"

All energy left him, and he fell back onto the floor. Floor? It felt more like the gritty bottom of a cave. From somewhere to the left, he thought he heard a hush of whispers.

"I'm disappointed," she said. "It has been a few hundred years, but I still thought you would remember." She sighed and pushed herself to her feet. Her booted foot fell on his chest, pinning him there. He felt like a bug on a board.

"Look around you," she said.

A low growl was building in his chest, and yet it wouldn't move through. It got stuck somewhere between his throat and tongue. It felt like a lump of meat too large to swallow.

"Let me the fuck up," he said.

A thrash, undignified, and yet a low-throated panic was building along with the growl, trying to change it to a scream. "Where is she?"

"Look around you, Flint," she said again.

This time the command was evident in her voice. She was used to being obeyed, he thought. Like his father, this female was used to having minions and thralls scamper to her bidding.

And that was the moment he understood. Thought of his father and the connection of relation freed something within him.

"Aiofe," he said, lifting his gaze to hers. "You're Blade's mother. The hellhound."

She shook her head. "Hellhound no longer, Flint." Her arms reached out sideways as if to encompass the area and draw his attention to the expanse of it. Because it was an expanse, he realized. It was large and dark and filled with shadowed energy.

"You know now where you are?" she asked, and this time there was pity in her voice.

A claw went around his heart. "The Darkness," he said. "The Stygian Darkness, where all fae go when they die."

Swallowing was impossible then. His eyes closed all on their own. The reason he was here. It was clear now.

"She's dead," he choked out in a flat tone. "That's why I'm here." *Die if she does.*

She'd died, and he'd taken his own life because of the vow. The damned vow. He'd given it freely all those centuries ago, and he'd accepted the weight of that order as his father gave it but he couldn't know then the price it would really demand.

And yet, he found it difficult to grieve the loss of his own life. He'd been alive too long already, it seemed, because it was her end that hurt the most.

"I'm dead." His eyelids tightened at the thought of Kit being gone. Now he'd live an eternity here, remembering it. "I'm dead and I'll feel it for a generation as penance."

Aiofe's low chuckle drew his eyelids open. "You've been told too many stories about me," she said. "Fae here, in this place are not dead. Merely...drained. The essence of them, their magic, wasted so much that they are mine to command."

She narrowed her gaze. "And I have no wish to swallow you, light bender. Nor do I need another thrall to scavenge for my attention." The boot on his chest pressed in harder. "I have too many already. So it might be useful for you to remember how you got here."

At that, her boots grew long spike heels that dug in to the muscles of his chest, so far he was sure the tips scored his ribs. She twisted without mercy.

And it came. The whole awful battle with his father's men, soldiers in the Shadow Court the same as he was. Sworn to the same blood oath to serve at all costs, at any price.

But though they were his peers, they were not his equal. He'd fought, yes, but his father had sent a gang of his best. There were too many of them. And she...she had been there when she shouldn't have been.

The sight of her face as she stepped out of hiding, a thick length of cold iron in her grip her only defense against creatures of powerful magic. She had no chance against them and yet she came for him just the same.

Her fear, the terror he felt coming off her in waves, was not enough to prevent her from offering herself as insurance against a threat she didn't understand. His brave, fragile dove.

And he'd let her down.

He knew those men. They were some of his father's best. Old soldiers. Trained as he was from the blush of youth to survive the harshest parts of Fae. Alone in the darkest thickets of forest, no food, no water, drained of magic and forced to waste unless they could restore it on their own.

And he knew their proclivities. He'd caroused with them in the taverns of the Iron Realm. He'd taken his magic from the light of human life the same as they had. Countless times.

These were the fae who held her. Males with no value save their own lives and the blood vow they'd given his father. They would use her and abuse her until she was a husk, of that he was sure. The master of the Shadow Court would only need her breathing to exact his vengeance on the hunter Ava Ashe.

A groan built in the back of his throat, but he refused to shed it. He couldn't let Aiofe see his worry for the mortal. Holding it in, imagining the things those fae would do to her...It made his stomach ache.

It made him murderous.

"Are you remembering?" Aiofe demanded as her boot scored another inch into his wound. "Do you have a good picture of the moment you came to me?"

He hissed through his teeth, an involuntary sound pulled from him under protest as the memory of Kit's face came to him. The way she looked as he'd fallen, distracted by her presence, leaving himself open to the cadre's blows.

A thousand years and he'd never been distracted during battle. A hundred mortal lifetimes and he'd not once met a human worth dying for.

He recalled that face, the trembling of her entire body as she held out that weapon, as she stepped on quaking legs toward him.

And something hard as flint cracked open somewhere deep inside his core. That this creature would keep him here when he had an oath to keep. The bowels of the darkness and the she-beast who kept it could not hold him here. He'd singe his soul in the heart of its fire if he had to, walk in darkness all his days, if that's what it took.

"She's alive," he said. "She's alive and they have her." The words built to a roar that rolled around inside him like thunder. "Don't you understand? She's alive and they have her and I'm HERE."

He launched himself like he was an arrow. Boots be damned. Wound be damned. Pain and weakness and God of the Darkness be damned to the hell master she served, he would leave this place.

In one swift, explosive movement, he was on his feet. Power surged through his veins, molten and wild, igniting the shadows around him as he surged upward. The ground cracked beneath him, a testament to his fury.

And then...then Aiofe's throat was in his hands, a soft bobbing thing of flesh and veins and blood. Velvet crushing beneath his palms.

He shoved her back, oh gods, he shoved her hard as he could into an expanse of bars where rabid, feral looking fae of all sorts scrambled to touch her, to drag her into the cells with them. He gave her all his power, everything that remained inside him, pulling from the pits of his marrow.

He slammed her against the bars, once, twice, three times, with all the violence in him. She didn't so much as flinch as her head struck the blacksteel bars.

Each time a hand, claw, or wing slid out to touch down on her face, they caught fire. Each creature hissed backwards, cradling their injured limb. More came, leeching from the shadows to find her flesh and touch it. Each of them drew back in pain.

Scores of lights winked in and out beyond the bars, but Aiofe just looked at him with those stoic eyes, the serpents of silver worming around the blood red of her irises.

He was giving her all he had, but it was nothing so powerful as the force of a silken scarf warming her neck.

She waited until he was spent before she took a breath. It swelled his palms, and he realized she could have broken free at any moment.

"Don't feel bad, warrior," she said. "Most fae don't get one chance to hurt me let alone...ten?"

His fingers tightened. They bleached out to white with the force of his rage.

"What do you want of me?" he hissed. "Why am I here if I'm not dead?"

Her fingers plucked at his, drawing them away from her throat as if they were wet noodles slung across her skin. Strong as he was, he couldn't resist her. Whatever he'd done to overpower her initially, it wasn't surprise or strength. He had the feeling she'd let him do so.

"You are dying," she said with an arch of her eyebrow. "That's why you're here."

She waved at the creatures behind the bars. "Like a thousand others who refuse to believe they are gone and waste here in madness expecting their magic to come at their command. When they have to wait for it. Those who have used it up as if it isn't as precious as breath."

"Then if I'm not dead, release me to my death. Let my body decide my fate."

"I can do many things, Flint from Terran, but that I can not do."

She looked aggrieved.

"She's dying up there," he said, waving at the cavernous ceiling. "They're likely killing her. They won't want to. They need her. But she's fragile. She won't be able to withstand the...the attentions they pay her."

She waved the comment away and pushed him gently to the side. "They are all fragile," she said, strolling toward the shadows that played over the chamber. He had the feeling she was about to meld into it and leave him there without answering, without a way out. "What is one more mortal life to me?"

"Stop," he said, the command in his voice reminiscent of his father's.

A look over her shoulder, disbelief on her face. And yet, she did halt.

"You would command me? For the sake of a mortal woman?" Her red eyebrow arched delicately. "Your father believed the same." Her eyes narrowed. "He always felt he was better than the she-hound of the Darkness. His high fae sense of superiority. And yet don't all fae come to me when it's over? Tell me, Lightbender, where do you think Terran will go when his end comes?"

He squared his shoulders. "My father's death means nothing to me," he said. "Only hers. Tell me how I may leave and save her."

She gave an undignified snort of laughter. "You wait, that's how. Your magic is wasted. You need to let it recharge."

His eyes narrowed. She was testing him, he was sure of it. "That's not the reason. My magic was not drained. I was killed."

Her head canted to the side. "Then I suppose you really are an anomaly here. Perhaps what you are seeing isn't real, Lightbender. Perhaps you're still lying on that sidewalk, bleeding out while the fragile mortal woman is being devoured bit by bit, thrust into inch by inch, within a lungful of her last breath by those comrades your father sent to retrieve you."

She tapped her boot three times, sharp raps that sounded too loud in his ears. "And if that's the case, then all you have to do is wake up."

Three more taps against the flagstones. Each one driving him to his knees, to his belly. His legs splayed and stretched out beneath the magic. The stink of sulfur rose to his nostrils. Hell's magic curling around him with each strike of her booted heel against the stones.

Thwack once. He felt his cheek against damp sidewalk.

Thwack twice. He smelled the fumes of traffic.

Thwack a third time and he felt his stomach burning as it slid out into the dirty street, his intestines collecting grit and filth.

The joy of the pain pulled a laugh from him. This was something real. This was life. With all its sensory inputs, all the agonies of it. The tarmac beneath his body was real and damp and stinking of tar and old rubber.

The flesh beneath his shirt began to knit. The viscera retracting into place with a faint slurping noise as if the magic in his veins was sucking them in with a straw.

He clung to the sensations, using the signals to force himself back into his body. He started to get up. His feet beneath him, the hope—such dangerous hope—fueling his muscles.

He could already feel a thread of light winding its way into his fingertips, coursing up his arm into his solar plexus. Her light, he realized. Dim and dimming, but she was alive.

And he knew where she was.

He just had to follow the thread like Theseus skeining up Ariadne's string.

He was already pushing himself to his feet, his mind centering on that light, working out the best way to travel the fastest to the fae sorceress's lair.

Liliah's. Of course, his comrades would take her there. It was the best place in the city to forge a portal. There would be fae magic there, residual energies of the sidhe sorceress left behind after the huntress Ava Ashe had taken her down. That magic, though he razed the place to the ground himself, would amplify the magics his comrades owned.

Because they would need all the help they could get. Forging a new portal took time. It took patient blending of blood and pain and death but it could be done.

That meant he might still be able to get to her before it was too late.

Just as the hope flared in his chest, he felt fingers tangle into his hair. His head was yanked back, sharp and hard, so that he was looking up into Aiofe's face. The smudge-colored shadows of the Darkness dropped back down around him. The street disappeared. All that remained was the dripping of condensation from the stalactites and the moaning of the creatures behind the bars.

And those crimson colored eyes gazing into his.

He'd heard stories about Aifoe the Hellhound of the Stygian Darkness. In his youth, he'd dared ask his father about the woman who kept suites in the manse, an entire section they were not allowed to visit.

Even for the likes of the Shadow Court, those stories were terrible, violent narratives.

And those stories came to life now in the visage that met his gaze. She was partially transformed, part shadow, part hellhound, and some part of her wearing the beauty of a fae face. Lies, all. She was not a creature of beauty. She was not fae.

"You've obviously misunderstood me, Flint," she said, her voice guttural and razor sharp. "I said perhaps you're on that street."

Teeth flashed at him long as a tiger's, thick as a python's engorged belly.

"Let me go to her," he ground out. "She won't survive without me."

There was a long pause. He felt her shadows collecting over his vision. She wasn't going to release him, he knew. His gaze drew a line to the bars and the creatures behind them, silent now, watching.

The air itself held its breath.

"I want something in return," she said.

The shadows began to recede. They merged strangely with scenes of the street. The streetlights flared atop a grossly misformed stalactite. The bus shelter housed two large ogres who stared at him through wart-covered eyes.

Hope flared again, a nasty emotion that rode his heart with iron spurs. But he refused to let it creep into his voice when he spoke. Instead, he schooled his tone like his mentors had schooled him all those centuries ago to sound unaffected. No emotion. Gods, no emotion could show or she might never agree. So when it came out even, when he'd mastered the twitch of nerves that fluttered over his cheeks, he said what she wanted to hear.

"Name it."

Her grin above his face softened, the play of shadow melting the terrible jaws into a soft line of feminine flesh. Pink. Full. Sensual. A mouth so pretty it might spout ancient fae curses and still sound like poetry.

"I was waiting for you to say that."

She leaned in, her perfume of sulfur and cinnamon, a musk so overpowering he railed back, forcing her to grip him by the back of the head. Her lips against his ear, she whispered against his skin. "But first, let me give you some truths to help you along the way."

Truths. He didn't think he'd hear such words spoken as truth in all his hard lifetime, but as she leaked the words into his ear, his eyes grew wider. His heart cinched up tight as if being ready to be ridden hard through a dense forest.

And the words were shocking indeed.

Wide Awake and Screaming

KIT

Kit woke screaming.

She'd been screaming in her nightmare, she thought. Shouting voicelessly through the darkness, with the sensation of razor sharp points jabbing into her skin. Hateful, mocking laughter crawled through her ears as she flailed and fought whatever was causing the pain.

In the dream, strobes of old-fashioned disco lights revealed creatures with strips of flesh dangling from mouths that looked an awful lot like predators' beaks. Hawks. Owls. Raptors of some sort, they all sucked the flaps of flesh into their mouths like noodles, slurping and smacking. Blood dribbled down their chins.

A long, wracking shudder snaked through her body at the memory of the dream. So real. It had been so real.

Except now that she was awake, all those horrors should evaporate like early morning fog dying beneath beams of sunlight. But they didn't. She still felt the raw scraped sensation of a skinned knee all over her body. The musty smell of damp cement leaked up her nose, visceral and pungent. And it was dark. So dark.

And in that impenetrable darkness, one thought rose to the surface, a leviathan breaching an ocean's worth of dread.

Something was wrong.

Panic bloomed like a mushroom in her chest, sending spores into the darkest depths of her marrow. Wherever was out there in the darkness, she had to get up. She had to get up *now*. Digging her fingernails into the floor beneath her, she tried to heave herself upward, a desperate attempt to sit upright, another futile attempt to twist herself sideways, arch herself backward...but she couldn't move. And it was only then that she realized something was pinning her to the damp concrete

Waves of air blew into her face, making her eyes water. A stinking smell of old cheese and decay...the battery post smell of blood. And oh God, she knew then that the weight above her was a sentient, living thing. That below that awful weight, pinned between it and the earth, she was naked. Bleeding.

And just as she registered that truth, a sharp pain struck down into her breast, an unbearable ache that radiated outward in shards of hot agony all the way to her collarbone. A scream tore through her throat, all the more painful because it turned into nothing but a rolling, gasp-infused din.

She tried to shrink inside herself, her shoulders bowing inward, curling her body over the unending hurt that rocked through it. Tried to tighten into a ball so small no pain could reach it, but there was no resistance against that strong suction pulling her breast tissue painfully taut. Instead of bowing to the pain, she arched upward, off the damp stone, surrendering to the upward draw in a futile attempt to lessen the stretch.

And then...screaming. It was all she could do except for the totally useless attempts to twist and turn out of reach of that weight, trying to buck it off, wrest herself out from under it. When that amounted to nothing but a painful blow to her cheek, she went still. Wept silently into her shoulder.

A wet, viscous trickle of warmth pooled in her cleavage. She smelled metal and the revolting stink of her own sweat. But at least it was over. The weight eased from her chest. The hot razors of pain subsided to dull aches that radiated down her torso. But at least....at least she was alive.

"My turn," someone groused in a needling, tinny voice. "Move. It's my turn."

The horror she felt at those words should have spurred her into another screaming fit, but she was too stunned at the realization there wasn't just one bastard biting down into her flesh, but two. There was no time to protest, to scream, or even to wrestle her body sideways out of range before a rasping tongue lapped between her breasts. And that was the thing that sent her into another, violent, thrashing bid for freedom.

"Stop," she yelled, her panic on overdrive. "Stop, please."

Miraculously, everything halted. The noise. The hateful, sharp pain of blunted ivory piercing her skin. Even the weight atop her shifted, easing to the side so she could catch a breath.

"Don't worry, sweetling We aren't going to kill you," said a voice, and a sudden flare of light blinded her. She would have shielded her eyes if someone wasn't holding her arms down. "We need you alive."

Smothered laughter. Some discussion in tones too low for her to make out. Or maybe it was in an unfamiliar language. She couldn't tell with all the roaring of blood in her ears.

But at least her eyes were beginning to adjust to the new light, and though pools of darkness still held the room together, she could make out that she was in a basement. Beyond her, a square shape outlined itself and she could see the tree line though it. A window. Woods beyond. The distant, winking glow of the city past that.

So she was in a basement somewhere, and there was a way out. That was something. At least knowing where she was gave her a sense of control that was so desperately out of reach that her stomach relaxed, just a little. Small comfort though it was, it was useful. If she was in a basement, someone might hear her. If she played her cards right, she could maybe climb through that opening to freedom.

That was all that was on her mind then. Get out. Get safe. Get away.

"What do you want?" she asked in a submissive voice, because she didn't think this was about sexual assault. This was something else entirely. Something that was evidenced in the raw way her skin felt. She'd fallen off her bike once as a kid. Skidded along the rough concrete of the skateboard park onto her hands and knees. The feeling of that flesh torn from her palms and her shins felt very much like this. Except it was everywhere. "Please. If it's about Ava, then I don't know what she's done. I haven't seen her for years."

A pinch of her skin as the one atop her lowered his mouth to her belly. Searing jolts of pain razored through her stomach, but she held on, gasping, tensing, every muscle doing its best to repel the teeth burying into her flesh. "Please," she gasped out. "Tell me what you want."

"I want you to lie still," he said. "Because if you don't I'm not sure I can fix you beyond repair after."

The words struck horror through her. "I don't understand."

"You don't have to," he said, lifting his face upward, peering into her eyes. He was so beautiful, she thought. His skin was luminescent in the gloom. Now that her eyes had adjusted enough to see him, she could tell his eyes had beautiful striations. They reminded her of a kaleidoscope. But the blood on his chin, and the strip of flesh that hung from his teeth, they made him look ugly. And knowing it was her blood, her skin, stole the light from his gaze. She thought she would pass out. She prayed she would.

The strobing started again, throwing everything into a dizzying array of movement, a slanting, skewed flash of images too fast to pin down yet each more horrifying than the last. Beneath that seizure-inducing dizzying array of pictures, her flesh suffered. Each image an echo in her bones and skin. It wasn't going to stop, she realized. It was going to keep happening until she lost enough blood to pass out.

That was when she began to pray for death instead of unconsciousness. That was when she begged them to at least drop her back into the terrific bliss of darkness.

"The lights," she said at one point. "They're making me sick."

"That's the magic, sweetling," someone said, the one with the beautiful skin. "And if we don't use it, we can't fix you."

And if they couldn't fix her, they couldn't keep doing this. She didn't need to hear the words to know the truth in them.

At one point, a face came at her from the webbing of shadow. She knew the face. She held onto the image as long as she could. It was one she'd seen a half dozen others out in the street. Someone she knew. Someone who made her feel safe. Someone who...

Oh Gods, she remembered.

These men killed Flint. She'd seen him fall. He'd known somehow that they'd come for her. This was what she needed protection from. This was what he'd tried to keep from happening.

But it was happening and as far as she could tell, it was not going to stop because Flint was dead and there was no one now who could help her.

Scavenges of Magic

FLINT

When Flint came to, there was nothing between his ears but a roaring howl so loud it deafened him to anything else. And somewhere in the back of his mind, Flint knew there should be something else. There should be reason and logic.

But sanity had fled. All that remained in its place was a driving need to find her. And in a small corner of that space, was a small but growing space where the need to kill lived. Faces came to him even before he pushed himself up from the sidewalk. Faces known to him half a hundred years or more. He named them in his mind, committing his body to their demise long before he met them again, so that he wouldn't balk, wouldn't pause out of some outdated sense of loyalty.

There was no loyalty anymore. There was only her. And he planned to send each one of her captors to the Stygian Darkness without a full body in pieces even Aiofe wouldn't be able to put back together.

Reisland the horned one, named so not because of a growth on his head, but because of a peculiar shape to his manhood that only certain females could accommodate.

Balzach the healer. Tristan, with his fair fae skin, the epitome of beauty, such that females had begged for his blood to bathe in, hoping they could attain the same glow. His skin as lustrous as an iridescent pearl disguised a rot beneath his skin so deep that it would rival a twelve-day-old peach at the bottom of a compost heap.

Wulven. Almand. Sigard the hungry.

All of those names, all of those faces, the catalog of their magics, Flint gathered to him like a shroud, and the sound of their names in his mind was the crutch that drove him to his knees.

The human realm was a sensory overload after the barrenness of the Stygian Darkness. The traffic hummed too loudly. Horns blared with an irritating frequency. Exhaust fumes and cigarette smoke stole over him, pulling an unexpected cough from his throat.

The young drug addict's body was gone. Presumably, the cadre took it with them. As a portal, the magic in her blood and from her death would be expended, but Sigard's people were descended from scavengers. Some of them could shift into ravens.

He'd never seen it of Sigard, but he had seen the male peel the skin from one of the Velvet Boar's indentures right in the main taproom before being tossed out onto the streets. And in the Kennel before the Shadow Bazaar's portals had gone haywire, Sigard had purchased a mortal woman for a night of pleasure.

She'd never come out of the room again.

What these males might be doing to Kit pulled Flint solidly onto his feet. He swung his head back and forth like a bear, sensing the direction, feeling the wind in his hair. Peering through the early dawn light to find that one dim thread of light that would lead him to her.

They wouldn't kill her. They couldn't. Their vows forbade it. But they would make good use of her and her pain until the portal gained the energy they needed to break through to Fae. He had no idea where the portal would open to, but creating them from scratch took a lot of dark magic, and dark magic was fueled by blood and pain.

He didn't doubt they would enjoy building the gateway. Another time, under different circumstances, he'd enjoy that journey as well. Another time, another circumstance, and he might have joined with them.

But these were not those circumstances. They were injured. One of them was dead, he couldn't remember which, but he knew it was truth by the way his magic itched beneath his skin, wanting more.

And in his head, banging around with wild abandon, was Aiofe's voice, a tickle in his ear, informing him in a rasping whisper that he'd marked her. That his natal magic had recognized her and imprinted on her wrist that night on the bus when he'd reached to hold her back.

So long ago now, it seemed. Too long ago. But the thread of light was there, glinting on the rosy dawn light. The chill in the air caught it much the same as it would a spider's silk, and it swayed, coming in and out of the shadows as though it was winking at him.

He stood and breathed fire into his lungs, exhaled fumes choking with sulfur. He was hell itself in that moment, the Stygian Darkness and its god all at once. And he would have his vengeance.

With a near rabid eye, he panned the streets. They had come alive around him while he'd been with Aiofe and her thralls. Whether any human noticed him lying flat on his face at the bus stop and tried to help him, he couldn't know. He couldn't know even if his body had been there or if the street had remained clear of foot traffic, if humanity's vehicles driving past were too busy to care that someone was dead on the sidewalk.

A chunk of wood lay in the abandoned lot just a few feet from him. An odd thing in a city this size. Perhaps the humans would find it peculiar and note the gnarled manner in which it resembled a man. Flint knew better. It was the remnants of the fae he'd killed. And by that form, he knew which one it had been and what their natal magics were borne in.

It didn't matter now who it was. It didn't matter that he was gone. All that mattered was ending the rest of them. So badly did he want to be the blade of that death that his fist tightened.

Something bit into his palm as he clenched his fist.

He uncurled his fingers to find a red pebble of some sort. He flattened his palm, studying the object. Smooth of surface. Tear drop shaped with bit of hook at the top end. It looked like both fire and blood thrived together within its depths. Liquid and flame twining around each other so tightly they could be one but for their warring natures.

He thought he heard it whispering to him. When he leaned down to press his ear against the smooth surface, he could almost make out the sounds of Fae: horses nickering, taverns filled with ruckus laughter, and a slight, high pitched keening below it all like the shadows that seamed the places where light couldn't reach.

Aiofe had told him what this was, hadn't she, after she'd sent him back into a body now knit back together?

He strained to pull the memory back, because it seemed important. Something about his father and a veil and sacrifice. Something, some ruse he had to pass along to Terran, but someone brushed past him. She shouldered her way by without comment or apology to settle onto the shelter's bench. She smelled of beer and someone else's sweat, and her presence cut through the vapor that tried to solidify in his mind. It broke into particles and drifted apart. Gone. Before he even had it.

He blinked at her, roving her with a cold gaze. She crossed her legs. Placed her purse on her lap.

"A woman died there," he said, anger seeping into his fist as he curled his fingers around the pebble, sealing it off from the fetid air of the human world. It warmed in his palm, sent brief shots of energy to his fingers. Magic. It held some power from his realm, maybe from the Darkness too. The magic was hot enough to make his palm sweat.

She furrowed her brow at him, then shifted her gaze. He knew it was so she could look for the bus. He made her uncomfortable.

A nasty smile collected on his lips as a thought occurred to him. "I said a woman died there last night." Was it last night? He couldn't be sure. Not that it mattered. Not now. All that mattered was his dove needed him and he was going to find her if it took the blood of an entire world to find her. "And another was taken."

The woman's profile revealed a whitened jaw line as she turned away from him entirely. She was scared. Her fingers on her purse strap tangled together. Her feet had started a shuffle that hinted that she would get up and leave at any moment.

He prowled forward. Ignoring the others that pushed past him, an unnervingly intimate turmoil that threatened to steal his air. He was aware that his entire spine was ramrod straight, a too tight harp string ready to snap at the slightest touch. Judging by the way she angled her body away from him, her little white running shoes aimed to flee, was a good indication of how terrifying he must look.

"I killed her," he said in a rasp as he drew close enough to lean against the shelter and peer inside. "Sliced my blade across her throat and let the world behind her spill out from her stomach."

He lowered his head, his intense stare demanding she face him. Everything inside him burned. Anger was a hellfire in his stomach.

"If you know what's good for you," he said, stopping in front of her finally. "You'll run."

He looked down at her. She held her ground, stared off into space as though he wasn't even there.

But her posture gave her away. She was trying to decide if she should run or stay and board the bus she'd come to take, but the conflict played out in her shoulders. He could see a scream building in her throat, but strangely, she sat there, stiff, unyielding. Stubborn.

"Why aren't you running?" he asked. The pebble in his hand became almost unbearably hot. He refused to let go even if it burned a hole in his palm. He needed its magic.

"Woman, I asked you a question."

When she turned to him, he saw grit in her expression. Her eyes were brown. Hard-edged. Curls escaped the hood over her head. Not a business woman, this. He'd been mistaken in assuming she was a woman on her way to work in the pre-dawn. The face was too seamed. Too aware. Hers was the bearing of a mortal who had spent too long in the pleasure taverns. She was more likely a woman on her way home from work than to it.

"You think I'm scared?" she asked, those red-rimmed eyes raking over him. She snorted. "Pretty boy, I seen a girl raped to death at a party for wealthy, elite mother-fuckers. Men took me three at a time sometimes. I've had bastards beat me until I couldn't walk. My boss likes to use boiling water as punishment. I've begged for death more times than I can count."

She leveled him with an unflinching stare. "Right now what I need is to get on this mother-fucken bus and get home to my kid because if I don't, her babysitter will just leave her there alone so she can get to work. What's a beautiful man like you going to do to me that I haven't already gone through?"

These humans could be a violent lot, he thought. He'd never felt such kindred with them as he did in that moment. She would be perfect.

He smiled for her then, the best he knew how, and her face bleached out at sight of it as he pulled his smile wider until he was sure all she could see was teeth.

When she jumped to her feet, he was in her way. When she dodged left, an expert maneuver that suggested she'd had more than once reason to execute it before, he blocked her. Didn't matter what she'd faced before in her brief, violent lifetime. She'd never met the likes of him before.

The tiniest of movements for him, really. Then a bit of light magic, dropping her back onto the bench like a rag doll. It didn't feel satisfying. Instead, it only heightened his need to kill.

But at least she slumped sideways, her whole right side leaning into the shelter wall. A bit too much magic, maybe. He'd likely broken her back. That, too, could be helpful since he preferred not to have to fight with her for long.

From somewhere behind him, he heard a gasp. A flurry of motion. Whoever it was, probably intended to call for help.

He canted his head at his companion, looking her over with a calm that seemed to have the pedestrian behind him—another woman, he guessed by the pitch of her voice—screaming into the phone that there was a killer hurting people right out in plain sight.

"She's not dead," he said in a flat tone, without looking over his shoulder. He didn't care what they thought, but he didn't want to delay by having to kill. He didn't want to use more magic.

His attention was wholly for the woman in front of him. She was the important one. She looked oddly like the woman from the night before in the way she curled over on herself. No blood showed anywhere, though. Her hoodie could be hiding a plethora of wounds taken and self-inflicted. But there was no blood, and that was important.

Because he would need all of it by the time he was done.

"I'm on the corner of..." the voice grew softer, more distant as it went on, and he guessed the good Samaritan had started running for her own safety. If he didn't act now, he might end up with a brood of murders on his hands and that would take far too much time and energy.

He scraped a hand over his hair, pushing it back out of his face. The world smelled of death and magic, or maybe that was just him.

With a sigh clawing its way out of his lungs, he bent to scoop the woman over his shoulder. She was heavier than he'd have guessed but he'd carried larger weights with less effort. It was the awkwardness of her hands slapping against his ass as he swung to face the street that bothered him more.

Traffic kept up, a city jaded by violence keeping its pace like a shark lest it drown. He understood that sort of activity. A creature could get bogged down in indecision and emotion.

He caught sight of the woman who'd called for help. She stood across the street, a phone to her ear, watching him.

With a lifted chin, he caught her eye. Smiled though he felt no humor, no pleasure. He didn't even enjoy the way her eyes widened or the way her mouth dropped as she pivoted sharply to grab the sleeve of a man passing by. He thought she pointed at him. She could have jabbed her phone in his direction, hollered at someone to do something.

But none of that mattered because he was on his way. His attention was on the light that threaded its way down the street and off into the distance. Somewhere out there, beyond the highly urban sections, lay a quiet block with woods and grass. And within that space of seeming-peace, he would find her. And he would find her tormentors.

And he would slake his rage with more violence than he could enjoy in a century.

He pulled in a bracing breath, gathering what magic he could from the sparse grasses around him, the few trees with branches climbing in a spindly ladder to the heavens. He found power in the dying street lamps and the headlights from oncoming traffic.

Everything went dim around him as the sun crept over the buildings and scraped along the grimy streets. Something fizzled as streetlights went out with a flare.

But he didn't draw from the woman on his shoulder. He merely plucked the stone from his pocket and squeezed. And then he murmured the words Aiofe had given him.

"Take me to my mate."

A Buoyant Rage

FLINT

He caught them in the middle of enjoying their work to create a portal home. He couldn't see them of course; they were in the cellar of the witch's burned out lair, and Aiofe's stone took him above them, straight to the middle of the scorched mess that was once Lilah's kitchen.

But he heard their voices and their laughter and the hairs on the back of his neck bristled at the sound of their pleasure. He recognized each voice in the words they spoke to each other.

Anger clamped a fist around his heart, and in reflex, his hands tightened on the woman draped over his shoulder. He'd almost forgotten her in the wash of emotion, and he suffered an almost irresistible urge to sate his anger on her.

But he would not give into the urge. Not yet. All that pent up energy was for the comrades below his feet. And when that time came, he would not hold back even the most terrifying of his anger. Because he had far worse things in mind for them than a quick, painful rampage that would end them in a rush of blood and fury.

That was too easy for them. Deaths such as he planned should be savored.

But it was difficult to hold back. The drive to feel their flesh beneath his teeth, their entrails in his grip, it was all-consuming. He wanted it deep in his marrow, where it burned and smoked just like this blackened fortress.

He had to close his eyes against the lust for it. In his mind, he sent her his strength, to hold out for a moment more. Along the lines of light that he'd followed, the one that moved straight to her wrist, he fed energy.

And he could feel her sucking it up, a desperate acceptance that helped his resolve. She was alive. She needed him.

Every mate bond was different, Aiofe had told him. For him, a light bender, that mark was made in energy, a phosphorescent symbol that burned bright for a moment before sinking into flesh and tying them together.

Should she be fae, she'd have felt it and responded. Were she fae, he'd have known the moment he marked her.

Instead, he was left to suffer the bond knowing she was terrified of him. And that was fine. So long as she lived and thrived, that was enough.

For an instant beneath his eyelids, he saw himself outside his own body, catching sight of Ava Ashe all those nights ago as she choked the life out of the fae sorceress and began this whole ordeal for her sister. An unwitting thing, no doubt, but a clearer path was not trod than the one he traced from there to this moment.

A skittering, shuddering undulation of agony moved through him, the longing, the ache of retribution was so strong. A time long gone by even if it was just half a dozen days. Despite the time that had passed, he saw the huntress clearly, and she looked nothing like Kit.

The huntress's pitch black hair was a match for the burnt timber and piles of ash that lay around him; it wasn't the fire that glinted in the locks of his mate. Though they were sisters, they were nothing alike.

He wished he'd killed Ava then. Had the huntress died that night at the fae sorceress's lair, her sister would not be here now, trapped with those beasts below his boots. If not for his father's decree, she might be living a life ignorant of the horrors of Fae.

The woman on his shoulder stirred, no doubt catching a whiff of the smoke and char that remained from the witch's lair. Maybe she even responded to the crunching of black embers beneath his boot or the tension in his shoulders that made his muscles so taut that they felt like bone on bone against her hips.

She made a small sound in the back of her throat.

"Shh," he crooned. "Quiet now."

A snap of her neck. That's all it would take. Frail things, they were, but this one, brave as she was, seemed a bit sturdier than most he'd encountered in his lifetime. He was lucky she came along at the moment he'd climbed free of the Darkness.

Her courage might have fed him during the days of his training had he found her all those centuries ago. She might have restored his magic with a single drain at her wrist. He didn't doubt she'd been boasting when she'd spoken of the things she'd faced. All he knew was those brutal, violent events would serve him well now.

Creating a portal from human flesh took dark, dark magic. And if it wasn't within the scope of a fae's natal magic, it would take a lot. This woman had lived through darkness. Her blood would aid him in building the gateway he needed to take Kit somewhere his father and Shadow Court would never find them. Perhaps the summer courts where her light would mask his darkness.

The bastards below were not gifted with that sort of power, and if all they had to use was Castor's discarded portal shell, they would find it a dud. And the scavenges of magic that remained in the ashes of the place would make it necessary to feed their own natal powers repeatedly from Kit to gain enough to cast that sort of spell.

And it still might not be enough. How many times had they found it needful to repair Kit as they primed the pump? Ten? Twenty? The thought became a burr beneath his skin, rubbing away at the fascia between his muscles. One time was too many. And they would pay for the mere notion of committing those atrocities.

His gaze drifted to the stone fireplace and the charred facade, followed it to the timbers that remained of the fire he'd lit to raze the place after Ava had fled. Flooring timbers still remained here and there where the witch had used black flagstone to cover the wood. No matter how hot his fire had burned, it hadn't touched at least half of the flooring.

It was a good sign some of the witch's protective spells remained intact. And it gave cover to the beasts below as they worked their magic with dark deeds.

A flare of rage nearly undid him at the thought, but he held it in check. Savoring it, delaying its admittance for when he could face them again. This time, the ending would be very different.

He took the time to dig a spot clear of rubble with his boot. Carefully, as silently as he could, he eased the woman he'd taken from the bus stop from his shoulder into his arms, cradling her there as he looked down into her face.

Kit would worry about her. She would want the woman cared for, not dumped in a pile of detritus and scorched things like a discarded doll.

So, for Kit's sake, he took care to splay the woman over what was left of the floor. Made sure she had a charred throw pillow beneath her head, a comfortable spot to recline where nothing could dig into her back or hips.

It took up precious time, put more time in the hands of those bastards below. Though he worked quickly, he knew how critical every moment was. He resented every second the task took from him. But he thought of that dove and its broken neck and he told himself that when Kit laid her eyes on him again, he would know he'd done this small thing for her.

"Don't move," he said to the woman, running his fingers over her eyes to draw shadows over them.

He could bind her with magic, blind her temporarily, but those things took from him and he needed every bit of power available. Slipping her into darkness was the best thing he could do.

Besides, she wasn't going anywhere. Her back was broken. He knew by the limp way she'd lain over his shoulder that she was paralyzed from the waist down.

"Sleep," he said, trusting the residual magic of the place would bring darkness to her, let her surrender to the shadows. It breathed over and through him and he knew by the sizzle of energy on his fingertips that the deed was done.

And then, he directed his attention to the chasm that remained of a blast of his own magic all those days earlier. A fissure he'd cracked open in the floor as he'd aimed for and missed Ava Ashe. It had been useless as a trap then, but it came handy now. Through it, he caught sight of them all. For an unearthly long second, he thought he might burst into flames, so great was the fury at what he saw below.

But something held him back. Some whisper he should let her have one moment of peace before he committed himself to such violent work. He should wait to make sure she was safely out of reach before he let loose the fury within.

They were so busy feeding, that they hadn't heard him. He couldn't see Kit's face, just watch as her legs, sagging open, jerking with the thrusts of the fae atop her as he fed. He knew what was happening wasn't a sexual thing. The fae were feeding their magic, taking what they could from her skin and blood and fear.

As he might have done a thousand years ago.

His eyes squeezed shut for a second, letting the rage gather. In the back of his mind, he thought he should explode into action, save her from one more second of agony. His vengeance should be swift and deadly. But he didn't take a single step.

Later, he might think his hesitation was because swift retribution wasn't enough for the bastards. He might convince himself that a fast end was not what he intended when he'd come here.

But the truth was, he was so caught up in the complete oblivion of fury that he couldn't move. The roar behind his ears was so loud he couldn't hear his own breath.

It might have been a mere heartbeat, but it was too long.

All he could think of was that he wanted to taste the savor of her vengeance in the back of his throat, store it there for the moment he could offer it back to her. He wanted the revenge to be sharp and cold and greater than the pain an entire world could suffer.

So when it finally built to a crescendo that had his entire body vibrating, the magic inside built to a painful brightness, he felt a smile pull at the edges of his mouth, drawing it up into something that would certainly terrify her should she see it.

He would use all the magic he had in him in sacrifice to this godless moment.

Only when he knew he'd gathered as much as he could, did he seal his mouth over the woman he'd taken to fuel this moment. He bit down hard on her tongue, pulling the blood from her in a swallow that took her screams as well. The sound of her terror and pain poured down his throat like the most delicious ambrosia.

It was painful for her, he knew. She spasmed beneath him. When she passed out, he knew he'd taken enough. He could feel the swell of her agony flooding his veins.

And then...then he dropped through the chasm.

He landed perfectly, with barely a crunch of his boots on the gravel in the basement. A terrible quake stole over him, shuddering him from the inside out. Head lowered, a bull about to charge, he charged forward. He parted his lips to speak, to issue an order so commanding they would piss themselves from fear.

What came out was a hiss, so low he barely heard it himself, but low, guttural. Semi audible as it was, they heard it.

"Get off my mate," he said.

Sigard looked back at him over his shoulder, surprised. The angle of his body, the slant of his shoulder revealed a woman so mangled by their attentions that he couldn't see his dove in there anywhere.

But she caught his gaze. Her amber eyes were lost in a glaze of magic and shock, and yet when she took him in as he stood there, he knew exactly how terrifying he looked because it was written all over her face.

He knew then, that she'd endured enough. That his vengeance on her behalf would be a straw too many.

"Don't look, Dove," he said.

In the split second he had before the rage took control, he threw shadows around her, so she could be saved the terrors he'd inflict on her attackers. And in that magic, he sent a merciful confusion, so she wouldn't know the horrors of what she'd hear and feel.

And then he let go the tenuous, flimsy thread he'd been clinging to. He could almost imagine it fluttering into the atmosphere. It stretched out and up like a string on a balloon, buoyant for an instant before the atmosphere whipped it out of sight.

And then there was no more reason. No more sanity.

There was only rage.

Taken

KIT

WHEREVER KIT WAS, IT was dark and cloistered with a heat that could only be created by being wrapped in too many blankets. Even the scents were off, not dusty pages and coffee the way the shop should smell. The energy was wrong too. The sounds of the bookstore, with its quietly ticking decorative train station clock and the gentle hum of the old-fashioned boiler registers were distressingly absent.

She wasn't in the shop anymore, apparently. Wherever she was, the place possessed a somber, tomb-like quiet. The very air felt stuffed with cotton batting, flannel cloths soaked in chloroform. The darkness was as deep and soft as the inside of the grim reaper's velvet cloak.

Only her heartbeat ticked off time in her ears. And as though her body sensed danger her mind held to the belief that she needed to be still as a deer in an open field.

It didn't help that the disorientation wore away as speedily as paint flaking in the sun.

She'd been sleeping, she thought. Evidenced by the way she felt stiff in places that hadn't moved in a long while. Maybe that was why she couldn't command her limbs to lift or kick. She was numb from lying in one spot for too long.

She waited for the pins and needles to mount an attack, even tried to wiggle her fingers, testing, forcing them in challenge for that telltale buzz to rise as blood flow resumed in tissues log-jammed by pressure.

Except the pins and needles did not raise. No electric shock lit up the nerves in her arms or legs. She couldn't even get a good sense of spatial awareness. As if she was lying in an isolation chamber, being robbed of sensory input.

All she was left with was darkness, and in that darkness, her mind dragged replays of Ava's voice through her mind like fingernails scrabbling over slate.

Some men were coming. Get out of town.

A groan slid free as she thought of that warning now. She hadn't got out. She'd stayed put, put her faith in some misguided belief that Ava was being dramatic, that her shit couldn't touch her anymore. She'd placed her faith in the distance she'd put between her sister and herself and it had done nothing. Nothing to save her.

But beyond that, confusion was a gelatinous mold of fruit salad.

She chewed the inside of her cheek. There was something, though. A nagging burn at the back of her memory that warned her not to poke about. She should know things, things that she did everyday and that should come back to her like a comfortable slipper sliding onto her foot after a long rest.

Things like taking the bus home, like walking up her steps.

She should remember more than the hazy sense of dread that tightened her chest so much she could barely catch a breath. More than the fact that she was leaning against something hard and cold.

There should be more to her reality than a thick darkness and the weight of fabric cloaked around her shoulders. A blanket of some sort she figured, heavy and smelling faintly of smoke and cloves.

She tried to shrug it off, but a sound froze her mid-motion.

Someone was moving around her. It was the stealthy careful, way an intruder moves when he's afraid to wake the resident of a house he's burglarizing.

Her breath caught almost too audibly. The footsteps paused. *Some men...some men were coming.*

"You're awake."

Oh God. She'd know that throaty voice anywhere. It was him. Flint. Her stalker.

A thousand images came back then to haunt the back of her eyelids. Flint holding a man by the throat. Flint stalking across the street as she knelt in front of a fallen bird. Flint slicing the tender throat of a woman at a bus stop.

And then...then Flint at that same bus stop, facing half a dozen or more men who seemed intent on killing him.

A scream was building in her throat, one that seemed trapped there as it tried to gather steam. In her mind's eye, a hood came down over her head, the memory so visceral, she flailed and fought against nothing until she ended up toppling over onto her side. The heavy weight of the blanket pinning her inside a tangle of fabric that she couldn't move against or through.

Tears welled in her eyes. There was something about the memory of that hood. Something...else. Something muddy after that memory, but too much sludge kept her from shoving her arm through far enough to pull it free.

She felt him kneel beside her, heard the faint rustling of his trousers. She flinched when a hand rested, lightly, on her forehead. Oh how she hated that it felt so damn warm. She should be terrified because why was she in the dark? Why couldn't she see him. Had he blindfolded her? Had he drugged her?

"You're safe now."

Safe? Somehow that didn't sound as good as it should. There was still a knot tied into her viscera, a prickling along her neck that told her she might never be safe again.

"Kit?" That palm roamed her waist in the pitch black. "Can you hear me? I said you're safe."

She felt him moving. A great weight lifted off her shoulders and a breeze invaded her core with a wave of air before it came back down again, shutting out the chill. Fingers tangled into hers.

"You were so cold," he said. "I didn't expect the magic to hit you that hard. If I'd known you were so susceptible, I would never have made him use it."

At that moment, something popped in her head. Like the unexpected release of pressure in a Eustachian tube hours after a long flight.

She tried to scramble out of reach, to pull her hand from his as panic took control. She tried to roll onto her knees and crawl away, anywhere, anywhere but there, but she was trapped between him and the damn wall. She collapsed. Laid her head back. He had taken her hand again, and she let him. What good was there in fighting when she couldn't see?

"You kidnapped me," she said, and the words came out like a bloom of dust. She coughed, ozone filling her throat with each breath.

"You were *taken*," he said in a slow voice that simmered with suppressed anger. But there was no regret in the tone. Instead, there was something else. Something she couldn't fathom. "But it wasn't by me."

She struggled with that information. She didn't remember any-thing after that hood came down. Try as she might, she couldn't peel the skin off the membrane that cloaked her memory.

Something grew warm on the flesh in her wrist, deeper than skin. It took a moment to realize he'd kissed her there. That his lips had drawn out of her pulse a heat that began to spread up her arm.

"Don't try to remember," he said. "It's over."

Little gnats were taking chunks out of her insides. She was too calm. Too numb. This wasn't shock. It was something else. Had he drugged her? She recalled feeling, thinking, as though she'd been drugged at some point. But she didn't think it was him who had done that to her.

She wanted to get up, claw the blankets away, because all of this was just adding to the confusion. She scraped the material off her chest and realized it wasn't wool that met her touch.

She felt a sleeve and what she thought might be a collar. The fabric was supple but cool to the touch. Leather, she realized. A jacket. His duster jacket.

He'd been wearing it when...

"I tried to help you," she said, another image flashing through her mind's eye, bringing home the first real memory since that hood had stolen them. "I didn't run like you told me to. I couldn't."

Her memory fed her more images then. Of a dark, cloistered area where he confronted several men. All intent on—

Oh my God, those men.

"They were going to kill you."

His dark chuckle moved over her hair. So he was closer than she thought.

"I'm not so easy as that to kill," he said. "But you..." his words choked off then. She could hear him swallow. "You don't have to think about it anymore."

"Why is it dark?" She wasn't quite so terrified now, just curious. Now that she knew he wasn't the thing in the shadows to be afraid of.

"Is it?" he asked. "I can see just fine. I see you, Dove. Your wide burnished green eyes with those burnished gold flecks. Your hair." She felt his fingers brush aside locks that had stuck to her cheeks. He tucked them behind her ear, lingering to cup her chin. "I see the sweetness of your face."

She trembled at his touch, leaning into it because it felt right. It felt safe. She reached for him and her fingers met a muscled thigh that lay beside her. A shudder wracked him, one that she felt against her side.

"I'm not in the bookshop." That information felt important.

"You haven't been at work for several hours."

A pause, then. The air felt tight. She ran her fingers around the space that surrounded her. Her palms moved across something cold and hard. Her fingers probed into nooks and crannies that felt rough.

"I'm on the ground," she said.

"Not completely true," he said. "You're on the floor of a basement."

Cold chills emanated from the floor, feeding up into her bones, now that she knew that. "And why am I on the floor of a damp cellar?"

A hitch of breath, caught in her throat as an image flashed through her mind. Something horrible. Something...awful had happened here. She tried to bolt to her feet, but his hand on her shoulder, preventing her, made her pause.

"Not yet, Dove," he said. "Wait for the magic to settle."

Magic. That smell of ozone. A slow, methodical unease prickled over her neck. Dogging her. She was sure someone had used the word before, and the use of it was a razor against her throat.

"Something's wrong," she said.

As if her words opened up a hole in the darkness, he came into focus then. His face, all of it, right there in front of hers. It was all she could see and it was both terrifying and comforting.

His finger slipped beneath her chin, lifted her face upward, drew her gaze to his. Something moved in the depths of his eyes. A violet flare.

"Everything is alright, Dove."

"Why can't I see anything except your face? Am I going blind?"

Did he just flinch?

"Am I scaring you?" he asked in a low voice.

She swallowed down her unease. "Yes."

His finger smoothed the skin from her chin all the way up to her jaw and cupped her face. Gentle. It felt so damn gentle that her throat closed up, and she couldn't understand why she felt so fucking grateful for it. Why she felt as though she'd just been pulled out from beneath a train's deadly path.

And the way he looked at her. It was strange and intense and filled with what she thought might be horror. Like he was afraid of her, not the other way around.

When he responded, his voice sounded as tight as hers.

"You're right to be afraid," he said. "I am a fearsome thing. Men may quake at my step, but I would never hurt you, Dove."

She blinked, training her focus over his shoulder. A half dozen lumps of blurred color hunkered throughout the space but she couldn't quite make out what they were.

The smell of smoke quivered on the air, congealing into some-thing more astringent. She squinted, curiosity a compulsion she couldn't resist until his finger urged her gaze back to his.

He shifted sideways, blocking her view.

"What lies behind me is not for your eyes," he said, his head tilting back, his gaze on the ceiling. "Best concentrate on leaving this place."

She followed his gaze. A tear in the ceiling above her, a wide seam that went off in three directions. Big enough everywhere for a person to crawl through.

"Come now," he said and hooked his arm around her waist. The jacket fell away as she leaned on him. It was all she could do not to collapse.

"I'm sore," she said as though that would somehow emulsify the sticky residue of lost memory.

It was true. She hurt everywhere. Even her hips ached as though she'd been riding a bike for too long and after too many years of inactivity. Her jaws ached like she'd been screaming.

"Sore is a good thing," he said. "Means you're alive."

She almost asked if there was some reason she shouldn't be, but she didn't think she wanted to know the answer to that. Not yet. Her legs. They were so weak. She had to sink back down onto her haunches even though he was supporting her. The cold stone of the basement wall didn't even feel like enough support.

"I can't," she said. "Not yet."

She peered up to see him looking at her. His lips thinned to a grim line. She noticed his chest was bare. That he was covered in blood and gobs of something that looked like tissue paper wadded into balls. His feet were planted in a defensive stance. The boots were covered in grime.

Something niggled at the back of her mind. Her gaze traveled past his legs. The forms beyond him, scattered amid rubble, looked like huddled masses of sleeping men, except she was sure they weren't sleeping.

"What did you do?" she rasped out.

"Signed my death warrant," he said flatly as he stooped to retrieve something from the floor at her feet. This he slipped over her shoulders. A shirt. His shirt. She realized she was shivering, and that seeing his naked torso was not helping.

"I don't understand."

He squatted in front of her. "You don't need to understand," he said, dragging his gaze from hers to something in his hand. He held it up for her to see. A small, reddish pebble.

"Can you trust me, Dove? Just this once? A small measure of time. Just enough to help you."

She thought that over as she studied the small red stone and the man who held it up to her gaze. This was the man who had stalked her. She sensed his possessiveness even now. He said he wanted to get her out, get her safe, but what did that mean? Why was she even here with him at all?

Things weren't right. Things were off. And it had everything and nothing to do with this man in front of her and those huddled, sleeping men beyond.

She nodded, lip caught in her teeth, as she made her decision. "I will trust you. But I want to know the truth. I need the truth."

Truth. She'd asked it of Ava and she'd asked it of Gideon and she knew they both lied. Whatever they were covering up, it had come to roost whether she knew the truth or not. She wouldn't hide her head in the sand for one more moment. Whatever this man had done, whatever it was he didn't want her to see, she needed to know that the feeling of protection, the sensation of safety wasn't a lie too. That what she felt was real.

He released an aggrieved sigh. Shook his head. "It's best you don't."

She curled her fingers around his forearm, feeling it flex, savoring the heat that radiated into her palm. "Please," she said as she tightened her grip. "It's the only way."

His swallow seemed hard. He could barely hold her gaze, but he finally nodded.

"I will show you the truth," he said. "Because you need it. But I won't apologize for what I've done."

What Needed to be Done

KIT

HIS VOICE PULLED A curtain open, and the world around her came into sharp, horrifying focus. Things she'd only caught whiffs of, the stink of char and sweat, the copper tang of metal and ozone, all of that was suddenly so strong it made her cough.

Her own hand, still on Flint's arm, looked as though she'd been punching concrete; the knuckles were bruised and bloodied. Three nails were peeled back or broken. She looked at them with her brow furrowed for a long moment, trying to make sense of it.

Sucking in a breath, she raised her gaze to his. His expression was pinched and tight with emotion. What emotion it was, she couldn't tell. He looked to be shaking. His body, his shoulders, his muscled neck, all of it was rigid. Braced for a blow.

"Careful now," he said. "I'm here. I'm here for you. Remember that, Dove."

She dragged her eyes from his and trained them over his shoulder. Braced herself. Because she sensed if she was still showing wounds and abrasions, then whatever lay beyond was worse.

And let herself see.

And oh the horrors that met her gaze then.

"My God what did you do?" she asked in a trembling voice, even though it was abundantly clear that he'd murdered several men in horrible ways.

"What I had to," he said in a rasp. "What needed to be done."

The fear ratcheted up then. She could barely swallow down the terror. Whatever had happened here, she'd taken some punches. Maybe more. But there was a hollowness in her that seemed so very wrong. As if her insides had been novacained.

She knew she looked as terrified as she felt. She didn't have time to hide it from him. And he saw it. Long before she could collect her wits and master her expression.

"Where is your trust, now, Dove?" he asked, bitterness an acid in his voice.

She shook her head, unable to answer. It was hard to pull her gaze from the horrors of blood and flesh that lay scattered over the cellar floor. She was sure the heads and the bodies were not even connected anymore.

Her stomach threatened to squeeze her intestines into a knot. She thought they were already twisting around her gallbladder, gathering the bile inside. She'd bring up bits of herself if she vomited.

She swallowed and swallowed, and it still wasn't enough to hold it back. She retched sideways, rolling over herself to expel the sick onto the floor.

There was nothing in her belly but strings of yellow fluid, but it wracked her frame as though she were trying to expel chunks of bone. Oh God. Bones. Fluid. She heaved again and this time she felt his hand in her hair, holding it back. He cupped her forehead, giving her something to sag into as the waves took her.

When she was done, she slapped his hand away. "Don't fucking touch me."

Her entire body shook, and she didn't care. This man was a monster. Whatever he wanted from her, it couldn't end well, even if he promised her safety. This kind of safety came at too high a price. She'd seen enough movies, enough crime shows.

She had to get up. She had to get out of there. She tried. She lurched to a stand, but her legs were weak. Shock. That's what this was. The shock postponed by that drug, that magic, come back to roost.

She tried to get up and fell back down. Something was wrong with her legs. Punching her thighs, she willed them to hold her, kept trying to make them move beneath the adrenaline dump until his voice snagged her attention.

"He couldn't heal you all the way," he said in a flat voice.

That didn't make any sense. Her brow furrowed in confusion. "What?" she snapped. "What are you talking about?"

His gaze trained itself on her face as he stood so that he was looking down at her. He looked...defeated?

"You asked to see, Dove, and I showed it to you. I would have spared you the things I did to save you, but you had to know. You wanted to *see* it."

"Fuck you, you monster. You saved me?" She swept her arm toward the fallen men. "Did you save these men too? Are you going to save me the same way?" Her voice broke into shards. She felt them slicing through her resolve.

Hysteria now. Great. She caught hold of her chest, feeling for her throat because she couldn't breathe all of a sudden. Her windpipe was a clogged straw trying to suck in air.

She rolled to her side so she could crawl onto her hands and knees. That made breathing easier at least.

"You fucking killed those men," she spat out, her eyes on the grey stone beneath her. She tried again to stand and collapsed onto her hip. A sob of frustration choked her.

He crouched down, his face in hers. Challenging. Angry. Oh, how angry.

"Yes, I killed them," he drawled in a tight voice. "And my only regret is that I let them die too soon."

He thrust his finger in the direction of a small man. The nearest of the bodies, the one sitting crookedly against the wall. His eyes were wide in death, the face contorted in anguish.

"Him, I let live long enough to heal you." His voice choked. "But I couldn't hold back the fury long enough for him to heal you all the way." He swiveled a pained gaze at her. "You were so broken, Dove. I lost myself."

"You're saying you did this *for* me?" she shrieked. "Fuck you. Fuck you, you monster."

She punched him. Flat on the chest. The blow stung her already sore knuckles, but she kept punching. It felt good to let go, especially since his chest was so hard it hurt. It hurt so good she couldn't stop.

And through it all, he remained as still as a mountain, letting her tire herself until her sobs came out with long drools of spit and tears.

By the time she had fallen against his chest exhausted and drained of adrenaline and unable to hold herself erect, her lungs were burning.

"You don't remember," he said in a soft voice as he eased her away, peeling her from his chest. "I understand your fury. I didn't show you all of it. Just my part because..."

He ran his palm over the back of his neck. "You only know what I showed you." Darkness claimed his expression, then. A stubborn decision made before he even spoke. "But I don't care. I won't show you more. Not even if it shows you why I did it.

"I am a monster, just like you say. But I've broken a vow a thousand years old or more, just the same. I've betrayed my family. I've laid bare and bloodied any future I might have. I've declared war on everything I know and made you the spoils. Can't you trust that?"

He dragged his fist over his hair, clawing his scalp at the back as if the energy coiled in his body was too much to bear. Even filthy, the scars, the tattoos, hinted at a violence endured long before this moment.

He'd given her his shirt, his jacket. And beneath the fabric she was wet with fluid: sweat, blood, smeared over her body as though he'd tried to wipe it off and clean her up but couldn't wash away all the evidence of violence.

She caught him watching her as she surveyed herself. His expression was painted in something primal and fierce.

"I'd do it again, Dove," he ground out. "No matter what you think of me. I'd do it a thousand times more to gain you a single breath. I would bring them back to life again a hundred times more just so I could tear them apart inch by inch, so I could hear them scream, so you could glory in their agony."

"But I didn't," she said in a tight voice, her hand going to her chest, understanding coming like cracks in fine porcelain. "I didn't glory in it, did I?"

He dropped his gaze but not before she caught the lethal flare of magic in them. "You did not."

He stepped around her and dropped down onto a nearby surface. A large wooden desk, she thought, judging by the shape and size of it.

Above it, a broken window, its frame a smudge against the gloom of pre-dawn. He looked backlit there, a halo of silver catching his hair.

He hung his head. "It was my gift to you. I wanted you to know they paid for what they did. But you're too soft, Dove. You didn't relish the retribution."

He looked back at her, flicked his gaze over her hair, and it felt like a caress so visceral, she could have sworn he'd touched her.

"I had the one of them with the natal magic for memory scrub you clean of the things they'd done to you. So you wouldn't have to think of it—any of it—ever again."

His gaze went to his hands where they gripped the edge of the desk so hard, his knuckles looked white as bone. And then his voice dropped to a low, throaty note.

"And then I killed them."

She shuddered at the ruthlessness in his voice. "And these things they did to warrant such a death—"

He shook his head, a dog clearing its ears. "Don't ask me that." He pulled the stone from his pocket and held it between them. "This relieved you of those things. Those memories are safe in here."

"I have to know," she said. "I can't live with myself knowing these men—"

"These were not men," he ground out. His fists curled into tight balls against the edge of the desk. "Don't you understand? Haven't you seen enough, suffered enough to know these were beasts of magic, bound to a fae court of violence and shadows."

His brow furrowed as he dipped down to look into her eyes. "The same as I am. A creature with no shame. No reason to live except to do my father's bidding."

He gasped, a sudden intake of air that seemed to surprise him. "Until you. You are my reason to take another breath now. You are all I have from now until the moment my father sees what I've done and takes my last agonized breath. Even then, I will feel the rightness of the work I've done this day, and yours will be the name I speak with that last exhale. I won't regret it. Even if you hate me for it."

The way his throat seemed to suck at the air, the rigid shoulders, the way every muscle in his body seemed to be quivering. It was clear he didn't have a hold on himself, but she was falling apart too. She needed to put some pieces back together. Find some sense in all this.

Magic. Creatures of shadow. Another place, a realm of sorts, where magic was a violent and awful thing...impossible as it was, she heard the truth in the words. She saw it in the sharpness of his features, the despair that shuttered his eyes. Magic—real magic—existed. She'd seen what he'd done to those...creatures. The way he'd sliced them apart with blasts of light and a weapon seemingly forged by the sun's own rays.

Whatever they'd done to her, he'd made them pay. For her. He'd faced it. For her.

And she softened then. "These...creatures... you're saying they were sent to... abduct me. To take me somewhere and then what?"

She waited for an answer, but he only blinked at her. His throat bobbed under several hard swallows. Whatever he was holding back, she knew she'd not get it out of him. Not this way.

She would have liked to stand, to appear somewhat in control, but she couldn't. All she could do was muster out a few words. A sigh scraped free of her throat. "I want to know what happened. I want to know all of it."

He shook his head. "I won't give those memories back to you."

She softened her voice as she reached up to wrap her hand around his muscled calf, the only place she could reach from the floor. "You have to give them back. Blind faith is fine for mortals and gods, but between a man and a woman, faith needs to be built on truth."

The stoic mask remained in place.

"Those are my memories," she prompted. "You had no right to take them." She lifted her chin. Crossed her arms over her chest and stared at him. She needed to know what these...fae...had done to deserve such death. She wanted proof. She thought of the drunk on the bus, the way he'd dangled from Flint's grip, and she tried to tell herself that what these men had done had to be worse. But was it? She couldn't remember.

The moment stretched out between them, a palpable thing, but she wasn't going to give in first. If she'd learned anything from Ava, it was that silence held power.

Finally, with a frustrated sigh, he aimed the red pebble at her, pinched between his finger and thumb. "This was given to me by Aiofe, queen of the Stygian Darkness. It holds enough magic gathered from each of the dead fae to perhaps give you your memories back. With luck, it would also make you numb to them, to heal the pain of what you'll see and remember."

"Is it that bad?" her voice was small.

"Oh, Dove," he said. "I would have killed these bastards for bumping into you at the market, but do you think I would have burned my entire world down if all they wanted of you was a game of chess?"

"You're trying to scare me."

He closed his fist around the stone. "Prepare you," he countered with a tilt of his chin. "Because luck does not favor those of the Darkness. It takes what it wants. It thrives on the pain and relishes the agony. The Darkness will give as much as it takes and none of it would benefit a mortal soul."

Pressing the heel of his fist against her forehead, he went on. "Would you take that, Dove? Would you want to be filled with darkness? Because there are better ways to let you savor the shadows than the things this stone will unleash upon you. Think now. Be honest with yourself."

She closed her eyes, thinking, feeling for a space deep within where those memories might reside. A vast darkness rested in her soul, one she felt was made of memories too vivid to recall. She remembered everything up to the moment the hood went down. She remembered waking here, with him crouching beside her. The rest...

The rest was a soft cushion of night air too dark to penetrate.

But one thing glowed in that darkness, a small pinprick that grew as she concentrated. She felt it warm her from the inside out, wrapping around her like a beautiful cloak made of lacey light threads. If she followed the skein it brought her his face. His voice. His hands. That was a darkness made of velvet. A blissful rest on a satin pillow. And even as she admitted it, she saw herself standing to save him. The way she'd confronted Ava's monsters. Against impossible odds, she knew she would take whatever was asked of her. For Ava, then. For him, now.

"If you ask if of me, I will show it to you," he murmured, breaking through her thoughts. "Only I pray you, don't ask it."

She heard him push off the desk, felt him as he crouched down in front of her. When she opened her eyes he was there, his gaze holding hers.

"What you would have back is more than most fae can stand in a hundred years of violence, but if you want it, I'll be there. When you fall apart, I will hold you fast, little dove. Believe that above all else, you are safe with me."

He held his arm out to her, letting her choose. Safety and oblivion or a storm with a harbor to anchor in.

She chose neither. Instead, she pushed herself to her feet. "Some day," she murmured. "Some day you will show me."

"Some day," he echoed. "Meaning there will be a day after this one."

"Perhaps," she said as she laid a hand on his shoulder. He flinched at first, but then turned into her, pressing himself deeper into the curve of her palm. The smile she gave him felt genuine and compassionate and he blinked as though he couldn't believe she would touch him of her own accord.

"I want to see it," she whispered. "This gift. I want to look at it."

He inclined his head slightly and brushed the backs of his knuckles over her cheek. "They are already returning to the magic that bore them," he said. "It shouldn't be too horrible to behold."

"Whatever it is, I'm ready for it," she said and hauled in a bracing breath. And then she began a slow, surveying trek around the basement.

She felt his eyes on her back as she walked. She swallowed hard on the ravages that were left of those moments. Even though the bodies were beginning to lose any resemblance to something human, and in some cases, looked more like unformed lumps of clay or wood—and in one case, like a stone—it was difficult to survey the work he'd done on her behalf, but she forced herself to do so.

Not because these brutes deserved someone to witness their end, but because Flint did.

He'd done it for her, he'd said. So she could glory in it. And that alone was the reason she took in every scorched bit of clothing and hair, every puddle and spray of blood. She'd pretend the stink of feces didn't cling to the air or that the smell of blood was already cloying and rotting as it drifted to her nostrils.

Because this was a gift. And she somehow knew that even in the midst of his fury, he'd held back because he wanted to spare her witnessing any more violence. A monster, yes.

But her monster.

She halted in place and turned to face him. His hands curled into fists at his sides. They flexed and let go a dozen times before she was able to let her breath go in a stream, her shoulders sagging.

Then she advanced on him, slowly, like a predator stalking a mouse, except she didn't feel strong enough for that. She felt like a flag buffeted in the wind. It was the hardest thing she'd had to do in her lifetime with the exception of watching Ava hang by her throat in an old gymnasium. Stalking him like he'd done her, showing what was left of her courage, fighting back the trembling that had taken over her core.

Because he needed to know his violence was worth something.

Her fingers reached for the hardness of his jaw, brushing over the stubble as she flattened her palm over the rigid curve.

"The things you did..." she said, her eyelids shuttering. "It's not for me to judge them. I'm not your god. If you say you did what you had to. I believe it."

His swallow looked painful, and she realized there was more going on behind his gaze than unspent rage.

A low rumble that superseded language moved up his throat. It was a primal, emotive thing beyond control. She felt it against her fingers as they trailed down below his jaw to his neck. Pausing on his pulse, she felt it hammering.

He was afraid. This large, lethally brutal fae was afraid of her.

And she understood with a start exactly why.

Just the Two of Us

Kit

THE TRUTH SHE SAW in his gaze was startling.

"You want me," she said, her voice tight with shock, eyebrows knitting together as she grappled with the things she saw in his face. Her foot stomped on the damp stone, the roughness of the surface, the uneven waver of it like marbles under her soles. "Here," she said. "Where you committed all this carnage, you want me. You want to *take* me here."

His lips curled back with a snarl. "Yes," he hissed out. "Especially here."

She felt as if air bubbles had invaded her veins. That she was a swimmer rising too fast from the depths.

"Here," she echoed in disbelief and her hands went to her throat. She was sure she couldn't breathe.

But he clasped his fingers around her wrist, and that heat between them spread from her pulse upward, hurtling toward her heart.

He held her wrist between them as his face worked through several emotions and anger winning out. She thought she saw a bright silver mark rise from the depths of her skin and shine with a luminescent glow.

"Yes," he growled. "I want to claim you in front of their bodies, with the last of their magic bouncing off the walls and ricocheting over the ceiling. I want to plunge deep inside you and fuck the memory out of you until all that remains is my face above you, my cock inside, my heart on its sleeve dying to give you the charred, dark world I live in."

She was shaking her head long before she could voice her response, and even that was so muffled she doubted he heard it. Gone was the short bloom of confidence and courage from before. Now, she wrapped her arms around her abdomen, curling inward, trying to find a way to tell him she couldn't do this. Not this. Not here. It was asking too much.

It didn't matter that part of her cried out for him, for an embrace that could make her feel safe. Even if she pulled to mind those fantasies from the night they'd met on that bus, brought to mind how much she ached at the thought of his strength when she needed it so badly.

That was when she made the mistake of looking up at him.

He was shaking. A predator fighting back the instinct to strike. Holding himself back. For her.

And all she could think was she wanted to feel safe again. To feel pleasure in the thought of an intimate touch. To know his was an embrace that would cocoon her, giving her space to dissolve until every sort of emotional damage was transformed into something magnificent. But she was afraid too. Afraid of the pain of that change. All these years, she'd wished she could easily dull the pain for Ava, knowing that the thing that made her sister strike out couldn't be erased without more pain. And she knew that to get rid of her own, she would have to face things she didn't want to face.

"I don't know if I can do that," were the words that whispered out of her.

He raked his eyes up to her face, and something shifted in his expression. Whatever went on behind his eyes, she saw it all as they moved through emotions too raw to recognize. In their purest form, they twisted his features like a sculpture would form and reform clay.

"It's because you see the real me, Kit," he said. "You know what I'm capable of. And you're not wrong." His chin lifted. She could see the way his throat bobbed with each determined swallow.

"Are you saying you would hurt me?"

He scraped his hand over his hair. "I'm saying for generations, I've hurt your kind. I'll hurt them again for generations more." He canted his head at her, his eyes narrowing. He saw something in her face, something that shifted the way he looked at her.

"But that's not the real issue, is it, Dove?" His voice dropped to a husky note.

She lifted her chin. Eyes flashing. And he inched toward her, challenging her to back away. "You're not afraid," he mused aloud. "You think you are, but you're not."

She held her ground, refusing to give him any quarter, even if she was shaking in the shirt, even if her teeth started chattering onto her tongue because she couldn't stop the trembling.

"Gods above and below," he said. "You want me too. Here. Right here. The same way I want you. With the same violent desperation."

Her heart skidded to a halt and lurched to life again.

"No." She was shaking her head, denying it to herself because here in this place what sort of woman would want to bed a monster? It was sick. It was shameful.

But it was a lie, and she knew it.

"Oh yes." He pressed closer, so close she could feel the air twine around them, joining them together in space. "That trembling you feel deep in your core, that's not terror. A mortal might be for-given for thinking that. Especially after what you've seen. But you don't know that pain. Those memories are not there. Not even your subconscious knows those secrets. All you know is the violence I committed for you. For your safety. And deep inside, you thrill to that."

When he leaned down, capturing her chin with his fingers, he twisted her face so he could examine every inch of her features. "Someday I might want to test that resolve," he murmured in a throaty voice. "I might relish the excitement of your fear, but not today. Today I will take the fire in your belly and turn it into light.

"Because I know you want me, Dove. I sense it. I can *smell* it. That quivering in your belly... It's desire. Maybe not for me. Maybe not because you're turned on by what you see. Maybe it's just a desire to reclaim yourself here the same as I want to claim you. In front of them, *because* of them. Somewhere inside you know that if you walk out of here without taking back what they took from you, you will always wonder what you lost. You might feel broken."

A smile brushed the corners of his mouth. "Oh, you are a fighter, Dove. Not a frail thing at all. These wounds you carry, they're not from the acts of these fae. These are old wounds. And I swear. Who-ever did that to you, whoever made you the shoreline that buffets a violent wind, that person will pay some day. I'll see to it."

He didn't so much as flutter his finger in the direction of the bodies behind him as he flicked his wrist in dismissal. The cant of his head as he examined her was too intense. What he saw in her expression, she couldn't imagine, but a quiver had took possession of her mouth as he studied her. Her pulse pounded in her throat.

His hand cupped her face, the thumb whispering over her cheek in languid strokes until it fetched up on her bottom lip. Her skin buzzed beneath his touch. She almost forgot where they were. For a moment, it was just them, and as if he realized how she felt, his touch became cruel, exploratory in a way that had her heart hammering.

Dipping his thumb ever so slightly into her mouth, he lifted his chin, inhaled sharply. She tasted cloves and cocoa on his skin. Oh god, exactly the way he smelled. She nearly sagged against him then.

A pause of that thumb, before he retreated, blazing a trail down her chin until it dipped beneath the crest, forcing her to tilt her face higher, to expose the delicate, vulnerable flesh of her throat. He examined it, tilting his head this way and that, his eyes half closed.

"Some monsters may only be slain by fear," he murmured. "If you think I'm not afraid too, Dove, then I haven't made myself clear. I'm terrified."

"Of me?" she asked.

His nod was slow. "I don't know if I can put you back together," he murmured, his gaze roaming her exposed throat and the pulse straining against the skin beneath her earlobe. "But maybe I can lend you the strength you need until you can seal the cracks on your own."

A shiver skated down her spine. She prayed he wouldn't step away, leave her standing on her own on watery legs that could barely hold her weight. Even as she thought it, his hand cupped behind her head. Strong fingers massaged her occipital bone. Tugged on her hair, pulled her head back.

"I want to help you gather the pieces," he rasped. "But I've never done that before. I've always torn things apart."

She watched him swallow down a knot and found herself doing the same, as if they were choking on the same emotion.

"You don't have to do this here," he said. "Just because I want it. But know that if you do, I've got you. I won't let you fall apart."

She breathed in resolve from the scent of him. Chocolate. Cloves. Hot spices in a warm mug on a cold night. Then, she willed herself to snake her arms up over his shoulders, to wind them around his neck.

As she tangled her fingers together, knotting them so she couldn't pull free, he groaned out loud.

He dragged her roughly against his frame, and though he seemed made of concrete, he softened like the most pliant clay. She didn't even have time to properly seal her lips over his, before he took control. His kiss was savage, masterful, the kind of experienced kiss of a man who had taken what he wanted from women for eons.

Her spine turned to warm liquid, a long bar of gold melting into the cracks that separated their bodies, drawing them together. And he molded her body to his as though he'd known the shape and size of her for a century.

She was terrified she'd come apart just from the way he held her. The bits that had been put back together with Aiofe's stone were gold-seamed, but they couldn't possibly withstand the pressure.

With each bleeding, leaking bit of space that filled, his body demanded she feel how badly he wanted her. She had to will herself not to push away. She wanted this. She knew she did. She'd made her choice.

But the ferocity of his response was an overwhelm of emotion, a rise too high over a jagged peak she might crash upon.

It was too much for the gazes of those dead eyes behind them.

As if his mind had heard hers, he pulled away, just enough to reassure her.

"I can make it so no world exists beyond our skin," he murmured against her mouth in a drunken, ragged voice. "It'll just be the two of us here. All sign of them will be gone for you. If that's what you need."

In a heartbeat, as though he'd anticipation her response, he cooed to her, a soft, whisper of sound that seemed to change the very air. A sizzling sort of energy coiled around her, around them. She felt as though she'd gone to the moon. That the sun had hidden itself behind the earth. That darkness in this damp cellar had pulled a sheet over them, giving them the privacy of shade.

And in that shadow, there was an echo, like a heartbeat thrumming against her own. Quiet at first, growing louder until it was a drum in her ear, a primitive rhythm filling her heart, her very marrow. It wanted more of her. It wanted to sweep her away.

She licked her lips, bracing herself for what she knew she was going to say even after all this. Because it was all necessary. Not just accepting him for what he was, but accepting the things he'd done for her. Like it had been for Ava.

"Do it," she whispered.

His gaze was shuttered, but between the half-mast lids, she could see the flash of a predator's gaze. She could even smell the threat of danger in the air, of blood and death mingled in the air currents.

"There's violence in me still, Kit," he said, his voice sounding like it was being rasped over shards of glass. "You need to know that."

She swallowed hard, knowing what he'd done to those who lay around them. And yet...that violence was done for her. On her behalf. It was an act of love, she thought. The only way he knew to show it. And she couldn't reject that. She didn't need to fear it.

With a trembling hand, she laid her palm against his chest. She was surprised to feel he was shaking as much as she was. His heart hammered against her palm, the muscles quaking.

His eyes squeezed closed as he drew in a long inhale, let it go in a wheeze that sounded small and powerless beneath the force of emotion claiming him.

"I know something about violence," she said. "I know what it feels like to give yourself to it for another's sake and have that sacrifice rejected."

The heat coming off him in waves tried to gather her closer still, but she held back, knowing instinctively that if she went too fast, he would strike. A cobra pulling a mouse to its mouth.

Peering up into his face, she forced herself to confront the brutality of his expression, telling herself it wasn't aimed at her, but for her. There was a difference in that, one she could gather courage from. One she could trust.

She thought of the sacrifice she'd made for Ava all those years earlier, a sacrifice repaid by more hurt, more anger. An act that drove a wedge between them that could never be pulled free and never be able to cleave through the knots of pain.

The violence of that moment had changed her in ways she was even still recovering from. That night she'd trailed her sister into the bowels of the worst neighborhood in the borough to an abandoned and dilapidated gymnasium.

She would never forget, could never forget, the sound of the ring her phone made as it sat on her bedside table, startling her out of a sound sleep. She was up in seconds, grabbing for the receiver. Answering the call that changed both their lives.

She hadn't bothered with clothes or a jacket. Just shoved on the hard-soled slippers that rested near her bed and ran from the house to the car in her pajamas.

She was wearing that plush flannel two-piece when she GPS-tracked Ava to that gym. As she crept through the old graffiti-covered halls, the lockers banged up, dented, and rusted. The floors a mess of debris that she had to kick her way through in slippers.

Her slippers had gained dozens of filthy stains by the time she stood in the doorway and caught sight of Ava hanging from the rafters, her feet kicking out at the air two feet above the floor tiles.

And she was terrified she was too late.

Everything Will Be OK

Kit

Now, she worried she'd be too late again, and she didn't want to be too late. Being too late had cost her the most precious things in the world. And she wanted more than anything to drive the wedge through the knot and break the trauma in two. She wanted liberation.

"What you did here..." Her voice broke, trembling as she swallowed the lump in her throat. "I know what this gift is. I know what it means—what it cost you to give it."

She pressed her cheek to his chest, desperate to hear the steady rhythm of his heartbeat, to anchor herself in the reality of him amidst the chaos that felt like a waking nightmare. "I may never truly understand the weight of the price you paid, but I swear to you—I will not just dismiss it."

She peered up at him. Waited for his response.

"It doesn't have to be this way," he rasped, but his voice sounded strung around barbed wire. "We can..." He swallowed down a thick note of almost unbearable desire. "We can wait." He cleared his throat, more sure now, it seemed. "I can wait. I don't have to do this. I can find a way to release the pent up energy."

"By murdering someone?" she asked, meaning to sound light but hearing a bit of tension in her tone.

His reply was a dark chuckle that would have warmed her heart on any other circumstance. "Do you have someone in mind?"

Despite herself, she smiled, and he tucked his finger beneath her chin, laid his forehead against hers.

"I want you," he said. "I think you know how badly. But I'm immortal. It will take more than a bad case of blue balls to take me out."

She couldn't help swatting his arm. "I didn't think you had a sense of humor."

"I don't," he whispered. "Make no mistake, I feel like I'm dying, but I can wait until you're ready for me the way I am for you."

She flicked her gaze over his shoulder, to the evidence of exactly how ruthless he could be. The evidence that was even now transforming into something less horrific, as though with their deaths the magic was changing them into something different. She was sure she saw smoke rising from one of the forms.

He'd been very clear about what he wanted and where. And yet he was willing to wait. If she wanted to. If she needed it. Despite the rage, the need all but overwhelming him, he was giving her the right of refusal.

"You know how I feel," she murmured. "I don't think I'd have the courage to admit it twice."

She expected a moment of respite, but an instant was all he gave her. Maybe it was all he had in him. A growl vibrated through him, one that she felt beneath her palms.

"While nothing would please me more than claiming you with the sight of those bastards in my eye sight," he said. "I know your kind doesn't find it exciting." He brushed his fingers over her lips. "Turn around, Dove."

Quaking, trusting, she pivoted on her heel. Her soles dug through grime and soot, scuffing through heavens knew what, but she turned completely around and planted her bare feet solidly facing the window.

He waited until she had her back to him, before he wound his arms around her midriff beneath the shirt. His nose dropped to the back of her neck. A gentle nuzzle, tentative and testing. She didn't pull away, and that mere acceptance pulled a groan, soft and rasping, from him.

"Good girl," he said, and the note of longing in his voice almost sagged her knees. Instead, she put her weight against him, letting his body curve around hers, lending her warmth. He felt strong and solid. Safe. Yielding her curves to his hardness seemed less intimidating this way. "My brave good girl."

She inhaled slowly, closing her eyes, shutting it all out so she could hold herself together. She would not think about the things that had been done here. She would come together, not come apart.

"Don't close your eyes, Dove," he murmured through lips that trailed down her shoulder, nudging the fabric aside. "Focus beyond the window."

Doing as he bid, she looked through the broken glass of the pane. Black fur notched its splinters of wood in places, speaking to a large animal driving itself through a gap too small to fit.

Strange how she'd not felt the breeze moving in through that window until that moment, but as it caressed her cheeks, she thought she caught a faint scent of chocolate.

Light gathered in the frame and swam over the scenery beyond the bits of broken glass. The woods and the trees came to life with winking fairy lights. Everything dimmed around her, as if shadows had come to court the pre-dawn and pulled down a privacy shade so they might play together.

Every dot of winking pinpoints changed color. Some silver. Some gold. Purple married with white and created an astonishing violet.

"It's beautiful," she breathed.

"It is beautiful," he said as the backs of his fingers brushed her shoulder. The lightest of touches, an almost impossible gentleness from a brutal creature. "I've never seen skin so lovely."

"I touched you once," he said absently as his mouth whispered against her skin. "Like this. While you were sleeping. Your skin felt as it does now, like Erachne's finest gossamer. I wanted to crawl into the sheets and wrap myself in you."

The tips of his fingers traced a line down to her elbow, sliding the shirt from her shoulder as he cupped her there, palming the curve, lending her warmth even as the room chilled her skin.

"Did you feel me, there, Dove? Did you know I was in your room, watching you?"

"Yes," she said, knowing it was true. She kept her eyes on the lights playing in the woods through the window, noticed they'd begun dancing.

"I woke you." His fingers were on the move, a painfully, agonizingly languid journey that eased the sleeve from her arm and slipped it free of her fingers. She drew in a shaky breath.

"Yes," she said. "I thought I saw you in the dark."

"I almost dropped the shadows, then," he said. "I wanted you so badly, I was ready to give up everything I was just to lie with you there."

This bald confession, in this place, as though she were a priest and this a closeted holy sanctum.

"You don't have to tell me your secrets," she whispered. "I'm not your confessor."

A low, throaty chuckle that despite her anxiety, warmed her core. "You're all the sin I can take, Dove," he said as his palm slid down her arm. "I've never gotten on my knees for any god. When you see me on mine, it'll be because I'm about to taste of a very wicked communion."

His hands skimmed over her ribs and dipped to her navel, feathering over her bare skin. She drew up on her toes, not sure anymore that she could take him so soon. Or even if she should ask him to wait, the way he'd suggested. But he'd already lit a fire in her core, and although she wondered what sort of woman would want this here, with a monster, she knew only that she did want it.

As if he'd understood her hesitation, he paused, his palm cupping her abdomen between the panels of unbuttoned shirt. It wasn't a threatening touch, but she flinched instinctively.

His voice lowered to a murmur. "Watch the lights, Dove," he said.

The thick tension in his voice suggested she was doing better than he was, that he was holding tight to the reins of control as if they would break free with a snap. She heard him swallow and almost turned to him, thinking she wanted to see his face. But he must have felt her movement because he slid a knee between her legs, preventing her from doing so.

"Keep watching, Dove," he said. "You aren't ready for me yet."

His lips dropped to her bared shoulder, nudging aside a veil of hair. She thought he drew in a long breath, could feel him shudder behind her. She was trembling, too, she realized, but it was a perfect match for the quaking of his body.

"You smell of vanilla and cherries."

Not blood. Not sweat and fear. Something soft and comforting. Something normal.

She ached to turn around, but he held her fast. He was already swollen and hard against her back.

"Look at the lights, Dove," he said in a low voice. "Violence isn't the only gift I have for you."

A flare of lights winked at her from the shadows, playing amidst the tree branches and the shrubs.

"Fireflies," she murmured. "That's what they look like."

"Searching for a mate," he murmured into her skin.

His lips had moved to the crook of her neck. "Did you know they have a unique pattern that attracts just the right partner?" A flick of his tongue, tasting her, making her spine feel like it was shrinking. "That's the manifestation of my magic," he said. "Maybe my magic knows its nature better than I do. Maybe I was something other than what I am now. Sometime before all of this. A firefly's light, perhaps, signaling in the darkness, looking for you."

The rhythm of his breathing had changed. It was coming faster. Air bubbles were popping in her veins. They fizzed like champagne when he urged her closer to the window, to the edge of the desk where he bent her forward.

His breath grew ragged the moment she bowed over it. She felt the hammering of his heart against her shoulders. "Or maybe I was yours before," he said in a drunken voice. "Claimed by you, inside you, maybe, borne of your body. I want that again. I want to be inside you. I want you to swallow me whole so I can be part of you."

Her legs felt weak at the huskiness, the smoke in his voice. His fingers dipped below the hem of the shirt, paused on her thigh.

She couldn't hold back the moan that slid free as he gripped her, more urgent now.

"Careful, Dove," he growled, low in his throat. "I'm barely holding on. And I want you to want this. I won't...I can't take you till you're ready."

In answer, she lowered her elbows to the desk. The desk surface was cold, but the lights beyond the window were flashing and dancing. It was a mesmerizing display. And he was right. This was easier.

"Don't hold on anymore," she said.

"You've given enough today, Dove," he said in a heated voice. And then he was doing the most delicious things to her with his hands. She didn't need to look down to know the same lights playing in the woods were on the tips of his fingers.

His touch was electric and warm and so gentle, coaxing her, teasing in places, letting the pleasure build in her so slowly she found herself grinding against his palm, lifting from his lap without a single thought to how wanton she might seem.

"Gods," he groaned. "You're testing me, Dove."

Something was emitting growls and curses, alternating with pleas and bargains, and she was surprised to realize she was the one making the noise. She was begging him. Cursing him. Demanding he stop the agonizing temptation of his fingers.

"You're ready for me?" he asked. "Gods, tell me you're ready. I can't wait any more."

"Yes," she said, frustration and primal need overwhelming her, erasing everything except them and that moment. "Yes, please."

He groaned aloud at her answer and nipped at her neck. A shiver of delight ran through her. She felt him. Swollen. Thick. When he entered her, she sucked back a hiss of pain. He was large. And he was ruthless in the way he buried himself. But once inside, he collapsed on her back, molding himself to her as though he couldn't stand on his own power a moment longer.

Lights sparked beneath her eyelids within seconds, and she realized she wasn't looking at the dancing fireflies anymore; she was finding something within her own darkness, lighting it up with the same dancing lights, as if she possessed the same sort of magic as he did.

She found herself planting her hands flat on the desk beneath her, straining to take more of him, aching to keep him inside. A moan, soft and urgent, built up in her throat.

"You like this," he rasped out. "You like my cock inside you."

The lights whirled in a frenzy. "Yes."

"You want to take more of me, don't you, Dove? You don't care if it breaks you apart."

She couldn't speak for the ache in her throat. Yes. Oh god, yes. That's what she wanted to say. She didn't care if she split in two. She didn't care if the pieces were so small they could never be put back together again, so long as he stayed sheathed within her.

She felt him plant his feet further apart as he draped himself over her back, gathering her even closer, pinning her beneath him, her thighs ramming into the edge of the desk. His weight seamed her from shoulder to hips, and he made the burden easier to bear by draping one arm over her collarbone, holding her shoulder with one hand, while pulling her hips tighter with his other.

And still it wasn't enough. She strained back, driving herself onto the root of him, reaching for the height of the sweet agony he was building inch by inch.

His lips were on her hairline as she flattened her cheek along the surface of the desk, seeking air, sucking it in with gusto.

"I've broken women like you," he growled against the shell of her ear. "Generation upon generation, I've watched the light leave their eyes. I've taken more than they could bear. Such fragile things, humans."

Another thrust, burying himself so deep inside that she cried out from the blissful pain of it.

"But you, Dove," he growled low in his throat, a rumble that seemed to have no end. "You, I want to put back together."

His withdrawal was agony. His return even more so. The burrowing, rooted tip caressed delicious nerve endings, and she wanted relief and she wanted more all at the same time. And he gave it. Masterful, rhythmic, ruthless strokes that built one on the other.

She felt his rage and she understood it. She was angry too. She swore out loud. She cursed herself for wanting this. She cursed him for giving it.

And yet there seemed to be no end to the brutal thrusts, no relief for the burning heat that ached so deep inside her, so massive a flame, she didn't think it could ever be quenched. Ruthless as he was, it wasn't enough to fill that hollow. No matter how deep he thrust, no matter how hard he pumped, she began to think he couldn't reach the end. That the chasm within her had no bottom.

She whimpered, wanting it to end, yet helpless beneath her own body's need to take more from him, as though breaking apart would be the only thing that could save her.

"I think you want the violence," he said at the sound. "Pain is all you know of love. That it costs you. That you have to pay for it with sacrifice."

He licked her ear even as the tip of his cock teased her entrance again. Her breath was ragged and too loud; it made her self-conscious. She tried to smother the sound in her shoulder, afraid he'd know how desperate she was.

"Don't hide your excitement, Dove," he murmured against her ear. "There's no shame in wanting to let go all that anger you've been holding all these years. Give it to me," he said. "I can drink your rage and savor it the way I've done for hundreds of years. I could shred you into a thousand pieces and leave you scattered to the winds." His breath was as ragged as hers and it rasped into her ear, drowning out the sound of her own gasps. "Is that what you want, Dove? Do you want me to fuck the pain out of you? Do you want to use my rage to obliterate yours?"

She might have responded, might have said, yes, that was exactly what she wanted, but he'd already peeled himself away from her back and spun her around in his arms. He planted his hands on the desk on either side of her, corralling her there. Lowering his head, he peered into her eyes until she was forced to hold the feral gleam of them.

That was when he smiled, slow and wicked. "That *is* what you want," he growled. "To be punished. You don't feel worthy unless you've paid for love with pain."

His hands left the desk to scoop beneath her bottom. When he hoisted her off her feet, she felt for a moment like something in her chest had taken flight. She closed her eyes, enjoying the liberation.

Then he set her down on the desktop. Stepped between her legs. His breath washed over her in a heated blast of cloves and smoke. She couldn't help drawing the fragrance into her lungs, holding it there as he smoothed his palms over her shoulders. Such a delicious sensation; she was lost to the way her skin felt like velvet beneath his calloused palms.

"But I know about punishment and pain, Dove, and that's not what you deserve," he rasped. "And it's not what you're going to get." His lips dropped to her shoulders as his hands slid down her arms to find her hips.

She thought he would draw away from her, leave her there, wanting him, wanting to be claimed but left abandoned. She dug into his hips with her fingers, trying to drag him closer, spread her thighs around him, used her heels to dig into his backside.

"You're scared," she said, accusing him. "You still think you'll break me."

"Oh, Dove," he crooned. "That's not what's happening. Can't you feel it? Can't you sense the shift? I'm not worried I'll break you." He swallowed. "The truth is you're breaking me."

Stunned, her knees sagged apart. She blinked at him. Powerful. Lethal. And completely hers.

"Lie back, Dove," he murmured as he brushed his lips against her inner thigh. "You're going to want to know there's something solid beneath you when I drag you to heaven."

And then his mouth was on her and she was full again, with his tongue, his fingers, his lips. He became light all over, his every touch was a hum and a warm, wet caress. She tangled her fingers in his hair and urged him further, to drive her harder and when she broke, it was with a cry of pleasure, not one of pain and anguish.

The seams of gold held. The cracks completely sealed over.

Her breathing evened out long before she felt him rise to his feet above her. She opened her eyes to see him watching her.

His expression was unreadable, and she smiled nervously. "I think you fixed my sciatica," she said in a soft, playful voice, the relief and release so palpable she felt like laughing.

A grin broke out over his face and it was good to see. An angel in the monster. And yet there was still that unbridled tension, a whickering of his skin like that of a horse eager to be given its head.

She reached for him, still feeling that warm rapture of release.

"Come to me," she whispered, hitching herself higher up on the desk. "Come let me put you back together."

His hand found her wrist and lifted it to his lips. Reverent. As though she was a sacred object to be washed clean. The touch was electric and warm all at once and a faint hum built behind her ears again.

"This skin," he said over the translucent skin, his breath skimming her flesh and shivered goosebumps all the way to her neck. "This skin isn't just worth killing for. It's worth dying for."

Her eyebrows gathered together. His tone. There was something in it.

"I want you to claim me," he said in a rough voice, an urgency she didn't expect. "I want to die as I am by your hands."

She cupped his face, not sure what she was agreeing to but wanting to give him what he needed. Eyes locked together, with an almost mesmerizing motion, he placed her palm over the powerful muscles of his throat, before grappling the other from the desk.

This too, he placed against his neck. He worked her fingers into a curling grip around the column of his throat. His muscles went taut and then relaxed. She felt him swallow beneath her palms.

He nudged her gently with his hip, edging in, brushing her knees aside.

"Let me in now, Dove," he murmured. "I promise everything will be ok."

She was shaking as she relaxed against him. He slid in easily, driving himself as far inside as he could. His face was close to hers, forehead to forehead, eye to eye. What moved inside his irises, she was sure moved inside hers.

"I don't know how to do this," she said.

His smile was bittersweet. "You'll find a way, Dove. I won't resist."

The Mark of the Beast

KIT

KIT HAD NEVER TRIED to kill anyone before. Never considered what it might feel like to have her hands around someone else's throat. But if he said it would be alright, then she believed him, and she gave the effort everything she had.

And he didn't resist.

She had to leverage herself against the desk, hooking him from behind with her feet, hauling him toward her as she pushed her energy into her hands.

It was harder than she realized to strangle another breathing soul. It was a slow, agonizing task. And it was exhausting. Her fingers hurt. Her forearms ached. Even her teeth hurt as she ground them together with all the energy she could muster.

Through it all, he kept his eyes on hers, placid, calm. But for the pressure of her fingers, the muscles working beneath her palms as they involuntarily tried to suck oxygen in through the straw of his windpipe, she might think she was having no effect at all.

But then his face blanched. The fireflies he'd captured for her swam over his features and blinked out one by one.

And still he didn't fight her.

Instead, as the life drained from eyes, he came to life slowly below the hips, stroking like a piston well-oiled and sure. A machine on automatic, driving onward despite the imminent failure of its engine.

Something came to life inside her as well. And it was such a surprising emotion that she gasped at the sensation that burned in her belly.

Rage. A need for vengeance. Flashes of images, painful and horrific painted the backs of her eyelids. The sound of Ava's voice in her ear tread around in combat boots, stomping on every tiny rooting flower that grew within her. The fear she'd felt as he'd stood up for her in that vacant lot. The things he'd done—had to do—for her.

He was all those creatures, fae and human, who had hurt her in those moments. He was the pain and the insult and he was the revenge all in one.

"Fuck you," she said in a hoarse voice, aiming the words at everything and everyone who had hurt her. The bastards in the cellar. Gideon. Ava. "Fuck you all."

She squeezed harder. Every ounce of pain and fury funneled down into her fingers and palms and forearms.

But Flint didn't waver.

He stroked faster. He burrowed deeper. In her mind's eye, she imagined the remnants of his violence. She saw again the things that were no longer humanoid, the masses of fabric and hair and blood that magic had whitewashed into something less horrific, and she knew them for what they were.

Rumors of a life she'd not truly lived. Secrets in the ashes of her own pain.

She squeezed harder, gritting her teeth against the pressure it took to dig her thumbs into his voice box. She gave him all the unspent fury she had in her.

And he found the air to drive himself deeper still, reaching a part of her finally that lit a spark in her core. The heat of an engine on override grew and caught fire. She met him thrust for thrust. Savage. Rabid. The need to finish this, all this, so great that she roared with a primal rage upward to the heavens.

The fear. The adrenaline. All that emotion in one magnificent knot tightened like a noose. She dangled there for a long, sweet moment, gasping for air.

A smile played at the corners of his mouth the instant she came. And then...then the knot slid free and let her go.

And everything in her went slack.

Her hands dropped from his throat, unable to exert a moment's more pressure. His eyes rolled back and the specter of pleasure playing on his mouth as a smile died as his features went slack.

He collapsed to the damp stone floor as though her grip around his throat had been the only thing holding him up.

His body splayed itself like a sacrifice at her feet, and her heart hiccuped in her chest at the broken way he lay against the stone. Like a downed bird, his arms splayed out at his sides. His trousers half-way down his thighs.

The world stopped. She was sure she heard it screech against gears too rusted to keep it turning. She was frozen in place for an entire heartbeat.

Terrified to check for life.

Terrified to stay put.

But then he coughed and his eyes fluttered open. His legs jerked. His back arched as he stretched the vertebrae into place one by one.

"Die if she does," he murmured.

At the sound of his voice, everything started to grind ahead again. She flew to him, tears wet on her cheeks, streaming down her chin.

"You're alive," she said, running her hands over his face, tracing his eyes, his lips. "Sweet Jesus, you're alive. I didn't kill you."

His low chuckle breathed air onto her palms. "I guess a fae can die from blue balls after all, Dove."

She leaned down, kissed him, finding the strange taste of chocolate on his tongue. His soft moan at her touch brushed over her mouth as he lifted his fingers to her cheek. She turned into his palm, letting it cup her face as she hovered for an instant, tasting his breath.

She wasn't aware her eyes had closed until he moved to kiss her eyelids. "Tears for a monster?" he whispered.

When her eyes fluttered open, it was to see his violet gaze had already locked on hers. Light moved around his irises, winking at her.

"Tears for my monster," she said.

A fleeting, half-smile of contentment ghosted his face before he hooked her with his arm and pulled her against his chest. He felt as solid as ever. She fit so nicely beneath his arm, tucked in as though beneath a protective wing, that she thought that was what it must feel like to have found true peace.

They lay together for several moments, quiet, letting their hearts settle into the same rhythm before she dared trust her voice.

"What were you saying?" she asked. "When you woke up?"

He rolled over onto his side, hauling up his pants before scooping her closer.

"My commission," he said. "I was told to chase you if you ran. Watch you while you slept." He canted his head at her, reaching up to cup her face. "Die if you did. And you died, did you not, my Dove? You came to life with me?"

She found herself nodding, tears burning the corners of her eyes.

He swiped his thumb along her jawline where tears had collected. "Then I've kept my vow."

They were facing the window, she noticed, and she could see the rising sun glinting in the broken glass. Black tufts of fur stuck to the jagged edges. She stared at them for a long while before she eased out of his embrace, rolling onto her hip.

"I remember you mentioning a vow to the men," she said, refusing to use the word fae, refusing to think about how they'd abducted her. They were just men. And they had no business being in her thoughts except for how they fit into the conversation. She wouldn't give them any more power than that.

"Males," he corrected. "We fae are called males and females. And yes. An oath does bind me. We take them very seriously."

She reached for the shirt that had pooled onto the floor where he'd scraped it off her shoulders. Pulling it over her arms now, she said, shyly, "There was something else, too." She pulled the panels closed, covering her chest. "You called me your mate."

"It's how I found you," he said in a rough voice. "The mate bond."

She tilted her head as he reached for her hand, lifting it between them, turning the palm upward. He traced her wrist with his finger, drawing an invisible symbol, teasing the skin.

"Aiofe explained it to me. When I touched you that first time at the bus stop. My light, my magic, recognized you. It marked you. Every creed of fae has a different bonding. Some with blood. Some with flesh." He kissed her wrist. "I have light and shadow, and the light in me knew the light in you."

She thought of that moment, how the mark disappeared into her skin, how she'd believed she'd been seeing things. It had seemed inconsequential at the time, but now, the way it radiated heat all the way through her body, the way it seemed to ache at his touch, she knew it meant something more than she understood.

She thought of the fairy lights he'd made for her, the light on his fingertips. The way he'd fought for her with that strange glow around his fists.

"That's how I knew you were there, in my room, isn't it?" she asked. "It's how I thought at times I could see you."

She shivered as his lips drew a line from her wrist to her palm, and she closed her fingers over his chin, holding him there with her.

"I'm not sure what it means," she said, brushing her cheek against his jaw. "But I've never felt anything like this in my lifetime. I never thought it was possible."

He took a button between his fingers and started to thread it through the hole of her shirt, pulling the panels closer together.

"As far as I know, humans don't have that sort of bond," he said, busying himself with the remaining buttons. "And I've watched mortals for a good many centuries." He dropped his gaze for a moment before skimming it over her mouth. "But I can tell you what the bond means for me."

She held her breath, watching the way his muscles moved in his chest as he finished buttoning the shirt together. He had scars, she noticed. So many of them. They crisscrossed and double-crossed and zigzagged over his skin.

He caught her looking at him, and his voice grew huskier. His gaze locked on hers, trapping her there. "It means you're mine and I'm yours," he murmured. "Nothing comes before you. Not my father. Not my brothers. Not my blood vow.

"It means I was yours before I even knew you, and I'll be yours long after the dust has taken you back to the earth. I may live another thousand years after you die, but I won't be alive."

His expression hardened then, his gaze lit too brightly. Manic almost. He used the panels of the shirt to pull her closer, sealing her against his body. Even naked, in the chilly damp of the cellar, he was still hot as a radiating furnace.

His mouth worked over something, and it took a while for him to continue.

"It's what drove me," he said. "It's why I needed you here. Why these males, who have been at my side, in my life for generations, had to die." His breath hitched. "And even if none of this meant anything to you, I would do it again. I wouldn't just kill for you, Kit. I have burned my world to ash for you."

Fear. Was that what she saw in his hardened, battle-scarred face? Was he afraid of her refusal? After everything she'd let him do, all the things she'd just surrendered to him?

She couldn't trust her voice, so she laid her palm on his chest, reassuring him the only way she knew, to feel for the hammering beneath his ribs, and as her fingers splayed out over his heart, his face lost that tightness that held his jaw so rigid it was white. His throat bobbed with emotion and his gaze dropped.

"You said you knew violence."

It was a quiet comment, murmured so low she doubted she'd heard it until he pulled her palm to his lips and kissed her there in the belly of soft skin. Whispered it again when she didn't answer.

A sigh threaded its way up her throat. Yes. This. She would have to confront it. But instead of answering, she slipped free of his hold to kneel before him, urging his legs apart until he stretched them out along the stones, propped his back against the desk.

She planted her hands on his thighs. His quads flexed and relaxed beneath his trousers, but the power in them didn't diminish. She took comfort in their sturdiness. Sensing it made it easy to ignore the things around them, to pretend it was just them there in that cold cellar.

"I've been on my knees before," she whispered. "In the face of violence. Like with you, I accepted it. I offered myself to it."

This place was not so different than that gym. An abandoned building. Someone who needed her.

He lowered his gaze to hers. A flash went through it. One of renewed anger, a lethal glance over her shoulder to where he'd ended those of his own kind. For her. Whatever they were now, chunks of stone, smudges of coal or puddles of water, she knew at one time they had been his friends.

"It's alright," she said, cupping his chin. The stubble was a soft brush against her palm. "It's been done seven years now. But it was for someone I loved. Like..." Her fingers inched up his thighs to find the taut bit of muscle above his navel. "Just like this time. I bartered the only thing I have for someone I love."

He blinked. Long and slow as though he'd forgotten how. She knew he was processing the words she couldn't say because they felt wrong in this place. To say them for someone she barely knew, who'd admitted to stalking her for a magical court, who had killed right there behind her. And she knew he was thinking all those same things and trying to wrangle the truth out of it, that she could love him. Despite all that.

But those things didn't seem to matter to him. What tightened his voice was something else, and it surprised her when he spoke it aloud.

"You offered yourself for someone before this?"

She nodded. "My sister," she said. "To save her life. I gave myself to someone who wanted to hurt her."

And because she needed to, she told him about Ava. She knelt between his legs on the floor and bared her soul and all the hurt that she'd suffered as her younger sister shunned all efforts of love and protection. How her affections had driven Ava into worse behaviors. How she had answered a call from a man she didn't know, telling her Ava owed him money, that he was going to take it out in blood unless she arrived at his 'place of business' in exactly twenty minutes.

"I got there three minutes too late," she said, anguish bleeding through her voice. "And he was as good as his word."

She closed her eyes, bringing it all to mind again. There was no telling how many times he'd pulled Ava up into the air by her neck by then, a frayed hemp rope noosed beneath that gorgeous mane of black hair.

That memory was the hardest, seeing her sister's feet kick out into the air, knowing she'd come to Ava's rescue too late. Thinking for years that maybe she'd taken a little too long to find her slippers when they were right there beside the bed. The way they always were.

Only when he swiped wetness from her cheeks into her hair, did she realize she was crying. His expression was a careful mask, but his voice gave him away, the words as brutal as the tone.

Darkness moved across his eyes. "Ava," he said. "She is good as dead."

"Would you kill someone who has my heart, who is part of me?"

His tone was fierce. "I would kill a man for bumping into you."

She laid her forehead against his. "I don't know how they do things in your world," she said softly. "But here we just give them the finger."

She lifted one hand to his cheek. A moth's kiss couldn't have been more gentle. "Besides," she said, her throat constricting so tightly that when she spoke, the words felt like shards of glass. "I think she might be dead already."

Surprisingly, he snorted. "She's not dead," he said, annoyance seething beneath his tone. "Not yet at least."

Her head snapped back, the unexpected information clawing at something in her chest. "What do you mean? How do you know?"

He pulled the shirt tighter around her, a casual, everyday gesture that did more to stoke her temper than the words he thoughtlessly dropped into the air.

"I know because she is in my father's dungeons. In the city of the dead. He's holding her. That's why my soldiers came for you."

Bubbles of nitrous oxide danced between her ears. Such calm words, such casual a statement, it was maddening that he didn't realize how much this news would affect her.

She planted her hands on her hips. "And you know this how?"

He bent to retrieve his leather duster from the floor and dropped it over her shoulders. The panels of it struck the floor and puddled there.

"You're shaking," he said.

"I'm not cold."

"I know. You're angry."

It was so very hard not to scream. If he knew she was angry, he wasn't working very hard at trying to discharge the fuse.

"What's going on, Flint?" She scraped the grounds behind him with a heated gaze to where he'd murdered members of his own court. Fae. All of them.

What had Ava got herself into?

"Flint?"

His heaving sigh suggested he did not want to answer. She had to slap him on the chest just to get his attention, and even then, all he did was grip her wrist right where the bond mark was. Dirty, dirty pool, that.

She yanked her hand away and pushed herself to her feet so she could tower over him. But even at her full height and him on his knees, he still came to chest.

"You owe me," she said, looking down into his face and watched a gamut of expressions move over his features before he raked both hands through his hair and dropped his head back, defeated.

With a sigh, he stood as well, and when he tried to take her hand, she pulled it away.

His mouth twitched, a white line seaming his jaw as he clenched it...twice before he spoke.

"I was sent to keep a tight watch on you as leverage against your sister." He waved his hand in the space between them, a swift, calculated gesture meant to quiet her since she'd already started to interrupt. "Don't ask me to tell you what we need her for. I will not put you in more danger by revealing that information."

"Am I still in danger?"

He glowered at the floor and didn't need to say more.

Because she knew the answer.

What's to Come

KIT

IT WAS HARD TO believe after everything, to know her life was still in danger. Hard to see him standing there in the middle of a damp basement, with scorched wood and broken glass and half a dozen dead fae, and know everything he'd done hadn't made a dent in the threat.

But all she could do was think that while she had this powerful fae to protect her, Ava had no one.

"And Ava?" she asked. "Is she in danger too?"

"If she is in danger, it's her own fault," he said and his eyes flared.

She refused to answer to that, and he growled a long, heaving sigh.

"I won't give you to the Shadow Court," he said. "I don't care what they do to me. Who they send for me." He clutched her arm and where his fingers touched, she felt a hum of electricity. "I don't care what they do to her. You are mine, do you hear me? You supersede any blood vow. You are more important than Ava. More important to me than all of Fae."

His voice broke, and she realized then, just how bad it was. It was a job to piece it all together, but she made some pretty good guesses.

"Ava is in Fae and she's in trouble," she said. "And you will suffer if I'm not delivered to your father's court."

"You will not be delivered," he said, heat in his tone. "I will not take you there."

She spun around, putting her back to him. "You're absolutely right on that," she said. "I will not be delivered. I will go on my own steam."

He grabbed for her wrist, right where the mark was. She felt something, an energy of sorts, a whisper somewhere in the back of her mind, as the flesh warmed. A command, she thought. But she couldn't be commanded to let her sister die.

Whatever the bond was for him, this was not the way humanity worked. She had choice. She would use it.

"That stone you have," she said, letting his hand stay on her skin but using it to draw closer to him, so she was in his face. Braver than she felt. "You told me it has enough magic to create a portal."

He must have guessed at her meaning, because he twisted her wrist, not painfully, just enough for her to see the light on her skin rising to the surface like a bio-luminescent creature from the depths. Everything in her hummed at the sight of it, but she held her own against the dizzying sensation of it, the desire to submit.

"You would suffer again for your sister's sake?" he demanded. "You would put yourself in danger? Again? For her? Face a violent end--because it will be a violent end, Kit. Make no mistake. There is no coming back from what awaits you there."

She put her hand on his arm. The jacket he'd slipped over her shoulders fell to the floor in a shroud of fabric.

"And your plan is to what?" she asked. "Find some cozy hovel in the lands of fae or run to the edges of the earth where your father can't find you? We've seen what they can do, Flint."

He stepped back, his boots clicking together. "Then I will let them take me," he said with a note of finality in his voice. "And each bit of torture I endure will only serve to remind me that you are living your days until the old woman inside you can claim her last dance with the grim reaper."

She snorted at the declaration. "I've had enough of martyrdom, Flint. It does nothing. It certainly doesn't help Ava?" She shook her head, her decision made. "No. I can't let that happen. I am going."

His expression hardened. "You are brave but stubborn, Dove," he said. "But you are not so stubborn as a fae who knows what waits for his mate. I won't let that happen. Not for Ava Ashe. Not for my blood vow. Not for the consequences I will face when my father knows I've broken it."

"Not for any of those things," she said softly. "Because I am not asking it of you." She stretched out her palm, silently insisting he put the stone in her hand.

He glowered at her, changing tactics as adroitly as a general. "The stone is nearly empty. I used the magic to heal you and then show you my deeds, ill-advised as that was." His mouth twisted into a wry line.

Grumpy. Sullen. But not a no. If he wouldn't help her, she'd find her own way. Eventually, his father would send someone else anyway if he wanted her that badly.

Sighing, she pulled her hand from his and turned away. The burn between her shoulder blades was a good indication of how upset he was as he watched her walk away, but she was confident by now, that was all it would be. He wasn't going to hurt her. But he wasn't going to help her either.

She was picking her way through the stone cellar, weaving her way past the first mound of greyish stone that had once been a body when she heard him pulling on his jacket. She didn't look anywhere but ahead, careful not to take in too much, letting her feet search for the way out.

Her sister needed her. That's all that mattered.

She had made it past the first puddle of drying blood and was stepping over a piece of wood that looked peculiarly like an arm, when she felt his hand on her shoulder.

She looked up into a carefully schooled expression.

"I can't let you go barefoot like that," he said in a low voice. Then he scooped her into his arms as easily as if she were a feather.

"My brave girl," he murmured, looking down at her.

"Not brave," she said. "Practical."

His low-throated chuckle vibrated the space between them.

"But are you brave enough for what's to come?"

"I faced you, didn't I?"

His mouth twitched, and for a second, she thought he might smile. Then he cleared his throat and adjusted her in his arms. He was all business then, serious as he looked down at her.

"Courage isn't all that's necessary. Mortals may not know of Fae and live," he said, his gaze lingering on her mouth with an intensity that made her squirm. "If we are to do this, if I'm going to let you go to Fae, then we must make sure my father believes I've delivered you. You must act as though you know nothing of your part in this, that you are ignorant of what I am."

"That's not hard," she said. "I don't know anything about what you are." It wasn't entirely true. She knew the heart of him, and she trusted him.

He was shaking his head. "My father has ways," he said. "I won't trust your life to happenstance. You will need to forget this, my dove. The stone can take most of the memories. Store them for you."

Something inside her cracked at the thought that yet more things would have to be erased from her memory, the worst of which was holding her right then. "Not you," she said. "You can't take that from me."

He smiled as he bent to touch his forehead to hers. "Never that. Just the bits of truth we need to keep hidden. What I am. That my men took you. That you even heard of the fae realm." His jaw clenched on the words and she knew he was thinking about what had happened when he'd found her. Things he'd still not shown her. "My men will have died trying to create a portal to return through."

"It won't be a lie," she whispered, thinking of the things he'd done to each of them.

"Not really," he said, smiling. "A half truth I can manage if I word it carefully."

"And you?" she asked. "How did you survive the creating of the portal?"

"I created my own portal to deliver you. Just the two of us. I brought a magic source with me," he said, jerking his chin upward to the floor above them, where the fissure in the surface zigzagged in different directions. "She's up there. I left her alive." He paused for a moment then said with a note of embarrassment in his voice. "Barely."

She had to shove down the comments she wanted to make. This wasn't the time to accuse. Only get information. Make plans.

"She?" she asked and felt confident that it sounded intrigued and not judgmental.

He nodded. "There may be enough magic left in the stone to fuel a portal and erase those memories if it has enough mortal blood to do so."

Kit's heart lurched at the insinuation. That Flint had recognized the young woman at the bus stop that Castor had climbed through immediately as a portal like that. That was why he'd tried in vain to halt the magic by decapitating her.

Kit put her hand on his chest. Rebuttal certainly, but softened by touch. In case it helped. Because she needed all the aid she could get.

"I won't use someone else's suffering for my own ends," she told him, trying to keep her tone light.

His lips pressed together, and she thought maybe he had suggested the woman as a means to show her how hopeless it was. And if he hadn't, if he'd truly given thought to creating that sort of gateway, then he had to know she would not resort to that sort of magic. She'd seen the results. Even for Ava, she wouldn't use it.

"There has to be another way," she said.

His mouth set itself into a grim line and his brow gathered into two knots instead of one. Then, he halted as if surprise had stolen his legs. He dropped his head back as though he couldn't believe he'd forgotten. "There might be another way. Another being of magic here in your world, one not bound by fae laws." He huffed a humorless laugh. "I'd thought him lost to death because of the way I came through, but it seems he's alive and well after all."

Her brow gathered together, as she tried to follow his reasoning. "You mean Castor?" She'd seen what he did already to create gateways to another realm. "No thank you."

He shook his head, excitement gathering on his face. "Not Castor. He's gone back home. Maddox the warrior. I caught sight of him in your shop after Gideon--" He stopped there, cutting his sentence off with a click of his teeth.

She squirmed in his arms, hearing the words he didn't want her to: that he was in the shop watching her even then. "You saw Gideon?" she asked, recalling how angry she'd been, how she'd cried after. She wished he hadn't seen that.

His eyes shuttered. "Another male I would like to murder." He hitched her up higher, settling her tighter against his chest. "But trust me, Dove, he'll pay for making you cry."

So he had seen that exchange after all, and he'd heard them discuss Ava. He'd heard her say she was done with her sister. That she wanted to move on even after Gideon said he was worried.

She might have felt ashamed except it was hard to feel anything except the warmth of his arms and chest as he held her. And that moment was not one she wanted to dwell on, least of all with him. It wasn't her finest of moments.

"So tell me more about Maddox," she said, thinking of the strange but handsome man who had gotten excited over what he'd thought was a grimoire on her bookshelves. For the first time in a while, she felt hope poke a tender leaf out from the soil of despair. "You saw him in my shop too? What makes you think he can help."

He was striding now again, this time with more purpose. The stink of old blood was dissipating with each step, thankfully.

"He's looking for something, would be my guess," he told her as he made the trek across the cellar floor. "I suppose he thought he might find it in your store." He peered down at her and smiled. "I didn't like the way he was flirting with you, but since I smelled another woman's mark on him, I didn't waste my magic trying to kill him. Now, I'm glad I didn't."

"You can't try to kill everyone who looks my way."

He shrugged as though to say 'watch me' but what he said was, "His realm has a dozen or more portals to worlds of every kind. But if he was in your shop, then he's not all the way dead."

His realm. A peculiar way to word it, as though it was different than the fae realm or this one. She decided she didn't want to know more. Lord knew he might start talking about vampires and werewolves and she was just starting to come to terms with the idea of fae.

"But you think he can help," she urged as he stopped in front of an old-fashioned root cellar door.

His jaw ticked to the side as he considered the question. "What I know is that his portals to this realm here in your city are tearing apart any magic they come in contact with. I found that out the hard way. If he's not fully deceased, then maybe they can be fixed."

He grunted, shifting her in his arms as he kicked the door open. Light clawed its way in and bathed her face. She peered up at him.

"You're just going to leave the bodies behind?" she asked. "Just walk through the door and leave all this out in the open?"

He planted a kiss on her forehead. "Such a tender heart for a warrior," he murmured. "But no. I'm not just leaving them. I would have burned them alive with my magic had I not used so much on their torture. Their fate is not mine. Aiofe will claim them for the darkness. They are hers now. What magic remains in this place will call to her, I'm sure. They might even be with her right now. And if that's the case, whatever it is that their bodies have become here will be soon too."

"I'm not sure I follow all that."

He smiled down at her. "You don't need to, Dove. All you need to know is that we are going to convince the master of portals that you have something in your shop that he needs. And then he'll be back. And then we'll find a safe way into Fae that will allow you to confront your sister on your terms and not my father's."

"And your oath?"

His eyelids shuttered. "Nothing for you to worry about."

He was climbing the cement steps to the ruins of the lawn by then, and she watched the birds harry away from the trees, squawking in alarm as though they knew a predator was in their midst.

She'd not seen the building when she'd been brought, and she was surprised to see it was built in the middle of a nice enclave of trees and grass. A garden shed squatted a dozen yards away, an ombre hue as the early morning sun dripped rays of gold over it.

His boots crunched over charcoal and twisted metal, enough debris that she was glad he was carrying her. With his shirt over her, she felt less naked but she was still wearing nothing beneath the fabric, and it was chilly. Whatever clothes she'd been wearing had likely been torn and shredded and bloodied. She thought about a pretty sweater she'd put on at some point and remembered the sound of it tearing.

She was still mulling it over when she noticed he was prowling toward a woman slumped beside a half standing wall of stonework.

There was only one reason why he would be doing that.

She tried to twist out of his grip, then, all images of devastation and trauma gone in the face of what she knew he was doing. "Oh, no," she said. "I told you; we can't use her. I won't let you."

"What you will and won't let me do, we'll find out later, Dove, but for now, I'm going to do what you'll just demand of me anyway."

He halted in front of the fallen woman. Broken, she thought. Just like she'd been except the woman's eyes were sentient. Exhausted and terrified, and almost manic with confusion.

He set Kit down in a place with little debris and pulled the crimson stone from his jacket pocket. Holding it up for her to see, he said, "I'm going to use what's left in this stone to heal her, wipe her memory, and send her on home. Presuming there's enough to do that."

"And if there isn't enough?"

He shrugged. "I'll just end her."

She gawked at him until he chuckled. "Your belief in my brutality is both astonishing and encouraging."

He toed the charcoal, kicking aside enough of it that she could move a bit more freely. "If there isn't enough, we'll take her with us. Maddox is known to be a healer of some repute. I'm sure he'll do what we can't."

She must have relaxed so visibly that the woman dropped her head back against the old chimney and closed her eyes. There was no telling what she'd heard below her as she lay there through the night, and Kit's heart went out to her. Even when Flint toed the woman with his boot, nudging her, the woman feigned sleep.

"Fortune is with you today," he said to her. "Pity you won't remember it."

He squatted beside her, murmured a few strange words. Electricity snapped in the air. Currents like lightning rose from the depths of the cellar, sizzling out from beneath cracks in the facade, rising from fissures all over the ground floor where the fire hadn't devoured it.

He pressed the stone against the woman's forehead, and she moaned. Her limbs twitched. A sigh escaped her lips as she slumped ever deeper against the bricks.

"I worked on her memory first," he said as he turned to Kit. Sweat beaded on his forehead. A vein throbbed in his temple. "That seemed the most important. And then the legs. Her arms are fractured but she'll be able to walk once she wakes."

"And then?" she asked. "What then?"

"Then she'll rise and wonder how she got there, but she'll go where she wants. Probably seek help for the rest of her wounds. But we'll be long gone."

He tossed the stone into the air, caught it without looking, and let it settle in his palm. He held it out between them, an electric, pulsing looking thing.

"There's still magic left, Dove," he murmured, his voice like a slow drag of a knife over silk. "Enough to make you forget. Enough to take your memories the moment we step through those gates."

His gaze lifted to hers, a gleam in his eyes that made her knees bow. "But before we take those steps, I'm going to find a quiet place in the grass." His fingers traced her wrist, featherlight, a contrast to the violence in his gaze. Each stroke drew the light beneath her skin to the surface.

His voice was a snake charmer's pipe, drawing the word from her in a trembling breath. "And then?" she asked. "What then?"

He smiled—wicked, knowing. A promise and a threat all at once. "Then I'm going to lay you down while you still remember what I am. While you still know the awful, bloody things I did in your name."

His arm slid around her waist, the heat of his palm melting her against his body as he pulled her flush against him, owning her. "I'm going to spread that shirt and spread your legs, and you're going to hold that image in your mind while the birds sing and the wind carries your moans to heaven. But when the sun kisses your bare skin, it won't be the Alpha and Omega you'll be crying out to."

He dipped his head, his breath a phantom against her lips. His voice curled around her, velvet and unshakable. "Because by then, Dove, I'll be tasting your manna—and you'll know exactly who your god is."

***

Author Thanks

Every new release I rely on some eagle-eyed BETA readers to help me finesse the story. Sometimes they remember more plot details than I do.

Kerry Taylor, Evelyn Dotson, Debra Martin (an amazing fantasy author, check out her work), Julie Pederick, Caroline Jenkins, Denise Sherman, and Joann Colantino.

I can't thank you enough.

But this time, I have some special thanks to a couple of brand-new-to-me beta readers who gave more than I could have asked

Sairs_readsandreviews and Kat (You know who you are)

I really appreciate you all.

-thea-